THE ORCHARD MURDERS

Robert Gott was born in the Queensland town of Maryborough, and lives in Melbourne. He has published many books for children, and is also the creator of the newspaper cartoon *The Adventures of Naked Man*. He is the author of the Murders series, comprising *The Holiday Murders*, *The Port Fairy Murders*, *The Autumn Murders*, and *The Orchard Murders*, and of the William Power series of crime-caper novels set in 1940s Australia: *Good Murder*, *A Thing of Blood*, *Amongst the Dead*, and *The Serpent's Sting*.

The ORCHARD MURDERS

ROBERT GOTT

SCRIBE

Melbourne • London

Scribe Publications
18–20 Edward St, Brunswick, Victoria 3056, Australia
3754 Pleasant Ave, Suite 100, Minneapolis, Minnesota 55409, USA

Published by Scribe 2021

Typeset in Janson Text by the publishers

Printed and bound in Australia by Griffin Press, part of Ovato

Scribe is committed to the sustainable use of natural resources and the use of paper products made responsibly from those resources.

Scribe acknowledges Australia's First Nations peoples as the traditional owners and custodians of this country, and we pay our respects to their elders, past and present.

978 1 922310 67 5 (paperback)
978 1 922586 06 3 (ebook)

Catalogue records for this book are available from the National Library of Australia.

scribepublications.com.au
scribepublications.com

For my parents, Maurene and Kevin. Always.

First, there was *The Holiday Murders* ...

IN LATE 1943, the newly formed Homicide department of Victoria Police in Melbourne finds itself undermanned as a result of the war. Detective Inspector Titus Lambert has seen the potential of a female constable, Helen Lord. She is twenty-six years old, and, as a policewoman, something of a rarity in the male world of policing. Lambert promotes her on a temporary basis to work in Homicide, alongside a young, inexperienced detective, Joe Sable.

On Christmas Eve, two bodies — of a father and son — are found in a mansion in East Melbourne. As the investigation into their deaths proceeds, Military Intelligence becomes involved. An organisation called Australia First has already come to the attention of the authorities through its public meetings and its pro-Hitler, pro-Japan, and stridently anti-Semitic magazine, *The Publicist*. A local branch of the organisation's enthusiasts has been trying to form itself into a political party, but they are essentially dilettantes. What they feel they need is muscle, and they find it in the person of Ptolemy Jones — a fanatical National Socialist. Jones has gathered about him a small band of disaffected men, susceptible to his dark charisma. Among these is George Starling, who calls himself Fred, a man in his late twenties who is dedicated to Jones.

Soon, Military Intelligence joins with Homicide to find the killer. Detective Joe Sable, for whom the atrocities in Europe are awakening the dormant sense of his own Jewishness, is given the task of finding his way into Australia First. He does so with the help of Constable Helen Lord and

Group Captain Tom Mackenzie, an air force officer who is also Inspector Lambert's brother-in-law. But the operation goes horribly wrong, and both Sable and Mackenzie are badly injured.

The Holiday Murders ends with the death of Ptolemy Jones, and with the sense that this case has not yet run its course. It has damaged the lives of everyone involved in it. George Starling, previously overshadowed by Ptolemy Jones, remains at liberty, and he is determined to avenge Jones's death and to step out of his shadow ...

And then there was *The Port Fairy Murders* …

SERGEANT JOE SABLE, of the Melbourne Homicide division, has returned to work, having suffered severe injuries in the course of an investigation into National Socialist sympathisers. The investigation has for Joe, who is Jewish, focussed his attention on what is happening to the Jews in Europe under the Nazi regime. Inspector Titus Lambert, the head of Homicide, is worried that Joe has returned too soon.

When a known Hitlerite, John Starling, is found dead at his property near Warrnambool, a town six hours south-west of Melbourne, Inspector Lambert, Sergeant David Reilly, and Constable Helen Lord make the long trip there to investigate. They're interested because John Starling's son, George Starling, is a known acquaintance of the brutal Ptolemy Jones, the man who tortured both Joe and Group Captain Tom Mackenzie, Lambert's brother-in-law. Both Joe and Tom were working for Military Intelligence at the time.

In Melbourne, two men are savagely murdered, and Joe's flat is burned to the ground. Now homeless, he is billeted with the wealthy businessman Peter Lillee, who lives in a grand house in Kew, along with his sister, Ros Lord, and her daughter, Helen Lord. Inspector Lambert organised the billet, and Lillee was happy to oblige. Here, Joe should be safe.

In a decision that will put both their lives at risk, Joe and Helen are sent to Port Fairy, a small seaside town near Warrnambool, to investigate the bizarre double murder of a brother and sister. Nothing about the case is straightforward, but nothing is as dangerous as the menacing George Starling, who has become obsessed with finding and killing Joe Sable, and whose shadow falls as far as Port Fairy.

Followed by *The Autumn Murders* ...

GEORGE STARLING, a murderous National Socialist sympathiser, sets sets out to exact revenge on Detective Joe Sable, of the Melbourne Homicide division. Homicide, which is riven by internal turmoil, has become a dangerous place for Joe to work. Corrupt police officers are targeting him to prevent him giving evidence against one of their own.

Helen Lord, no longer with the police force, suffers a tragedy in her family, and she and her friend, Dr Clara Dawson, set out to discover the truth of what happened.

George Starling, having completed his preparations for finding Joe Sable and killing him, returns to Melbourne where he begins to settle old scores with people he considers his enemies.

An old friend of Joe's, Guy Kirkham, damaged by an incident in New Guinea, comes back into Joe's life. Together with Tom Mackenzie, an air force officer who suffered terribly at the hands of Starling's Nazi mentor, Ptolemy Jones, they set a trap, with the help of Helen Lord, to catch Starling before he catches them. Inspector Titus Lambert, the head of Homicide, considers this foolish and reckless, and the consequences for everyone will change their lives.

1

May 1944

Zac Wilson heard Peter Fisher before he saw him. It was a strange sound, a kind of blubbering and gasping and choking. Wilson was checking his crop of pears, walking the rows, looking for blight and hoping to Christ that this year's harvest would be better than last year's. Fisher stumbled into view at the end of a row. He was some distance away, clutching something to his chest. He fell to his knees and stayed there. Wilson walked towards him, and as he got closer he saw that Fisher's face was contorted and that snot was oozing from his nose.

'What's wrong, mate?' Wilson called. As Wilson reached him, Fisher raised the towel-wrapped bundle like an offering.

'Dead,' he said. 'All dead.'

'Who's dead?'

'He killed them.'

Fisher pushed his bundle towards Wilson, who reflexively took it in his hands, which were made clumsy by the gardening gloves he was wearing. The towel was soaked with blood, and when Wilson looked down at it he saw what once had been a baby, but was now a pulpy mess. He dropped the bundle as if it were hot, and as it hit the ground the towel unravelled to reveal the body of Sean Fisher, the two-month-old son of the man who knelt, his hands on his knees, his nose dropping a string of mucous onto his shirt. Wilson saw that Fisher's clothes were soaked like an abattoir worker's apron. Appalled by letting go of the small corpse, Wilson gathered it up and, not knowing what else to do, handed it back to Fisher, who took it and hugged it to him.

Wilson, flummoxed, said, 'Christ, mate.'

'He killed them,' Fisher said again, and releasing one arm from holding the bundle, indicated behind him in the general direction of his farm, a few paddocks over.

'Who? Who are you talking about?'

'He's dead, too.'

'Who? Who the fuck are you talking about?'

Wilson's raised voice jolted Fisher to his feet.

'Him. I'll show you.'

Fisher began to walk back towards his own property. Wilson, his nerves frayed, followed. They had to duck under two barbed-wire fences, and Wilson was glad of the gloves, although at the second fence he misjudged his manoeuvring and caught his shoulder on a barb. It ripped through his shirt and dug into his flesh. As he moved to extricate himself, it tore his skin. The sharp stab of pain distracted him for a moment, but it vanished when he looked up and saw Peter Fisher's house, now just 50 yards away. It was a good, solid place with a handsome, wide veranda. There were two chairs and a table where Fisher and his wife, Deborah, might sit in the early evening to watch the gloaming settle over Wilson's orchard. There wasn't a breath of wind, so the body hanging from the veranda rafter was rigid. When Wilson mounted the steps, the boards creaked under his weight, and the corpse moved slightly so that the rope slung over the beam groaned. Fisher stayed at the bottom of the two steps.

'The prick's name is Emilio,' he said. 'Go inside and see what he's done.'

Wilson, who'd only seen one dead body in his life, and that had been the wizened, desiccated remains of his grandfather, was both morbidly fascinated and repelled by the depending figure. The sight in Fisher's bedroom made him physically sick. It took a moment to make sense of the bloody mess on the floor beside the bed. It was a woman, although Wilson only glanced at the face, now cleaved and hacked into unrecognisable mash and bone. He bent double and vomited onto the mat at his feet. He didn't linger in the room, but needed the wall, spattered with blood, to support him on his way out. He hurried past the hanging man into the yard. Fisher was nowhere to be seen.

'Peter!' he called hoarsely, his throat sore and his mouth filled with the acid taint of vomit. There was no reply. Wilson walked around the house. Where had Fisher gone with his murdered baby? He heard a sob and followed it to behind the outside dunny. Fisher was sitting propped against the toilet wall, the baby in his lap. There was something in his mouth. It looked like a candle. Fisher looked at Wilson blankly and struck a match. The fuse fizzed, and Wilson, knowing now that this was a stick of gelignite, backed away, but stumbled and fell. He heard the explosion before the obliterating darkness of unconsciousness overwhelmed him.

INSPECTOR TITUS LAMBERT watched as Martin Serong photographed the unspeakably awful scene at Fisher's farm. The 12-year-old boy who'd come upon the slaughter had been delivering mail and bread. Fortunately, Titus thought, he'd only taken in the hanging man and had bicycled to the post office in Nunawading, where he'd stammered out a description of what he'd seen. The postmistress had telephoned the police, and the machinery of investigation had been set in motion. The crime-scene attendants had gathered and were waiting impatiently for Serong to finish. Among them were detectives who were inexperienced in seeing the gruesome tableaux of killing. The Homicide division of the Victorian police force had been made a discrete unit just 12 months earlier, in 1943. Its head, Inspector Lambert, was now grappling with the legacy of a case that had depleted his team, particularly those closest to him. Sergeant Joe Sable had resigned. So, too, had constable Helen Lord. They were young, but Lambert had trusted each of them, and in Helen Lord's case, he'd admired her intelligence and skill. He'd seconded her into the division against the advice and directives of those above him. Lambert's critics now felt vindicated. The experiment of placing a woman in Homicide had failed.

'What do you see, Martin?'

'I see what our species is capable of, Titus, and it sickens me more and more. You never get used to this.'

There was something in Martin Serong's voice that Titus hadn't heard before. It sounded like despair.

'No, Martin, you never get used to it. Murder is never just about the perpetrator and the victim. So many lives are tainted by it.'

'This is a bad one, Titus.'

Lambert trusted Serong's eyes almost as much as he trusted the close examinations of his crime-scene specialists, the men who found evidence in microscopic analysis. Serong's photographs had often guided him towards a vital clue. He'd been helped by Maude, his wife, whose analytical skills were subtler than his own. Titus kept nothing from his wife. If police command knew that Inspector Lambert took crime-scene photographs home for Maude's perusal, he'd have been disciplined, demoted, or probably dismissed. For Titus, the risk was worth it.

'Give me a thumbnail sketch, Martin.'

'The bloke hanging from the rafters looks about 17 or 18. It's hard to tell, though. The woman in the bedroom is so disfigured, all I can tell you is that she's a woman and that the person who attacked her did it in a rage. The body behind the shed is only half a body. Forensics is going to have to find as much of him as they can. He's fairly intact from the waist down. There was an infant in his lap, who weirdly escaped the worst of the explosion, and I'd say he or she was dead before the gelignite went off. I'm assuming it was gelignite. The baby's injuries are still very obvious, and I'd say they were inflicted with the same axe that was used on the woman.'

'We're presuming that's the axe that's leaning against the wall near the hanged man?'

'Precisely.'

'There's a survivor, of course.'

'He'd been taken to hospital before I got here.'

'He hasn't regained consciousness yet. What do you think happened, Martin?'

'I can tell you what we're supposed to think happened. We're supposed to think the young man on the veranda wielded the axe and then hanged himself, and maybe that's what happened. As for the others, I have no idea. It's so grotesque it defies speculation. Your turn, Titus. What do you know?'

'Not much more than names, and we're assuming the woman and the male torso are the people we think they are. The young man is Emilio Barbero. He's 17 years old. Italian. The woman is Deborah Fisher, 25 years old, the wife of the gelignite victim. He's Peter Fisher, 35 years old. He owns this place. The baby is their son, Sean, two months old. The survivor is an orchard grower named Zachary Wilson. His orchard is across the paddock. We need him to pull through, because at the moment it's like someone threw a jigsaw puzzle into the teeth of a gale. The pieces are all over the place, and the key pieces could be anywhere.'

'Is there a Mrs Wilson?'

'There is. She's at the hospital with her husband. She hasn't been allowed in to see him, and there's a policeman with her. She's very distressed. I don't think it's occurred to her yet that her husband might be a suspect.'

'I'll have the photographs developed as quickly as I can, Titus. I'll get them to you by this afternoon.'

Again, Titus heard a weariness in Martin Serong's voice. This troubled him. Serong was always on the side of the victims, whoever they might be. He couldn't preserve their dignity. The brutal intimacy of the photograph stole this. What he could do, and what he always tried to do, was expose in his pictures some detail that the naked eye might miss. He'd said to Titus once that when photographing victims he was attempting also to photograph the killer. The thought of investigating a murder without Martin's presence was as unthinkable to Titus as investigating it without Maude's assistance.

JOE SABLE AND Guy Kirkham were sitting in the library in the late Peter Lillee's house in Kew. Peter Lillee had been dead for only a few weeks. His sister, Ros Lord, and his niece, Helen Lord, had assured Joe and Guy that there was no reason for either of them to move. Joe had been living in the Lillee house since his flat had been destroyed by arson, and Guy had only recently found sanctuary there, having been invalided out of the army. Neither of them felt entirely comfortable, and Ros Lord's refusal to accept rent added to this unspoken discomfort. Joe could, after all, afford to pay rent, despite having resigned from the police force. Guy had a small reserve of cash to draw on, but no income and no prospect that his wealthy parents would help out. The bridge between him and his parents, if not actually burnt, was smouldering and unsteady.

'You should marry her, Joe.'

'Who? Who should I marry, Guy?'

'Helen Lord.' He paused for effect. 'Then you could live here permanently.'

'There are a few things wrong with that suggestion, Guy. Firstly, I don't want to live here permanently. Secondly, I don't want to get married. Thirdly, when I do get married, it won't be to secure accommodation somewhere. Fourthly, Helen doesn't have a very high opinion of me. Shall I go on? I've got a lot more reasons.'

Guy laughed.

'She must have a reasonable opinion of you. She's given you a job. She hasn't given me a job. That might be because I have absolutely no qualifications or experience. And I do fall asleep without warning. Still ...'

Dr Clara Dawson, Helen Lord's closest friend, had explained Guy's narcolepsy to Joe, and he understood that the benign expression 'falling asleep' really meant that Guy slipped unpredictably into unconsciousness. These episodes might last seconds or minutes. The cause, whether physiological or psychological, was uncertain, although in Guy's case the condition had appeared after an incident in New Guinea. Whatever it was that had provoked the condition, it had led to the death of a young soldier. Guy had fallen asleep at the wheel of a jeep, which had overturned. He hadn't yet found a way to live with this, and he'd become afraid of sleep. The horrors he could corral during the day broke from their restraints at night.

'Trust me, Guy, Helen doesn't think my detective training has made me a good detective.'

Guy leaned back in the armchair.

'Are you a good detective, Joe? I've never asked you that. We were all surprised when you became a copper.'

'The army wouldn't take me. The police force needed men, and they weren't bothered about my arrhythmia. Am I a good detective? I think I was learning to be one. Inspector Lambert made me feel incompetent. Not deliberately. Just by comparison.'

'I like Lambert's wife. What's her name?'

'Maude.'

'Maude. Yes. She's very impressive.'

'I always feel clumsy around her, and there's a lingering sense I have that she still blames me for what happened to Tom. She's assured me that this isn't true, but of course how could it not be a bit true? How could you look at your brother and his injuries, and not blame the person who put him in danger?'

Guy stood up. The mood in the room had changed suddenly.

'Blaming yourself is much harder to live with than being blamed by someone else,' he said. 'Believe me, I know.'

Tom Mackenzie had never given his body much thought. At 32, he'd remained lean, and none of the women he'd slept with had made unflattering remarks. He'd taken it for granted. It was fit for purpose, serviceable, perhaps to some eyes even attractive. Now he stood before a full-length mirror in his house in South Melbourne and surveyed the damage done to him a few months earlier at the hands of two torturers. The cigarette burns had healed, but had left ugly circles of puckered skin. He forced himself to look at the ruined flesh over his shoulders and on his chest, the legacy of a vicious scald. He still had a splint on one hand. His right hand had healed much faster than his left, and those splints had been removed. The breaks in his right fingers had been cleaner than the breaks in his left. The bruising and swelling on his face had gone. He wasn't a vain man, but he wondered if women would be repulsed by that raw, angry scald. He'd been assured by his doctor that it would settle down, although it would never repair itself into invisibility. It would be a permanent, physical reminder of what he'd suffered.

Whether or not the psychological damage would recede was more problematic. The nightmares had eased. He wasn't sure if the visits to his psychiatrist were helpful or not. He supposed they must be. He liked going, at any rate, which surprised him. He'd always been suspicious of psychiatry, and his sister, Maude Lambert, had been astonished at his willingness to seek help in that quarter. Until recently, Maude and Titus had shared Tom's house. It had been unsafe for them to stay in their own house in Brunswick. The danger that had made this so had passed, and Tom now had the place to himself. He still approached sleep nervously, but his dreams were mostly untroubled.

Tom knew that the day was coming when the air force would demand his return to Victoria Barracks. The thought of re-entering his tiny office, accepting the salutes of those junior to him, and giving salutes to his seniors, made him feel ill. It had been the monotony of his job that had led him to accept Joe Sable's request for assistance. The fact that it had gone badly for both him and Joe hadn't made him crave the safety of his desk. What would he do if he resigned his commission, and was this even possible in a time of war? He envied Joe Sable and his new position in Helen Lord's private inquiry office. He understood that there wasn't a place for him. It was a business, and he wasn't a detective. Helen Lord wasn't much interested in amateurs. Simultaneous with this thought was another that took him by surprise. He was interested in Helen Lord.

HELEN LORD WAS unequivocally pleased, almost in fact happy. This situation was so rare that her friend Clara Dawson couldn't help but draw attention to it. They were sitting in an office in East Melbourne, late on a Saturday night. Clara was exhausted, having finished a punishing shift at the Royal Melbourne Hospital. As one of only a handful of female doctors, she spent a good deal of every day dealing with people, both men and women, doctors and patients, who found her sex anomalous to her position. Men didn't want her looking at their 'bits', and some women thought it unseemly that she would poke around theirs. Helen had heard this conversation many times, and had always found it both depressing and reassuring that it wasn't just the police force that dismissed women as congenitally unsuited to 'manly' professions. Until recently, Helen had been a policewoman and had endured the daily derogations because she knew she was good at her job; better than most of her colleagues. Inspector Titus Lambert had seen this and had rewarded her. She'd lasted long enough in the Homicide unit to learn to respect Lambert more than she resented him, although a small ember of resentment held residual heat still. She couldn't quite forgive him for suspending her from the unit, despite her knowing that this hadn't been his decision.

'Helen Lord and Associates,' Clara said.

'That's what it says on the door, Clar, so it must be true.'

'This office is pretty flash. It's a proper suite, isn't it?'

'Three rooms plus bathroom and kitchen.'

'It's nicer than where I live.'

'I love your flat.'

'Or as I like to accurately call it, my bedsit. This must be costing you a fortune in rent. Is the private inquiry business in Melbourne sufficiently lucrative to offset that?'

'I have no idea, Clar. That's what I'm going to find out. However, I have one serious advantage over my competitors, and there are only a few of those anyway.'

'Oh?'

'I've done my accounting and, thanks to Uncle Peter's legacy, I've calculated that, taking all overheads into consideration, including wages and sundry expenses, Helen Lord and Associates can run without making a profit for something like ...' She paused for effect. '... thirty years.'

Clara laughed.

'So, you see, I don't need to panic about the bottom line until 1974. Ideally, of course, we will turn a profit.'

'I can't see you spying on wives for jealous husbands, or vice versa, and that's the bread and butter of this sort of business, isn't it?'

'There might have to be a bit of that, but I can afford to pick and choose. I don't really care if wives are cheating on their husbands.'

'You don't have a very high opinion of men, do you?'

'I haven't met a sufficient number of impressive men to believe that that's the norm.'

'Apart from Joe.'

The mention of Joe Sable's name caused Helen to blush lightly. This often happened when Clara spoke about him, because Clara Dawson was the only person privy to Helen's great secret — that she was in love with Joe Sable. This was a situation that infuriated and excited Helen in equal measure. She'd shared an office with him in the Homicide department, but she'd felt, wrongly she now knew, that she hadn't shared Inspector Lambert's respect equally. He was young, and had been promoted to sergeant so quickly that other policemen at Russell Street headquarters despised him. The promotion had been partly the result of personnel shortages. Those same shortages would never benefit Helen in the police force. Women weren't even required to wear a uniform, because extra stripes of office would never be conferred on them. If you were a woman, you went in as a constable, and no matter how hard you worked or how talented you were, it might take you 20 years to reach the giddy professional height of senior constable.

'Joe is a good man, Clar, but I'm a much better detective. He knows that, and I think it only bothers him a little bit.'

'He's working for you, so it can't bother him too much.'

'Am I doing the right thing, Clar? Is this all going to end in tears?'

'Working with friends is always risky. Actually employing them strikes me as fraught.'

'Joe is the only one on a full-time salary. He's the only qualified detective, so that's fair enough. Tom Mackenzie will have to go back to the air force eventually, once his wounds have properly healed. And Guy Kirkham, well, I don't know much about him, apart from the fact that he has courage and that he has nightmares.'

Clara laughed.

'When you line them up like that, Helen, it's like roll call at a casualty station. They're each recovering from injuries, physical and mental. Guy Kirkham has narcolepsy, for fuck's sake. Joe has an irregular heartbeat, and he's carrying the scars from torture. And Tom, my god, I'm surprised he's not a complete cot case after what happened to him. Maybe you should change the name to Helen Lord and Outpatients.'

'The thing is, Clar, they're my outpatients. When I turn up for work every day, I won't be breathing the same air as people I have no respect for.'

'You know you can count on me to help out whenever I can.'

'I'm absolutely counting on it, Clar.'

2

ZAC WILSON'S MEMORY of what had happened at Peter Fisher's house was uncertain. He couldn't piece things together into a coherent whole. He'd woken up in hospital, but had no idea how this had happened. There'd been something wrong with his hearing. Voices had seemed muted, echoey, and distant.

A week in hospital had eased a severe concussion, his hearing had improved, and his bruised body had turned various impossible shades of blue, green, and yellow. He knew his own name, he recognised his wife, and he began to worry about being away from the orchard. But the man who stood at the end of his bed wasn't familiar to him. He introduced himself as Inspector Titus Lambert, and he asked Zac if he felt up to answering a few questions.

'Of course. Are you from the police?'

'Yes. Homicide.'

'What's that?'

'We're a new division. We specialise in investigating suspicious deaths.'

'You mean murder?'

'Yes, murder.'

'Who's been murdered?'

Inspector Lambert looked at Zac Wilson and tried to determine if that question was genuine or disingenuous. Wilson's doctor had told Lambert that concussion had unpredictable consequences, and that every brain responded differently to trauma. Zac Wilson's memory might be affected, and that effect might be temporary or it might be permanent; it might also be partial. This made Wilson a problematic witness to the events at Fisher's farm.

'Your wife has been to visit you, I believe.'

'Yes.'

'Did she talk about what happened?'

'No. She said there was a tragedy at Peter Fisher's place. An explosion.'

'And you remember nothing about the explosion?'

Wilson closed his eyes. There was something forming behind them. A vague shape that resolved itself into the figure of a man walking towards him. He was holding something in his arms. The shape dissolved.

'Mr Wilson, I have to warn you that you are in serious trouble, so serious that your memory loss looks convenient.'

'I don't understand.'

'You know Peter Fisher?'

'Of course I do. He's my neighbour.'

'And you know his wife?'

'Deborah. Yes. She had a baby only recently.'

Lambert waited.

Wilson's face drained of colour so that the bruises under his eyes became stark.

'He showed me the baby,' he said. 'He was holding him, wrapped in something, a blanket maybe. There was blood.'

'When did he show you the baby?'

'It must have been ...' Wilson tried to concentrate. 'I don't know exactly. He was walking towards me, holding something, and then he said, "Dead. All dead."'

14

Wilson's face was contorted into puzzlement, as if his own words made no sense to him.

'And what happened next, Mr Wilson?'

'He said, "Dead. All dead." And then … why can't I remember what happened next?'

A voice behind Inspector Lambert, a voice he recognised, said, 'I think Mr Wilson needs to rest, Inspector.'

Lambert turned to greet Clara Dawson, a doctor whose abilities had impressed him greatly.

'Dr Dawson, I didn't know Mr Wilson was your patient. I was briefed by another doctor.'

'Strictly speaking, he isn't. The female ward is my usual stomping ground, but I'm plugging a gap temporarily here.'

Lambert turned to Zac Wilson.

'I'll need to speak to you again, Mr Wilson. If you remember any other details of the explosion, please let me know immediately. There's a constable here in the nurses' station who you can speak to.'

Wilson didn't ask why a constable had been posted in the hospital, but he nodded and instantly regretted it, as the nod seemed to unleash a headache of sudden ferocity.

Clara sat with Titus in a small, untidy room at the end of the ward. It was essentially a store cupboard, the nurses' station being too busy for privacy.

'I don't think I ever congratulated you on your evidence at the inquest,' Titus said.

'Thank you. I was pleased that the coroner didn't dismiss it as fanciful.'

'Can you give me a frank assessment of Mr Wilson's condition?'

'Where any injury to the brain is involved it's difficult to be either confidently predictive or properly accurate. What I can tell you is that he was incredibly, freakishly lucky not to have been burned.

The force of the explosion threw him beyond the heat. He has extensive, deep-tissue bruising, and he suffered a severe concussion. As far as we can tell, there isn't any significant brain damage. His speech is unaffected, and he has full movement of his limbs. He has memory loss, which is not unusual. This seems to be improving.'

'Could he be exaggerating or even faking these memory gaps?'

'I suppose that's possible, but why would he do that?'

'We have four dead bodies and one live one. It might be convenient for the live one to have no recollection of what happened.'

'You think Mr Wilson might be implicated in those deaths?'

'He was there.'

'There's something else, though, isn't there?'

'There are anomalies, but I can't discuss them with you.'

'It would be handy to know if you think we have a dangerous killer on this ward, Inspector.'

Clara almost called him 'Titus', but decided to stick with formality.

'My instinct tells me that Mr Wilson is a peripheral victim, but there is some evidence to suggest otherwise, and given the nature of these crimes I have to err on the side of safety. I'm going to arrest him, and I need to know when it's medically safe to place him on remand.'

'I read about those murders. The papers really enjoyed themselves. I can't believe Mr Wilson attacked a woman with an axe.'

'When can I arrest him, Doctor?'

Clara stood up and tried to disguise the dismay in her voice.

'Mr Wilson was due to go home tomorrow. He should be here longer, but we need the bed, and he's considered to be stable now. So I suppose you can arrest him now. How comfortable are the cells in the Magistrate's Court?'

'I wouldn't want to spend the night in one.'

'I'll organise Mr Wilson's clothes and belongings. I don't want to be here when you do this, Inspector.'

Titus got to his feet. He put his hand on Clara's arm, a gesture that took her by surprise.

'Doctor. Clara, I don't want to do this either. Can I be frank with you?'

'Of course.'

'We are so short-staffed and this case is so strange that I don't believe we're equipped to deal with it efficiently. My department has been so stripped of good detectives and so disrupted by recent events that I know we need help. Outside help. If I said that out loud at Russell Street, Commissioner Cottrell would demand my resignation. I'm exhausted, Clara.'

'I can recommend a first-class investigator. She's discreet and can work invisibly.'

Titus smiled wanly.

'Could you let Helen Lord know that I'll call at the house tonight at 7.30? I don't want any telephone trail that might indicate that I set up the meeting.'

'I'll telephone her and tell her to expect you.'

Before leaving the small office to give Zac Wilson the astonishing news that he was being arrested on suspicion of murder, Titus said, 'And, Clara, Mr Wilson's life might depend on Helen Lord's skills. I can't tell you how tangled the threads of this case are.'

Clara walked ahead of Titus and out of the ward. A policeman passed her. She turned to see him greet Inspector Lambert where he stood at the foot of Zac Wilson's bed.

IN THE WEEKS since Peter Lillee's death, his sister, Ros Lord, had made no changes in the huge house she'd inherited. Lillee's

17

portrait still hung in the dining room. The pictures he'd carefully chosen, some of which Ros knew to be valuable, remained hanging throughout the house, and his bedroom and its contents hadn't been touched. None of this was due to squeamishness, reverence, or denial. There was simply no pressing reason to remove the evidence of Peter's life. Despite four people living in the house, there was no need to free up space. The house could easily accommodate four more without Peter's room being called into service.

Ros had suggested to Joe Sable that he might like to move into Peter's bedroom, with its private bathroom, but Joe had declined the offer. His stay in the house wouldn't be permanent. As soon as he could find alternative accommodation he'd do so. Building a new house was out of the question at the moment. Materials for such an enterprise were scarce, and the war economy meant anyway that new builds were restricted. He'd have to buy an existing property, which he intended to do. It was simply a matter of finding one. There was no urgency, although Joe had never felt entirely at ease in Peter Lillee's house, despite every assurance that he was welcome. He'd accepted Helen's offer of employment, though, without hesitation. She'd assured him that he wouldn't be spying on the wives of disgruntled husbands.

Joe's experience in policing was limited. He'd been promoted quickly, too quickly, and the promotion had been a mistake. It had created resentment at Russell Street, and he'd disappointed Lambert, who'd made this clear and who hadn't discouraged Joe's resignation. He wasn't sure what private inquiry agents actually did. He'd always thought of them as vaguely sleazy, more associated with the lubricious *Truth* newspaper than either *The Argus* or *The Age*. He'd had a frank discussion with Helen before he'd accepted her offer of employment. His heart had sunk a little when she'd said that he'd need to do some work on book-keeping, not because the finances of Helen Lord and

Associates would be his concern, but because she imagined that corporate fraud might form a part of their investigations. Joe hated accounting. But what skills did he bring to this position? He'd been to detective school — that title belied the seriousness of the training he'd received there — and he had a good knowledge of European art and some acquaintance with Australian art. These were not particularly impressive credentials. Helen had told him that he was underestimating his abilities and that what he had in spades was a quality that no amount of training could provide: courage.

Joe was in his room reading when Inspector Lambert arrived to speak to Helen. Ros Lord answered the door. They spoke briefly about the sadness and distress of her brother's recent funeral, and she took him into the library, where Helen was waiting. Titus found the opulence of Peter Lillee's house — now, more correctly, Ros Lord's house — disconcerting. It didn't marry at all with what he knew of Helen Lord, and he felt slightly ill at ease, a feeling he didn't care for. The last time he'd felt like this had been inside St Patrick's cathedral. For her part, Helen too was uncomfortable. Here was Inspector Lambert, the head of Homicide and until recently her superior, sitting in her house, the house she'd grown up in and the grandeur of which she'd long since become inured to, and he was coming to her as a professional equal. Clara had passed on Lambert's request for a meeting and had said that it involved the recent deaths in Nunawading. She hadn't said any more than that. Despite the closeness of their friendship, Clara's discretion, until she was released from the need for it, was a quality that Helen admired and that she knew she could depend on.

Inspector Lambert took in the impressive room. The walls were crowded with pictures of various sizes. He supposed Joe Sable would know what each of them was, but to him they were simply a gallimaufry of shape and colour.

'Dr Dawson no doubt explained why I wanted to, needed to, talk to you.'

'Only in the sketchiest terms, Inspector.'

'I think we can dispense with the "Inspector", Helen.'

'I'll try, but it feels strange to call you "Titus". I've never thought of you as "Titus", only as Inspector Lambert.'

Lambert smiled. 'Well, I'm still that, but under the circumstances ...'

'I will try, Titus. Clara said that this was about those awful deaths in Nunawading. The newspapers had a bit of a field day.'

'They did, but they got nowhere near the truth, which is why I want to talk to you.'

'Four bodies, Titus. It's astonishing.'

'And one survivor.'

Lambert paused.

'He's a man named Zachary Wilson. He was injured in the explosion and has been in hospital with no memory of what happened, which may or may not be convenient. At the moment, for him it's inconvenient, because I've arrested him on suspicion of murder. And because the case has attracted such public notice, bail has been refused. Apparently, people won't feel safe in their beds unless they're assured the killer has been locked up.'

'You're not convinced, though, are you?'

'No.'

'Why arrest him?'

'This is where I hope you'll come in, Helen. My being here is, as you know, irregular, and irregular in a career-ending way if it got out.'

'You didn't need to say that, Titus.'

'Yes. I'm sorry. The information I'm about to give you is known to a handful of people inside Homicide.'

Lambert reached inside his coat and withdrew an envelope.

20

There was the slightest hesitancy in his movement, which Helen noticed and which she read as uncertainty about the course he'd chosen to take. She understood that what was about to happen represented a stunning breach of protocol, a breach for which Inspector Lambert ought rightly to be dismissed by his superiors. A small part of her wondered if she could trust a man capable of such a breach, despite the fact that he was demonstrating enormous trust in her. He handed Helen the first of four photographs — four from among the dozens taken by Martin Serong. Helen looked at the first photograph.

'The young man hanging from the rafter is a 17-year-old Italian farm worker named Emilio Barbero.'

Lambert was unsurprised when Helen immediately noticed the axe leaning against a wall, even though in this photograph it was out of focus.

'The axe was used to murder this woman.'

He passed a picture of Deborah Fisher to Helen. It was a wide shot of the bedroom, with Fisher's body, and the damage done to her face, clearly visible.

'I imagine there are more graphic photographs of this than you've chosen.'

'Yes. Her name is Deborah Fisher. She was 25 years old, and married to this man.'

He produced a small portrait photograph of Peter Fisher, borrowed from the house.

'He was 35. This is what was left of him.'

He gave Helen the final photograph. Again, this was a wide shot so that the bottom half of his torso was visible, as was the small, starkly white corpse of the baby in his lap.

'The man you've arrested for murder ...'

'Mr Zachary Wilson. He's an orchardist who owns the neighbouring property.'

'Which of these people is he suspected of having killed?'

'At this point, all of them.'

'So, to put it crudely, Mr Wilson took an axe to Mrs Fisher, strung Mr Barbero up, knocked Mr Fisher unconscious, or killed him, and then blew him up, and killed a six-month-old baby as well — not necessarily in that order.'

'That's certainly what we're supposed to believe, but there are complications.'

'How could this possibly get more complicated?'

'Emilio Barbero's are the only fingerprints on the axe handle, which would be suggestive, except that the autopsy revealed that he'd been dead for at least 12 hours before Deborah Fisher's death.'

'And I presume it was that axe that was used to kill her and the baby?'

'Blood and tissue from each of them was on the blade and on the handle, so we're assuming that was the particular weapon, yes.'

'So whoever wielded it wanted to implicate Emilio Barbero? But he was inconveniently already dead. He must have worn gloves — the killer, I mean.'

'Zachary Wilson was wearing gloves, gardening gloves, and there was blood on them. Deborah Fisher's blood. Peter Fisher wasn't wearing gloves, and his hands did have blood on them, but he was holding his dead son after all.'

'This looks too much like a lay-down misère to be an actual lay-down misère.'

'I haven't got to the complication yet.'

Lambert reached into his pocket again and produced a folded piece of paper.

'This is a piece of information that was withheld from the press. It's an accusation, typed, but signed by Peter Fisher. As far as we can tell, the signature is correct. It was found between the pages of a family Bible — a Fisher family Bible that dates back to the nineteenth century. Forensics have the Bible at the moment.'

'I presume you think the Bible itself might be of some significance.'

'Of great significance, but the nature of its significance is a mystery to me.'

Lambert left the implication unsaid that Helen Lord might solve that mystery. He passed her the typed accusatory letter.

'That, of course, is a copy, typed by me. We know that the original was typed on a machine in Fisher's house.' He didn't need to explain how they knew this. Idiosyncratic letters must have matched idiosyncratic keys. Helen read the letter.

'Zachary Wilson plans to kill me. He is a withersnake. He will kill us all. Peter Fisher.'

'What is a withersnake?'

'It isn't a word I was familiar with either. It's an archaic term with religious connotations. It means something like a betrayer.'

'A traitor?'

'Not exactly. Well, yes, but it's closer to a word like "apostate". Given where the note was found, there seems to be some sense that Mr Wilson was guilty, in Fisher's eyes at least, of some sort of religious betrayal.'

'What do you want me to do, Titus?'

'I want you to do some discreet snooping out in Nunawading. I can't pay you, and I can't give you any overt help.'

Helen handed all the material she'd been given back to Titus.

'I don't think I ever thanked you properly for making sure I was granted my licence, Titus. Helen Lord and Associates is now in business, and is happy to take the case, as they say.'

She reached out her hand, and Inspector Lambert leaned forward and shook it.

3

Joe Sable, having become used to the noise at Russell Street Police Headquarters — even with the doors closed there was never real silence — found the quiet at Helen Lord's office disconcerting. It wasn't absolute silence; there were sounds that came up from the street, but there were no telephones ringing, or voices raised, or muffled laughter. He had his own office, and it was generously proportioned. All of the furniture had been brought from the house in Kew. There were rooms in that house that were rarely used, or even entered, but Peter Lillee had never thought of any room in his house as just a place to store superfluous furniture. Each of them was neatly and deliberately arranged. Helen, with her mother's permission, had raided the spare rooms for chairs, desks, and even beautifully finished filing cabinets.

The desk Joe now sat at was large, and had been made in the 1920s by a skilled cabinet-maker. Its modern lines were at odds with much of the furniture in the Kew house, the contents of which was mostly a fastidiously curated collection of Edwardian splendour. This desk was much more to Joe's taste. Helen's desk was heavier and more ornate. With his door open he could see into the reception area. Two armchairs and a couch failed to crowd this room, and Helen had placed a table with six chairs at one end of it. Her office was next to his, and next to that was a small kitchen. The remaining room was a bathroom. This had been an expensive refit, and must have been done before the start of the war. The indoor lavatory and shower stall were luxury features for an office. Clearly, it had been designed to attract well-heeled tenants, and Helen Lord was certainly that.

Joe had read the detailed brief that Helen had prepared for him about the murders in Nunawading. There were descriptions of the photographs, but Inspector Lambert had taken the actual photographs away with him after his meeting with Helen. The brief was clear, concise, and dispassionate. It included a summary of the autopsy report on each of the bodies. It offered no speculations, but drew attention to certain anomalies or peculiarities. These included the absence of Zachary Wilson's fingerprints, the use of the Bible to conceal Peter Fisher's vaguely religious *J'accuse*, and the discrepancy in the time of death between the young Italian man and the other bodies. Whatever speculations might be made in this case would be made initially only in conversation. Helen believed that writing them down might secure them too firmly in their thinking, which might in turn misdirect them.

Joe was re-reading the final part of the report when Helen came into his office.

'What do you think?'

'I can't grasp the connections. Why was the Italian bloke hanged so much earlier?'

'What did you notice about his autopsy report?'

Helen saw Joe tense at her question and realised how it must have sounded to him.

'Sorry, Joe. That sounded like an exam question. I wasn't testing you. It wasn't something I picked up immediately. Clara drew my attention to it.'

'Clara has read your brief?'

'Of course she has. She was looking after Zac Wilson in hospital. You're my only employee, Joe, but we need Clara's expertise. She'll accept wine from Uncle Peter's cellar as payment. Apparently, the ligature marks around Emilio Barbero's neck are deep and more consistent with strangulation than hanging.'

'So he was strung up after he died?'

'Or at least at the point where he couldn't put up a fight.'

'This Zachary Wilson, is he guilty?'

'Clara doesn't think so, and she's met him and observed him closely. Inspector Lambert is ambivalent, I think, but leans more heavily towards his being innocent. I have no idea. We can't rule out Peter Fisher just because he's dead.'

Joe wondered, but only for a moment, if a father could take an axe to his infant son. Of course he could. Small children were being murdered in concentration camps in Europe in numbers that defied rational belief. There was no act so vile that someone, somewhere, couldn't commit it.

'I think we should start with Emilio Barbero,' Helen said. She handed Joe an address in Nunawading. 'He was a boarder with this woman, a Mrs Suckling, which is a hideous name.'

'It's a noble English name. Sir John Suckling was a great poet.'

'Probably not related to a woman in Nunawading. Anyway, thank you for plugging a gap in my knowledge. Uncle Peter's car has a full tank of petrol, but I don't think we'll be able to maintain the level-three exemption to the petrol ration that he'd been given. Mum is trying to sort that out. We may be able to get some sort of exemption as a legitimate business necessity. Uncle Peter had influential friends.'

'Peter must have had the inside running on critical shortages before any restrictions were introduced. There are six tyres in the garage.'

'We couldn't run this business without a vehicle.'

'It's a pretty flash vehicle to be beetling about in.'

Helen laughed. 'We all have to make do, Joe. There's a war on.'

MRS SUCKLING'S HOUSE in Nunawading sat beside a vacant block of land that was thick with thistles. The foundations of a house had been laid there, but the build had been abandoned. There were three similarly abandoned properties in the street. Joe, who'd lived in Melbourne all his life, had never ventured this far into the eastern suburbs. He'd been surprised on the drive out here at how quickly dense housing had given way to orchards and paddocks. When the war was over, and its conclusion now seemed inevitable, would he want to build a house out here? No, he thought. He didn't crave open space. He would rather look into a painting than out at a view.

There was a woman in the front yard of Mrs Suckling's house. She was perhaps in her sixties, although she may have been younger. Estimating women's ages was a skill Joe lacked. He was better with men, but was prepared to admit that he wasn't much better. The woman was wearing an apron and had her grey hair tied up in a scarf. She stood with her hands on her hips, and watched as Joe came towards her.

'Nice car,' she said. 'Yours, is it?'

'Strictly speaking, no. It's the company car. Mrs Suckling?'

'And what company would that be?'

Joe stayed at the gate.

'May I come on to the property?'

Mrs Suckling stepped forward and opened the gate.

'Please, come in.'

'My name is Joe Sable. I'm a private inquiry agent.'

'What's that when it's at home?'

'A private detective.'

'Handsome, too. Just like in the pictures. The wallopers have already been here about poor bloody Emilio. I presume that's why you've driven all this way in your big car.'

Joe couldn't get a handle on Mrs Suckling's demeanour. He wasn't sure if she was hostile or not.

'I would like to ask you some questions about Emilio Barbero, yes.'

'Why?'

That question was certainly hostile in tone.

'I want to find out why he died, Mrs Suckling, and I'd like to know something about him.'

'But why? That's the job of the police. Why are you involved?'

Joe ought to have been prepared for this question, but it flummoxed him briefly. He couldn't mention Inspector Lambert. That would have been an indiscretion. Instead he was vague, and hoped that Mrs Suckling would be satisfied.

'I'm representing a third party who has an interest in finding out who killed Mr Barbero. I can't tell you more than that.'

'So this third party doesn't think the police are up to it.'

'I can't discuss that, I'm sorry.'

'You'd better come in.'

Joe was relieved. Mrs Suckling's curiosity had overcome her suspicion, or Joe supposed that this was the case. At the front door of the house, Mrs Suckling hesitated.

'You'd better show some sort of identification. How do I know you didn't kill poor Emilio and now you've come to kill me?'

The question was intended to be humorous, but Joe detected a slight, nervous quaver in Mrs Suckling's voice, as though she'd suddenly realised she was taking a risk. Joe showed her his card, which she read closely.

'So you're a proper private detective, all registered and everything.'

'Yes, Mrs Suckling, I am.'

She opened the door, and Joe followed her into the house, which was stuffy and smelled of rendered lard. The living room was furnished cheaply, and the only art on the walls was a discoloured print of the ubiquitous 'Monarch of the Glen'. A narrow mantle held a few gewgaws, which told Joe all he needed to know about Mrs Suckling's taste.

'I'll make us a cup of tea.'

This wasn't a request. It was assumed that Joe would share a cup.

'I don't have any sugar,' she said.

'Black is fine.'

The tea was dark and bitter, and Joe sipped at it to be polite. He took out a notebook.

'Very official,' Mrs Suckling said.

Joe smiled. 'I don't trust my memory, Mrs Suckling. Tell me about Emilio Barbero.'

'Well, he was a lovely looking young man. Italian, of course, although his mother was Australian.'

'So Emilio was born here?'

'Oh yes. His father came over from Piedmont. I think that's right. Back in 1925, I believe. It wasn't a good marriage, or so Emilio told me. His mother's people couldn't accept that she'd married a dago. He barely spoke English and she didn't have any Italian, so god knows what they talked about. He left to get work up north in the canefields. She stayed behind with little Emilio. He never came back, not even when his wife died. Emilio would have been 16 then. This was just last year. That's when he came here to me. I advertised for a boarder, and he turned up. Nicely spoken, he was, and very easy on the eye, so I took him in.'

Joe found Mrs Suckling's slightly louche insistence on Emilio Barbero's attractiveness off-putting.

'He found work on that farm, just as a hand. We'd natter away over dinner.'

'Who would want to kill him?'

'No one.'

'Did you meet his employer? Mr Peter Fisher, I believe his name was.'

'No. Emilio said he had a young wife. Nice-looking woman, he said.' Joe noted the unspoken implication. Mrs Suckling watched as he jotted something in his notebook.

'You needn't be thinking there was anything between Emilio and Mrs Fisher. She was expecting a baby when he first started working there. It wasn't Emilio's baby, if that was where your mind was headed. I don't think he'd had any experience with women. He was only 17. He wouldn't go after another man's wife, especially when she was expecting.'

'Did he ever talk about Mr Fisher?'

Mrs Suckling put down her teacup.

'Oh, you're representing one of those people, aren't you?'

Joe hoped his face betrayed neither puzzlement nor sudden interest.

'Which people might they be?'

'They came here once or twice, talking to Emilio. I heard them. Sacrilege it was, and him a Catholic.'

'I'm sorry, Mrs Suckling, I don't understand.'

'Of course you do. They're paying you.'

Mrs Suckling picked up her teacup again, and as she was bringing it to her lips she said, 'Was Emilio sacrificed?'

Joe couldn't disguise his startlement.

'Sacrificed?'

'Well, they got up to all sorts of nonsense, didn't they? I don't know much about them, but Emilio told me a thing or two. He wasn't taken in by them. That's why they killed him, isn't it?'

'Mrs Suckling, I don't know who "they" are, but if "they" killed him, why would "they" hire me to investigate the death?'

Mrs Suckling thought about this for a moment. She nodded.

'Yes. That makes sense. So you're investigating them then.'

Joe tamped down his exasperation.

'Tell me about "them", Mrs Suckling.'

'The Messiah people. That Mr Fisher was one of them. And some of his neighbours.'

'You said they came here to talk to Emilio. Do you have any names?'

'Oh, so you *are* after them. I'm happy to help out then. Creepy, they are. I only knew one of them. He's a bloke named Anthony Prescott. Nasty man. Runs an orchard here in Nunawading. He was with a woman. I don't know her name. Not his wife, though. Half his age. They came here twice. The second time was just before Emilio died. Prescott got quite heated.'

'What about?'

'I wasn't listening at the door, Mr Sable. I'm not a nosey person. I mind my own business.'

'Of course, but if this Prescott was loud, you couldn't help but hear.'

Mrs Suckling accepted this as absolution for her nosiness.

'Well, I was in the kitchen, but I could hear him, clear as a bell, accusing Emilio of having betrayed them. He used a word I don't know. Apos … apos … something.'

'Apostasy?'

'That's it. Don't know what it means. Do you?'

'Yes, I do. Did Emilio say anything?'

'He was always very quiet. Never raised his voice, so I couldn't hear what he said. Afterwards, when they'd left, he came out of his bedroom and looked as pale as a ghost. Prescott had given him a fright, that's for sure. He said he was going to leave Fisher's farm as soon as he could find another job.'

'Did Prescott threaten him?'

'He was loud and angry. That's threatening, isn't it?'

'Did you tell the police about Prescott?'

'They didn't ask. Besides, I didn't like the policemen who came here. Untrustworthy looking. Shifty. And rude. I should have told them, but I just wanted them off my property. They thought they could poke about like they owned the place. I was going to write something down and post it to them. I don't have a telephone. But you turned up, so now I don't need to.'

Joe wondered who these two clumsy Homicide detectives were. Inspector Lambert couldn't have been one of them. He wouldn't have mishandled the interview so badly. Only a few weeks had passed since he'd resigned from Homicide and from the police force. He knew that the unit had been severely disrupted, so perhaps the two men who'd called on Mrs Suckling were recent, inexperienced recruits. Lambert liked to hand-pick his detectives, but the war had stripped a lot of good men out of the force.

'And you know nothing about the young woman who was with Prescott?'

'She didn't say anything. She was pretty enough. She wore her hair like Veronica Lake. I think she was there to catch Emilio's eye.'

She thought for a moment.

'I think she was bait. Prescott must have thought Emilio would go to their meetings if there was a pretty girl there.'

'And did he go?'

'He must have, mustn't he, if Prescott turned up here accusing him of aposathingummy. What does it mean?'

'It means the renunciation of a religious belief. Once upon a time, you'd be burned at the stake for it.'

Mrs Suckling laughed.

'I'm in trouble then. I used to be C of E. What about you?'

'I'm Jewish, Mrs Suckling.'

'Are you now? How very interesting. My sister, Eunice, married a Jew. Caused a fuss in the family, I can tell you. Not with me, mind. I thought he was a lovely bloke. I've lost touch with them. They moved to Germany, oh, 25 years ago. He was a German boy. So, two strikes against him — a German and a Jew. Dad disowned Eunice. Good riddance, he said, when they moved to Germany. She converted, of course. He'd have disowned her if she'd married a Catholic, so you can imagine. A Jew was beyond the pale. I worry about them over there. He had a good job. Came from a good family, so I'm sure they'll be all right.'

'Do you read the papers, Mrs Suckling?'

'I glance at them, but I can't bear to read them too closely.'

Joe wondered if Mrs Suckling knew what was happening to Jews in Europe. He decided against discussing it with her, particularly as he was sure that the chances of her sister and brother-in-law being alive were slim. He'd been collecting articles about Hitler's program of ridding Europe of Jews, but despite the unimaginable nature of the crimes described, they never made it to the front page. Small articles tucked away among competing news detailed acts of monstrous inhumanity. For Joe, the few words that were written about it were deafening howls of suffering. Those around him seemed oblivious to them. Joe worried that the ignorance of even his friends was poisonous, and in low moments he allowed himself to suspect it wasn't ignorance at all, but indifference.

'May I see Emilio's room?'

'Of course. I haven't tidied it. It's just as he left it. He didn't have much.'

Joe wasn't sure what he was hoping to find in Barbero's room. There were only a few items of clothing. A 17-year-old farm hand doesn't accumulate much in the way of a wardrobe. There was a framed photograph of a couple Joe presumed to be Emilio's parents, a string of rosary beads — which, given their feminine design, had probably belonged to the late Mrs Barbero — a few books, and a copy of *Modern Screen* from 1938. Joe checked the wardrobe, under the mattress, and under the bed. There was no trunk, no cache of letters, no photograph album.

'Not much to be going on with, is there?' Mrs Suckling said when Joe returned to the living room.

'When he arrived, did he have a suitcase?'

'No. He brought all his belongings in a hessian bag. He didn't even own a razor. Well, he didn't need one when he first got here, he was that young. He started to use my late husband's just recently. He had nothing much more than the clothes he stood up in.'

'You don't know where he lived before he came here?'

'No, sorry. Somewhere in Fitzroy, I think he said, but he never mentioned an address.'

'I've taken up enough of your time, Mrs Suckling. Thank you. If you think of anything else, could you telephone me or drop me a note?'

Joe gave Mrs Suckling his card.

'Just one more thing,' he said. 'Did Emilio speak good English?'

'Well, of course he did. He was born here. His mother was Australian. He was smart, too. What a strange question. I did tell you that already. You need to pay closer attention if you're going to be a proper detective.'

She smiled, but Joe felt stung.

'Just double-checking, Mrs Suckling.'

On the drive back to the Helen Lord and Associates office, Joe allowed himself the luxury of feeling pleased that this initial interview, the first in his job as a private inquiry agent, had gone well, despite that final, small dig. He had a name, Anthony

Prescott, that the police had failed to discover, and even a possible motive, although the idea of some sort of Messianic cult seemed absurd.

HELEN LORD WASN'T in the office when Joe returned. He typed up his notes and checked the telephone directory for Anthony Prescott. There was one A. Prescott, but the address was in Sunshine, a suburb on the opposite side of the city to Nunawading, where Mrs Suckling had said his orchard was. He telephoned, just to be sure, and was told that a Mr Albert Prescott, retired, lived there.

When Helen came back, Joe outlined his interview with Mrs Suckling and handed her his typed summary.

'We're already ahead of the police,' Helen said. 'Well done. What do you make of the religious stuff?'

'When people throw words around like "apostasy" it makes me nervous. It's a word I associate with fanatics, and fanatics operate beyond logic and reason. Fanaticism is how you end up with four people dead.'

'I want to talk to Zachary Wilson's wife. She might be able to give us an address for this Prescott character. I'll need the car tomorrow morning.'

They talked generally about the case and specifically about Inspector Lambert's sense that an innocent man might be on remand. Joe wasn't convinced that Lambert was so sure of Wilson's innocence. Why would he arrest him?

'I presume,' Helen said, 'he was under pressure to calm the public down. Remember the hysteria about Leonski? All the press rubbish about Australia's Ripper? And the press loved this one. So much blood and gore, and four dead. Lambert would have been told to do something about people thinking they might be murdered in their beds. Having a suspect in custody is bad for the suspect, but good for Mr and Mrs Melbourne. Lambert's not happy about it. That's the sense I got from him anyway.'

'Lambert could be wrong.'

'Our job is to find that out.'

Guy Kirkham slipped into unconsciousness twice while waiting for Clara Dawson to leave work at the Royal Melbourne Hospital. He was nervous, and his narcolepsy attacked him whenever he felt anxious, or so it seemed to him. In fact, it was more unpredictable than this. Clara wasn't expecting him, which was the source of his nervousness. He knew that her shift at the hospital was due to finish at 4.00 pm — he'd wangled this information out of Helen Lord. He stood at the corner of Swanston and Lonsdale Streets, although he sat down against the wall he'd been leaning against after the first narcoleptic episode. This had lasted only a few seconds. It had been so brief that he hadn't fallen over. He reckoned that it would be safer to sit. He'd be less likely to end up prone and the object of attention.

He could see the front door. When Clara hadn't emerged by 4.30, he began to think she might have used a back exit. He supposed, though, that a doctor's shift would never run according to the clock — it would be subject to hold-ups and last-minute emergencies. He'd give her until five o'clock before abandoning his plan. Not that asking someone to the pictures constituted much of a plan. Clara had already turned him down once. She'd done it with good humour, though, and had given Guy the impression that he might meet with success on another occasion. Guy could understand her reluctance. What, after all, could he offer her? She was highly intelligent, skilled, and employed. He was unemployed, possibly unemployable, strapped for cash, and, for all intents and purposes, homeless. He was no one's idea of a fine catch. Still, he was good company, and he'd been told by more than one of his intimate companions, both men and women, that he was good at sex. This wasn't something he felt he could boast about. Clara didn't strike him as the kind of woman who'd respond well to any sort of boastfulness, let alone that sort of boastfulness.

At five, Clara came out of the hospital. Guy got to his feet and began waving his arms to attract her attention. She saw him, and signalled that she'd done so. He crossed the street to her.

'You're wearing a hat,' she said.

'I thought I'd make an effort and try to impress you.'

She laughed.

'And you think all it takes is a hat.'

Guy tried to look sheepish.

'It's all I've got. Just a hat.'

'Is it your hat?'

'No. It's Joe's hat. We have the same size head, only there's more inside his than in mine.'

'So, not even a hat, Guy, to call your own. Maybe I need to take you to the pictures.'

'Yes, please.'

'Why don't we go to a café instead? I'd like a decent cup of tea.'

They walked to the Liberty Bell Café in Collins Street. In 1942 the Liberty Bell had been busy with American servicemen, and it had kept its doors open until late in the evening. Now there were fewer and fewer Americans in Melbourne, but the Liberty Bell maintained its late trading hours. Joe had mentioned this café to Guy. It was here that he'd met the people who would lead him into the brutal investigation that had left him and Tom Mackenzie badly wounded. Guy was interested to see the place, and it was he who suggested it to Clara.

'Oh, I know the Liberty Bell,' she said. 'Yes, let's go there.'

There was, of course, nothing about the café to suggest its role in Joe Sable's case. It was crowded, but Guy and Clara found a table at the back of the room. Despite its busyness, conversation was possible without having to shout across the table.

The social niceties had been exchanged on the walk to the café, so Clara felt able to ask Guy a personal question.

'Have you had any narcoleptic episodes recently, Guy?'

'Is this a free medical consultation?'

'Well, you know, I am a doctor. I'm interested. You're the only narcoleptic I know.'

'I had two small ones while I was waiting for you.'

'So just thinking of me puts you to sleep.'

Guy laughed.

'I'm awake now. Ask more questions. Strike while the iron is hot.'

They ordered tea, and when they'd drunk it they realised they were hungry, and settled on lamb chops with vegetables and gravy. Everything was overcooked, but neither of them cared particularly. Clara spoke about her friendship with Helen Lord, and answered Guy's questions about working in a large hospital. He was a little disappointed that Clara didn't interrogate him. He would have been willing to have been unguarded in most of his responses, but she didn't ask him many questions, and the questions she did ask were inconsequential. What was he reading? What movies did he enjoy? Did he read *The Age* or *The Argus*? It wasn't awkward exactly, but it was small talk, and Guy thought the incident at Peter Lillee's wake ought to be raised.

'It's amazing that no one was hurt, don't you think?' Guy said.

'Someone was hurt, Guy.'

'He doesn't count.'

'You were brave. If you hadn't been there, things would have been a lot worse.'

'It was just instinct.'

Now that the subject had been broached, Clara asked Guy

what he thought of Helen's decision to set up as a private inquiry agent.

'I don't really know her,' he said. 'She and Mrs Lord have taken me in off the street, and I can't tell you how grateful I am for that, but I met Helen for the first time just a few weeks ago. She's given Joe a job, which is great. What do you think about it? You know her much better than I do.'

'Helen is the smartest person I know, but I hate the idea of her putting herself in any sort of danger. I couldn't do it. I meet enough unpleasant people just accidentally in the course of a day. I can't imagine deliberately setting out to find them, and that's what a private inquiry agent does, isn't it? The ugly behaviour of others becomes your bread and butter.'

'I hope some of that bread and butter falls my way. I can't work as a private detective, but Helen did say that there are no laws about me helping out with stuff like surveillance.'

'Actually, Guy, I think there might be laws about that.'

'I suppose she meant that there are ways around them.'

'Your family doesn't live in Melbourne, do they?'

The non sequitur threw Guy for a moment. The last thing he wanted to talk about was his family.

'No,' he said, and he said it so emphatically that Clara understood that further questions along this line would be unwelcome. There was a change between them after that. It was subtle, but each of them was aware that the light-heartedness with which the evening had begun had darkened a little. They spoke of other things, and it was pleasant, but neither of them tried very hard to extend the evening. Clara wasn't in any way offended. She liked Guy's company. Guy, however, felt he'd spoiled their meeting, and he couldn't find a way of retrieving it. He'd wanted to impress Clara, to charm her, and instead he'd revealed to her a truculence that she no doubt found unattractive.

Guy offered to walk Clara to her flat in East Melbourne. She declined the offer, and seeing that Guy had taken this as a kind of reproach, she said, 'You know, Guy, I would like to go to the pictures with you. It's just a matter of finding the time.'

'Are you serious?'

'Absolutely. You're good company, Guy, and good company is rare and precious.'

Rare and precious. Guy thought seriously about having those words tattooed somewhere on his body.

4

MEREDITH WILSON HAD pondered on more than one occasion whether she'd have married Zachary Wilson if she hadn't been pregnant. But she had been pregnant, so the luxury of choice had been denied her. Having the baby out of wedlock had been out of the question. Within two months of the marriage, Meredith had miscarried, and in the ensuing ten years she hadn't become pregnant again. Sometimes she looked at her husband across the table and thought that, if she'd just waited, someone better might have come along. He didn't disgust her. He was quite good-looking and he hadn't let himself run to fat, and he was clean. He wasn't dull — he could make her laugh — but the grinding rhythm of orchard farming stifled passion. How many conversations could a person endure about gall wasps and leaf mould?

The orchard provided the Wilsons with a living, but profits fluctuated, and Meredith had come to know that Mother Nature was a bitch with no interest in the welfare or wellbeing of the pathetic creatures who depended on her largesse. She'd shrivel or swell a crop with an equal show of indifference. There were few luxuries in the Wilson house, not that Meredith craved them. What she craved was company. Her brother visited sometimes and stayed overnight, which would have been fine if she'd liked him.

She didn't. The nearest neighbour was Peter Fisher. Fisher had a young wife. Meredith had spoken to her once or twice, but what did she have in common with a 25-year-old? Mrs Fisher had had a baby, and maybe they could have found common ground there. But there was that nonsense that her husband Peter preached, and which her own husband had been seduced by. They'd had rows about that, ugly rows. Meredith thought she'd married an intelligent man, not a gullible one. He'd discovered that he'd been a fool, but Meredith had seen the weakness in him, and it diminished him so that now, as he sat alone on remand, she felt neither grief nor dread. She didn't believe for a minute that he was guilty of these crimes, but his suffering failed to touch her somehow. His absence meant that she had to walk the rows of trees. She thought she'd despise this, but the exhaustion that almost overwhelmed her that first night was glorious. Why had she been confined — why had she confined herself (Zac had never demanded it of her) — to the farmhouse?

HELEN LORD STOPPED at the Fisher place first. She hadn't expected anyone to be there. There was someone there, though, and it was someone who didn't want to be seen. Helen stepped from the car and was aware of a movement, almost the memory of a movement, behind one of the windows. Was it a shadow shifting, or the faintest shiver of a curtain? It was furtive, and it signalled to Helen that she needed to be wary. She'd checked with Inspector Lambert, who'd told her that the Fisher house was unoccupied and that forensics had completed all their work on it. Perhaps it was a member of Peter Fisher's family, or his wife's family. Someone, after all, had to have an interest in the property. Helen had intended to simply walk about to get a feel for the scene of this hideous crime. She'd had no expectation that she'd get into the house. Now, though, she thought it was worth trying to do just that. She'd been spotted, so knocking on the door seemed logical. There was no answer. She moved to the veranda, and stood where Emilio Barbero's body had hung. There was no evidence of his pointless death. She returned to the door and knocked again. Did someone move within? Helen tried the doorknob, and it turned. Whoever was inside had entered with a key. Why was he, or she, reluctant to answer the door? Four people had died in this place. Helen's heart was pounding as she pushed the door open and entered the house.

It was an ordinary house with a living room well lit by the morning sun. Could something unspeakable really have happened here among the knick-knacks and domestic disorder of ordinary lives? Helen stood still, conscious that there was another person taking breaths in here, and that that person didn't want to be discovered.

'My name is Helen Lord,' she said, loudly enough to penetrate every room. Silence.

Helen identified the door to the bedroom where Deborah Fisher's body had been found. It was closed. She felt slightly foolish, but she knocked on it, gently, as if Mrs Fisher and her baby might still be woken from a slumber. She went into the bedroom and stood at the foot of the Fishers' bed. It had been stripped of its bedclothes, but the mattress showed the dried wash of blood that had flowed from Deborah Fisher's body.

There was, too, a horrible odour that made Helen gag. She put her finger under her nose, and was unprepared for the hard shove in her back that propelled her onto the foul mattress. She hit it with sufficient force to feel dazed, but the awareness that her face was in contact with Deborah Fisher's dried blood made Helen recoil and scramble to her feet. She felt ill, and had to wait while she quelled the bile that was rising in her stomach. When she'd regained her composure and her alertness, she began to search for her assailant. She checked every room in the house, her initial tentativeness on entering rooms giving way to indignation at having been manhandled. There was no one in the house. She hurried outside, but whoever had pushed her had fled. She turned on a tap attached to a water tank and washed her face. She tried to assess the strength of the hands that had assaulted her. Were they a man's hands or a woman's?

Having gained a clear idea of the murder scene, Helen drove to the neighbouring orchard. Meredith Wilson wasn't expecting her, and she would doubtless be suspicious of a woman claiming to be a private detective. Helen hoped that Meredith's desire to have her husband released from jail, and from suspicion, would allow her to speak freely, particularly about Zac Wilson's relationship with his neighbours.

There was no answer to Helen's knock on Meredith Wilson's door. There was a small truck in the driveway with 'Wilson's Fruit' printed on its doors. Unless they also owned a car, which was unlikely, Helen surmised that Meredith must be somewhere on the property. She walked to the back garden, which was unkempt, although perhaps it looked that way because it had largely been given over to growing vegetables — and vegetables, Helen thought, always looked unruly and ungoverned even when they were carefully tended. She saw the figure of a woman in the middle distance, reaching up to prune a tree. Helen walked towards her. She was noticed quickly, and the woman stopped what she was doing. She let her arms drop to her sides and simply waited.

'Mrs Wilson?'

'Yes.'

'My name is Helen Lord. I want to prove that your husband is innocent.'

'Why?'

This was not the response to her cool declaration that Helen had expected, and when she reflected on it later, she realised that it pointed to something formidable in Meredith Wilson.

'I'm a private inquiry agent, Mrs Wilson.' Helen produced her identity card. 'I'm interested in justice, and I think the police have arrested the wrong man.'

'You're also in business, Miss Lord. I wonder how proving my husband innocent might be financially rewarding to you. Are you hoping I'll pay you?'

'I have no financial interest in this at all, Mrs Wilson. I'm not being paid by anyone, and I'm not expecting payment from anyone.'

Meredith removed the gloves she'd been wearing.

'I am half-sick of crusading, Miss Lord,' she said wearily. 'Still, you'd better come into the house. Talking to you is the least I can do for my husband.'

Her tone suggested to Helen that the least Meredith could do might be her preferred option.

Meredith didn't offer Helen a cup of tea. The stove had no fire in it, so it would have taken an effort Meredith was unwilling to make to begin the process of tea-making. She wasn't intimidated by Helen's presence, and she sat across from her at the kitchen table, looking directly at her.

'You've spoken to the police, of course,' Helen said.

'Of course. I wasn't very helpful. I wasn't deliberately unhelpful, but I don't think I was of much use to them. They've been back a couple of times. I got the impression they think I know more than I'm telling them.'

'And is that impression correct?'

'Well ...'

'Did you, for example, mention anything about the Messiah?'

Helen had intended to introduce this shred of information much later in the conversation. She'd hoped, in fact, that Meredith

Wilson might mention it unbidden. It seemed right to her, though, having met and assessed Meredith, that she should produce it early. It was risky, because she had nothing to back it up with. It was bluff. The effect on Meredith looked at first to be minimal. She straightened slightly, and her lips, which had been parted, closed. These small reactions disguised a rush of emotions that if separated would have included dismay, relief, astonishment, and fear.

'None of the policemen mentioned that,' she said.

'I'm not a policeman, Mrs Fisher.'

Helen had fired her one piece of ammunition, and knew instinctively that the worst thing she could do was attempt to direct the interview at this point.

'My husband was a fool. A complete fool. Imagine believing that that unimpressive little Peter Fisher was the Messiah. It's laughable, or it would be if it wasn't so bloody stupid.'

Helen wished that Joe was here with her. She felt ill-equipped to wrestle with anything to do with religion. She'd had a desultory acquaintance with it at Methodist Ladies' College, but neither her mother nor her uncle had been religious, so she'd never experienced, or even witnessed, zealously expressed faith. Joe wasn't religious either — she knew that — but he had a better grasp than she had of the arcane workings of various institutions. Helen tried to maintain the fiction that nothing Meredith Wilson was saying was new to her.

'Did your husband talk to you about his belief?'

'There were a few months when he talked about nothing else. It was as if he'd lost his mind. I mean, have you ever seen Peter Fisher?'

'Only a photograph.'

'He was unprepossessing, to say the least, and he had a high, wheedling voice. That, I said to Zac, is not the voice of God. He realised that himself soon enough, of course, but not before he'd given Fisher hundreds of pounds. He's embarrassed about it now.'

'And angry?'

'That's a disappointingly obvious leading question, Miss Lord.'

'Is there a disappointingly obvious answer?'

'There is,' she said. 'Zac was more ashamed of his gullibility than he was angry about it. So, no, he wasn't so enraged that he went berserk and murdered four people.'

'It must be upsetting to have him on remand.'

'It's upsetting for him, certainly.'

Helen liked the frank lack of ambiguity in this answer. Apart from anything else, it lent credence to Meredith's claim that her husband was innocent, or at the very least it lent credence to her belief that he was innocent.

'I know what you must be thinking, Miss Lord: if not Zac, then who?'

'Tell me about Anthony Prescott.'

'So you know something about these people already.'

Helen decided that Meredith would discover fairly quickly that all she had was a name, and the vaguest idea about some strange religious goings-on. Her instinct was to come clean.

'To be honest, Mrs Wilson, I was trying to create the impression that I know more than I do. I know the barest details, and none of them makes much sense to me. Anthony Prescott is just a name that was mentioned by someone connected to Emilio Barbero. You can safely assume that I'm working in the dark. Any light you can shine would be appreciated.'

'You had me fooled,' she said.

'I don't want to fool you. I want to find out what happened at the Fisher house.'

Meredith folded her arms and looked directly at Helen.

'I've got work to do. If you walk with me along the rows, we'll

47

talk. Peter Fisher was a madman, and somehow his madness was contagious.'

She stood up, put on work gloves, and. with Helen following close behind, left the house.

Tom Mackenzie wasn't expecting visitors. Just a few months earlier, a knock at the door might have aroused annoyance, or curiosity. Now, it made him jump. His flinch made him realise that despite feeling stronger, residual damage to his nerves remained. There was no need to be nervous. The threat to his personal safety had been removed. Whoever was at the door hadn't come to kill him. He knew this, and even though he understood that it was irrational, he was afraid.

There were two men on his doorstep. One of them was facing him; the other had his back turned, watching the street. Tom didn't recognise them, but recognised their type. They wore suits, and not the cheap Dedman suits that men had been encouraged to buy once the war had got under way. These suits had both cuffs and pockets. Their hats were also of superior quality.

'You blokes are supposed to be invisible,' Tom said. 'You might as well carry a big sign reading Military Intelligence.'

The man who'd been surveilling the street turned around, and smiled. It was he who spoke.

'Group Captain Thomas Mackenzie.'

'Are you asking me or telling me?'

The man who'd knocked on the door removed his hat to reveal a carefully oiled head of well-cut, copper-coloured hair.

'I've seen you around the corridors at Victoria Barracks, sir,' he said. 'May we come in?'

'I'm not in uniform, so you don't need to call me sir.'

'We, however, are in uniform. Apparently,' he said, and smiled.

Tom, in the face of both the deferential tone and demeanour of each of these men, was conscious that his hostility was unwarranted.

'How do I know you are who you say you are?'

'We haven't said who we are yet, sir, but your first impression was correct. I'm Benjamin Newman, and this chap' — he unexpectedly put his hand on the man's shoulder — 'this chap is Vincent Deighton.'

Deighton removed his hat. His hair was dark and receding at a rate that, Tom thought, probably bothered him, given that he looked no older than thirty.

'We're stationed in hopelessly cramped conditions at Victoria Barracks, in the Office for Native Policy in Mandated Territory.'

'So, Military Intelligence,' Tom said.

'Precisely.'

'You'd better come inside.'

When both visitors were seated in Tom's living room, he offered them tea, which they declined. Benjamin Newman placed his hat on the arm of his chair. Vincent Deighton held his, and moved it around between his fingers. Newman seemed to Tom to be the senior of the two, although they were close in age.

'It won't surprise you to know, sir, that we've read the report on your …' He paused to find the right word. 'Ordeal. May I say that your physical recovery has been remarkable?'

Tom liked the discretion shown by the use of 'physical' and the slight emphasis Newman had given it.

'You weren't, of course, working for us.'

'I was voluntarily alleviating the boredom of my job. Are you here to tell me I've committed some sort of offence?'

'I won't beat about the bush, sir. You weren't working for us then. We'd like you to work for us now.'

Tom made a small, involuntary noise, somewhere between a cough and a laugh.

'That was not what I was expecting you to say.'

'We were going to wait until you were fully recovered.' He nodded towards the splint on Tom's left hand. 'But now that your sister and brother-in-law have moved out, we'd thought we'd approach now.'

'How do you even know that Maude and Titus were staying with me?'

'We've been watching you. In a desultory kind of way, you understand. Nothing round-the-clock or intrusive.'

Tom wanted to be outraged, but he liked Newman's tone too much to challenge him. He was not at all what he expected a Military Intelligence man to be. He noticed the faintest odour of coconut in the air, and realised that it was coming from Benjamin Newman's hair. He associated that pleasant smell with his grandfather, who'd kept his thick hair in order with Macassar oil.

'We've sorted out the details with the air force wallahs, or the top wallahs, at any rate. You would have returned to work in a few weeks, but we'd like you to bring that forward. When I say we want you to work for us, we don't want anyone in your section to know this. You will be Group Captain Thomas Mackenzie, as you were before, in your air force clobber, parked away in requisitions. You will, however, be reporting to Military Intelligence.'

'Why?'

'A not-unreasonable question. I'll let Vincent explain.'

'It's delicate. There's a man who has recently been posted to Victoria Barracks. His name is Flight Lieutenant Winslow Fazackerly.'

'I've never heard the name before.'

'No. He arrived soon after you went on leave. He comes with connections. Old Melbourne money. His father is a KC and a member of the Australia Club. His mother is related in some obscure but socially useful way to the Mountbattens. His sister lives in England, and is married to some toff. All in all, he's pretty well set up and has managed to have, so far, a cosy war. He keeps to himself, and he presents as a decent bloke. He doesn't lord it over anyone. He just goes about his job quietly and efficiently.'

'There's a big "but" waiting to come out of the gates, isn't there?'

'We want you to cultivate him, get to know him, gain his trust.'

'Why?'

'We think he's a fifth columnist, which sounds melodramatic, but there it is.'

'A Nazi sympathiser?'

'Oddly, no. We think his loyalties are with Japan.'

'How very peculiar. When do I start?'

Benjamin Newman and Vincent Deighton stood up.

'Tomorrow is Thursday, which is an odd day to return to work,' Newman said. 'But we'd rather you didn't wait until Monday.'

'Tomorrow is good.'

'Thank you, sir. A man named Tom Chafer is our immediate boss. He'll meet you at 7.00 a.m, in the Office of Native Policy for Mandated Territory. It's tucked away.'

'I know where it is. This meeting with Chafer, it was already scheduled, wasn't it?'

Benjamin Newman put his hat on.

'Yes, it was. We weren't expecting you to say no.'

On the way out, Newman said, 'Oh, just one more thing, sir. When you meet Tom Chafer, you won't like him, and the more you'll get to know him, the less you'll like him. That's a simple fact and not a state secret.'

'I've met Chafer, and the memory isn't a rosy one.'

✸

MEREDITH WILSON CARRIED a stepladder with her, and as she came to each tree she examined the low-hanging fruit, and then mounted the ladder to look at the higher fruit.

'It's strange,' she said, 'but after doing this a few times you get to know every single piece of fruit, and losing even one is upsetting. Isn't that ridiculous?'

'I've never really liked pears.'

'These aren't ready yet. If they were, I could convert you with a really good one, straight from the tree. But you're not here to talk about fruit, Miss Lord.'

'Can you tell me anything about Anthony Prescott?'

'Not much. I stayed well out of all the nonsense. I've met him, and I can tell you where his orchard is. I didn't like him. He was here one night, with Fisher, talking to Zac, or rather trying to get more money out of him. Prescott struck me as a bit of a thug. I was dismissed as irrelevant as soon as he realised my position. Only he wasn't just dismissive — he was rude and aggressive. What upset me about that was that Zac didn't leap to my defence. He should have thrown Prescott off the property, but at that stage, with Fisher in the room, he thought he was in the presence of God. Laughable. Prescott was Fisher's main apostle, but I thought he was actually running the show.'

'So Prescott believed that Fisher was a god?'

'Not a god, Miss Lord. God himself. The Messiah come to Earth and made incarnate in the unimpressive body of Peter Fisher. This was a man who never bothered to shave properly. He missed bits and cut himself. You'd expect the Messiah to be presentable, wouldn't you?'

Helen laughed.

'I'd say that's the minimum I'd expect,' she said.

'Zac had an answer for that, of course. The whole point was, he said, that God would choose to return as an ordinary man. Jesus was a lowly carpenter. He's not going to come back as Cary Grant. That wouldn't test anyone's faith.'

'How many people did Peter Fisher take in?'

'Oh, dozens. He had quite a following. They must be a bit confused now. Fisher's death puts a bit of a dent in his claim that he was immortal.'

Meredith climbed down from the ladder and faced Helen.

'That was his claim, Miss Lord. Your incredulity is the proper response. None of this will make much sense until I've told you everything that Zac told me, and even then it will beggar belief. I have documents back in the house that will fill in the background. It's fascinating, in a macabre sort of way, or it would be if it had remained in the past.'

Helen looked quizzical.

'This is all about the past, Miss Lord, and a huckster who Peter Fisher claimed as his great-great-grandfather.'

'A huckster?'

'A conman, whose ridiculous claims have fallen out of history. When we get back to the house, I'll introduce you to the Nunawading Messiah.'

Helen couldn't contain a snigger of disbelief.

'Those are two words that don't feel like they belong together,' she said.

'And it doesn't matter how often you repeat them, they still seem wrong. And yet in 1871 hundreds of people fell hook, line, and sinker for the first Peter Fisher.'

HELEN LORD PASSED a leather-bound document case to Joe. She'd told him about her visit to Fisher's place and that she'd been

shoved hard from behind. She'd also relayed her impressions of
Meredith Wilson.

'I like her. It must be disappointing when you discover that your
husband is a nong, even when he comes to realise this himself.
I've read the documents she gave me. They are bizarre. They
originally belonged to Peter Fisher. Meredith doesn't know how
Zac came to have them. She thinks he may have taken them from
Fisher's house at some stage. And I don't understand why Fisher
kept them. You'll see what I mean when you read them.'

There were many yellowing and fragile pages from newspapers,
which Joe put on the desk in front of him.

'These have been handed down in Fisher's family,' Helen said.
She leaned across and took two of the reports from the pile.

'Start with these two. They give you the gist.'

Joe picked up an article headed 'The Nunawading Messiah.
Extraordinary disclosures'. It was taken from *The Age*, and dated
14 July 1871:

> Considerable excitement has been raised in Nunawading,
> Oakleigh, and that neighbourhood, during the last few days,
> by revelations made as to the impostures practised by one
> Fisher, a charcoal burner, in Nunawading, who claims to be
> the Messiah. One of his dupes, named Andrew Wilson, has
> charged him with obtaining money under false pretences, and
> the case was on the list for hearing at the Oakleigh Court of
> Petty Sessions on Saturday last.

Joe looked up from the paper.

'Fisher and Wilson? So Peter Fisher is a descendant of this Messiah
Fisher. What about Wilson? Is he related to this Wilson here?'

'That's something that might be important. I don't know. It
could be coincidence, although farming families do tend to stay

in one place for generations. It gets more intriguing, believe me. Read on.'

The following is a statement made to our reporter on Saturday evening by Wilson in the presence of his wife and a number of his acquaintances:–

'I am a member of the Wesleyan body and one of those who look for the coming of the Messiah again as a man, and not in the clouds. For ten years or so past the claims of Fisher to be the Messiah have been talked of in Nunawading, and about six years ago I was led to communicate with him, with a view of ascertaining whether he was really the Messiah. Shortly after I came in contact with him, I saw enough to convince me that he was not the Messiah. I now look upon him as a rank impostor, but he was certainly very lucky in the prophecies by which he obtained his present ascendancy over the minds of many people. There are considerably more than a hundred who believe in him implicitly — most of them residing in Nunawading, although there are some in Prahran, Ballarat and other places. He calls himself the Son of God, Jesus Christ — and they all believe that he is. He says he will never die, and that none of those who believe in him will ever die, nor their wives and families, provided they are staunch in their belief. He does not mean only that their souls will never die, but that they will never die on this earth. All who follow him believe this, and that the millennium has commenced during which the saints are to live until they are translated. When I came to have faith in him, I believed that I would never die, nor my wife nor any of my family. Once a child of mine fell ill. Fisher said, "The child cannot die, Wilson. Only believe." Then he came to my house, poured some wine over the child's face, and prayed. The child did get well, and that made my belief stronger than ever. However, Fisher's mother-in-law died, and this set people enquiring. Fisher said it was a judgement on her, sent direct from him, and that he had struck her with a paralytic stroke which killed her. I asked him why, and he said, "She is gone the way of Ananias and Sapphira. She told me she had no money, but I knew she had, and after she died, £100 was found secreted in the house.""

'I don't understand this bit about Ananias and Sapphira.'

'Neither do I. Does it matter, do you think?'

'This is so strange, I need to know. It's biblical, so maybe Guy's Catholic education will help. I know it's ridiculous, but I can't finish reading this until I know. He's at your house. I'll telephone him.'

Ros Lord answered the telephone and said that Guy was working in the garden. As soon as he came on the line, Joe said, 'Who are Ananias and Sapphira?'

'I can honestly say that no one has ever asked me that question before.'

'Do you know who they are?'

'Keep your shirt on, Joe. Yes, I know who they are. Has this got something to do with the deaths in Nunawading?'

'Yes, Guy.' Joe's impatience was evident.

'All right. The story of Ananias and Sapphira is in the Acts of the Apostles, which is why you're not familiar with it, you heathen. Ananias sold some land and donated the proceeds to Peter, only he didn't donate the lot. He kept some for himself. Peter wasn't happy when he found out, and told Ananias that he'd lied to the Holy Spirit, and Ananias just dropped dead. Then Mrs Ananias, that's Sapphira, arrived, and she told the same lie about the money, and she dropped dead. It's a heart-warming story, isn't it? Does that help solve your baffling mystery?'

'One small corner of it.'

Joe went back to reading the newspaper article:

'Fisher said once that a man who had scoffed at him would be struck in a mysterious manner in a year or two. Strange to say, the man went insane afterwards, and was sent to the Yarra Bend. Once I had two cases in the court. Fisher told me I could not possibly lose them for he would influence the mind of the judge with his power. Sure enough I won both the cases. Afterwards, Fisher came to me and said, "Wilson, I told you how it would be. When you thought Judge Pohlman was speaking, it was me. I entered into his spirit and spoke through him." All these things made me believe most implicitly. Fisher looked upon me as one of the faithfullest among his disciples, and indeed I had not a particle of doubt. He let me more and more into the secrets of the religion. Milk, he said, was for babes, and strong meat for men. While men who were yet young in the faith were only allowed one wife, those more advanced might have several. Fisher himself lives with three women, who are sisters, and their father is one his devoutest believers. There is a fourth sister who is married. Fisher says he is bound to have her too, and that her husband will die when he wills it.

When I became a regular member of the church, Fisher hinted that I would have to show my faith by giving him something. I gave him £10 at once, and for a considerable time paid him £1 a month. All together he has had about £35 out of me, and it is on account of this that I proceed against him for false pretences. I can tell you all about his villainy, and I will. Before putting myself away from his connection, I openly denounced him in the chapel at his house in Nunawading. I called him an impostor. He said he was quite willing to submit the question to the Church of the First-born. The meeting of the chapel came to nothing, except that Fisher's party all affirmed their unshaken belief. Afterwards I learned that they expelled me from the Church, one only of the "apostles" voting in my favour.'

'How completely extraordinary,' Joe said. 'So Peter Fisher modelled himself on this Fisher and declared himself the new Messiah, and people actually fell for it.'

'They fell for it, and they gave him money. But how does this end in four people dead?'

'One, or more, disgruntled apostles?'

'Read the other articles, Joe. There are details that are missing from the first article. They're all worth reading. They'd be entertaining in a lurid sort of way, except that they're a depressing catalogue of human gullibility and predation.'

Joe read, with mounting incredulity, three more articles that detailed Fisher's extraordinary claims, and the accusations against him, not just of polygamy, but of seducing away from her husband one of three sisters. He named them Truth, Justice, and Prudence. He fathered eight children with these women, according to the account, and blithely overrode complaints that the Bible was adamant that a man may not take another man's wife by simply declaring, 'The Lord may do as he pleases.'

'Meredith Wilson said that Peter Fisher had declared himself the Messiah?' Joe asked.

'And that he was the descendant of this Fisher, whose name was Jimmy, by the way.'

'I didn't know Messiahs had descendants. I thought you either were or you weren't.'

'Oh, Jimmy Fisher wasn't born the Messiah. Somewhere among the other documents, we're told that a woman lost her baby and that Fisher had a dream that the baby's spirit had entered a cabbage in Fisher's garden, and that if he ate the cabbage the spirit would enter him and turn him into the Messiah.'

Joe laughed.

'I suppose,' he said, 'it's no more ridiculous than the Ananias and Sapphira guff, or that Christians believe in a three-person god, one of which is a pigeon. They call it a dove because it sounds classier, but a dove is a pigeon no matter what colour it is.'

'Peter Fisher and his dupes, to use the newspaper expression, seem to have run their sect using the 1871 sect as a template, and something went horribly wrong.'

'There's really only one way to find out, isn't there?'

Helen turned pale.

'I know what you're going to suggest, Joe. You can't go under cover, not after ...'

'This is completely different, Helen, and it's exactly why you formed your agency.'

'Joe, one of these people took an axe to a baby. What would they do to you? I can't ask you to do this.'

'I'm volunteering. No, I'm insisting.'

There was silence between them. Helen stood up and left the room. She'd felt on the edge of tears. It had never been her intention to put Joe at risk, and she realised that she'd begun her business not just with optimism, but with naivety. Of course a private inquiry agency would involve personal risk, and of course Joe was right that the only way to find out about the Church of the First Born was to get inside it. Her contact with Meredith Wilson made it impossible for her to assume that role. Meredith had seemed hostile to the Church, but her contact with it would make Helen's anonymity insecure. Joe had interviewed Emilio Barbero's landlady, but her connection to the Church was tenuous, almost non-existent. Helen knew, too, that allowing Joe to undertake the infiltration would be an expression of trust in his abilities. She calmed herself and returned to Joe's office. Before she could say anything, Joe said, 'We need Guy to go with me.'

'What about his ...?'

'I need someone I can trust, and I trust Guy absolutely. His illness might work in our favour. Charlatans like these people like nothing better than performing miracles, and having someone to play with who has come to them for a cure is perfect. It also gives us what looks like a legitimate excuse to approach them, and Guy knows his way around the Bible. That, I imagine, will prove useful.'

Helen nodded, but it was a reluctant nod of approval.

5

The Office of Native Policy for Mandated Territories was difficult to find, and when you did find it there was nothing on the door to suggest that you were in the right place. Victoria Barracks had begun to resemble a Piranesi drawing with its confusion of temporary offices, some of them thrown up in sections of corridors. Finding your way around the old building had been bad enough, but after four years of functioning as the heart of Australia's military management of the war, and housing the War Cabinet and its myriad functionaries, it was now a rabbit warren. It was home to at least one of the branches of Military Intelligence. There may have been others that Tom Mackenzie didn't know about, although he did know that several units operated out of Brisbane. He suspected that the Netherlands East Indies Force was a cover, but he didn't know for sure. At 7.00 am precisely, Tom knocked on what he knew to be the correct door.

'Come!'

Behind the door was what once had been a large room, but now consisted of three mean, partitioned offices. Like Tom's own office, the partitioning had paid no attention to the windows in the room. There was a narrow reception area at the front, so narrow that when the door was opened fully it almost touched the partition that ran across the width of the room. There were three doors in this temporary wall, one of which was open. The man seated behind the desk in that room didn't look up when Tom entered. He knew from his own experience that Tom Chafer didn't make a good first impression, and that subsequent impressions didn't make any improvements. They shared a first name, and Tom decided to use it.

'Tom Chafer.'

Chafer looked up, and the disdain on his face suggested that he disapproved of the intimacy. He was younger than Tom Mackenzie, but unlike his fellow Intelligence officers, Newman and Deighton, he didn't pay Mackenzie the courtesy of calling him 'Sir'.

'Sit down, Mackenzie.'

Tom, who'd never liked being called 'Sir', nevertheless felt the slight, and it put him on edge. Chafer hadn't changed much since their last meeting a few months prior to this one. His hair was cut very short, and was slightly darker than his thin, blond moustache, which he no doubt grew to prove to an observer that he was an adult. He was thin, so thin that he looked unhealthy, and everything he wore looked too big for his frame. Chafer didn't bother to welcome Tom back to Victoria Barracks, or to express any gratitude that he had volunteered for this intelligence work. On the contrary, his first objective was to put Tom firmly in his place.

'Your last bit of work for us ended exactly as I thought it would end — badly. You were inexperienced and, in my view, foolish. Others disagree, and admire your bravery. The fact that you survived is down to luck, not bravery.'

'I have never claimed that I was brave, but I wonder how someone as physically frail as you would have fared in the same circumstances.'

Tom Chafer's prominent ears flared red.

'I would never have been stupid enough to find myself in those circumstances.'

Tom Mackenzie's fists clenched, and the involuntary action forced resistance in the still-braced fingers of his damaged left hand. The sharp bolt of pain made him impatient to be away from Tom Chafer's presence.

'If all you plan to do is trade insults, Chafer, I'd rather be briefed by your partner, Dick Goad. He seemed like a reasonable man.'

'Goad is not my partner, and he never has been. We worked together briefly. He's been moved into the Fleet Radio Unit, not that it's any of your business.'

'Well, maybe you shouldn't have told me. That sounds like carelessness. Loose lips.'

Chafer pushed a folder towards Tom.

'The only reason you're here, Mackenzie, is that you're the senior officer in your section and you've already been given a security clearance, so I'm stuck with you. Inside that folder is what we know about Winslow Fazackerly. The folder doesn't leave this office. Take it into the room next door and read it. Don't take notes. Bring it back when you're finished.'

Chafer indicated that there was nothing more to be said by pushing a bony wrist from his sleeve and ostentatiously beginning to write something on a pad. Tom picked up the folder and took it into the room on the other side of the flimsy partition. Chafer had told him nothing, and Tom wondered what on Earth a man like that — he couldn't have reached 30 yet — was doing in such an important position. Perhaps he had hidden talents. Perhaps he had a genius for cryptography, although if that was the case, surely he'd be in Frumel, and not Goad. Working with him was going to be a nightmare, and yet Tom realised that this was where he wanted to be, with only a thin wall between him and one of the most immediately detestable people he'd ever met.

He opened the dossier on Winslow Fazackerly. There were several photographs, only one of which showed Fazackerly's face clearly. His hair was black and well cut. He was clean-shaven, and looked to be about 30. Tom checked his date of birth and discovered that he was in fact 35. Perhaps the photograph flattered him. All of the pictures showed Fazackerly from a distance, meeting various individuals. On the back of each of the photographs was the date and the words, 'Unidentified Asian. Possibly Japanese.' Tom peered at the images, but they were too blurry to establish Fazackerly's ethnicity, let alone his companions'.

His background was sketched in with no more detail than Newman and Deighton had provided. He was well connected and well educated. He was married to a Japanese national named Etsuko Endo. In his twenties, Fazackerly had travelled extensively in Japan, and was known then to his friends as an unapologetic Japanophile. He had met his wife-to-be in the Hiroshima prefecture, and had married her against her family's wishes when he was just 22 years old. She was 17. They returned to Australia in 1933 without any challenge being launched under the *Immigration Restriction Act*. The dossier had nothing to say about their marriage. There was a note to the effect that Etsuko may have formed connections with the handful of Japanese then living in Melbourne. All of these people were currently interned either at Camp No. 4 at Tatura, in Victoria, or Camp No. 14 at Loveday, in South Australia. It was also noted that many of these internees were elderly and poor, their poverty exacerbated by being ineligible, as aliens, for the old-age pension. This was underlined as if the person who'd prepared the dossier thought it was significant. Tom couldn't see how.

In 1938, Etsuko returned to Japan alone. There was no explanation as to why. She didn't make any visits to her husband in Melbourne between 1938 and 1942 when Japan unequivocally showed its expansionist hand by bombing Pearl Harbor in 1941 and Darwin in 1942. After that, a return was impossible, and even if it had been possible, Etsuko would have been interned at Tatura.

On a small square of paper, probably inserted recently into the dossier, was the name Yokito Torajiro, and beside it the words, 'Male, Loveday Camp 42. Corresponding with Fazackerly?'

These were just shreds of information. It wasn't stated, but Tom assumed that Fazackerly spoke Japanese, which would have made him a useful Intelligence man, except Intelligence didn't trust him. Putting him in Requisitions was a way of keeping him close, but as Tom re-read the dossier and committed details to memory, he began to suspect that Fazackerly wasn't the only one being tested. He closed the folder and returned to Chafer's office.

'There's not much here,' he said.

'Your job is to plug the gaps. Is he one of us, or one of them? Either way, he'll be useful to us. Just don't fuck this up. He's never met you, although he was told yesterday that you'd be returning to work today after an accident. You can decide what sort of accident. Just don't tell him it was an undercover operation that went pear-shaped.'

'Do you always assume the person you're talking to is a moron?'

'It's usually a safe assumption. We need to know about him quickly. I don't care how you win his confidence. I don't care if you have to fuck him — just find out if he's passing information to the Japs, so we can hang him if he is.'

Chafer pulled his sleeve up his hairless arm to reveal a watch, which needed the thickness of his forearm to remain in place.

'He's due in at 8.30.'

Again, Chafer began writing to signal that the meeting was over.

ON HIS WAY back to his office, Tom passed Benjamin Newman — headed, no doubt, to occupy one of the offices next to Chafer.

'You've had your meeting, sir?'

'Yes. Tom Chafer and I have exchanged pleasantries.'

'And how did you find him?'

'He lived down to my expectations, but remember, I have met him before.'

When Tom entered his own office in Requisitions, or, rather, the half-room that had been assigned him, he discovered that it was much tidier than he'd left it. Not that he was slovenly, but no one could accuse him of obsessive tidiness. Whoever had occupied the office in his absence had imposed order. As he was familiarising himself with where things now were, Winslow Fazackerly came into the room. He stopped when he saw Tom, and saluted.

'Flight Lieutenant Fazackerly, I presume. We can dispense with the saluting inside the office.'

'I've been looking forward to meeting you, sir.'

Winslow ran his eye over the room.

'I haven't tampered with your system of doing things. I've just tidied up.'

'Please, Winslow, sit down and get me up to speed on the underwear and boots situation.'

Winslow smiled, and Tom looked for the sinister face of the fifth columnist behind the smile. He couldn't see it. His first impression of Flight Lieutenant Winslow Fazackerly was that he was urbane, easygoing, and probably excellent company. After a few minutes of conversation, he found it difficult to believe that this man was a traitor, passing information to the monsters who'd perpetrated horrors in Asia.

JOE DIDN'T HAVE to sell the idea of infiltrating the Church of the First Born to Guy. Guy jumped at it. They decided against using aliases. Allowing these people to see their identification papers, should that need arise, would help underline that they were genuine acolytes. Joe wouldn't declare that he was Jewish, however. He suspected that the anti-Semitism revealed in the newspaper reports he'd read from 1871 wouldn't have shifted much. Indeed, it was likely that it had become an entrenched part of the sect's teaching. Joe's cover was simply that he was bringing his friend to Prescott, but that he was not himself interested in religion of any kind. Guy's story was of bitter separation from the Catholic Church, which no longer offered him solace or direction. This would be an easy role for Guy to play, because it was essentially true.

They had a name, Anthony Prescott, and an address. Guy had read all the material provided by Meredith Wilson, and, like Joe and Helen, he was astonished by people's gullibility, although less astonished than they had been, because he recalled his own childhood fervour for the rituals and credibility-straining beliefs of the Catholic Church. Faith did strange things to a person's willingness to look too closely at what was being offered up as truth.

Prescott's property, a sizeable orchard in Nunawading, proved difficult to find. The road into it was unmarked, and was more track than road. Peter Lillee's car was an incongruous presence where Joe parked it, at a point where the track met a closed farm gate. They decided to leave the car there, climb over the gate, and walk towards what they could see was a substantial house. Joe had been expecting a modest, perhaps run-down house. This place had been embellished by money. Its core was a simple dwelling, but it had been extended until it now sprawled on either side of an impressive front door. An elegant veranda ran the length of the house, and down two sides. The garden and lawns were maintained at a high pitch of neatness.

'Wow,' Guy said. 'Someone works very hard to keep this place looking like this.'

Two women came into view on the veranda. Both of them were dressed identically in a simple, grey linen tunic, gathered at the waist and falling to the ground. Guy and Joe were some distance from the house, but their presence seemed to alarm the women. They each put down the buckets they'd been carrying and hurried through the front door into the house.

'We've been spotted,' said Joe. 'I think we've come to the right place. Those tunics were described in one of those articles.'

'If the outside of this place is anything to go by, I'd say this Prescott bloke runs a tight ship.'

'It's a lot flasher than Fisher's house. If I was the Messiah, I'd rather live here.'

They continued walking towards the house. As Joe placed his foot on the lowest of the front steps that led up to the veranda, the front door opened, and a man wearing a tunic of a softer cloth, the hem of which fell only to his knees, emerged.

'Why are you trespassing on my land? You have not been invited here.'

Joe's immediate reaction was that this was the rich voice of an actor. It was measured and weighty, as if every utterance was worthy of being heard in the back row of the balcony.

'You are the man I saw in my dream,' Guy said. 'I have come to inquire after your gospel.'

The man at the top of the steps hesitated. The remark had taken him off-guard. There was a slight quiver in his eyes, which made his gaze disconcerting. He looked from Guy to Joe.

'I had no such dream,' Joe said simply.

The frankness of this response seemed to impress this man, and he smiled. There was nothing sinister in the smile. It softened his features, and Joe saw in him a dangerous charisma. This had to be Anthony Prescott. If it wasn't, Guy had made a bad miscalculation.

'And how did you find me?'

'Some people might call it luck. I call it destiny.'

Joe had no idea where Guy was going with this. He had no doubt that Prescott was a fraud, making money from the credulousness of others. Would he see through Guy, or accept him as one of the desperate people eager to believe?

'I didn't understand the dream,' Guy said, 'so I prayed and I read my Bible, and I prayed, and I found you.'

Joe's heart was in his mouth. Surely Prescott would press Guy to fill the gaps in this absurd story. He didn't. He said, 'You are welcome,' and signalled with a sweep of his arm that they should follow him into the house.

The room Prescott took them to was off the kitchen. It was large, and had probably functioned once as the estate office or the gunroom. It was now a domestic chapel. There was no altar, but there was a lectern, with 15 chairs lined up before it. To one side was a desk. Prescott sat behind it, and Joe and Guy took two chairs and sat in front of him.

'My name is Guy Kirkham, and this is my friend, Joseph Sable.'

Prescott nodded. It was now clear that he wasn't going to introduce himself as Anthony Prescott, although that was undoubtedly who he was.

'I've come here to be healed,' Guy said.

'Your friend here, Mr Sable, thinks you're foolish. He is not a person of faith.'

Guy feigned astonishment.

'How did you know that?'

Joe picked it as a lucky guess, although he acknowledged to himself that Prescott was a skilled observer. He'd noticed the difference in Guy's and his demeanour, and had accidentally hit upon half the truth, the whole truth being that neither of them was a man of faith. Prescott smiled, and this time his smile had a faint air of self-satisfaction about it, as though he was confident that his seduction of Guy had begun.

'You have a nervous disorder,' Prescott said, 'and it is this that you want healed.'

Joe would have been properly impressed if Prescott had diagnosed narcolepsy, but nevertheless this was an adept guess. Guy must have been exhibiting small tells that he, Joe, had become so used to that he no longer noticed them. Prescott was a man they needed to be wary of.

'Are you working, Guy? May I call you Guy?'

'Of course. No, I'm not working. My condition makes that impossible.'

'How do you support yourself?'

Joe glanced at Guy, curious to know how he'd reply.

'I have a private income,' Guy said. 'I was lucky in my choice of parents.'

Was that the slightest of smirks? Or was Joe imposing that on Prescott's face?

'And what about you, Joe? You're not an enlisted man?'

'I have a heart condition.'

'Ah. Two men in search of a miracle.'

'I'm not here for a cure. Guy asked me to drive him here.'

'From where?'

'Kew.'

There was no advantage to lying about the bare details of their lives. Lying was a recipe for being caught out. It was easy to forget fictionalised snippets, easy to get them wrong.

There was a knock on the door to the chapel, and without waiting to be acknowledged, a man in his late sixties entered. His hair was long and grey, his beard unkempt, and he smelled of sweat. He was wearing a rough tunic. The cloth under his armpits was wet with perspiration, and mixed with his body odour was the scent of earth and mud. He said nothing, but passed Prescott a piece of paper, and left. Prescott read the note.

'Is that your car parked outside the gate, Joe?'

'It is.'

Prescott gave an appreciative nod.

'Did you get lucky in your choice of parents, too?'

'My parents are dead. I don't call that lucky.'

'We never really die, Joe. I could prove that to you.'

Joe affected a small hesitation, as if just for a moment he was taken with the idea.

'Joe doesn't believe in miracles,' Guy said.

'And yet here you both are. That's a small miracle in itself.'

'Amen,' Guy said. His chin quivered, and his eyes filled with tears.

'Why don't you go back to Kew, get some things together, and come back tomorrow. I'll organise a room here for you. And Joe, you're welcome to stay with your friend, just to make sure he's safe and that being here is a retreat, a sanctuary. Just for a few days.'

'I'm happy to drive Guy back here tomorrow, but I won't stay.'

'Think about it. You might change your mind.'

In the car, on the way back to Kew, Joe and Guy analysed closely what had transpired. Had they fooled Prescott, or had Prescott fooled them?

'He liked the idea that I had money,' Guy said. 'That seemed to blunt any suspicions he may have had, and when that old bloke passed him the note about this car, I think we had him.'

'You had him when you produced those tears. How did you do that?'

'Oh, that's easy,' and to prove the point he produced them again.

'You should go on the stage,' Joe said.

'This is better than the theatre. Much, much better.'

*

Tom Mackenzie knew perfectly well that he was bound by the secrecy provisions of the *Crimes Act*, and he also knew that any breach of those provisions amounted to treason in a time of war. Nevertheless, having invited his sister, Maude Lambert, and her husband, Titus, around for dinner, he had no intention of not discussing his first day back at work. He knew that Titus had met Tom Chafer, and he was eager to hear his view of the man. Tom was certainly not going to exclude Maude, who had nursed him back to health and who had been privy to his lowest moments, from the details of his new position. Chafer had said that he was to use whatever means he had to lure Winslow Fazackerly into betraying himself. He couldn't do this inside Victoria Barracks. He needed to gain Fazackerly's trust, and he thought that bringing him into his own family, although a risky strategy, would be the most efficient and practical way to do this. He'd suggest bringing him round for dinner. Fazackerly presented well, but if he really was a fifth columnist it would be like bringing a viper into the nest. Titus and Maude would be watchful and discreet. Maude especially had a gift for drawing people out, and for seeing through their shams. If Fazackerly was a spy, Maude Lambert would probably be the first to know.

Tom managed to turn unappealing and fatty chops into a rich stew, which he called a daube because he'd used beer in which to slowly braise them. He would have explained the process fully, but he knew that neither Maude nor Titus was particularly interested in culinary techniques. They did, however, enjoy the result. Neither of them knew he'd returned to work, and that took both of them by surprise. Maude had assumed that he'd wait until his left hand had been freed of its splint.

'I had no intention of going back, until I got a visit from two blokes from Military Intelligence.'

'Not that awful little arsehole Chafer?' Titus said.

'Not him, no, although I'll tell you about my meeting with him in a minute. And he is an arsehole. No. It was two very reasonable men who suggested I might like to come back to work sooner rather than later, and by sooner they meant today. I suppose I could have said no, but I got the sense that no wasn't really an option. For them, my saying yes was plan A, and there was no plan B.'

'Intelligence doesn't do plan B.'

Tom told them as much as he knew about Winslow Fazackerly and about Chafer's instructions. There was no need to raise the delicate matter of the *Crimes Act*. Both Titus and Maude knew that Tom was breaching it, but they were pleased that he was. Maude particularly saw this as proof that her brother had fully recovered. There had been times, and recently, too, when she thought this might not be possible.

'Do you know anything at all about Japan, Maude?' Tom asked.

'Only what I've read in the papers, and none of that is good, even adjusting for propaganda.'

'Titus?'

'Nothing. I've never met a Japanese person. I have some vague idea that they dived for pearls up around Broome.'

'So convincing Fazackerly that we share his passion for all things Japanese isn't going to work.'

'I think our ignorance might work in our favour,' Maude said. 'But I don't think all three of us should try to win him over. He'd see through that. Only one of us should attempt to gain his confidence.'

'That's my job,' Tom said.

'I think it should be me,' Maude said. 'I presume he's not stupid, so he'll be on the lookout for anyone inside Victoria Barracks who starts asking him questions. I, on the other hand, could reasonably express great sympathy for his wife, and be wide-eyed about whatever he tells me.'

'I can't put you in any danger, Maude.'

Pre-empting Tom's as-yet-unexpressed plan, Maude said, 'Invite him here for dinner tomorrow night. What's dangerous about that? I'm not planning on meeting him in a dark alley to discuss helping out with the Japanese invasion of Australia. All you need is evidence of his treason. I think I can get that more quickly than you can, simply because your position will be a barrier to intimacy.'

'Chafer helpfully suggested I should seduce him, only he wasn't so polite in his language.'

Maude laughed. She leaned across and kissed Titus on the cheek.

'Don't worry, darling. I won't sleep with Mr Fazackerly, not even for my country.'

'Thank you, Maudey. How very reassuring. What if he looks like Dana Andrews?'

'Oh well, if he looks like Dana Andrews I'll start learning Japanese immediately.'

DR CLARA DAWSON was used to male patients, and even some female patients, refusing to allow her to examine them. She'd once told Helen Lord that the easiest patient to deal with was one who was in a coma. Generally, resistance to her ministrations vanished after the first examination. Soldiers were the most amenable. Whatever modesty they'd suffered in civilian life had been knocked out of them by the forced closeness of army life. Men in their forties and fifties were the worst. It was not uncommon for them to suggest that Clara couldn't wait to get a look at their private parts. Clara had discovered that the best way to deal with this was with frankness, and she would tell them that the sight of their cocks would add nothing to her day, and in some cases perhaps less than nothing.

Clara was mostly confined to the female ward, but night shift and short-staffing meant that she went to wherever she was needed in the hospital. She knew that she copped more night shifts than the male doctors, but she hadn't got very far in challenging this. In time, she'd come to prefer night shift, because many of the people who let her know daily that they considered her a glorified nurse worked normal hours and were absent.

It was just after 10.00 pm when Clara was called to the bedside of a man who'd been admitted that evening suffering a head injury and a shallow knife wound to the stomach. His injuries were superficial, but they bled extravagantly, especially the head wound. Clara shaved his belly and sutured the shallow slash, and bandaged his head. He was lean, but not underfed, and he wasn't drunk. His dark hair was thinning, which made him look slightly older than the 45 he'd given as his age. His name was Kenneth Bussell, and he said that he worked for the railways. He'd given all this information to Clara as she'd set about cleaning him up. He'd shown no reluctance to being examined by a female doctor, although he'd expressed surprise when one of the nurses had addressed her as 'doctor'.

'How did this happen, Mr Bussell?'

'I was minding my own business, just walking through the gardens near the Shrine. I was concentrating on not falling into one of those bloody air-raid trenches they've dug all over the place when some bastard jumped me. He clocked me on the head, and it knocked me out. When I woke up he was gone, and I discovered that the cu— … Pardon me, I discovered that he'd stabbed me.'

Clara had no interest in filling the gaps in this absurd story. Whatever had happened hadn't happened the way Bussell had told it.

'You're a lucky man,' was all she said, and left him to attend to another patient. She would check on him at the end of her shift, and would recommend that he be discharged. The police could deal with him from there on.

Clara gave no further thought to Bussell. Her shift had been busy, and she was on her way out of the hospital when she remembered him. She found him sitting on the edge of his bed, redressed in his bloody clothes. The doctor who was with him was a man for whom Clara had little respect, either as a practitioner or a human being. Dr Gerald Matthews made no secret of the fact that he believed women were barely tolerable as nurses, and intolerable as doctors. He never spoke to Clara, unless it was to pass a snide remark. He'd seen her enter the ward, so it wasn't possible for her to avoid him.

'This man tells me you've given him permission to go home,' Matthews said, and his tone managed to suggest the decision was the result of incompetence.

'No. I told Mr Bussell I'd assess him at the end of my shift, which is why I'm here and not on my way home.'

'I think I'd better do that assessment.'

Bussell looked from one to the other.

'The lady doctor stitched me up. You haven't even looked at me, mate. I think I'd prefer her to look at me again.'

'She stitched your wound, did she? Show me.'

Clara retained her self-possession in the face of this attempt to humiliate her in front of a patient.

'Open your shirt,' Matthews snapped, and Bussell, with a little sneer of reluctance, did so. Matthews made a show of looking closely at Clara's sutures, and sniffed as if in disapproval, but said nothing. There was nothing to say. The sutures were neat, and the wound was clean. He didn't bother checking the head injury.

'He's all yours, Dawson. I'm happy to leave you with the paperwork.'

'He's a bit of a prick, isn't he? Pardon my French,' Bussell said.

6

Winslow Fazackerly didn't consider himself an agent of the empire of Japan. He knew that his marriage and the time he'd spent there would have made him a person of interest to the authorities. In fact, he was amazed that no one had yet openly questioned his loyalty to Australia. No doubt, his family's impeccable social credentials had helped protect him. He had no career ambitions in the air force — he was only there because his father had insisted that some form of military service was inescapable. He had no desire to see action. He wondered sometimes if this made him a coward or a pragmatist. The thought that he might be a coward didn't appal him. He'd never admired heroes, either in fiction or in life — and real-life heroes were mostly fiction anyway. Heroes were stupid people who managed to survive their stupidity. That was Fazackerly's view.

The moment he met Tom Mackenzie, he liked him. Mackenzie was personable, and seemed to be intelligent. He'd offered no explanation for the splint on his left hand, and Fazackerly made no inquiries about it. He wasn't incurious, but his instincts told him that his discretion would be appreciated. Fazackerly also knew instinctively that Group Captain Mackenzie had been deputised by someone to keep an eye on him. Fazackerly didn't mind being watched. There was nothing to see. He'd be suspicious of all overtures of friendship, but he saw no reason to reject them. Good company was rare, and by the end of Mackenzie's first day he'd proved himself to be good company.

For his part, Tom hoped that Fazackerly wasn't a spy. His immediate impression had been favourable. Fazackerly was witty and relaxed about the tedious nature of the job he was required to do. Air force people needed shoes, socks, and underwear, and Fazackerly said he'd rather be requisitioning them than wearing them. Tom was certain that Fazackerly was smart enough to know that he was being watched. It would be a strange dance that they'd be doing — each aware that the other couldn't be trusted, and each determined to keep this knowledge from the other. Despite this, Tom wondered if a friendship might be possible.

At lunchtime on Friday, Winslow and Tom walked down St Kilda Road and into the city, where they managed to find a seat at the Hopetoun Tearooms in the Block Arcade. The lady who pushed the trolley between the tables was particularly attentive to the two good-looking men in uniform.

'We get mostly air force in here,' she said. 'A cut above, don't you think? Rarely see a bloke from the army in here.'

'The air force is definitely a cut above,' Tom said.

'The corned-beef sandwiches are good today,' she said, and so that was what they ordered.

'Why the air force, Winslow?'

'I liked the uniform.'

'You don't strike me as a person who's comfortable in a uniform.'

'Well, unless they're tailored they're always a bad fit — and I know that's not what you meant. I was encouraged, shall we say, to join a branch of the services by my family. My father called in some favours, and here I am, safe in a stuffy office in Victoria Barracks, and back living in the family home. Do you have your own place?'

'Yes, I have a house in South Melbourne. It's not flash, but it doesn't leak, except in one spot, which I wish I'd fixed every time it rains.'

'I'm about your age and I don't have a place of my own. Not in Australia, anyway.'

Tom's face must have betrayed him, because Winslow said, 'You weren't expecting me to tell you that?'

'Well, I'm not sure what it means.'

'I don't have a place in Australia, but I do have a house, or my wife's family has a house, in Hiroshima, in Japan.'

'Your wife is Japanese?'

'As I think you know, Tom. May I call you Tom, outside the barracks?'

'I hate being called sir, so please call me Tom whenever there's no brass around to accuse you of insubordination.'

Tom was stalling for time, unsure how to answer Winslow's comment. If he lied, Winslow would know it and any hope of getting close to him would be lost.

'I'm sorry, Winslow, that was disingenuous of me. I was given your dossier, which has nothing in it that wasn't supplied by you. I think Intelligence thought I should know, so that I didn't go running to them with the exciting news that you were married to a Japanese woman. Believe me, if you were considered a security risk, you wouldn't be working in Victoria Barracks.'

'Or maybe that's precisely where I'd be. Keep your friends close, but your enemies closer. That sort of thing.'

'Your wife is in Japan.'

'I haven't seen or heard from my wife since 1938. It's the greatest grief of my life.'

'It looks like the war won't go on for much longer.'

'I'd be about as welcome in Japan as Etsuko would be here, and yet if I could get to her in Hiroshima tomorrow, I'd go. Does that make me a traitor?'

'Your wife isn't responsible for what the Japanese army is doing.'

'But that's not how people see it, is it? She's the enemy, and the enemy is cruel and not quite human. And you have to admit, the Japanese army has done a pretty good job of reinforcing that view.'

'You lived in Japan, didn't you?'

'Listen, Tom, I make no secret of the fact that I love Japan and the Japanese people, although I no longer say that out loud. I don't, however, love everything about it unconditionally. I don't understand, and loathe, emperor worship. What kind of god-emperor needs thick spectacles? The culture of obedience is unsettling to me, but despite everything, Tom, there's something there that draws me in. I can't describe it, but I've been seduced by it.'

'I think people might be more forgiving than you think after the war.'

'No. Why should they be? Their sons or brothers or friends have been tortured, starved, murdered. Brutality is hard to forgive. The truth is, my wife doesn't belong here, and will never belong here, and I don't belong there. I'm what the Japanese call a *gaijin*, which is an outsider, an alien, and, depending on who's saying it, a potential enemy.'

Tom wondered if this honesty was the clever strategy of a different kind of potential enemy. He couldn't see it. Winslow Fazackerly, if he was a spy, was a clever one. He was anxious to get Maude's opinion of him.

'My sister and brother-in-law are coming around for dinner tonight. Would you like to come? Titus is the head of the Homicide department.'

As soon as he'd added this detail about Titus, Tom wished he hadn't. It sounded like he was big-noting himself.

'If you come with me straight from work, you can help chop the vegetables.'

'I'd love to come, but I'll go home first and change into civvies. I don't want to spend any more time in this uniform than I have to.'

Tom knew that Fazackerly was staying in his parents' house in Middle Park, which meant that he lived within walking distance of Tom's house.

'Should I bring anything?'

'A couple of beers, if you have them.'

'I can run to that. I've got some decent cognac as well.'

Having settled on this, Fazackerly spoke further about his life in Japan, astonishing Tom with his description of communal bathing in the neighbourhood *onsen*. They returned to Victoria Barracks and the mundane work of requisitions.

JOE HAD BEEN against Guy's staying at Prescott's place on his own. Helen had at first agreed with Joe, but had been persuaded by Guy's argument that Joe was needed on the outside, if only to be able to get Guy out in an emergency. She said it was important that Guy's role be formalised, and entered him into the agency's books as a consultant on a limited contract and a generous remuneration. Guy said that he'd do the work gratis, but accepted Helen's terms when she insisted upon them.

Joe drove Guy to Prescott's gate. A few hundred yards back from the gate and well out of sight of the house there was a large tree stump, the remains of what had once been a majestic and ancient river red gum. There was a split in the stump, and Joe and Guy had settled on this as the best place for Guy to leave his written reports and observations. There was no other way for him to communicate with Joe. Prescott had a telephone, but it was in the hallway in the main house, and any call from there would be overheard. Leaving a note in a tree stump was primitive, but the nearest post office wasn't within walking distance. Guy was confident that he could leave the area of Prescott's orchard without being seen. He'd do it at three in the morning if he had to. And, yes, he understood that taking notes would have to be done carefully.

'I know you're the trained detective, Joe, but I'm not actually stupid.'

Joe turned to Guy.

'I know that, but there are possibly very unpleasant people inside, and I don't like the idea of you being here on your own.'

'Listen, Joe, everything that is wrong with me will work in my favour. They'll know I'm damaged goods when I have my first nightmare, or when I suddenly lose consciousness. And I can carry off the ecstasy of belief much better than you could, because you've never felt it.'

'And you have?'

'Every good little Catholic boy has felt the pleasurable rush after Confession, until common sense intervenes and intelligence asserts itself.'

'I'll come by tomorrow afternoon and check the stump.'

'No. Give me 48 hours to get settled and get some idea of the rhythm of the place. Check the stump on Sunday night.'

Guy shook Joe's hand, collected his suitcase from the back of the car, and entered Prescott's property. Joe watched as his friend walked towards the house. He saw Prescott emerge and stand on the front step. Joe's heart began to beat erratically, and the familiar onset of nausea forced him from the car and onto all fours on the ground, where he vomited up the sour dregs of his breakfast. When he returned to his seat behind the wheel, dizzy and sweating, Guy and Prescott had disappeared into the house. Joe was filled with foreboding.

ANTHONY PRESCOTT DIDN'T shake Guy's hand when he entered the house. Instead, he placed an open palm on his shoulder and slowly folded it over so that Guy could feel that here was strength withheld. He took Guy into the room that served as the chapel, and insisted that Guy leave his suitcase outside. The seats had been pushed to one side. Prescott said very little beyond a carefully modulated, 'Welcome.'

Here in the chapel, he stood behind the lectern and indicated that Guy should stand before him. Prescott took hold of a rough shepherd's crook and rapped it three times on the floor. The old man, whom Guy and Joe had seen on their first visit here, entered. He was accompanied by a younger man. They each wore a simple tunic, similar to the tunic worn by the women, but the cinch was more masculine than the cinch that gathered the women's tunics. A tunic was draped over the arm of the older man. They approached Prescott and stood beside him.

'Guy Kirkham,' Prescott said, 'do you come here of your own free will?'

'I do.'

'Your friend isn't with you.'

'He thinks I'm a fool.'

Prescott smiled, and despite being wary of this man, Guy felt its warmth. It would be easy to be beguiled by him, and difficult to believe that he might in any way be implicated in the deaths at Fisher's property. Prescott came to Guy and placed his hands on his cheeks. He leaned in and kissed him gently on the forehead. Guy smelled lavender. Very quietly, Prescott said, 'You will shed the skin of the man named Guy Kirkham. Close your eyes. Trust in me. Do you trust in me?'

'I do.'

'You must close your eyes and shed your clothes, and I will make sure that there are no marks of the devil on your body. Then you will don your tunic. Do you understand?'

'What is the mark of the devil?'

'I will know it if I see it.'

Guy had not been expecting this and he knew its purpose was to disempower him, perhaps even to humiliate him, but he'd never been physically shy or modest, so the act of disrobing in front of three strangers was inconsequential to him. He had no tattoos and no birthmarks, so he guessed he'd get the all-clear when it came to devil's marks. He took off his clothes, keeping his eyes closed, and without being asked, raised his arms in the attitude of the crucified Christ. He heard Prescott move around him, searching for satanic signs.

'Raise your arms above your head,' Prescott said. Guy felt the surprisingly soft cloth of the tunic being fitted over his arms, and when it had fallen over his body and tied at the waist, Prescott said, 'Open your eyes. You are welcome here among us, Absalom.'

Guy opened his eyes. The three men who stood before him bowed their heads, and Guy found himself affected by the solemnity of the gesture.

'Nepheg will take you to your room,' Prescott said. The young man stepped forward, and Guy reached down to retrieve his clothes.

'Leave them,' Prescott said. 'Someone will bring them to you later.'

Guy followed Nepheg out of the chapel. He noticed that his suitcase had been removed.

The room to which Guy was taken was in a bungalow behind the main house. It reminded him of convict quarters attached to grand squatters' homesteads. The room was sparsely furnished, but clean. There were two beds in it.

'This is our room.'

'I didn't realise we'd be sharing,' Guy said.

Guy's suitcase had been placed on his bed. It was open and empty. The door to a small wardrobe had been left ajar, and Guy could see that his clothes had been hung up and his toiletries placed on a shelf. He couldn't see the notebook or the bottle of ink he'd brought with him. He crossed to the wardrobe and checked. He decided to say nothing to Nepheg.

'If you want to be alone for a while, I'll leave you.'

'No, no. I'd like to ask you some questions and maybe have a look over the place.'

'I won't be able to answer all your questions. Only the Master can guide you properly.'

As he said this, a woman brought the clothes that Guy had left in the chapel. He took them from her, and, as he placed them in the wardrobe, felt for his fountain pen. It wasn't there.

'I think my pen must have fallen out of my pocket. It was a gift from my father.'

'The Master will have your pen. It will be quite safe. For the moment, you don't need a pen. Writing is a distraction from prayer.'

'Fair enough.' For the first time, Guy felt a small fizz of trepidation. There was something about this young man, Nepheg, that unsettled him. He lacked warmth. There was nothing about him that spoke of contentment, nothing that suggested that proximity to Prescott had raised him to a state of grace. He wasn't surly, exactly, although perhaps that was what surliness ameliorated by faith looked like.

'Nepheg is a strange name.'

'It's the name the Master chose for me.'

'How many people live here on the property?'

'There are five, and many more come to worship.'

'Five?'

'Three men and two women. Yes. We tend the fruit and the chickens and the livestock.'

Guy thought this self-consciously biblical turn of phrase might try his patience.

'Can I have a look around?'

'I'll come with you. There are some areas men are not allowed to trespass.'

Nepheg didn't take Guy into the main house, but showed him the outbuildings, and indicated the various plots and what was growing in them. Guy counted three women and the man named Abraham at work. In the distance there was a small structure, shed-like, but with a roofline that made it look more substantial.

'What's that?'

'That is a place where men are not permitted. That is where the women must retreat to until their bleeding has passed and they are clean again.'

Guy had a vague memory of having sniggered when he was a boy at a passage in Leviticus that insisted that everything a menstruating woman touched or sat upon was befouled. There was a great deal of washing involved.

'We all work in the fields,' Nepheg said, 'even the Master, and you will be expected to do your share.'

'Of course. I wasn't expecting to be pampered. I want to be a part of this community.'

'There's a tunic of rough cloth in our room. You'll wear that when working. The one you're wearing now is to be worn at all other times while you're on the property. You're not required to wear it outside the Master's demesne, although you may wish to if attending a service at the house of another disciple.'

'There are others?'

'The Church of the First Born has many followers, too many to fit in our small chapel. We worship wherever we are, and the Master visits where and when he can.'

Until he felt the hand on his shoulder, Guy hadn't been aware that Anthony Prescott had come up behind them.

'Absalom, walk with me and I will show you who we are, and who I am. Nepheg has been away from his work for too long.'

Nepheg nodded and headed back to the room he now shared with Guy — presumably, Guy thought, to change his tunic. Prescott and Guy walked around to the front of the big house.

'We'll have tea,' he said, and invited Guy onto the veranda, where they sat opposite each other across a sturdy table. A young woman came out of the house carrying a tray, which she placed on the table.

'This is Justice,' Prescott said. 'And this is Absalom.'

'I'm happy that you've come to us, Absalom,' Justice said. Guy had been expecting her voice to be meek. It wasn't. It was harsh, confident, and nasal, with no hint of subservience in it. Guy guessed she might be 22 or 23 years old, although the sun had already etched lines around her eyes and mouth. If the look she was going for was plain and simple, Guy thought, she'd achieved it. She didn't stay to pour the tea.

'Justice will cook our meal tonight. It will be palatable, but not as pleasant as the meals prepared by Prudence. Still, she does her best, and I don't demand more than that.'

'I don't know what questions to ask you.'

'I can hear your unasked questions, Absalom. You want to know why the others call me Master.'

Guy manufactured a startled look.

'I was afraid to ask you that,' he said.

Prescott smiled his warm, inviting smile.

'I didn't choose this path. It was chosen for me. There was a man I'd been told about who claimed that he was Jesus Christ and that he had the power over life and death. I was searching for some kind of truth and I met this man, and for a while I believed in him. He was false. His falseness was shown to me in a dream. God's arm came down to me, draped in white, holding a book. *In you is the spirit of David and the spirit of my son, Jesus Christ. This is my book and you are chosen to unfold my law. You are anointed, and you alone. Go and claim my kingdom. You are David, and who you save will be saved, and who you damn will be damned. This is the power I invest in you.* I reached out and took the book, and the laws came into me and I knew them.'

He paused to gauge the effect his words were having on Guy. Guy had opened his eyes to be marginally wider than usual — creating, he hoped, an illusion of enthralment.

'My followers call me Master because God has named me so. I have never insisted on it. You may call me David, but I hope you will also come to see me as your Master.'

Prescott took a sip of tea.

'I can cure you, Absalom. If you believe in me, I will cure you.'

For a fleeting moment, Guy wondered if this might be true after all. This momentary lapse bothered him. He'd never thought of himself as being available to the crude seductions of religious shysters, and yet there it was, a sudden glimpse of weakness. Illness, he reminded himself, makes you vulnerable to hope.

'I believe you, David.'

Prescott seemed to accept this, and began to explain to Guy the arcane practices of the Church of the First Born. He began with the tunics, explaining that in accordance with God's law one must not wear a garment of cloth made of two kinds of material. Much of what he said was vaguely familiar to Guy, because it was drawn from Deuteronomy and Leviticus, the two Old Testament books that schoolboys trawled for its unfettered violence and darkly erotic references to rape, testicles, and menstruation. Where else but in the Old Testament could you read with a clear conscience about incest, bestiality, and masturbation? He and his friends had sniggered often about Onan spilling his seed on the ground. When Prescott used Leviticus to justify stripping him naked, Guy recognised the passage. Prescott's mellifluous voice, as he recited it, failed to disguise its ancient grotesqueries:

None of your offspring throughout their generations who has a blemish may approach to offer the bread of his God. For no one who has a blemish shall draw near, a man blind or lame, or one who has a mutilated face or a limb too long, or a man who has an injured foot or an injured hand, or a hunchback or a dwarf, or a man with a defect in his sight or an itching disease or scabs or crushed testicles. No man who is the offspring of Aaron the priest who has a blemish shall come near to the Lord's food offerings; since he has a blemish he shall not come near to offer the bread of his God.

'So you see, Absalom, why it was necessary to uncover your nakedness. My father is not a soft God.'

'God shouldn't be soft, but will he cure me?'

'God's mercy flows through me. I am holy, and you shall be holy.'

In the course of the conversation, Prescott never explicitly claimed that he was Jesus Christ, but he came close. He didn't reveal the position of the women in the house. The theology of the Church of the First Born, apart from the as-yet-unspoken belief that Anthony Prescott was God incarnate, was closely aligned with the Old Testament and seemed to draw selectively from its bizarre laws, with a smattering where convenient from the New Testament. After 15 minutes, Prescott saw that Guy's concentration was waning.

'It's a lot to take in at once. You'll come to understand us slowly, but don't be afraid to come to me with any questions. You will have doubts. Don't be troubled by them. Doubts are a sign that your mind is alive. I will banish your doubts.'

How good are you, really, Guy thought, *if you haven't seen through me?*

'We eat together at 6.00 pm. There will be a place set for you'

Again, Prescott exercised his smile. Guy stood up and left the veranda. Prescott leaned back in his chair and said quietly, 'Absalom, Absalom. I think I've named you correctly.'

'I LIKE HIM,' Tom Mackenzie said. 'I don't believe he's a spy, but if he is, he's a bloody good one.'

Tom was rolling out the pastry for a steak-and-kidney pie. Maude Lambert was in the kitchen with him. Titus hadn't yet arrived. He was often late, so this was normal, and besides, Maude had arrived early — in order, as she said, to offer her clumsy help in preparing the meal. As always, Tom didn't require any help, although he'd telephoned her just after lunch and asked her to use her meat ration to fill out the small amount of beef and lard he'd been able to buy. It wasn't good-quality meat, so Tom planned to cook it slowly for a couple of hours before putting it inside the pie. This meant that they wouldn't eat until 8.00 pm, but he had beer, and Maude had brought a bottle of sherry.

Winslow Fazackerly arrived just after 6.30. The house smelled pleasantly of the rich stew. Winslow, apart from the cognac, had brought a gift for Tom. It was a small, squat figure made of papier-mâché and painted red. It had the face of a rather fierce-looking bearded man, with two blank, white circles for eyes.

'It's called a *daruma*,' he said. 'It's meant to bring you luck and help you achieve an ambition.'

Tom took it and balanced it on the palm of his hand. Winslow flicked it with a finger. It swayed, and righted itself.

'I've never seen anything like this,' Tom said.

'You draw in one eye and only draw in the other when whatever you wanted to achieve has been achieved. Then you can ceremoniously burn the daruma.'

'How marvellous,' Maude said. 'Do you have one yourself?'

'I have several. They each have one eye drawn in. When I meet my wife again, I'll draw in the other eyes.'

Winslow's easy, unguarded reference to his wife made it comfortable for Maude and Titus, when he arrived, to ask questions about Japan. As he had earlier been with Tom, Winslow was honest about the fact that his status in Japan would always be that of an outsider.

'That feeling of not belonging was good training, because that's exactly how I feel here.'

'Do you speak good Japanese?' Titus asked.

'It's reasonable. I'd never pass for a native, but it's better than conversational.'

'Surely that would be useful to our intelligence services.'

'Oh, they approached me, but I was feeling bloody-minded at the time, so I turned them down, which made them suspicious of me, of course. No one was willing to say anything out loud. That's the advantage of coming from a rolled-gold family.'

'Do you mind if I ask what made you bloody-minded?' Maude asked.

Winslow took out his wallet, and unfolded a piece of paper from it. It had been creased and uncreased so often that the folds were now on the point of tearing.

'I've had this in my wallet since 1942. And I look at it from time to time to remind me that this is how Australians view my wife. Read it out loud.'

Winslow slid the page towards Maude.

'I remember seeing these on telephone poles, after Darwin was bombed,' she said. She began to read:

Every one a spy. We saw plenty of them in Australia. They followed many lines of business. One sold silks, another chinaware, one bought wool, another wheat, one fished for whales, the other for pearls — they asked lots of questions; they took plenty of photographs. They smiled, bowed, scraped and though we tolerated them we hated their obvious insincerity, their filthy tricks of snide business, and we weren't so very impressed with the 'Co-prosperity sphere', which sounded to us mightily like a policy of forced annexation, murder and rapine. How right were our instincts. The Japanese who came to spy out our land now attempt to return and enslave it. Every one a killer. The record in every conquered country is one of falsity, violence, demoralisation and hateful brutality. In Formosa it has driven the aborigines again and again to rebel. Each time the Japs have put them down by massacring them in thousands. In Korea a reign of terror still persists as the Japanese attempt to totally subdue the inhabitants. In Manchuria it has meant the complete harnessing of all manpower and resources of the Son of Heaven's chariot. In the Marshall and Caroline Islands it has meant criminal neglect and the degradation of the people. Half the deaths among the natives are caused by tuberculosis; venereal disease is widespread. In Nanking it meant murder, rape, unbridled, unlicensed looting and robbery. In Hong Kong, 50 British officers were first bound then bayoneted. This is Japan's New Order, worked out to include Australia too. But it won't get here. Every white Australian, backed by the generous help of our allies, is ready to carry the war right back to Japan. Every man and woman is at his post — determined, forever, to halt Japanese aggression and throw back the Jap where he belongs. We've always despised them — now we must SMASH them.

No one said anything for a few seconds.

'It's ugly,' Maude said.

'But it's not all lies, is it?' Winslow said.

'It's that final sentence,' Tom said. 'The call to hate them all.'

'And that would include my wife. There were plenty of other posters like this one.'

'Stamp out the Jap,' Tom said. 'That campaign is still running.'

'Look,' Winslow said, 'the Japanese army is the enemy, and I want them defeated as much as the next man. And I don't doubt for a second that the atrocities they've been accused of are real and not exaggerated. I had the misfortune, perhaps, to fall in love with a Japanese woman. I don't know what that will mean for us when the war is over. Japan is going to be defeated. That's becoming increasingly obvious, but every fibre of their being is trained to find surrender unthinkable. How does an entire nation commit harakiri?'

Feeling that the conversation had become too serious, Winslow added, 'There just aren't enough sharp swords in Japan to cope with the demand.'

Maude wasn't quite ready to abandon the conversation.

'Will you bring your wife here when the war is over, or will you go to Japan?'

'Can you imagine how she'd be received here? I couldn't put her through that. I won't be welcomed by the family there either, of course. We've got a better chance of being happy if I go there, to Hiroshima. There's an island nearby called Shikoku. Etsuko and I have been there a few times. I don't even know if it will be possible, but I'd like to buy a place there and just live quietly, living off investments. It's a fantasy, I know, but if you could see how beautiful it is, if you could come with me to the Dogo Onsen, you'd see why I love Japan.'

'Come with you where?' Titus asked.

Winslow explained the etiquette and ritual of the Japanese bath house.

'Everyone is naked together?' Titus said.

'The sexes are usually, but not always, segregated. Believe me, all it takes is one visit and you'd be converted.'

'I'm not sure I'd enjoy sitting around in hot water with a lot of naked men,' Titus said.

Winslow laughed.

'That's what I thought,' he said. 'Turns out, it's marvellous. Clothes define us. Get rid of the clothes, and Jack is as good as his master.'

'I don't want to see Jack or his master naked,' Titus said.

'You don't have to look, darling,' Maude said. 'Modesty can be exercised by the observer as well as the observed.'

'That's a very Japanese idea, Mrs Lambert.'

At the end of the evening, Winslow left first, which allowed Titus, Maude, and Tom to do a post-mortem on him. Maude was unequivocal.

'He's not a spy. I think he's a lovely man who loves his wife and misses her terribly.'

'If he is a spy,' Titus said, 'being so open and frank about his relationship with Japan is a strange strategy. He's made it impossible for Intelligence not to be wary of him.'

'It might be a brilliant strategy,' Tom said. 'Hide in plain sight. I don't think so, though. I'm tempted to come clean with him about bloody Tom bloody Chafer.'

'That,' Titus said, 'would be a very bad mistake.'

Tom sighed.

'I know, Titus. God, I loathe Tom Chafer.'

7

Dr Clara Dawson always had trouble sleeping after night shift. She read the papers, dipped into a book, and ate something, trying to reproduce the rhythm of the end to a normal day. This might have been easier if the night shifts followed one after another, but they didn't. Her next shift wouldn't begin until Sunday evening, which would give her most of the weekend to recover, but her disrupted sleep patterns wouldn't fully realign. As she stretched out on her bed on Friday afternoon, she wasn't hopeful of drifting off easily. There were several patients she was worried about, and she couldn't quite shake the irritation she was feeling about Gerald Matthews' ugly behaviour. She knew he was married, and pondered how thankless it must be to be his wife. Perhaps he was a different man at home. She doubted it.

She managed to fall asleep, and woke again just after midnight. Was it the front door opening and closing? It was too late for either of the two women with whom she shared the house to be getting home. Both of them kept regular hours, but it was Friday, so perhaps one of them had stayed out unusually late. She was sufficiently curious to get up, unlock and open the door to her room, and check the corridor. Pat, the schoolteacher, was irritatingly careless in leaving the front door of the house unlocked. She hadn't been in Melbourne when the American soldier Eddie Leonski had murdered three women and terrified the city. She'd grown up in the country, where doors were never locked, and she hadn't got into the habit of turning the key.

The corridor was dark, but illuminated by the light from Clara's room. She checked the front door, and found that it was unlocked. She'd say something, for the umpteenth time, to Pat the next time she saw her. On her way back to her room, she noticed an object on the floor beside the doorjamb. It looked like a wallet. She bent down to pick it up, thinking that perhaps Pat had dropped it. It was sticky, and as she brought it into her room, she realised that the stuff on her fingers was blood. She put the wallet on a table and stared at it. Blood didn't usually disgust her, but this blood did, and she hurried to the sink to wash her hands clean. When she returned to the table, she gingerly flipped the wallet open. There was a small photograph visible behind a clear pocket. It was Gerald Matthews, and Clara knew with a dreadful certainty that the wallet had been taken from his corpse. *Kenneth Bussell*, she thought. *Kenneth Bussell*. She went cold as she realised that he might still be in the house.

The telephone was in the corridor. She tried to think clearly. She had to call the police. Did they work this late? What would she tell them? She opened her door and called into the darkness. 'Pat! Pat! Susan! Susan!' She was aware that there was an edge of panic in her voice. She ought to have just knocked on their doors. It was too late now. There was no immediate response. It was reassuring that Bussell didn't show himself, but what if this meant that both her housemates were dead? Clara uttered a small gasp, and felt suddenly weak. *No, no*, she told her body, *do not go into shock; do not go into shock*.

Both Pat and Susan emerged from their rooms at the same time. 'What's wrong? What's happened?' Susan asked.

Clara felt a moment of relief, followed by a spike of white-hot anger.

'You didn't lock the fucking door, Pat! Why didn't you lock the fucking door?'

Pat, taken aback by Clara's fury, became self-righteous. 'For God's sake, Clara. What's the big deal?'

'The big deal, Pat, the big fucking deal is that a fucking murderer left something on my doorstep.'

'Please stop swearing, Clara,' Susan said. 'It doesn't help anything.'

'Yes, it fucking does, Susan. You should try it sometime. Did you both hear what I said?'

'You must have had a nightmare,' Pat said.

'A man's wallet, covered in blood, is on a table in my room. It was left outside my door.' Clara was now speaking quietly. 'The person who left it there might still be here, in the house.'

Susan clutched at the collar of her nightdress. Pat looked stricken. 'That's what happens when you don't lock the fucking door, Pat.'

Pat gathered herself. 'I'll check the rest of the place,' she said, and before Clara or Susan could stop her, she'd headed towards the back of the house. They followed her. With all the lights turned on, and having established that there was no one else there, they each felt more secure. Pat, in an act of courageous atonement, went out into the backyard with a torch. When she returned, she poked the embers in the stove and goaded them into a flame. She put a kettle on the hob.

'You call the police, Clara,' she said. 'I'll make us some tea.'

'I'm sorry I lost my temper,' Clara said.

'I'm sorry I didn't lock the fucking door.'

Hearing Pat — who, like Susan, never swore — use Clara's favourite expletive made all of them laugh.

After Clara had made the telephone call, all three of them sat in

Clara's room, waiting for the police to arrive. Now that they were all calm, they looked at the wallet lying on the tabletop. They didn't touch it. Clara, who'd been impressed by Pat's courage and by Susan's absence of hysteria, told them that she knew the man in the photograph.

'I had a run-in with him, just before my shift ended. It was in front of a patient, a strange bloke who stood up for me, in a way.'

'We don't know that this Dr Matthews is actually dead, though,' said Pat.

'No, we don't. I've just jumped to that conclusion, because why else would someone steal his wallet and present it to me?'

Susan sipped at her tea and said, 'You think this is like a cat bringing home a dead rat, or a dead bird?'

'That's a perfect analogy, Susan. It's a trophy.'

Two constables arrived just after 1.00 am. When Clara let them in she couldn't resist pointing out that more than an hour had passed since her phone call. The older of the two constables, a man in his forties, said, with mild sarcasm, that finding a man's wallet didn't constitute an emergency.

'Lost property isn't the same as murder,' he said.

'That's very funny,' Clara said, and she meant it. If she were a policeman, stuck on night duty, called out to look at a wallet, she hoped she could summon a bit of wit. She liked this constable, whose name was Barclay.

'However, this isn't exactly a lost wallet. I'd describe it as the bloody trophy from a corpse you haven't found yet.'

'That's your professional opinion, is it, Miss …?'

'Doctor. Dr Clara Dawson. It's not an opinion. It's a hypothesis.'

The young constable was about to pick the wallet up when Barclay snapped, 'Don't touch that, Jim.'

His sharp tone suggested he wasn't dismissive of Clara's claim. He stood over the wallet, and moved it carefully with his fountain pen.

'What happened?' he asked simply, and Clara described the events leading up to the finding of the wallet outside her door. Constable Barclay took copious notes. Using a handkerchief, he slowly removed the contents of the wallet. There was £20 in notes, which Barclay noted was a large amount of money to be carrying around.

'And a large amount not to steal,' Clara said.

There were Matthews' identification papers, a crackled photograph of a woman, and a photograph of two children. There was also a piece of card with several telephone numbers on it, including one labelled 'home'.

'It's after 1.00 am.' Barclay said. 'It's very late to be telephoning Mrs Matthews.'

'If my husband was missing,' Susan said, 'I'd want to hear from the police. She might be sitting at home worrying herself sick. And if Dr Matthews is there, he might appreciate knowing his £20 is safe.'

Barclay agreed, and went into the corridor to telephone the number on the card. He closed the door behind him so no one could make out what he was saying. When he returned, he said, 'We have a missing person. Dr Matthews didn't return from his shift. Mrs Matthews said her husband was often late home, but that this was unusually late. She was just about to ring the police. She'd already rung the hospital and been told that Dr Matthews had finished his shift on time, and had left the hospital.

'How did she sound?' Clara asked.

'Matter-of-fact. Sensible. Calm.'

Barclay put the contents of the wallet back, and wrapped it in his handkerchief.

'We might get some prints off this,' he said.

'My fingerprints will be all over it,' Clara said.

'It might still be a storm in a teacup. If your hypothesis turns out to be correct, you'll need to come down to Russell Street to have your prints taken, for elimination purposes.'

'Unless, of course, I killed him.'

'Clara!' Pat was genuinely horrified.

'It's no secret that I couldn't stand Dr Matthews, Pat. I'd have to be a suspect, surely, wouldn't I, constable?'

'That is true, Dr Dawson.'

'So my fingerprints might incriminate me, as well as eliminate me.'

'It can't be both,' Barclay said.

Clara ignored the gentle correction.

'Let's hope Kenneth Bussell's prints are there as well.'

Within two hours of the two constables' departure, Clara's hypothesis had been proved correct. Dr Matthews' body was found in the Fitzroy Gardens, lying face down in a puddle of stale water at the bottom of an air-raid ditch.

'THIS ONE LOOKS pretty straightforward, Titus.'

Martin Serong stood on the edge of the air-raid ditch looking at the body that at its bottom.

'Nothing is ever straightforward about murder, Martin,' Titus said.

'I was speaking comparatively, I suppose. A single body in a ditch looks less complicated than four bodies on a farm. Motives, of course, are never straightforward. But I just take the pictures, Titus. Motives, and all the rest of it, that's your job.'

'We've got a head start on this one. The victim is Dr Gerald Matthews. We even have a suspect — a bloke named Kenneth Bussell. All this is courtesy of Dr Clara Dawson, whom you know.'

'She should be working for you, Titus. She's wasted in medicine.'

'You think good doctors are less important than good detectives?'

'When you put it like that, no. By the time you're involved, it's too late to expect a full recovery.'

Titus, as a general rule, didn't approve of police officers who engaged in banter around a corpse. He didn't buy the idea that black humour was a coping mechanism. Now, though, he was relieved to find that Martin Serong seemed to have lost the worrying edge of despair he'd revealed at Fisher's farm.

'So, open-and-shut case then?' Serong said.

'Wouldn't that be nice? We don't know for sure how this man died.'

'He could have drowned. There's water down there.'

'And, unfortunately, Kenneth Bussell isn't cooperating by turning himself in. And, as you know, Martin, having a name is a long way from having a conviction.'

CLARA DAWSON SAT alone in Inspector Lambert's office at Russell Street. It was Saturday lunchtime. She'd managed to sleep for a couple of hours, but the sleep had been shallow and not restorative. Her eyes felt scratchy. She was due back on night shift the following day, so between now and then she simply had to get some sleep. Titus entered, and apologised for being late.

'Does the head of Homicide normally take witness statements, Titus?'

'Well, you're not really a witness, and this isn't really a statement. You've already given that to Senior Constable Barclay.'

'Who's very good at his job, may I say. Why is he languishing on night duty?'

'I have no idea, but that is good to hear. I've read the statement, and it's surprisingly free of spelling mistakes. You make no secret of the fact that you didn't much like Dr Matthews.'

'I thought he was a frightful man and a workmanlike doctor. Nothing more. He was arrogant, and from what I'd seen of his interactions with patients, unsympathetic and undiplomatic. He wasn't good with people. Impatient and dismissive. He should have been a vet. Animals don't know when someone is being rude to them. No, I didn't like him.'

'Tell me about this Kenneth Bussell.'

'He presented with a shallow stab wound and a flimsy story about how he'd acquired it. It isn't my job to dispute his account. He was well nourished and clean, so he wasn't living rough. What he was doing in the park, where he said he was attacked, at that hour of the night, is his business, however unsavoury it might have been. He was polite and cooperative, two qualities that I appreciate in my job. I didn't think he needed to be admitted, but I wanted him to stay until I'd finished my shift, just to be sure I hadn't missed anything. I actually forgot about him, and when I went to check on him, Dr Matthews was there dispensing his unique brand of medicine. This involved questioning my judgement in front of a patient and ostentatiously checking the quality of my sutures. I left and thought no more about it, until the wallet appeared at my door.'

'You'd never met Bussell before?'

'Never, and I understand the meaning behind the question, Titus. Why would this stranger become my champion?'

'It bothers me that he knows where you live, Clara. He must have followed you, returned to the hospital, waited for Dr Matthews' shift to finish at 6.00 pm, and then ambushed him. The time of death is estimated to be between 8.00 and 10.00 pm, on Friday. What was Matthews doing in the two hours between the end of his shift and his death? Was he with Bussell all that time?'

'How did he die?'

'We're not sure yet. He'd been struck in the back of the head with something heavy but blunt. The skin wasn't broken, but the skull was. That would certainly have rendered him unconscious. Martin Serong suggested that he may have drowned.'

'Drowned?'

'He was face down in a deepish puddle of muddy water. If someone held his head, it's entirely possible that he breathed in the water and drowned. We won't be sure until the autopsy.'

'Kenneth Bussell was lean, but he was strong.'

'He gave no personal details? No address?'

'If he'd been admitted he would have filled out the forms, but he wasn't admitted. I was with him for maybe ten minutes when I assessed him.'

'Did he strike you as disturbed?'

'Only in retrospect. He was calm. But he'd been in some sort of fight, so he's no stranger to violence. I feel strangely responsible for all this, Titus. And Matthews has a wife and children.'

'Adelaide Matthews is coming here. In fact, she should be here now. She wanted to come. She said she didn't want to be at home on her own. The two children are at boarding school, apparently. I'll take her to formally identify the body.'

'Christ, Titus. It's all so fucking awful.'

'We have to find Kenneth Bussell, Clara.'

'I have to get Pat to lock the fucking front door.'

Before ending the interview, Titus asked after Helen and Joe. Clara wasn't able to tell him much, except to assure him that Helen's investigation into the Fisher murders had begun and that, as far as she knew, some progress was being made.

'Helen is very happy, Titus. Leaving the police force is the best thing that's happened to her.'

'It's not the best thing for us, Clara.'

IN THE FOYER of police headquarters, Clara observed a well-dressed woman asking the receptionist for Inspector Titus Lambert. On an impulse — an impulse she might have resisted, had she thought about it — she approached the woman.

'Mrs Matthews?'

'Yes, I'm Mrs Matthews.'

It was an educated voice, a voice Clara associated with her teachers at the Methodist Ladies' College, where she'd completed her final year. She took in how Adelaide Matthews' hair had been artfully peroxided and cut short, with soft curls rolling back over her ears.

'I'm Dr Clara Dawson. I was a colleague of your husband's.'

'Oh, I see. I'm afraid my husband didn't consider you a colleague, Dr Dawson. He used to refer to you as "the unfortunate anomaly."'

Adelaide Matthews' tone had no acid in it.

'I was aware that he didn't approve of me.'

'He didn't altogether approve of me. I wonder if we could have a cup of tea, or something stronger, after my meeting with the policeman? Do you have time?'

'Yes, of course,' Clara said, and realised that curiosity might have smothered her common sense.

'Oh, I just realised that I have to identify my husband's body. Perhaps you could come later to my house.'

Clara knew that grief was often suppressed initially to allow the practicalities around death to be dealt with. Even so, Adelaide Matthews' measured response seemed peculiar. It wasn't cold, exactly, but Clara didn't suppose this woman's grief would ever amount to uncontrollable sobbing. She accepted the offer, and Mrs Matthews jotted her address in Drummond Street in Carlton on a piece of paper.

'I'll be home by three o'clock.'

Clara wondered what Titus would make of this coolly elegant and composed widow.

✗

CLARA HOPED THAT Helen Lord was at her office in East Melbourne. She wanted to see her. She didn't want to take a taxi to Kew. It was expensive, and anyway there were fewer and fewer of them about, as worn tyres became impossible to replace. She telephoned Helen Lord and Associates, and Joe Sable answered. Helen was there. It would take Clara 15 minutes to walk from Russell Street.

'Tell Helen to put the kettle on. I have much to discuss.'

When Clara arrived, Joe opened the door to let her in, and not for the first time she examined him and pondered the mysteries of attraction — or, more specifically, Helen's attraction to him. He wouldn't turn heads when he walked into a room. On the other hand, once he'd been noticed, people might agree that he was pleasant enough to look at. For Joe's part, Clara's presence continued to make him regress into awkward boyishness. He knew perfectly well, because Guy had made no secret of it that he, Guy, intended to pursue Clara. Joe had said nothing, and had managed to dampen the mean jealousy he felt.

Clara kissed Joe on the cheek in greeting. Their shared experience at Peter Lillee's wake had made such an intimacy possible and unremarkable. Helen came out of her office and embraced her friend.

'Joe said you had much to discuss.'

'I have just been called "an unfortunate anomaly". I can't tell you how thrilling that is.'

Clara and Helen went into Helen's office. Joe interrupted them to bring them tea. They didn't stop talking when he entered, and he caught the tail end of Clara's story.

'Stay, Joe,' Helen said. 'You should hear this.' She then précised what Clara had said.

'We need to find this Kenneth Bussell,' Helen said, 'and you should come and stay with us at Kew until we do.'

Clara refused, saying that she couldn't just leave Susan and Pat in the house.

'And no, Helen, they can't stay at Kew. Your poor mother. It's a house, not a hotel for strays.'

As soon as the words were out of her mouth, she realised her faux pas, and Joe's deep blush confirmed it.

'Oh, fuck. Clearly, present company excepted. I ...'

'It's okay, Clar, Joe knows he's not a stray.'

The colour of Joe's face indicated that this was not entirely true. To cover the general embarrassment, Helen hurried on.

'Kenneth Bussell must live somewhere. And he was well dressed, you say?'

'Well, he was clean. I don't really notice men's clothes. He didn't smell, and he'd shaved that day, I'd say. He had decent shoes, I remember that. And good teeth. He didn't smoke. There were no tar stains on his fingers or his teeth, and there were no scars on his body. He was fit, but he wasn't living a hardscrabble life. Finger and toenails were clipped and clean. I could describe his genitals for you, but it doesn't seem relevant at the moment.'

'You're a marvel, Clar.'

'I wish I was better at noticing clothes. All my training is about the body underneath, though.'

'It's what's inside the head that is disturbing,' Joe said.

'The police artist is knocking up a likeness.'

'That might be useful, if it's good,' Helen said. 'I wonder if Inspector Lambert would give us a copy.'

'I can't see why not,' Joe said. 'What really worries me, Clara, is that this Bussell bloke has been inside your house and knows which room is yours.'

'Oh, God, I hadn't thought of that. He knew which door to

leave the wallet near. It wasn't just a lucky choice, was it?'

'No,' Joe said. 'Somehow he'd discovered which room was yours. Was he inside the house already when Susan and Pat came home, so he saw them enter their rooms?'

'That gives me the creeps.'

'It's more likely,' Helen said, 'that he was waiting outside, saw that a light was on in your room, and then saw Susan and Pat come home and turn the lights on in their rooms.'

'Unfortunately, Helen, we haven't got around to taking the blackouts down.'

Joe's theory, however unsettling, now seemed the most likely.

'It makes me shudder to think about it, but at least it might indicate that he doesn't intend to do me any harm.'

'He went to a lot of risk and trouble, Clar. He's going to want something in return, surely.'

When Clara told them that she intended calling on Gerald Matthews' wife, they each expressed surprise and disapproval.

'It's just a courtesy visit.'

'Oh, Clar, I don't believe that for a minute. It has the whiff of prurience about it.'

'I don't think you can smell prurience, Helen, but you're right of course. I am interested in finding out about Gerald Matthews. I know it's awful, but he's more interesting dead than when he was alive. You can't talk me out of it. I'm due there in an hour. I was invited. I didn't inveigle an invitation. After all, what's so peculiar about it? A colleague has died, and I'm visiting his wife.'

Both Joe and Helen folded their arms in an act of coordinated scepticism. Clara laughed.

'Anyway, I'm going. Perhaps you won't be interested in what I find out.'

'You have got to come around for dinner, Clar.'

Clara declined that offer, saying that she needed to sleep, but promised to telephone if she learned anything of interest.

'In a novel,' she said, 'it would turn out that Adelaide Matthews and Kenneth Bussell knew each other.'

THE MATTHEWS' HOUSE in Drummond Street was handsome. It was double-storeyed, with an ornamental fountain set in the path to the front door. Adelaide Matthews opened the door to Clara's knock.

'Thank you for coming,' she said.

The front room where they sat contained an eclectic mix of modern and Victorian furniture. There was, Clara thought, a controlling hand behind the mix so that it was aesthetically pleasing rather than chaotic. Clara suspected that that hand was Adelaide's.

'Would you mind if we bypassed tea and went straight to brandy? Good brandy?'

Clara would have preferred tea, but accepted brandy. Clearly, Adelaide Matthews preferred not to go to the bother of boiling water.

'I know your husband didn't like me, Mrs Matthews.'

'Adelaide, please.'

'Adelaide. But I'm genuinely sorry for your own loss.'

'Thank you. I'm sorry, I don't know your first name.'

'Clara.'

'I did love my husband, and of course this is devastating for the children. I don't think the finality of his death hit me until I saw him lying there in the morgue.'

Clara was listening for any querulousness in Adelaide's voice that might indicate deep emotion, but she couldn't detect any. Adelaide was obviously conscious of the discrepancy between her words and her feelings.

'I must seem rather detached,' she said as she poured brandy into balloons that looked expensive. 'The truth is, I feel rather detached. I should be throwing myself on the ground and tearing at my hair, but somehow those emotions just won't come.'

'Everyone deals with these things differently, Adelaide. There isn't a correct way.'

'Yes, I know. My children are coming home tomorrow. I need to be strong for them. You see, Gerald wasn't an easy man to love. He wasn't warm, or particularly loving, but he did love me, and he certainly loved the children. He could be demanding and short-tempered, but he wasn't a violent man, which makes the way he died so awful. I can understand that people didn't get on with him, but who would hate him enough to kill him? Who would hate him enough to rob two children of their father?'

Clara sipped her brandy and wished her palate was more sophisticated. Should she tell Adelaide about Kenneth Bussell? No. There couldn't possibly be a connection between them. That idea was ludicrous. They belonged in different worlds, and besides, Bussell's appearance at the hospital had been entirely random in its timing. But should she warn Adelaide that this man was out there? What if Bussell turned up at the Matthews' house? But why would he?

'The man who killed him might have been a stranger, Adelaide.'

'The police said his wallet was found some distance from his body, but that no money had been taken from it.'

So Titus hadn't been specific about where the wallet had been found. He must have had a reason for withholding this information from Adelaide. Clara was glad she hadn't mentioned Kenneth Bussell.

'I think whoever took Gerald's wallet must have panicked and thrown it away,' Adelaide said. She poured more brandy into her balloon. 'I'm very grateful that you came, Clara. I wanted to meet the female doctor my husband railed against. He was old-fashioned. Women were nurses. Men were doctors. He had firm ideas about the limitations of the female brain. Women were too emotionally unstable to make safe and reliable diagnoses. He used to say that. Our biology is against us, apparently. We're good at other things, like childbirth, but too prone to mood swings for science. I stopped arguing with him years ago. It was out of boredom, really, not acquiescence, although that's how it must have appeared to him. I'm sorry, I'm prattling on.'

'If it's any consolation, Adelaide, Dr Matthews wasn't the only male doctor to consider me an unfortunate anomaly — which, by the way, has become an immediately favourite expression.'

Adelaide managed a small laugh.

'Gerald would have been disappointed that you're not offended by it. Of course, it says more about him than it does about you, doesn't it?'

It didn't seem to Clara that Adelaide was in any need of consolation, but she reassured her that Gerald wouldn't have endured prolonged suffering, although she couldn't be certain of this herself.

'So,' Adelaide said, 'no reckoning made, but sent to his account with all his imperfections on his head.'

Clara recognised the quote from Hamlet, and assumed it meant that Gerald Matthews had been a religious man.

'Was your husband Catholic?'

'No. We're nominally C of E, but Gerald didn't care for institutional religion. If he worshipped anyone, it was Norman Lindsay.'

Clara knew very little about Norman Lindsay, beyond the fact that he was an artist who produced rather louche pictures.

'I'm not sure what that means, Adelaide.'

'I'm sorry. Gerald used to carry on about him so often I

sometimes forget that he's an acquired taste.'

Clara hadn't noticed until this moment that the walls of the room had no pictures hanging on them. Scuff marks indicated that art of some sort had until recently hung from the picture rail that ran around the room. Adelaide noticed Clara's eyes moving around the walls.

'This used to be the Lindsay room.'

She gave no indication when the pictures had been taken down. Surely not in the last 24 hours? Would stripping the walls of Norman Lindsay pictures be the first thing Adelaide Matthews did after being told that her husband had been murdered?

'What was it about Lindsay's art that so intrigued Gerald?'

'It wasn't the art so much, although he did love that. Inexplicably. I think it's frightful and vulgar. My opinion didn't count, though. Mr Lindsay didn't much care for the opinions of women. Feminine minds are only half-formed, you see. Half-minds, that's what we have. Half-minds.'

Clara couldn't suppress a cough of disbelief.

'Let me show you something.'

Adelaide stood, and despite having downed two generous brandies, left the room without any hint of a stagger. She returned quickly and handed Clara a book.

'This,' she said, 'was Gerald's Bible.'

Clara took the book and turned it towards her so she could read the title. *Creative Effort: an essay in affirmation*. Adelaide poured herself a third brandy.

'It's all in there — Gerald's rules for living a good life. It poisoned his mind. It made it impossible for him to be happy. Nothing in Gerald's life lived up to Mr Lindsay's aesthetic ideals.' She paused for a moment and then indicated the walls. 'I took all the pictures down an hour after I'd been told that Gerald was dead. That must seem callous, but some instinct made me do it, and somehow it helped me cope. I can't explain it. I wasn't trying to expunge him from my life, not completely, just the worst of him, and that's what those big-breasted Amazons represented — the worst of him. He was essentially a good man, Clara. I wonder if you can believe that.'

'I wouldn't presume to judge your husband, Adelaide, although it would be dishonest of me to pretend that I liked him. I never saw the best of him.'

'But there was a best part of him. That's why I wanted you to come here. I think you must know how he felt about you.'

This had already been declared, and Clara had no wish to return to it. Adelaide, however, continued.

'He loathed you, Clara. I mean, he actively loathed you. He thought you were a danger to the running of the hospital.'

'Why are you telling me this?'

'Because I think it must have made you hate him, but you see, he was envious of you, which is a sort of perverted admiration, isn't it? I'm not explaining this at all well.'

'Adelaide, it doesn't matter what your husband thought of me. All that matters is that you've lost him, and that the children have lost their father.'

Adelaide emptied her brandy glass, but didn't refill it.

'I need to put some pictures up before the children get home.'

Clara took this an indication that she should leave. After a warm farewell and invitation from Adelaide to call in again at any time, Clara left. As she made her way back to her room in East Melbourne, she rehearsed what she would say to Helen when she telephoned her. The meeting with Adelaide Matthews felt more peculiar with each step she took. It had been pleasant enough, but what had it been about? Adelaide's desire to rehabilitate Gerald Matthews' character was odd, and it lacked conviction, although Clara reminded herself yet again that people's emotions were unpredictable in times of great stress. She imagined that having to welcome two children home to a world that no longer had their father in it would disrupt normal behaviour.

8

ZACHARY WILSON'S MEMORY of what had happened at Fisher's farm began to reform itself piecemeal, and it reached a point where it crashed in on him, fully realised in all its hideous detail. How could the police think that he was the perpetrator of these atrocities? His head ached terribly, so terribly that it made him nauseous and made sleep almost impossible. He'd been told that his wife was coming to see him that afternoon, and his initial reaction was to feel ashamed that she should see him like this, in prison. Of course she knew he was innocent. Of course she did. And yet there was a tiny seed of doubt. She'd lost faith in his common sense when he'd fallen victim to Fisher's absurd claims. He could barely credit it himself now. Had the suggestion that he might be guilty, that he might have wreaked terrible vengeance on the man who'd exploited him, come from Meredith? What other explanation could there be for his incarceration?

The pain in his head was fierce, but not so fierce as to obliterate his horror at his surroundings. His bleak cell, among the cells attached to the Magistrates' Court, did not reflect the presumption of innocence accorded to prisoners on remand. The lavatory, with no lid or seat, was doubtless an extravagant improvement on the nineteenth-century facilities, but it was foul-smelling nonetheless, and the sounds that came from the cells around him excited in him an emotion he'd never before felt, even at the lowest points in his life — despair. He sat on the edge of his mean bed, aware suddenly that one of the sounds that echoed around him was coming from him. It began as a groan and declined into a guttering whimper. This was how the guard found him when he opened the door and announced the arrival of his visitor.

'Your wife's here, mate. You might want to clean yourself up a bit.'

Zac felt in his pockets for a handkerchief to mop at his streaming eyes and nose. There was nothing there. With no other option, he lifted his shirt to dab at his face.

When Meredith saw her husband, the first thing she did was give him a handkerchief. He cleared his nose and wiped his eyes. She'd known it was unworthy of her, but as she'd driven from Nunawading to Russell Street in the city, she'd been more concerned about the amount of fuel being consumed than about the welfare of her husband. She'd assumed that Zac would be uncomfortable, but that the discomfort would be temporary. She hadn't been expecting to find him broken. She couldn't contain the gasp that escaped her when he was brought into the room. He barely noticed her response. He felt dizzy and on the edge of fainting. He sat down opposite her, accepted the handkerchief, and began taking deep breaths. Meredith reached across the table and took his hand.

'Zac, look at me.'

He raised his distracted eyes, but was unable to speak.

'I have a lawyer, Zac, and there are people, private people, not just the police, investigating this.'

'The baby,' he said. 'They killed the baby. They killed the baby.'

He began to sob, and the sobs escalated quickly until his body shook. Meredith, who'd never seen her husband weep, was disconcerted and appalled.

'They think I did it. How? How could they think that? A baby? Why am I here? Meredith, you have to tell them. I didn't do these things. I saw Fisher blow himself up.'

Meredith leaned towards him and spoke sharply in the hope that her voice would cut through Zac's hysteria.

'You have to pull yourself together, Zac. Of course you're innocent. You're here because you were there, that's all.'

'I'm remembering things. Awful things.'

'You have to tell the police.'

'I can't stay here, Meredith. I can't stand it. It will kill me.'

'It will not kill you, Zac. Axes kill people. Ropes kill people. Unpleasant prison cells do not.'

Zachary was too distraught to be wounded by his wife's seeming lack of sympathy. Meredith looked at the floundering man in front of her and found herself unable to be moved by his suffering. She felt that he was weak and that his behaviour was degrading. Of course he was weak. He'd been conned by Peter Fisher. She realised that he'd never won back her respect after that. Their lives had returned to a kind of normality — he farmed, she cooked and cleaned, they made love — but for Meredith, everything had a dulled, muffled quality about it. She didn't want to be here in this room with him, and she couldn't contain the impulse to get away. Without a word more, she stood up and left, leaving Zachary bewildered and the guard smirking.

SUNDAY WAS A day of rest on Anthony Prescott's property. That is to say, it was a rest day from working in the orchard and the fields. There was no respite from the demanding schedule of observances, prayers, and sermons in the Church of the First Born. Guy had been expecting a large crowd to arrive, but there were only two people from outside the property. Fuel shortages and the decreasing roadworthiness of many vehicles made this unsurprising. The visitors were a married couple, neither of whom spoke, but both of whom sat rapt by Prescott's theatrical mix of thundering, hectoring, and cloyingly reassuring warmth. These were the tactics of the bully.

The congregation sat with their heads bowed. One hour into the service, Prescott stopped. There was silence for a moment and, as if unbidden, but obviously the result of custom, each of the congregants rose to his or her feet and declared his or her faith in Prescott as the way, the truth, and the light. The women gave thanks that they'd been chosen as handmaidens. The men offered to lay down their lives in defence of the Master and to root out false prophets and those who made sacrilegious claims to being the source of revelation. No mention was made in the course of the service of the deaths at Fisher's farm, but perhaps this had been addressed at earlier services and was now considered done with.

The afternoon was spent in silent contemplation. Having returned to their room together after the service, Nepheg told Guy — although he called him Absalom — that four hours of silence would begin at 1.00 pm, and that this silence could not be broken without penance being exacted. The penance was determined by the Master: it might be harsh or gentle, depending on his mood, but it was always just. You were not required to keep to your room, but could walk about the property so long as you kept close to the house. No one was to enter the orchards or the paddocks. The temptation to bend and retrieve fallen fruit had to be avoided. Eye contact with others was to be resisted during this time, and physical contact was a breach that would be punished severely. These strictures seemed absurd and pointless to Guy, but given the small number of people who lived on the place, he didn't suppose anyone found them too onerous. The mention of punishment unsettled him. He should have known, he told himself, that obedience was guaranteed by fear as much as it was by faith. Self-appointed messiahs didn't bind people to them with love. Always, always there was fear.

Nepheg said that he'd stay in the room and pray, although Guy suspected that by pray he meant sleep. Guy had no intention of traipsing around the outside of the house for four hours, but he was curious to see how the others managed this forced contemplation. One of the women was walking about. The other, the woman called Prudence, must have remained in the building. Abraham was seated on the veranda next to Prescott. Their postures were so self-consciously contemplative that Guy suspected they would begin chatting to each other as soon as everyone was out of sight. Despite the stricture against eye contact, Guy was conscious that Prescott was watching him as he passed by the veranda. Prescott was suspicious of him. Why? His suitcase and his clothes had been thoroughly searched. Had he left some tell-tale clue that he wasn't a serious acolyte? He didn't think so. The pen and the notebook were ordinary objects carried by lots of people.

After half an hour of mindless perambulation, Guy began to realise that four hours was a very long time indeed. Around the back of the house, he stopped and looked across at the small outhouse that was forbidden to men. Had Prudence retreated there? As he was considering this, Prudence appeared beside him, as if he'd conjured her up. She paused for a brief moment, and spoke, in contravention of the rules.

'You have to leave.'

That was all she said before quickly moving away. He would have followed her, but Prescott walked into view, and Prudence headed towards him. They passed each other without acknowledgement. He couldn't possibly have heard Prudence's words — Guy himself had barely heard them. Prescott, though, had an extraordinary ability to read signs in others. Had Prudence betrayed herself with some small shift in her demeanour as she passed him?

Prescott approached Guy, and, instead of passing him, he reached out and placed his open palm on Guy's chest. Could he detect the sudden change in Guy's heartbeat?

'Absalom.'

His voice was low. Obviously, the rules forbidding physical contact and speech didn't apply to Prescott. Rules rarely applied to the people who made them. Guy had known this since childhood. Nevertheless, he was taken by surprise whenever he saw it realised.

'Nepheg has come to me with a confession. He lay on his bed during this silence and fell asleep. Sleep is not contemplation. He has requested penance. Come to the chapel at 5.30. You will be a witness to his acknowledgement of weakness.'

Guy was about to respond when Prescott said, 'Do not speak, Absalom. 5.30.'

Prescott moved away, and Guy returned to his room. Nepheg wasn't there. Guy sat on the edge of his bed. He wished he could put trousers on. The tunic might have been comfortable in summer, but the late-autumn coolness played along his bare legs, and Guy had never liked being cold. Joe would be expecting a note detailing his first impressions of Prescott and this community. He'd make the long trip from Kew early the following morning, and he'd find nothing in the tree stump. There was no way that Guy could warn him unless he entered the main house when people were sleeping and used the telephone. That was too risky; he'd be discovered. The only solution was to get down to the stump later in the evening and leave something there to signal that he was all right, something that Joe would understand to mean that his pen and notebook had been confiscated. Could he spell something out, just a word or two, with twigs? This seemed so much like some sort of schoolboy jape that it made him laugh. This was, however, the only solution.

At 5.30, Guy entered the chapel. Prescott, Abraham, and Nepheg were already there. Nepheg was standing, bare-chested, his arms stretched out. There were welts across his back — some almost healed, the legacy of earlier whippings.

'Absalom,' Prescott said, 'Nepheg stands here before us, guilty and penitent. What is it that you want from us, Nepheg? How do you wish to atone?'

'I slept, Master. I slept in the room I share with Absalom, and I have defiled that place with my weakness. I ask forgiveness from Absalom.'

'Do you give it, Absalom?' Prescott asked.

'Yes, of course.'

'I ask that Absalom exact my penance.'

Guy felt sick. He saw what was expected of him.

The old man handed Guy a thin, whippy branch, stripped of its leaves but with sharp protrusions along its length. These weren't thorns, but the ragged ends where twigs had been snapped off.

'Nepheg has requested ten strokes,' Prescott said. 'If no blood is drawn, the penance will not be complete, and ten more strokes will have to be made.'

Guy took the branch. He felt his hand shaking, and it was at this point that he lost consciousness. When he woke, he was seated on a chair against the wall. Anthony Prescott was standing in front of him. The branch was lying across Guy's lap.

'You fainted,' Prescott said.

'No. I fell asleep.'

Prescott laughed. 'You were so bored that you fell asleep?'

'Narcolepsy.'

Guy explained his condition, and said that it was this that he'd hoped to cure.

'I've never heard of such a thing, Absalom.'

'Soldiers in the first war were afflicted by it. Some of them would fall asleep even as they began to run towards the guns. I feel fine afterwards. It's not like fainting. I don't feel peculiar.'

'Good, because Nepheg is waiting to do his penance.'

Nepheg was still standing, his arms outstretched.

'How long was I unconscious?'

'Less than a minute.'

'How did I get to this chair?'

'Nepheg carried you. Are you ready now?'

Guy nodded. He stood and willed his body not to let him down, although simultaneously he wondered how he would bring himself to whip Nepheg until he bled. He approached him and said, 'I'm sorry.'

'You have nothing to be sorry for, Absalom.'

Prescott said, 'Begin.'

'If he bleeds after the first stroke, will that be sufficient?'

'He has requested ten strokes.'

Guy raised his arm and brought the branch down sharply across Nepheg's back. Nepheg flinched. No blood had been drawn. As Guy raised his arm again, he consoled himself that this was a fetish of Nepheg's and that, far from doing him harm, he was satisfying some peculiar urge in him. The fourth stroke produced a thin beading of blood. The fifth and sixth opened a partly healed welt, and by the tenth blow Nepheg's back was sufficiently running with blood to satisfy Prescott that Nepheg's penance had been achieved. Abraham stepped forward and, with a tenderness that surprised Guy, sponged Nepheg's back with carbolic. The muscles twitched and jumped, but Nepheg didn't utter a sound. He pulled his tunic back over his shoulders.

At dinner, no mention was made of Nepheg's penance. The spots of blood on his tunic were evidence enough of what had happened. Prudence avoided Guy's eyes, and Prescott spoke with sudden fierceness about false prophets and apostates. Guy didn't speak. He assumed what he hoped was an attitude of humble attentiveness. As he listened to Prescott, he knew with awful certainty that this was a dangerous man and that he wasn't safe. Why had Prescott named him Absalom? Who was Absalom? Before going down to the tree stump to leave Joe his coded message, he would scour the pages of the Old Testament and find out who Absalom was. Prescott didn't name people by accident.

CLARA'S SUNDAY-NIGHT SHIFT had been quiet. A baby had been born; an elderly man had died; a young man had broken down and been transferred to the secure ward at Willsmere Asylum. There was talk among the nurses of Gerald Matthews' death, and Clara overheard a reference to Adelaide Matthews as his 'uppity wife', although little affection was expressed for Gerald.

By the time Clara left the hospital, the dawn had broken, and the day promised to be cool and grey. The street outside the hospital was already busy, and Clara's eye fell on a figure standing stock-still among the pedestrians. He was some distance from her, on the opposite side of the street, but Clara recognised Kenneth Bussell. His hands were in his pockets. Their eyes met. Bussell smiled, took one hand from his pocket, and made a gesture that might have been a small wave. Clara froze, uncertain how to proceed. What was he doing here? She thought about going back inside and telephoning Inspector Lambert, and she half-turned to do so. She looked down at the ground, and when she raised her eyes, Bussell was gone. Clara saw a man who might have been him joining the general hurry. As Clara walked towards her flat in East Melbourne, she felt that Bussell was somewhere behind her. She checked over her shoulder again and again. By the time she reached her flat, she was both panicked and angry. Pat and Susan had left for work already. She made doubly sure that the doors were locked. It was too early to telephone Titus Lambert, and it was him, not an underling, she wanted to speak to. She made herself a cup of tea, and telephoned Helen at home.

'You can't stay there, Clara.'

'I have to get some sleep, Helen. The doors are locked.'

'Get in a taxi and come here. You can sleep in one of the spare rooms. No one will disturb you.'

'He didn't follow me home, Helen.'

Helen, her frustration evident, snapped, 'He's watching you, Clar!'

That bald statement pulled Clara up short.

'All right,' she said.

'I'd get Joe to pick you up, but he's taken the car out to Nunawading. I'll wait until you get here, and then head off to the office. Does Bussell have a car?'

'I have no idea. I doubt it. He didn't strike me as wealthy man. I'll keep an eye out for a car following me.'

Clara arrived at the house in Kew with her nerves jangled by constantly checking the traffic behind and around the taxi. She was confident that she hadn't been followed, but she asked the driver to circle around the block before dropping her three doors up from her destination. The driver didn't query her instructions. The last woman who'd made odd requests had been a high-class prostitute. This woman didn't look like a prostitute, but then neither had the other woman.

Clara checked her surroundings before walking towards Helen's place. By the time she reached the gate her courage had returned, and with it came anger that a creature like Kenneth Bussell was controlling her life.

Ros Lord welcomed Clara into the house, and Helen showed her the room where she could sleep. Clara then telephoned Inspector Lambert, who took down the details and expressed his relief that she was staying in Kew. He reassured her that they were doing as much as they could to track Bussell down, but that they weren't having much luck. No one of that name had a criminal record. They'd checked boarding houses and hotels, and had distributed the sketch of him far and wide. Thus far, they'd had no luck.

'It's as if he's a figment of my imagination,' Clara said. 'The only people to have seen him are me and Gerald Matthews, and he's dead.'

'Dr Matthews wasn't murdered by a figment, Clara.'

Clara read for a while, and, feeling safe inside the great house, managed to sleep deeply and well.

IT HAD BEEN Joe's intention to reach the tree stump before dawn. The roads were empty of traffic when he left the house, and he was in Nunawading sooner than he'd thought he would be. He was worried that he'd lose his way on the unlit roads and unmade tracks that ran past orchards. His sense of direction was poor at the best of times, and the landmarks he'd noted during his daylight visits to this distant suburb weren't visible. More by luck than design, he found the road that ran down to Prescott's orchard. He switched off the headlights and crept forward in the moonlight. He stopped well short of the tree stump, even though he knew it wasn't visible from the house. As he walked towards it, he saw a figure bent over the stump. Joe squinted, hoping to recognise Guy. The clothing suggested it might be a woman. Whoever it was was wearing what looked like a dress, but the pale legs were masculine. It was the brief cough that reassured Joe that this was Guy, and he said his name quietly. Guy, startled, straightened up and peered into the darkness.

'Joe?'

Joe stepped forward to where he could be seen. They shook hands.

'What were you doing?'

'I was trying to construct some sort of message out of twigs, and I know how ridiculous that sounds. They've confiscated my pen and notebook.'

'Are you in any danger?'

'No.'

Guy said it quickly, hoping that his doubts about his own safety were disguised.

'If you have the slightest suspicion that they're on to you, come back with me now.'

'I'm not leaving my fountain pen here, let alone my clothes. I don't have enough coupons to buy new ones.'

Guy gave Joe a detailed account of all that had happened on Prescott's property. He withheld the fact that Prudence had advised him to leave. He knew that Joe would insist on pulling the plug, and that would mean he'd come away with nothing. There was no doubt in Guy's mind that Prescott and the Church of the First Born were implicated in the deaths at Fisher's farm. The only way to find out for certain was to remain where he was.

'He calls me Absalom, but I don't know why. Everyone here has a biblical name.'

'Do you think it means something? Who was Absalom?'

'If you weren't such an ignoramus about your own religion you might be able to tell me. I've had a flick through the Old Testament, but I can't find it.'

'Maybe Prescott just likes the sound of it.'

Joe told Guy about the death of Dr Gerald Matthews, and its connection to Clara Dawson. He was half-hoping that Guy might want to hurry to her protection. As he said goodbye to his friend, who was shivering in his tunic, he once again experienced a deep dread.

'Please, Guy, please be careful. You're among wolves.'

INSPECTOR LAMBERT WAS surprised by the deterioration in Zac Wilson's appearance. He'd been bruised and swollen when he'd seen him in hospital, but the man who sat opposite him in a room in the remand section that had been set aside for interviews looked drained, emptied out. He looked defeated. Was the vanquished demeanour the result of guilt, or of innocence? Until he'd met him face to face like this, Lambert hadn't believed in his guilt. Now he wasn't so sure. If he wasn't guilty of all four murders, perhaps he'd been responsible for some of them. The murder of Emilio Barbero had occurred 24 hours before the others. It was an anomaly that might be explained if there'd been more than one perpetrator at Fisher's farm.

'Why am I here?' The desperation in Zac's voice was obvious.

'Perhaps you were in the wrong place at the wrong time.'

'You can't arrest people for that.'

'In this case, Mr Wilson, we really didn't have any choice. The awful truth is that at the moment you're our only credible suspect.'

'I can't bear it.'

'Prison is dreadful.'

'It's not just that. I can't bear that when people look at me they think I killed a baby and the others. They think I'm a monster.'

He lowered his head and began to shake.

'Mr Wilson! You are the only person who was there. You have to help yourself. I need you to tell me everything you can remember. Everything.'

Wilson pulled himself together sufficiently to give Inspector Lambert a coherent account, as he now remembered it, of the moment he saw Fisher coming towards him to the moment he saw him put a stick of gelignite between his teeth. It was coherent, but sketchy.

'What was your relationship with Peter Fisher?'

Lambert had been expecting an obfuscatory answer. Helen Lord had relayed to him, as she'd agreed to do, the information she'd learned from Meredith Wilson. To his astonishment, Fisher simply told him the truth.

'I was duped by him. For a short while, I believed he was Jesus Christ.'

He looked at Inspector Lambert.

'You already think I'm crazy. What do you think now?'

'My opinion isn't something you should be thinking about. Tell me how this happened. How did he convince you to believe this?'

'It's difficult to explain. My wife says I'm gullible. She means stupid, of course. At the time I must have been looking for some sort of guidance.'

'When was this?'

'Last year. I didn't really know I was looking for anything. Fisher saw something in me, and played me for the fool that I was. At first I thought it was ridiculous that this ordinary man was claiming that he was God, but there were others who believed in him. I got caught up. One afternoon, the wind was blowing so hard I was worried about the blossoms on my fruit trees. Fisher came down to my orchard, raised his arms, and commanded the wind to stop. Almost immediately, it died down. I see now it was a coincidence, but at the time it removed my doubts, and I started to attend services at his house. My doubts returned pretty quickly, and I soon realised that he was a fraud. I told him he was a liar and a conman. He told me he'd dried up my wife's womb so that we'd never have children. I was expelled from the Church, and declared anathema.'

'Anathema?'

'The Church of the First Born is a hybrid. A bit of Catholicism, a bit of Protestantism, a bit of paganism. Anathema is excommunication. No one from the Church was supposed to speak to me, or do business with me.'

'Did you lose customers for your fruit?'

'You think that was my motive for killing him?'

'I'm just trying to put all this together, Mr Wilson.'

'It didn't affect my business at all. None of my buyers belong to the Church. After my expulsion, I only saw Fisher in the distance. He didn't visit me, and I didn't visit him.'

'What do you know about Emilio Barbero?'

'I don't know who that is.'

'He was a farmhand. He was the young man hanging from the rafter.'

'Christ.'

Wilson suddenly sat up straight.

'He must have done it! This Barbero bloke. He must have done it and then hanged himself. It's obvious, isn't it? Why haven't you figured that out? Why have you arrested me?'

'Is that what you wanted us to think, Mr Wilson?'

Wilson looked confused.

'Emilio Barbero had been dead for many hours before any of the others. Dead men don't wield axes.'

Wilson slumped in his chair.

'I didn't know him. I'd never heard his name until you said it. You think I killed him first, don't you?'

Inspector Lambert said nothing. Wilson uttered a moan, and began to cry. These weren't great, racking sobs. His shoulders barely moved, but his eyes and nose streamed.

'Mr Wilson.'

Wilson turned away from Inspector Lambert.

'No,' he said. 'No. No more. No more.'

He sniffed, took the handkerchief from his pocket, and made a desultory dab with it at his face. 'No more. I can't.'

It was clear to Lambert that he'd get nothing more out of Wilson. There was, however, one question he needed to ask.

'Where were you the day before Fisher came to you with his dead son?'

Wilson whimpered. 'No more.'

Inspector Lambert stood up. On his way out, he spoke to the warden of the remand section and suggested that Wilson be watched carefully.

'He seems very fragile,' Lambert said. 'I don't want him hurting himself.'

'I'd be more worried about the other prisoners. No one likes a baby killer. Presumption of innocence means nothing in here, Inspector. Still, none of the other prisoners are here for violent crimes, so he ought to be safe. I'll keep an eye on him, though.'

Inspector Lambert didn't feel buoyed by this reassurance as he left.

9

Winslow Fazackerly had decided that Tom Mackenzie was essentially all right. He knew without a shadow of a doubt that Mackenzie had been instructed to attempt to form a friendship with him. In fact, there was an unspoken understanding about this between them. No real friendship was possible under these circumstances. There would always be something of the cat and mouse about their encounters, however open Winslow was about his relationship with Japan. Japan was the enemy, pure and simple.

On Monday morning, as Fazackerly prepared to leave his parents' house, he bent down to pick up an envelope that had been pushed under the front door. Both his parents were in London, having been caught there at the outbreak of war.

Winslow knew instinctively that the envelope was for him. There was nothing written on it. Inside was a piece of paper, roughly torn from a notebook, and grubby at the edges as if it had been handled by unwashed, earthy fingers. The writing was in Japanese, katakana, which Winslow could read easily. He would have struggled if it had been written in kanji. There was no signature, but Winslow knew who'd written the note. Who, though, had delivered it? The author was a man named Yokito Torajiro, and Torajiro-san was currently interned at Loveday in South Australia. The note was disturbing. It said simply that Etsuko, Winslow's wife, was gravely ill. That was all it said. 'Etsuko gravely ill.' There were no further details. Winslow's mind began to race. How could Torajiro-san know this? Surely it wasn't possible for information to get from Japan to a camp in South Australia. And how had he managed to get the note out of the camp and all the way to Melbourne? Its brevity was alarming. He put it in his pocket, and set off for Victoria Barracks.

Tom Mackenzie was there ahead of him. They exchanged pleasantries about the dinner at Tom's place, with Tom directing the information to stress what lively company Maude Lambert was, and how fascinated she'd been by Winslow's descriptions of life in Japan.

'She'd love to hear more,' Tom said.

If Winslow hadn't been distracted by the note in his pocket, he might have spotted that this was a clumsy attempt at gaining his confidence.

'That would be fine,' he said. 'Always happy to talk about Japan. It's not something most people want to hear about.'

'Maude is definitely not most people.'

'She did seem like an interesting person.'

There was a vagueness in his tone that Tom detected.

'Is everything all right, Winslow?'

'Yes, everything's fine.'

Winslow thought briefly about reaching into his pocket and producing the note. As a man with nothing to hide, he ought to have done this, but he realised that in handing over the note to Tom, and in acknowledging that it had probably been sent by an interned Japanese man, he would have been condemning that man to interrogation. Yokito Torajiro had been interned on the basis of his race alone. He wasn't an apologist for the Empire of Japan. He'd worked hard as a tailor, and had troubled no one. Winslow had been introduced to him, and a few of his compatriots, when Etsuko had lived with him in Melbourne. He'd kept up the contact after Etsuko had returned to Japan in 1938. Torajiro-san and his friends provided him with an opportunity to speak Japanese and to eat something that resembled Japanese food. He'd enjoyed their company, even though he was aware that they maintained a distance from him. It was unspoken, but Etsuko had assured him that their politeness hid an essential suspicion and disapproval of his marriage. Nevertheless, he'd managed to forge a relationship with Torajiro-san that he valued, and he worried about the old man's health. Internment wasn't comfortable, and Yokito Torajiro was 70 years old.

The more he thought about the note, the more he thought it must be a trap. Set by whom? By Tom Mackenzie? Winslow couldn't be sure the handwriting was Torajiro-san's. It looked hurried. It was certainly written by a Japanese person. The characters showed no hesitancy, and although it was brief, there was a colloquial quality to it that suggested a native speaker. How, though, could he possibly have access to information about Etsuko? Winslow would have to find out.

As TOM MACKENZIE prepared to leave work on Monday afternoon, he asked Winslow if he'd like to join him for a drink at Young and Jackson's. Winslow declined, saying that he needed to get home. Tom didn't believe him, and he didn't like how this made him feel. He experienced a sharp stab of detestation for Tom Chafer, whose poisonous suspicions about this perfectly decent man in some way spoiled all their interactions. Tom realised, with shame, that when Winslow left Victoria Barracks he would follow him.

The foot traffic down St Kilda Road towards Flinders Street Station was quite heavy. Winslow paused outside Wirth's Circus to read the garish advertising. He was smart, and Tom worried that this pause in his walking was a way of checking to see if he was being followed. Tom's wasn't the only air force uniform among the pedestrians, and the deepening twilight as winter approached offered him some cover. Winslow didn't seem to look behind him, so Tom assumed that he'd stopped out of curiosity — although, as Winslow passed Wirth's Circus every day, it was odd that he would halt there on this day. Tom was relieved to discover, as he passed the circus, that a new hoarding had been put up, promising new and daring attractions.

Winslow turned right at Flinders Street and walked east, past the Treasury Gardens and the Fitzroy Gardens, turned into Clarendon Street, and then into George Street. Tom had kept a fair distance back from Winslow and had removed his cap so that if Winslow happened to look behind him, the silhouette of the distant figure wouldn't read as a military man. Tom turned the corner into George Street just in time to see Winslow go through the gate of a house at the far end. When Tom reached it, he noted the number. It was a small house, single-fronted and showing its age. He decided to wait half an hour. It would be dark by then, so there would be little chance of his being discovered. He stood opposite the house and a few doors down in the deep shadows of a laneway. He hoped Winslow wasn't intending to stay the night. As it happened, he emerged after just 15 minutes. A woman walked with him the few steps to the front gate, but Tom couldn't make out any of her features. The light cast from the open front door was too dim even to provide him with a clue as to her age. There was no physical contact between them, so Tom surmised she probably wasn't a lover.

Tom, already feeling slightly nauseated about intruding on Winslow's privacy, decided not to pursue him from this point. This general sense of queasiness was compounded by the knowledge that he would have to report this meeting to Tom Chafer. He accepted that this was an obligation he'd undertaken to honour, despite it not sitting well with him. He'd leave it up to Chafer to find out the woman's identity. All he wanted to do now was to get home and take a bath.

WINSLOW WAS WARY, but a nagging concern that his wife might actually be ill, and that there might be something he could do about it — this was irrational, he knew — overrode his wariness. He'd read and re-read the note, turning it over and holding it up to the light, hoping to find something. Nothing. He'd looked again at the envelope. It was pristine. Unlike the note, it hadn't been crushed into a pocket or handled with greasy fingers. At first sight, there were no clues to be found on it, but he'd noticed when he'd looked closely that on the right-hand corner, at the very bottom and in faint pencil, were two tiny initials: K.H. He knew who that was. Katherine Hart. This lent credence to the authenticity of the note. Katherine Hart's husband was Japanese, and interned at Loveday. Winslow had met her a couple of times, but Etsuko hadn't liked her and had told him that she found her haughty and dismissive. She'd never shown this side of herself to Winslow, and Etsuko had said that of course she hadn't — her marriage had taught her the art of deference to men. With another woman, her true nature was undisguised. Winslow trusted his wife's judgement, and consequently his relations with Katherine Hart were glancing and cool. Those small initials on the envelope were an invitation, though, and it was an invitation he couldn't ignore.

After he'd left Victoria Barracks, his eye had been snagged briefly by the new line-up at Wirth's Circus — he had a weakness for the vulgarity of circuses — but after that he'd been barely aware of the world around him. The thought that Etsuko might be desperately ill had taken hold as a fact, and he could think of nothing else. The idea that she might be in pain clutched at him. There had to be something he could do.

He'd been to Katherine Hart's before. He and Etsuko had had dinner there, in early 1938. He'd seen her once since then: he'd visited her to offer solace after her husband's internment in 1942.

When she opened the door and invited him in, she showed no surprise at his being there. She'd aged, he thought. Her hair was greyer than he remembered, and there was something rather doleful about her manner. After just ten minutes in her company, he decided that doleful wasn't strong enough to describe her. She was miserable. She offered him a cup of tea, which he refused.

'I knew you'd find my initials, Winslow.'

'I almost didn't.'

Winslow decided to curtail the small talk.

'How did you come into possession of that note?'

'Mr Torajiro handed it to me himself.'

'You've been to Loveday?'

'It took months to get approval to visit my husband, and then I had to get the travel permission. It was awful. I thought I'd never get there.'

'And how did you get there?'

'I took the train from Adelaide. I wasn't allowed to stay there, of course, so I stayed overnight in Barmera and headed back here the next day. At least I know that Toshiro is well. They don't feed the Japanese as well as they feed the others, but he's healthy. He's lost weight, but that's because he's working in the vegetable gardens. He didn't complain. He said the Japanese didn't treat their prisoners this well. That's true. I understand why people hate them. But that's not the Japanese we know, is it?'

'War perverts the whole world. When did you get back from South Australia?'

'Two days ago. I got the note to you as soon as I could. I told Mr Torajiro that it would upset you and that there was nothing you could do about it. He said you'd want to know.'

'How did Torajiro-san know that Etsuko was sick? How could he possibly have heard?'

Katherine Hart stood up and crossed to a small table. She opened a square, black lacquer box, and took from it a folded piece of paper.

'I was told to give you this, but only in person. It's nothing mysterious, Winslow, or seditious. It's a name and an address, that's all. Well, not a full name. Just initials.'

'It sounds both mysterious and seditious.'

'Family members visit Loveday whenever they can get permission. Mr Torajiro wouldn't tell me who, but someone came into the camp who's known you and your wife. Whoever this person was had heard from a third party who'd been in touch with people in Hiroshima. I don't know how, and I don't want to know how. If the authorities knew, they might accuse me of consorting with the enemy, which I am not. All that I've told you is all that I know. The initials in that note mean nothing to me, although they gave me the idea of putting my initials on that envelope.'

'The vagueness of all this is troubling. It feels like a trap.'

'I'm not part of any trap, Winslow.'

'Not knowingly, I'm sure.'

'Anyway, what sort of trap? All I've done is pass on some initials and an address, and I only agreed to do it because I thought you might want to find out about your wife's health.'

The unappealing note of pique in Katherine Hart's voice made Winslow certain that Etsuko's assessment of her character had been accurate. He had no wish to linger in her house. She'd pushed the note under his door reluctantly; he'd come to her reluctantly; he'd reluctantly taken what she'd given him. The only thing he hadn't done reluctantly was leave her house.

CLARA HAD SLEPT well at the Kew house, and was still asleep when Helen and Joe returned from the office. Over a dinner of corned beef and vegetables — the smell of which had brought Clara downstairs — they repeated, for her benefit, Joe's concerns about Guy. Helen had reassured Joe that Guy was capable of taking care of himself, and that Prescott knew that he, Joe, was expecting Guy to return, and that a failure to do so would invite suspicion and possible police intrusion. Neither of them believed this, but it helped a little to say it anyway.

Visitors were rare at the house, so the knock on the door at 8.00 pm made everyone nervous. Joe opened the door to find Inspector Lambert standing there, his hat in his hands.

'Titus.'

Joe was pleased at how easily that informality now came to him.

'Is Dr Dawson still here?'

'She is.'

'An informal discussion with all of you would be good.'

Once, Joe might have found such a request coming from Inspector Lambert intimidating, with the probability that it implied an imminent dressing-down. He didn't feel that now.

Ros Lord brought a bottle of red wine into the library, and discreetly retreated upstairs to read. None of them knew the first thing about wine, but they assumed that it must be a good one, because it went down easily.

Titus began by saying that there'd been no progress in finding Kenneth Bussell. Clara told him about her meeting with Adelaide

Matthews, which Titus was frank in expressing his disquiet about. Clara was mildly stung.

'I was responding to a grieving woman's need to talk to someone, Titus.'

Titus held up one hand in a gesture of capitulation, but his eyes betrayed that he was sceptical of this claim. Clara read his scepticism, and it was she who capitulated.

'All right, Titus. I can see that you don't believe that my purpose was so pure, and of course you're right. I was curious. I wanted to see what kind of woman would shackle herself to a man like Gerald Matthews.'

'And what kind of woman did you find?'

'I suspect a frequently drunk one and one who endured a bad marriage for the sake of her children.'

'Did she love her husband, do you think?'

'There is no yes-or-no answer when it comes to love, Titus. Maybe "sometimes" is as close as we get.'

As far as Titus was concerned, there was a yes-or-no answer to that question. Did he love Maude? Yes. It was simple, and unnuanced.

'I presume there's no difficulty about you staying here for a few days?'

'That might be sensible, but I'm not going to do that, Titus. I was shaken when I saw Bussell, but I'm not shaken now. Now I'm just royally peeved, and I'm not going to have my life cabined by Kenneth fucking Bussell. Or anyone else.'

She glanced at Helen and Joe.

'Besides, I couldn't just leave Pat and Susan there on their own.'

'They could come here,' Helen said.

'Oh, for goodness sake. I know this is a big house, but it's not a fucking hotel. I can't tell you how good it feels to swear in a room as swanky as this.'

Despite further protestations from her companions, Clara remained adamant that she intended to return to her shared house. Of course she would take precautions. Of course she would be brutal with Pat about locking the fucking doors.

Inspector Lambert, who'd been instrumental in ensuring that Helen was granted her private inquiry agent's licence, was nevertheless uneasy about her decision to allow Guy Kirkham to go undercover on Anthony Prescott's property. Helen wasn't offended when he expressed his unease. On the contrary, she admitted that she shared it, but that the suggestion had come from Guy himself, and he'd convinced her that he was capable of looking after himself. He'd also made the point that it was precisely the kind of work that the police force was unable to do.

Joe felt compelled to support Helen, so he didn't tell Titus that he was worried sick about Guy. He detailed his impression of Prescott and the strange set-up of the Church of the First Born. Helen spoke at length about the Nunawading Messiah, and both Titus and Clara were mesmerised as she piled detail upon detail.

'I know,' Helen said, 'it beggars belief. It's a shame that there's not a law against being stupid.'

'If there were,' Clara said, 'every second person would be locked up — which isn't such a bad idea.'

'From everything you've told me,' Titus said, 'there isn't anything illegal happening at Prescott's place. No one is being held against his or her will.'

'In the 1870s case, the ludicrous Messiah was polygamous. He collected the whole set of Prudence, Justice, Truth, and Meekness. If Prescott is doing the same thing, surely that's against the law,' Joe said.

'You only suspect that. Anyway, I imagine the marriages wouldn't be registered, and a marriage ceremony performed inside the Church of the First Born wouldn't be considered a legitimate marriage.'

'So all it means is that he's sleeping with more than one woman, which might be frowned upon, but isn't illegal,' Clara said.

Helen laughed. 'You went with "sleeping with", Clar. That was uncharacteristically discreet of you.'

'Well, I didn't want to shock Titus, or cause the wallpaper to start peeling by swearing a second time.'

'Was anybody killed in this 1870s cult?'

'No,' Helen said. 'From all that I've read, there was petty in-fighting, but there's no record of anyone being murdered, or sacrificed.'

'That's disappointing,' said Clara. 'You'd expect any decent cult to sacrifice *something*.'

'I am concerned,' Titus said, cutting through Clara's levity, 'about Zachary Wilson. We had to oppose bail, given the hysterical public response to these killings, but he's not coping with imprisonment. He looks terrible, and he's an emotional wreck. He needs to be either condemned or rescued as quickly as possible.'

'Can I see him to assess his medical condition?'

'I can arrange that. It's irregular, but I can arrange it.'

'I can go straight from my shift, so 8.00 am tomorrow?'

'I'll let them know you're coming.'

They spoke for another hour, with Titus asking Helen and Joe to expand on their respective meetings with Meredith Wilson and Emilio Barbero's landlady. At ten o'clock, Clara said that she'd have to leave for work. Titus insisted on driving her. The hospital was more or less on his way home. In the car, Clara asked him how police command would feel about him sharing information with a private inquiry agent.

'Helen Lord and Associates is sharing information with me. I'm not providing them with any information that would compromise the safety of my officers or the integrity of the investigation. But how would they feel about it? I have no doubt at all that I'd lose my job.'

'Is it worth the risk?'

'For Zachary Wilson's sake, I hope so.'

GUY HAD SPENT Monday morning harvesting strawberries. His back ached. Nepheg harvested beside him, and for him it must have been agony, given the rawness of his back. Lunch that day had been served by Justice, a young woman whose shyness had made her all but invisible in the household. At least Guy assumed it was shyness; it might have been an extreme expression of reticent humility. She had delicate features and pale skin, which would suffer under Prescott's regime of farming. Her hair, which she wore long, was gathered away from her face and constrained within a head scarf. She was beautiful, Guy thought, and the way that Prescott's eyes followed her as she served the soup suggested he thought so too. When she placed Prescott's soup before him, she leaned in close. She didn't say anything, but the movement was intimate.

In the afternoon, Guy found himself working alongside Justice in the pear orchard. Conversation with the women who lived in Prescott's house wasn't forbidden, but there was something about Justice's manner that made talking to her seem transgressive. He'd heard her voice only once. It wasn't harsh or unpleasant, but it was unrefined and unmusical. He had his back to her when she unexpectedly spoke to him.

'The Master says you are welcome here, Absalom, and that I am to cut your hair and wash your clothes.'

Guy turned to face her. Her lovely features were blank. They showed neither resentment nor acceptance.

'Thank you. You don't need to do that.'

'Yes, I do,' she said simply.

'May I ask you something?'

'Nepheg will answer your questions.'

'It's not a question Nepheg can answer.'

'Then it's not a question you should ask.'

Guy realised that he'd underestimated this young woman. It was easy to assume that Prescott's acolytes were unintelligent, because how could an intelligent person believe that he was the master of anything?

'Is the Master your husband?'

'The Master is my Master.'

'I've accepted him as my Master too.'

'No, you haven't, Absalom. You can't disguise the doubt in your eyes. When he shows you a miracle, you will believe.'

'Blessed are those who have not seen and yet believe.'

'Perhaps he should have named you Thomas.'

'Who was Absalom?'

'Nepheg will tell you.'

'Is it a good name?'

'The Master gave it to you, so it is a good name.'

'I do have doubts.'

'Stay long enough to witness a miracle.'

There was feeling in this statement, and Guy didn't doubt that it was genuine. The fact that it was so counter to Prudence's warning made Guy wonder if there was tension between the two women.

'Prudence wasn't at lunch today.'

'My sister is in the women's house. It is her unclean time.'

'Your sister?'

'Leave your laundry outside your bedroom door, and come to me when you need a haircut.'

With that, Justice moved away from Guy, leaving him unclear about her relationship with Prudence. Was 'sister' simply an affectionate term, or did it denote a familial relationship? He watched her as she walked among the pear trees. Emilio Barbero's landlady had said that Anthony Prescott had visited Barbero, accompanied by a young woman whose hair fell across her face so that she resembled Veronica Lake. He hadn't seen Justice's hair free of its scarf, but she did look vaguely like the movie star.

It would be impossible to raise Emilio Barbero's name without exposing the falseness of his position at Prescott's orchard, but Guy wondered if he could somehow encourage someone to mention him — or Fisher, for that matter — inadvertently. Prescott would never make such a mistake, and Guy had made no connection at all with the old man, Abraham, so a casual conversation with him was unlikely. Nepheg struck Guy as being deranged by religious fervour, but such derangement might lead to him blurting something useful about Fisher's competing claim to be the Messiah.

It was Prudence, though, who offered the best hope of providing information, or so Guy believed. He had nothing to go on, except her sudden warning, but the intensity of that warning hinted at the possibility that Prudence wasn't the surrendered acolyte that Prescott supposed her to be. It would be dangerous, but Guy decided he would visit her later that night, in the outhouse forbidden to men. Nepheg was a sound sleeper who drew in long, deep breaths, without snoring. Guy had been aware, on his first night, that he'd had a nightmare. He'd woken himself and had heard his own small cry. Nepheg, just a few feet from him, hadn't stirred. So deeply asleep was he that Guy thought he might have taken some sort of draught.

Dinner that night was a mutton stew, but the meat portion was small. Each of their plates was crowded with vegetables, for which Prescott praised the earth for its bounty. Abraham praised Prescott for his bounty, and Prescott bowed his head in gracious recognition of this deference.

Guy studied Abraham throughout the meal. His beard was full and white, except for tar stains around the mouth, which indicated a smoking habit that Guy hadn't yet seen him indulge. Perhaps this was a vice that had to be kept private in the Church of the First Born. Who was he before he grew a beard and swapped his clothes for a tunic? Guy tried to imagine him clean-shaven and in a hat and suit, with skin unroughened by working outdoors. He might have been an accountant or a lawyer. He made a convincing rustic, but there was an intelligence in his eyes, and a self-assurance in his manner, that made Guy think that his reverence for Prescott was a performance. Or was this the thinking of a sane man who couldn't bring himself to believe that anyone could be taken in by Prescott? However, his own upbringing was proof that religious fervour dimmed the light of intelligence. He remembered how he had once sincerely believed in the Holy Trinity, and had invested in dull-witted priests the power of transubstantiation. Perhaps Abraham was simply a damaged man who'd been seduced by the false hope of immortality that Prescott offered.

Prescott announced to the table that Prudence was indisposed. This was for Guy's benefit, he supposed, because he also reminded the men that the women's hut was off-limits. Neither Nepheg nor Abraham would have needed such a reminder. Had Prescott somehow intuited that Guy intended to break this rule?

Conversation over dinner was sparse. Nothing was said about the war or politics. Indeed, no reference was made to the outside world. Guy realised that he'd seen no newspapers, no books, and no radio. This was a closed society that depended on Prescott for any information that it might need. And yet there were adherents outside the property who gave Prescott money and who believed in him. The inconsistencies and contradictions that secured Prescott's position were incomprehensible to Guy. Such things were glossed over as faith.

There was a brief prayer meeting after dinner, during which Prescott once again warned of false claimants and false prophets. He also warned each of them to be wary of those who would seek to tear down the Church of the First Born.

'They seek to silence the word of God, and they will be silenced instead.'

'Amen,' Abraham said.

Lying in bed, Guy wondered if those words had been directed at him. When he'd spoken them, Prescott hadn't been looking at him, so perhaps it was a routine admonition. They'd only just switched off the light, and Nepheg was still awake.

'Nepheg? May I ask you a question?'

'Of course, Absalom.'

'The Master has mentioned false Messiahs and false prophets more than once. Has there been a false Messiah?'

'There have been many throughout history. They are always found out.'

'Have there been any here, in Melbourne?'

Was the question too direct? Nepheg answered it without hesitation.

'There was a man near here. He claimed he was immortal. He's dead now.'

'So, not the Messiah then.'

Nepheg then did something extraordinary. He laughed.

'No,' he said, 'not the Messiah after all.'

'Do you know much about him?'

'His name was Fisher. He used to call himself a fisher of men.'

'You met him?'

'No. Never. Prudence and Justice knew him. He was their brother-in-law.'

Guy took a moment to sort out the implications of this. Fisher's wife, so savagely murdered, was the sister of Prudence and Justice.

'Did the Master know this Fisher bloke?'

'Of course. And the Master knew him for what he was — a liar.'

'How did he die?'

'I don't know. The master told us that he'd died, that's all.'

This seemed incredible to Guy, but challenging it would be risky. It was possible, of course, that Nepheg hadn't seen a newspaper or listened to a radio since the murders had been discovered. This was indeed probable if he hadn't left Prescott's property.

'The Master said unbelievers would be silenced. Do you think the Master struck Fisher down?' Guy tried to inject a note of awe into his voice.

'If you mean physically, no, but there are other ways to gather sinners. All flesh is grass, and God's scythe is sharp and quick.'

If a scythe wasn't handy, maybe an axe would do, Guy thought.

'Nepheg, when you say "God", do you mean the Master?'

'The Master is an incarnation of God. He is one of three persons.'

'So God the father moves independently of his son?'

'It is all one.'

'Yes,' Guy said emphatically, as if Nepheg's explanation made perfect sense. 'Thank you, Nepheg. One last question. Why did the Master call me Absalom? Who is Absalom?'

'He was the third son of David.'

'The Master calls himself David. He named me after one of his sons? I don't deserve such an honour.'

'The Master is wise.'

'Where will I find Absalom in the Bible?'

'The Book of Samuel.'

Guy felt relieved. If Prescott had named him after one of David's sons, perhaps he wasn't suspicious of him after all. He lay awake waiting for Nepheg to fall into a deep sleep. It was just after 2.00 am when he stood up and made his way towards the women's hut.

It was a cool night, and a light drizzle and a brisk wind made Guy shiver uncomfortably. His tunic was no defence against the chill. As he began walking towards the hut, he regretted his decision to go barefoot. The sharpness of stones and twigs alternated with the crunch and squelch of snails and slugs underfoot.

The hut was in darkness, unsurprisingly, given the hour. Guy wasn't sure how to proceed. He'd have to wake Prudence, and being woken at 2.30 in the morning would be unsettling. He'd have to take the risk that Prudence would be prepared to speak with him. He was on the point of knocking when voices from inside the hut made him draw back into the shadows. The door opened, and Prescott emerged, naked, his pale skin stark against the hut's brown walls. He stood stock-still before tilting his head up to the night sky. The drizzle had turned into rain, and Prescott allowed his body to run with it before wiping it from his flesh, as if he was bathing. He seemed impervious to the cold. Guy was sure that he couldn't be seen, but just for a moment Prescott seemed to look right at him. It was fleeting, and he gave no sign that he'd seen Guy, so after a moment of panic Guy relaxed. Prescott finished his ablutions, if that's what they were, and calmly walked back towards the house, his naked form slowly vanishing as it retreated.

Guy waited a few moments and then knocked on the door. A faint light swelled, as if Prudence was turning up the flame of a kerosene lamp, and she opened the door. She was wearing a loose, lined tunic, and her hair fell freely over her shoulders. Her reaction to finding Guy at her door was muted, as if she'd been expecting him. She held the lamp up to illuminate Guy's face.

'Absalom.'

'May I come in?'

'It's forbidden.'

'But not to all men.'

'When my husband comes to me, he comes naked as Adam, the first man. Nothing is forbidden to him.'

Adam, David, the Master — this, Guy thought, was a fluid and flexible theology.

'The Master is your husband?'

Guy thought that when Prudence began to move the door she was closing it. In fact, she opened it and silently indicated that he should enter.

The interior of the hut was sparsely but not meanly furnished. The single bed looked comfortable, and there was an armchair and a prie-dieu that gave the room a strangely Catholic, monastic quality. He could smell Prescott's recent presence. Prudence directed Guy to sit down, and then extinguished the hurricane lamp. When his eyes had adjusted to it, the darkness wasn't absolute. He could make out Prudence's form seated on the side of the bed. Guy saw no advantage in beating about the bush.

'Why did you warn me to leave here?'

'You're not a believer.'

'Justice said that all I needed was to witness a miracle.'

'My sister's faith is very strong.'

Guy wanted to ask if Prescott had married her as well, but thought the indelicacy might end their conversation.

'Am I in danger?'

'Your immortal soul is in danger.'

'Well, it has to leave my body before that becomes an issue. Is my body in danger?'

'The Master's disciples are immortal.'

There was something rather rote about that response, and it annoyed Guy.

'I don't think you believe any of that stuff. There's no conviction in your voice. There's no conviction in your eyes.'

'Don't presume to know me, Guy.'

The use of his name showed her hand, and Guy understood that it hadn't been a slip of the tongue.

'Too many people are dead,' she said.

Guy was startled.

'And do you know who killed them?'

'Yes. I know.'

'Prescott.'

'This is what you've come here to find out, isn't it?'

'I'm not a policeman or a detective.'

'So who are you?'

The conversation had hurried so quickly to this point that Guy felt swept forward by it.

'An innocent man has been arrested for the murders at Fisher's farm, a man named Zachary Wilson.'

'I know him.'

'And you know that he's innocent, don't you?'

'Yes.'

'Why are you protecting your husband? Are you afraid of him?'

'My husband has killed no one, Guy. The man who murdered my sister is beyond the reach of the law.'

'Nepheg told me that Mrs Fisher was your sister — your other sister.'

'We were three sisters, yes.'

'Why? Why would Peter Fisher suddenly kill his wife and child?'

'She was going to leave him. She was coming here.'

'But the baby ...'

'It wasn't Fisher's. It was my husband's child. David had chosen Truth to join us.'

Guy was glad of the darkness. His face would have betrayed his astonishment. Prescott had collected the set — Truth, Justice, and Prudence.

150

'Bigamy is against the law,' he said.

'Such an ugly word. Whose law? Not God's law. And how would you prove it? Our marriage is sacred, not a profane entry in the registry of births, deaths, and marriages. I'm telling you this because you have to go away from here. I don't know who sent you, but now you know the truth. There is nothing further you need to know.'

'Zachary Wilson is in prison.'

'God will protect him.'

'You have to go to the police.'

'No. We don't want them here. Besides, they've already paid us a visit.'

'But surely you know I'm going to tell them what you've told me.'

Prudence was silent. She stood up, and Guy watched her shadowy form move to the door. She opened it, and a rush of cold air entered the room.

'You must do as your conscience demands,' she said. As Guy passed her, she reached out and touched him. 'Our husband is not guilty of these crimes. Please don't destroy our lives.'

Guy stepped out into a thin, icy drizzle, and the door closed behind him. He'd almost reached his room when he realised that he hadn't asked Prudence any questions about Emilio Barbero, and she hadn't mentioned him either. When he began to analyse the encounter, he thought he'd been clumsy and inept in his questioning. He hadn't extracted from Prudence any information that she didn't want him to have. She'd known what she'd been doing, while he had bumbled along. Had she been telling him the truth? The intimate details of polygamy may well have been a smokescreen for far-greater crimes. Was he supposed to be seduced by this honesty into believing that this was the whole truth? It had certainly been a remarkable intimation, especially the claim that Mrs Fisher had given birth to Prescott's child. Would this knowledge have made Fisher's infanticide easier for him to perpetrate? This was Guy's last thought before a blow to the back of his head rendered him unconscious.

10

WHEN CLARA DAWSON left the hospital at 7.30 on Tuesday morning, there was no sign of Kenneth Bussell. She'd decided that if he'd been waiting across the street, she'd go up to him and ask him just what the fuck he thought he was doing. *If he'd wanted to kill me*, she thought, *he'd have done it by now.* Gerald Matthews' death had, after all, been his gift to her. She'd felt brave about her decision all through her shift. She didn't leave the hospital without trepidation, however, and she was relieved when Bussell wasn't there to test her mettle.

By 8.00 am she was at the Magistrates' Court. To her surprise, Inspector Lambert was waiting for her — but as police headquarters was across the street, perhaps she ought not to have been surprised. Lambert was there to make sure that the bureaucracy of the watch house didn't prevent Clara from gaining access to Zachary Wilson. He had told them that Dr Dawson was coming, but he wanted to make certain she was admitted quickly.

He went with her to Wilson's cell, and said he'd wait to hear her assessment. The prison officer slid back the peephole.

'We don't want to interrupt him if he's taking a shit,' he said, and immediately apologised when he saw the look on Inspector Lambert's face. The officer peered into the cell, and began fumbling with the key to open the door.

'Jesus,' he said. 'Jesus,' and his voice had panic in it. He opened the door, and all three of them entered the cell. Wilson was hanging, his toes barely touching the ground, from the bars of the cell window set high in the wall. It must have taken some effort to accomplish this. He'd torn his bedsheet in two, twisted it into a rope, looped it around the bars, tied one piece to the other, formed a noose, and launched himself from the edge of the toilet bowl. Titus rushed to him and held him so that the sheet was no longer taut. The stink that came off him told Titus that he was dead. His body had evacuated its waste.

When Wilson had been cut down, Clara confirmed that he was dead and that the cause of death was most likely to have been asphyxiation by hanging. When Clara looked at Titus's face, she couldn't read the range of emotions that were playing across it.

'I arrested this man,' he said. 'I hope to God he's guilty, Clara.'

'This isn't your fault. If he's not guilty, he's another victim.'

'Well, the public can feel safe now, can't they?' He spat these words out. 'The newspapers won't be happy. Fear sells more papers than comfort. Still, they'll get a good 24 hours out of it.'

Later, in Titus's office, when all the initial paperwork had been done, Clara could see that he was struggling to contain anger, frustration, and guilt. She hadn't associated any of these emotions with Inspector Lambert, and it worried her.

'I'm not letting some local constable deliver this news to Mrs Wilson. I'm driving out to Nunawading.'

'Would you like me to come with you?'

'Yes, I would, but that isn't possible, I'm afraid.'

As he said this, a uniformed constable appeared at the door of Lambert's office.

'The car is ready, sir.'

'Thank you Alexander. Oh, I should introduce you. This is Constable Alexander Forbes. This is Dr Clara Dawson.'

Alexander Forbes stepped into the room.

'Dr Dawson. I read your evidence at Peter Lillee's inquest. I thought it was brilliant.'

Clara admired this young man's confidence. He couldn't have been more than 23 or 24, but there was nothing in his demeanour that suggested that the proximity of Inspector Titus Lambert was in any way intimidating. He wasn't brash, exactly, but he exhibited none of Joe Sable's reticence or uncertainty.

'Thank you very much,' she said. 'Do you read many coroner's reports?'

'I'm new at this. I read whatever I can.'

'Constable Forbes is coming with me to Nunawading,' Titus said.

Clara looked at Forbes, expecting to find eagerness in his face. She was glad it wasn't there, glad that this young constable wasn't approaching this task with unseemly and expectant curiosity. She sensed his awareness that his imminent exposure to Mrs Wilson's grief was both a responsibility and an awful privilege. Titus must have seen in him the qualities he saw in Helen Lord and, to a lesser extent, Joe Sable. Both of them would be interested to know about Constable Alexander Forbes.

MEREDITH WILSON KNEW as soon as she'd opened the door to the two men — one in a suit, the other in a uniform — that her husband was dead. After they'd identified themselves, she invited them in and offered to make them a cup of tea. They accepted. Constable Forbes held his helmet on his knee. Titus noted the nicety of not placing it on the table. It was a small thing, but it mattered. He also noted, when Meredith had gone to the kitchen, that Forbes's eyes flicked around the room, picking up details that might help in building a picture of the Wilsons.

When Meredith returned, she thanked them for giving her time to compose herself, and said she knew that the news they'd come to report was bad.

'Yes,' Titus said. 'I'm sorry to inform you that your husband died this morning.'

'He took his own life, didn't he?'

'Yes. I'm sorry.'

Constable Forbes poured a cup of black tea and handed it to Meredith.

'Thank you,' she said. She took a sip and placed the teacup on the table. 'My husband wasn't a strong man. He was a good man, but he wasn't strong. I think being in that cell did more than demoralise him. It terrified him, and shamed him in a way that's difficult to understand. I saw when I visited him that he'd never recover. Even when his name was cleared — and it would have been. He didn't commit those crimes. He was too broken to ever be healthy.'

She took a deep breath.

'And God help me, Inspector, I felt contempt for him. Isn't that dreadful? Driving home from the watch house, I decided that I was going to divorce him. I couldn't bear looking at him.'

She looked up at Titus and then at Constable Forbes. Alexander looked back at her. She saw no judgement in his face, but she said, 'You must think I'm a cold fish.'

'Honesty requires courage, Mrs Wilson, not an absence of emotion.'

Titus, who was struggling to keep his own emotions under control, was impressed by Forbes's response. What was a young man of such intelligence doing in the police force? Joe Sable, whom Titus liked and admired, would have been incapable of such an accomplished, pitch-perfect reply to Meredith Wilson's remark.

Meredith poured each of them a cup of tea, and Titus realised that Forbes had deliberately poured only one cup in order to allow Meredith Wilson the distraction of pouring the other two.

'I'm the police officer who arrested your husband, Mrs Wilson.'

'I don't blame you, Inspector, if that's what you're thinking.'

'I want you to understand that it wasn't on a whim. With the information we had ...'

'Please, Inspector, please don't justify yourself. It makes me think you actually *knew* he was innocent and arrested him anyway. I couldn't bear that.'

Titus immediately regretted his clumsy attempt to expiate his guilt. If he wasn't so exhausted he'd be thinking more clearly.

Throughout the conversation that followed, Meredith Wilson maintained her composure. She answered each of Titus's questions without obfuscation. She told him everything she'd told Helen Lord. Titus didn't reveal that Helen had briefed him.

'Did Peter Fisher ever come here, to your house?'

'No. Zac knew how I felt about him. I took food up to the house when the baby was born. I met him, and thought he was a pathetic, angry little man who spoke badly to his wife, and in front of me, which is poor form for a messiah, don't you think? I really can't explain how my husband could have been so foolish, and now he's dead. Peter Fisher claimed that he could give him eternal life. All he managed to do was drive him to suicide. Peter Fisher is responsible for my husband's death, Inspector, not you.'

Constable Forbes asked no questions. Once or twice he was tempted to request clarification on a point, but knew that his inexperience would make such an interruption look like impertinence.

'What happens now, Inspector?' Meredith asked.

'There will be a coronial inquest, and I'm afraid suicide will be a foregone conclusion. Your husband's body will then be released to you.'

In the car on the way back to Russell Street, it was Constable Forbes who broke the silence.

'Meredith Wilson is an impressive person.'

'She is.'

'I don't think we should eliminate her as a suspect, sir.'

Forbes was driving. Titus looked at his lean profile. He had done precisely that — he had eliminated her, and he was discomposed that this young man had correctly surmised this. *Alexander Forbes*, he thought, *has the makings of a great detective*. Maude needed to meet him.

TOM MACKENZIE WASN'T looking forward to Tuesday morning. The first thing he needed to do, to get it out of the way, was report to Tom Chafer and give him the number of the house Winslow had visited. Chafer, as Tom knew he would, berated him for not following Winslow after he'd left the house.

'Were you just too lazy to do it?'

'I think there should be a "sir" at the end of that question, don't you?'

Chafer curled his lip and refused to oblige.

'I'll do your job for you, shall I,' he said, 'and find out who lives at that address?'

'It would be nice to see you do something.'

Chafer's face turned red, but he didn't take the bait.

'Come back here at 2.00 pm,' he said quietly, and managed to inject venom into every banal syllable.

When Tom got to his office, Winslow was already there. Tom couldn't detect any change in his demeanour. They talked about that morning's newspapers and settled down to the necessary drudgery that was requisitions. They had lunch together, and Winslow talked about his love of Japanese art. Tom had never heard of Hokusai or Ukiyo-e. Winslow said he'd bring in some prints he'd collected.

At 2.00 pm, Tom knocked on Chafer's door. He was aware that he'd offended him earlier, but this didn't worry him. In fact, he was looking forward to offending him some more.

'Come in.'

Chafer was seated behind his desk, his thin arms folded, his face set into a smug rictus of self-satisfaction.

'We were right to have our doubts about Fazackerly. The woman he visited is married to a Japanese.'

'So?'

'She's been most cooperative. She's been visiting her husband, and we made it clear to her that his life could become difficult unless she told us why Flight Lieutenant Fazackerly had paid her a visit.'

Chafer didn't invite Tom to sit down.

'And?'

'Fazackerly has found a way to make contact with people in Japan.'

'I don't know what that means.'

'Neither do we, exactly. That's where you come in.'

Chafer pushed an envelope towards Tom.

'Inside that envelope is the name of Katherine Hart's husband — Katherine Hart is the woman Fazackerly visited — and other information you'll need when you get to Loveday. It includes your travel permits and a sealed letter to the commanding officer at Loveday camp.'

'I don't understand.'

'You will be flying to Adelaide in a couple of hours and taking the train to Loveday tomorrow morning. There are persons of interest in Loveday who know a lot more about Fazackerly than he wants us to know.'

Tom felt his stomach lurch. This was the last thing he wanted to do. Following Winslow had been relatively benign, and he'd hated doing that, but this, this was spying on him in a profound and damaging way. When Winslow found out that Tom had done this — and he would find out — the excuse that 'I was just doing my job' wouldn't wash. No friendship could survive such surveillance.

'When you go back to your office, tell Fazackerly that you're being sent to Mildura to sort out a local fuck-up. You'll only be gone for two days.'

'What if he checks?'

'Why would he? If he does check, that will be revealing, won't it?'

Chafer opened a ledger on his desk. This was a soundless dismissal. Tom took the envelope and left.

At the very moment that Tom Mackenzie entered Tom Chafer's office, Guy Kirkham, miles from Victoria Barracks in the distant Dandenong hills, died. It had been a slow, drawn-out death, and he took with him information that, had he had it in time, and had he been able to pass it on, might have saved Zachary Wilson's life. As it was, it all came too late. In the final moments of his suffering he thought the pointlessness of his death was a just punishment for the death of the young soldier in New Guinea. Guy, who'd known that he shouldn't have been driving, had fallen asleep at the wheel of a Jeep. It had overturned, and Private Harry Compton, aged just 20, had been killed. In the closing of his life, it was this young man's name that Guy Kirkham uttered.

The blow to the back of Guy's head had been delivered with such force that it had cracked his skull. He'd remained unconscious for more than three hours. He'd come to briefly and passed out again as the competing agonies of his head injuries and sharp pain emanating from his neck overwhelmed him.

Abraham watched him, pleased with his work. They were in a thick forest high up in the Dandenongs, well away from any track. The air was damp, and smelled of eucalyptus and leaf litter. It had taken Abraham a long time to find the right tree. He'd been looking for a tree with a forked branch close enough to the ground to enable him to manoeuvre Guy's neck into the fork. He hadn't been gentle. He'd lugged Guy's unconscious form up a steep slope, and he was in no mood to be careful. The skin on Guy's neck had been broken, and a sharp protrusion on one of the branches dug deeply into his flesh. Guy's feet were touching the ground, but his weight was borne by his wedged neck. To secure him to the tree, Abraham had tied a cord firmly around his waist and the trunk of the tree.

After a while he grew bored with waiting for Guy to regain consciousness, and threw a cup of cold water into his face. Guy's eyes opened. He tried to move his head, but it was trapped somehow. He seemed to be standing up. And he was cold. Very cold. He could smell and taste blood, and in the grey dawn light he saw Abraham standing in front of him.

'I named you Absalom,' he said. 'I knew as soon as I saw you that this is how it would end.'

'Where …?'

'Oh, no one knows where you are. No one will ever find your body. Not even the Master knows. My job is to protect him from people like you. Your blood is on my hands, not his. But he warned you. He warns us all that there will be a reckoning for unbelievers. You've arrived at yours.'

Guy tried to move his arms, but they were held by the rope that bound him to the tree. Slowly the world around him came into focus, and despite the intense pain in his head, he began to make sense of his predicament.

'You killed Peter Fisher, and his wife and the baby.'

Abraham approached Guy. Their faces were almost on the same level.

'No,' he said. 'Fisher killed his wife and child, and, like the coward that he was, he took his own life.'

Abraham ran his hand through his beard as if he was considering whether or not to say any more. He couldn't help himself.

'I delivered retribution to the young Italian boy. The Master thought he could convince him to join us.' Here he laughed. 'Well, he did join us, for half a day. He walked all the way from Fisher's farm to the Master's orchard. He'd come to see Justice. He was quite open about it. He said he wanted to speak with her. It was Justice's unclean time, and she was in the hut. He was told it was forbidden for a man to visit the hut. He was young, stupid, and he'd walked too far to resist the temptation. He pretended to leave the property, but doubled back and entered the hut. He stayed in there for an hour. I know this, because I knew he'd return and I was waiting nearby. Justice didn't cry out and I'm forbidden to enter the hut, so I waited for him to come out. When he did, I strangled him. Simple as that. My hands are strong, and his body wasn't yet a man's body. Justice didn't know that I'd done this, and neither did the master. Justice didn't speak of the young man's transgression. Perhaps all they did was talk. It doesn't matter. When he crossed the threshold into the women's hut, he committed a sin so grave that expiation could only come with death. Oh, I prayed for his soul, Absalom. I prayed and prayed. I took him down to Fisher's farm and hung him up there. What sort of miracle would Fisher generate to explain the presence of a hanged man on his porch? Fisher couldn't perform a miracle. All he could do, all he could ever do, was wreak havoc. He must have thought that he could kill Truth and the Master's son. It wasn't Fisher's son. He was sterile. The Master made him so. He must have thought he could kill them and blame it on the Italian bloke.

That might have worked if he hadn't lost his nerve and blown himself up. Why don't you say something?'

Guy was incapable of saying anything. He began to drift in and out of consciousness, and nothing Abraham was saying made any sense to him. The old man came close to Guy, leaned in, and whispered in his ear.

'I'm going to kill you. You have betrayed the man who is your father, and, like the first Absalom, you must pay with your life. And the Master, like the first David, will grieve for you.'

He began to walk around the tree, intoning lines from a Bible he held:

And the king commanded Joab and Abishai and Ittai, saying deal gently for my sake with the young man, even with Absalom. So the people went into the field against Israel and the battle was in the wood of Ephraim; for the battle was there scattered over the face of all the country; and the wood devoured more people that day than the sword devoured. And Absalom met the servants of David. And Absalom rode upon a mule and the mule went under the thick boughs of a great oak, and his head caught hold of the oak, and he was taken up between the heaven and the earth; and the mule that was under him went away. And a certain man saw it and told Joab, and said, Behold I saw Absalom hanged in an oak. And Joab said unto the man that told him, And behold, thou sawest him, and why didst thou not smite him to the ground? And I would have given thee ten shekels of silver, and a girdle. And the man said unto Joab, though I should receive a thousand shekels of silver in mine hand, yet would I not put forth mine hand against the king's son: for in our hearing the king charged thee and Abishai and Ittai, saying, Beware that none touch the young man Absalom.

He paused in his reading, walked a few paces away from Guy, and picked something up from the ground. Guy, groggy and nauseated, couldn't make out what it was. He returned to Guy.

'Just for today, I am Joab.'

He tore Guy's tunic from his shoulders so that it fell to his waist, held there by the rope. The air was so cold against his skin that for a moment Guy's senses returned. He saw Abraham take three long nails, new and gleaming, from the pocket of his tunic. He placed the Bible on the ground, so that now he held the nails in one hand and a hammer in the other. He came to Guy and touched his chest in three places, pressing the skin with his finger.

> Then said Joab, I may not tarry thus with thee. And he took three darts in his hand, and thrust them through the heart of Absalom, while he was yet alive in the midst of the oak.

It was the third nail, hammered through the bone and into the heart, that killed Guy Kirkham. His body convulsed, and then it was suddenly still, his eyes wide. 'Harry Compton,' he'd whispered.

Abraham heard it as a meaningless sound. He waited a few moments to make sure that Guy had died. He ought to have taken him down and buried him under rocks, as the biblical Absalom had been buried, but this was too much effort. Finding a tree with a forked branch in it, even if it hadn't been an oak, had been effort enough. No. The body could stay tied to the tree until it fell apart. In summer, a fire might go through there and remove all trace of him.

CLARA DAWSON SAT with Helen and Joe in the Helen Lord and Associates office. As a doctor she'd seen dead bodies, and been present when patients had died, but the ghastly sight of Zachary Wilson hanging from the window bars in that grim prison had upset her deeply, and in an unexpected way. When she'd left Inspector Lambert's office she'd begun to feel an unwelcome and, she knew, irrational creep of anger directed at him. He was blaming himself, and Clara had reassured him that no one believed him responsible.

However, as she'd walked from Russell Street to East Melbourne, she realised that she did in fact blame Titus for Zachary Wilson's death. He'd arrested him, after all, and he'd done so without having any real evidence to justify it. It had been an expedient, crowd-mollifying arrest. The more she thought about it, the angrier she became. By the time she'd finished telling Helen and Joe about Wilson's suicide, she was unequivocal in her condemnation of Inspector Lambert. Joe tried to defend the arrest, but Clara dismissed his defence with a withering claim that he had a policeman's brain, and that that wasn't a compliment. Joe blushed, and then blushed even more deeply as he worried the initial blush might have revealed his attraction to Clara. She saw that she'd embarrassed him, and mistakenly assumed that it was simply a result of the insult. Her anger was still too hot to allow for an apology. Helen came to Joe's defence.

'Do I have a policeman's brain, Clar?'

'No, you have a detective's brain.'

'All right,' Joe said. 'Clearly, as one of the lesser primates, I have nothing to contribute, so I'll leave you to it.'

He stood up and left the office before Helen could stop him. As soon as he'd closed the door, he felt foolish. Clara would interpret his departure as a childish tantrum, and this would lower her opinion of him even further. No wonder she preferred Guy's company. He was amusing, and unburdened by a 'policeman's brain'. The thought of Guy drove his small humiliation in front of Clara from his mind. The dread he'd felt when he'd left Guy on Monday morning rose in him again. He didn't believe in telepathy or any spiritual nonsense, but he couldn't suppress the feeling that something was terribly wrong.

'Is Joe often petulant?' Clara asked.

'No, Clar, he isn't, but you caught him at a vulnerable time.'

Clara looked sceptical.

'He's worried about Guy.'

'I'll apologise to him later. Guy will be fine. Despite everything that's wrong with him, he can look after himself.'

Clara began to calm down.

'I suppose the "policeman's brain" crack was a bit much, although it's interesting that Joe immediately assumed it was pejorative.'

'It was the tone, Clar, as you know perfectly well.'

'I'm just so pissed off about Zachary Wilson's suicide. Why didn't someone at that fucking jail notice how desperate he was?'

There was no answer to that. Clara told Helen that Inspector Lambert intended visiting Meredith Wilson to break the news of his death in person.

'It's decent of him, I suppose, but it's the least he can do.'

'I'm sorry, Clar, but I'm not blaming Inspector Lambert for Wilson's death.'

Clara ignored this.

'He has a new favourite: a Constable Alexander Forbes.'

'Oh? Someone else with a policeman's brain?'

Clara managed a laugh.

'Actually, Helen, he's an impressive young man, and he's a bit gorgeous, and sharp. Very sharp.'

'How very interesting. I can't wait to meet this paragon.'

'Maybe you should poach him. Offer him more money.'

'I'm quite happy with Joe, thank you.'

Clara was about to say that Alexander Forbes was a lot smarter than Joe, but thought better of it. Antagonising Helen was the last thing she wanted to do. Helen's attraction to Joe was a mystery, but attraction was always a mystery.

11

WINSLOW FAZACKERLY KNEW that Tom Mackenzie wasn't telling him the truth when he announced that he'd been sent to Mildura to sort out some problem with requisitions. He knew that no such problems existed. Tom couldn't possibly know about the note from Torajiro-san, could he? To be in the least quizzical about Tom's story would be a mistake, so he simply commiserated with him about how tedious the train would be, not to mention the accommodation.

Tom left Victoria Barracks at midday. Winslow waited a full hour before he took the small square of paper with the address and the initials from his pocket. He turned it over and over through his fingers. The address was in Dalgety Street in St Kilda. He didn't know that part of Melbourne very well, but he could get there easily by tram. He'd have to go home first and change into mufti. He didn't want to turn up at a risky rendezvous in uniform. And he did intend to turn up, despite all his instincts warning him against it. He'd lain awake for most of the previous night, worrying about Etsuko. He had to know. He simply had to know. What if the news was terrible? What if she'd died? This thought had so disturbed him that he'd paced his bedroom and made his decision to visit the address in St Kilda.

✳

WHEN JOE RETURNED to the office, Clara had left. He felt sheepish, but Helen pre-empted any apology by saying that Clara had been out of line and that she would have walked out too, if it had been her on the other end of Clara's barb.

'She contradicted herself as soon as you'd left. Apparently, Inspector Lambert has a new trainee. He's very young. Constable Alexander Forbes. She was very impressed with his policeman's brain — and with the head that contains it, I might add.'

'Still, I shouldn't be so thin-skinned.'

'Also, she's so angry with Inspector Lambert that you were a convenient displacement target.'

'I think I was stung because I feel like Guy is doing the job I'm supposed to be doing. And I'm worried about him.'

'They know you're expecting him to return, Joe. Look, why don't you drive out there and pay him a visit? It would be a perfectly reasonable thing for a friend to do. If he feels like he's in any danger, just bring him home. And it might be a good idea to have a look at Fisher's farm. There might be something there that I missed. In fact, I'm sure there's something there that I missed.'

'Homicide would have been over it with a fine-toothed comb.'

'Different eyes. Different comb. And we know a bit more now, so there just might be something, the significance of which was missed.'

Joe almost said something about whether his policeman's brain was up to it, but knew that self-pity was an unattractive emotion and that Helen would have little patience with it.

FISHER'S FARM WAS already beginning to have an abandoned air about it. The overcast skies and persistent drizzle didn't help. It had only been a couple of weeks, and the horrors perpetrated here had kept vandals at bay, so no damage had been done. Nevertheless, there was something palpably desolate about it, and as Joe walked around the house, he thought he wouldn't like to spend the night here. Not that he believed in ghosts, but places where cruelty had been inflicted and suffered retained their power to unsettle. How, he wondered, could anyone live comfortably, when the war was over, in the shadow of those places whose names he'd seen in the newspapers — Treblinka, Auschwitz, Dachau? He stood near the place where Fisher had blown himself up.

'We are truly dreadful,' he said out loud. The walls of the outhouse had been knocked down by the blast, and the drop toilet was alive with the hectic hum of flies. Joe moved away, not wanting one of those creatures, carrying some tiny, ghastly morsel from the excrement, to land on him.

He climbed the stairs to the veranda, and stood where Emilio Barbero's body had hung.

He could see across the paddock to the neighbouring orchard where Zachary Wilson and his wife lived. The front door of the house was locked. The back door was open, and Joe entered. He waited in the kitchen, and listened. The house was silent. He didn't know why, but he felt compelled to make as little noise as possible, as if a sudden sound might rouse something hideous. Perhaps he was more susceptible to superstition than he'd thought he was. He moved through various rooms, opened drawers and cabinets, and looked under furniture and behind gewgaws. If Fisher was God, God had execrable taste in knick-knacks. There were no pictures on the walls, and no religious ornaments. Had someone stripped the house of such objects, or had Fisher imposed on the family a severe, Baptist-like abhorrence of representation?

He left the bedroom until last. Its door was closed. With

reluctance, Joe turned the doorknob and opened the door. The smell was awful, even so many days after the murders. He put his handkerchief to his nose and entered. There was a woman lying on the filthy sheets, her head on a pillow that was brown with Deborah Fisher's dried blood. The woman was on her back, her hands by her side, her eyes closed. Joe's heart lurched, but didn't lose its rhythm. Was she dead? Joe moved closer. She was breathing. Joe recognised the tunic. He'd seen it being worn at Prescott's farm. Why was this woman here? How could she bear to be in contact with the awful evidence of Deborah Fisher's murder? And the smell — how could she tolerate the smell?

Joe was uncertain what to do. The decision was made for him when the woman opened her eyes. She sat bolt upright and screamed, 'You're dead! You're dead! Monster!'

Joe held out his hands in a placatory gesture.

'It's all right. It's all right. You're quite safe. I'm not here to hurt you.'

At the sound of his voice, the woman calmed down. She swung her legs over the edge of the bed, but didn't stand up.

'I thought you were him. Who are you? What are you doing here? Are you like that woman, poking around?'

'What woman?'

'There was a woman. I pushed her over.'

'My name is Joe Sable. The woman's name is Helen Lord. I haven't come here to do anyone any harm.'

'You're doing harm just by being here in this room. This is a holy place.'

'Holy? A terrible thing happened here.'

The woman lay back down on the bed, and again settled her head on the foul pillow.

'That pillow isn't clean.'

'It's my sister's blood, and my sister's blood is sacred.'

'Deborah Fisher ...'

'Her name was Truth.'

She closed her eyes. 'I've seen you before,' she said. 'You came to the Master's house with a friend.'

'Guy Kirkham, yes.'

'Absalom.'

'I'm going to visit him.'

'He isn't there. He left last night.'

'He left? How?'

'The Master didn't say. He just said that Absalom wasn't a believer and that he left in the night.'

Joe's heart began to race. He tried to keep his anxiety out of his voice.

'I'm going there now. I have a car. Would you like a lift?'

The woman sat up.

'My prayers are done. Yes, I would. Thank you.'

She didn't offer her name. She simply passed by Joe and walked to the front door. As they emerged onto the porch, a car pulled up and parked next to Joe's car. Inspector Lambert and Constable Forbes got out. Joe couldn't read the expression on Titus's face. Was he annoyed to find him here? So focused was he on Lambert that Alexander Forbes barely registered with Joe. He was a uniformed constable, that was all. The woman moved closer to Joe, as if he might suddenly be an ally against these two strangers.

'These are policemen,' Joe said. 'You don't need to be afraid.'

'I'm not afraid. I'm not a child.'

She said this quietly so that only Joe heard, and there was a fierceness in her tone that reminded him that he'd yet again made assumptions that were lazy. Helen would never be guilty of making such assumptions. Would his capacity to read people ever improve?

The two policemen came up onto the veranda. Justice stepped

back, away from them. She'd lived long enough with Anthony Prescott to have acquired his suspicion of and distaste for all policemen. They meant trouble. They liked to poke around where they weren't wanted and where they had no business being.

Before Titus could speak, Justice retreated into the house. He didn't follow her. He'd speak to her after he'd spoken to Joe.

'Joe, I'm glad you're here. This is Constable Forbes. He's helping with the investigation. I thought he needed to get the feel of this place.'

Alexander Forbes held out his hand, and Joe shook it.

'Joe Sable.'

'Inspector Lambert has mentioned you. It's good to put a face to the name.'

Joe couldn't see why Clara had been so immediately impressed with this young man. He was confident, without being brash, and Joe supposed that that might be an attractive quality. An unwelcome twinge of jealousy passed through Joe. He'd experienced this recently when Guy had declared an interest in Clara Dawson. He hated feeling like a schoolboy with a crush, and after his last encounter with Clara he felt less able than ever to approach her. It wasn't Alexander Forbes' fault that he'd caught Clara's eye in a way that Joe had failed to do, but this produced in Joe a reluctance to like him.

'Who is the young woman?' Titus asked.

'I don't know her name. She was here when I arrived, lying on the bed — the filthy bed. It was all a bit weird. She's Mrs Fisher's sister, and lives on Prescott's property. I need to get out there. She said Guy left last night, which can't be true. How could he have left?'

The alarm on Titus's face was apparent, which made Joe more concerned.

'I need to talk to her,' Titus said, and he hurried into the house. He was back on the porch almost immediately.

'She's gone. She's headed off across the paddocks, presumably back to Prescott's place, although that's quite a way from here.'

'It's about three miles.'

'It's time Mr Prescott had another visit from the police. We'll have a quick look around here, and then go to see him.'

Joe was anxious to get going, and suggested that he go on ahead. Titus thought for a moment.

'This is awkward, actually, Joe. You can't come with us on police business.'

'That woman is going to mention that we were all here together. I told her my name, and Prescott knows who I am.'

'All the more reason for you not being part of an official visit. What you do after we leave is up to you.' Titus paused. 'Just give us a few minutes here. We'll follow you.'

Joe waited in his car while Titus and Constable Forbes quickly explored the house. When they came out, he said, 'I'll park my car where it can't be seen and wait for you to leave before driving up to see Prescott. He'll be surprised to see you. I don't think he'll be surprised to see me.'

Alexander Forbes took his helmet off and ran his fingers through his hair.

'Prescott was interviewed by a constable the day after the murders. There was nothing in his report about Mrs Fisher being related to anyone on his farm. At least, I don't think there was.'

'There wasn't,' Titus said. 'It was quick interview, a part of doorknocking in the area. A wide area admittedly, but we interviewed everyone within a five-mile radius. It is interesting that Mr Prescott failed to mention such a pertinent fact. Let's go and ask him why.'

Joe pulled over into the spot where he knew his car wouldn't be seen, and allowed Constable Forbes to drive past him. At the gate, Titus got out and opened it, and Joe watched as the car headed up to the house. No one came out to meet the visitors. Titus knocked on the door, and when no one answered it, Joe saw the two policemen walk around to the back of the house. Joe ought to have stayed where he was, but his impatience was too great. There seemed to be nobody about, so he began walking towards the house. His approach went unnoticed. The woman he'd met at Fisher's place couldn't have made it back yet, but where was the other woman?

Keeping close to the side of the house, Joe made his way towards the back. He stopped when he saw Titus and Alexander talking to three men. They were some distance away. Prescott was leaning on a shovel. The other two, one of whom was the old man, held pruning shears. They were each wearing tunics and were bare-legged. To Joe's left, there was a bungalow. To reach it, he would need to cross open ground. There was a risk he'd be seen if one of the men glanced this way, but they were each turned slightly away, and seemed to be focused on Titus and Alexander.

Joe crossed to the bungalow. There were two rooms. Joe checked each quickly. Neither door was locked. The second of the rooms was unoccupied. The two bunks had been stripped of their bedding. The first room smelled of human occupation — stale sweat and dirty socks. Both bunks were made up. Between the bunks was a wardrobe. Joe opened it. It was divided into two sections marked by a block in the middle of the hanging rail. There were clothes on either side. Joe recognised Guy's shirt and coat. The neatly folded trousers were also Guy's. He checked inside the hat that sat on the trousers. 'Guy Kirkham' was written on the band. The previous night had been cold and wet. If Guy had left, what on earth had he been wearing?

Joe left the small room. There was now no sign of the five men, and Joe assumed they'd gone into the main house. He returned to his car to wait for Titus and Alexander to leave. He'd then drive up to the front door and confront Prescott.

✳

WHEN NO ONE answered his knock, Inspector Lambert was tempted to try the doorknob and let himself in. With no reason to enter private property, however, he decided against this. Instead, he and Constable Forbes walked around to the back of the house. There were three men working among pear trees, and the two policemen began walking towards them. One of the men noticed them and called to the other two, who looked up and moved to join him, so that by the time Titus and Alexander had reached them they stood side by side. They each wore tunics of rough, sturdy material. Two of them, the youngest and the oldest, held pruning shears, and the third, whom Titus took to be Anthony Prescott, held a shovel.

'We knocked,' Titus said. 'There was no answer.'

'And who is "we"?' Prescott asked.

'Inspector Titus Lambert, Homicide, and this is Constable Forbes. We're investigating the deaths at Peter Fisher's farm. You are Mr Anthony Prescott?'

'So some people call me. A policeman has already been here to ask questions.'

Prescott's tone was perfectly pleasant. He didn't demand to see any identification.

'Let's go inside and complete the introductions there. You've come a long way from the city. I'm sure you'd like a cup of tea.'

As he said this, he saw a figure cross the space between the house and the bungalow. He gave no indication that he'd seen this, but politely ushered Titus and Alexander towards the house.

In the well-furnished front room, Anthony Prescott introduced his companions to Abraham and Nepheg. Titus asked if these were their real names.

'While they live here, this is who they are.'

'I'll need their real names.'

'Abraham is my real name,' said the old man. Before I was Abraham I had a name that meant nothing.'

'I was no one before I was Nepheg.'

'Make these gentlemen a cup of tea,' said Prescott.

Titus waved away the offer. He was exasperated by the nonsense about the names, and his exasperation increased when Prescott said, 'Outside this place there are people who might want to call me Anthony Prescott. Here, in this place, I am David. As guests in my house, I would ask you to call me David.'

'I don't care if you choose to call yourself King Kong, Mr Prescott, but please don't expect me to play along.'

This didn't get a rise out of Prescott. Alexander Forbes noticed that the old man bridled at Inspector Lambert's frankness. It was a slight movement in the muscles of his face, but it was definitely there.

'Why are you here, Inspector?'

'I want to know why, Mr Prescott, you didn't mention to the officer who spoke to you that the murdered woman was the sister of a woman who lives here with you.'

Forbes was watching Prescott's face closely when Titus asked this question. The man's discipline was remarkable, but there was a narrowing of the eyes and a tiny shift in the nostrils that hinted at the unexpectedness of the question.

'I told your policeman that I knew Mr Fisher, as a neighbour, and that Mrs Fisher was known to me. There's no mystery, Inspector. The woman you're referring to, the woman who lives here, is indeed Mrs Fisher's sister. Given that there is no connection between this fact and the ghastly murder, I saw no reason to mention it. Justice's grief is profound. The last thing she needed was to be interrogated by some clumsy, inexperienced constable. Or are you suggesting that Justice had something to do with their deaths? Because if you are, I can assure you that at the time these murders took place, all five of the people who live here were on the property. We can vouch for each other on that point.'

'What was the nature of your relationship with Mr Fisher?'

'He was a neighbour.'

Titus deliberately let his annoyance show.

'Do you imagine, Mr Prescott, that we are such dullards that we don't know about this …' He paused, and chose a word he knew would irritate Prescott. '… establishment? We know all about the Church of the First Born, and about Peter Fisher's absurd claims to have been the Messiah.'

'With the greatest respect, Inspector, you know nothing about the Church of the First Born.'

'You are, I believe, its current Messiah.'

The contempt in Titus's voice caused the old man to clench his fists. Forbes saw this, and saw, too, that the young man's face flushed pink. Prescott, however, was unfazed.

'I am as you find me. Nothing more and nothing less. Your conscience and your beliefs are your affair, Inspector. I don't presume to judge them. You might apply that courtesy to this place and the people who choose to live here.'

'I'm not interested in your religious beliefs, or anyone else's for that matter. I am interested in the deaths of four people just a few miles from your doorstep.'

'No one here can help you. As I said, we were all here and accounted for at the time of the tragedy.'

No one had sat down during this discussion. Constable Forbes knew that Inspector Lambert was in control of his emotions, despite his apparent shortness with Prescott. He'd made no mention of Guy. Given that Joe Sable was about to pay these people a visit, this made sense. He didn't want Prescott to know that there was any connection between him and Joe. That connection would be established when the young woman arrived, but Alexander figured it would take her at least another half an hour to cover the distance on foot. Inspector Lambert needed to give Joe this time to question Prescott. He was relieved when Titus indicated that he had no further questions for the moment. Prescott was gracious as he accompanied Titus and Alexander to the veranda.

As they drove down towards the gate, Titus said that he'd wait until Joe had finished with Prescott, and that he'd return to the house and question Abraham and Nepheg separately, and the two women.

'The other woman must have been somewhere on the property, and the one we met should be back soon. Give me your impressions, Constable.'

'Prescott is a smart man. The old bloke, Abraham, he didn't take his eyes off you, and he wasn't looking at you with affection.'

'And the young man?'

'He looked mostly at Prescott, with what I'd describe as an uncritical gaze. He didn't strike me as being very intelligent.'

'And Prescott, apart from being smart.'

'You have to admire his composure, but it's self-control, not some beautiful state of grace. He's a shyster, a sideshow huckster.'

'A murderer?'

'No. I don't think so. He wouldn't like to get his hands dirty. He might not object to someone else doing the dirty work. He didn't strike me as a man prone to qualms.'

Inspector Lambert smiled. *Maude will love Alexander Forbes*, he thought. It was time they met.

INSPECTOR LAMBERT STOPPED briefly to tell Joe what had transpired, and to reassure him that neither his nor Guy's name had been mentioned.

'There's no need to wait,' Joe said, and turned on the ignition of Peter Lillee's very expensive car.

Abraham was standing on the veranda when Joe pulled up.

'I've come to see Guy Kirkham.'

'You're too late. He didn't like it here. He failed.'

Prescott came outside.

'Joe Sable, isn't it?'

'I'm here to see Guy Kirkham.'

'That's odd. I was sure he'd have let you know. He chose to leave us yesterday. It was unkind of Abraham to say that he failed. Perhaps we failed him. Didn't he telephone you? We have a telephone. I felt sure he would.'

'He didn't telephone, no.'

'Please, do come inside.'

There was not the faintest hint of menace in Prescott's voice, and although Joe was wary of the invitation, he accepted it. Prescott pointed out the telephone in the hallway.

'Your friend was free to make use of it.'

Abraham was nowhere to be seen.

'Sometimes people come to us with great optimism, and they are disappointed.'

He walked towards the room that doubled as a chapel, and Joe followed him. Once there, he invited Joe to sit down, as he had done on Joe's first visit.

'Mr Kirkham found our discipline not to his liking. You know him better than I do. I don't think this would surprise you. I thought when I met the two of you that you knew he wouldn't stick it out.'

Joe wasn't seduced by the languid reassurance of Prescott's tone.

'What time did he leave?'

Prescott performed thoughtfulness.

'I think it was about an hour after dinner. It was dark.'

'And he just walked out?'

'Yes. He just walked out. He wasn't upset or angry. He just left.'

'What was he wearing?'

Prescott leaned forward. He spoke slowly.

'He was wearing the clothes he wore when he came here.'

Joe heard only the first part of this sentence. The blow to the back of his head rendered him unconscious before Prescott had finished speaking.

'How LONG SHOULD we wait, sir?'

'As long as it takes for Joe to drive back down here and tell us what he's discovered, if anything.'

Constable Forbes had parked the car out of sight, and he and Titus were standing where they could see the house. After twenty minutes of watching, they saw Justice emerge from a thicket to the left of the house.

'That's the woman we saw at Fisher's place,' Forbes said. 'There must be footpaths all over the place between these orchards.'

Justice entered the house. She had been gone for barely a minute when the front door was thrown open and she hurried out onto the veranda. She ran around Joe's car. There was something frantic in her movements. She stopped, shielded her eyes, and looked down towards the gate. Titus stepped into view and waved his arms. Justice began to run down the path towards him. When she reached the gate, she clutched the top rail and tried to catch her breath.

'They're taking his body away,' she said.

'Whose body?'

'The man called Joe. They killed him, and they're taking his body away in the truck.'

Titus would later wonder how he managed it, but he doused the fires of panic that threatened to engulf him.

'Is there another way out of here?'

'Yes, yes. Up there, around, behind. There's a track.'

'Show us.'

Justice sat in the front of the car. She directed Alexander to drive to the right of the house. At the back there was a track, which Titus hadn't noticed before. It was partly obscured with the drooping branches of low-growing wattles on either side. As they drove towards it, Titus looked behind and saw Anthony Prescott standing by the back door, watching them. Dealing with Prescott would have to wait.

The track was rough, and Alexander was forced to drive slowly. The truck, which wasn't visible up ahead, must have been making much faster progress. At a fork in the road, Alexander stopped.

'Left or right?'

'Right leads back into Nunawading,' Justice said.

Alexander turned left. This road, although unmade, was well maintained, and he was able to pick up speed. It wasn't a straight road, so if the truck was in front of them it was remaining stubbornly out of sight. They came to another fork.

'It's a chance we have to take, sir, but I'd say he's heading for the Dandenongs.'

The unspoken addition to this sentence was that the Dandenongs would be a good, remote place to dispose of a body. *Joe can't be dead, though*, Titus thought, and he spoke this thought to help secure it.

'I agree. Joe's life might depend on us being right.'

'The man called Joe is already dead,' Justice said. 'I saw his body. I saw Abraham drag it to the truck.'

'Do you know where he's taking it?' Alexander asked. The use of 'it' hit Titus like a punch.

'There! There!' Justice said, and pointed towards a small plume of dust some distance from them. They drove for another 30 minutes, never within sight of Abraham's truck, but occasionally spotting rising dust. It was only an assumption that this was the old man, but it was all they had. The road rose into the hills, and the bends became tighter. No traffic passed them. Justice said that she was beginning to feel car sick.

'Do you need me to pull over?'

'No. Not yet.'

She wound the window down, and cool air filled the car. Justice closed her eyes. Titus hoped she wouldn't need to be sick. Their chance of catching up to Abraham was already slim. If they had to stop, they'd lose him.

As the road rose into the hills, it became narrower and rougher. Alexander drove faster than he would normally have done in such conditions, and the sight that met him as he rounded a bend made him slam on the brakes. Titus was thrown forward, and his nose hit the headrest in front of him with sickening force.

'Fuck!' he said, and the expletive was as shocking to Alexander as the blood that began to flow down Titus's chin. There was no time to assess the damage to Titus's face. There, just a few car-lengths ahead of him, was Abraham's truck. It was parked off the road in a small clearing, and the old man was standing with Joe's body slung around his shoulders like the carcass of a sheep. Without displaying any signs of panic, his eyes locked on Alexander's, and he dropped Joe with casual indifference into the mud at his feet. He walked calmly to the truck, and drove off. Following him was out of the question. Both Alexander and Titus, a handkerchief pressed to his nose, ran to where Joe lay. He was face up, his skin pallid and one arm twisted awkwardly under his body. Titus knelt and felt for a pulse at his neck. His hand was shaking so violently that he couldn't still it. He had the sensation that Joe's neck was warm, but he couldn't discipline his fingers to find a pulse. Alexander knelt and pressed his fingers into Joe's neck.

'There's a strong pulse, sir. He's very much alive.'

Titus pulled himself together.

'We need to get him to a hospital.'

'We need to get you to one as well.'

As carefully as they could, they carried Joe to the car. He lay on the back seat, his head cradled in Titus's lap. The drive down from the hills was frustratingly slow, with Alexander trying to minimise bumps and jolts.

'Why there?' Titus asked Justice. 'Does that spot mean anything to you?'

'No, nothing. I've never been there.'

Titus wished that he'd looked around, but even if he had, even if he'd looked up the slope above the place where Joe had been dropped, he wouldn't have seen Guy Kirkham, whose body hung in a tree that couldn't be seen from the road.

TOM MACKENZIE HATED flying. Given that he wore the uniform of a group captain in the RAAF, this was a fact he felt constrained to conceal as he boarded the plane at the RAAF base at Laverton. It was late on Tuesday afternoon, and the weather wasn't promising — at any rate, it wasn't promising not to cause turbulence. The flight hadn't been arranged especially for Tom. It was a regular military transport, delivering personnel and equipment to Adelaide. The equipment was principally machinery parts for the army's armoured division. This information was shouted at him conversationally by an army officer — one of those people who feels a compulsive need to engage with those around him. In the noisy cabin, Tom had to strain to hear him, which made the uncomfortable flight even more uncomfortable. The plane was buffeted irregularly, and there were moments when Tom thought he might embarrass himself by bringing up his lunch.

Three hours after taking off, they landed in Adelaide. Tom was driven by a mercifully silent driver to Keswick Barracks, where he would spend the night before taking an early train the following morning to Barmera. Tom Chafer had provided him with a folder of information about Loveday Camp. He'd been unable to read it on the plane — just the thought of that had made him feel queasy — and although he began looking through it in his room at Keswick, he'd fallen asleep. The train trip was 235 miles long. He'd have plenty of time to read then.

12

JOE'S HEAD WAS pounding. It was bandaged, and Clara had assured him it wasn't to keep his skull together. Although the blow, from what was probably a cosh, had resulted in a spectacular contusion, it had also split the skin, and the bandage was there to contain any blood flow. As far as she could tell, no bones had been fractured, which was evidence of a thick skull, because the blow had been brutal. In many people such a blow might have resulted in a serious fracture and possibly death.

Joe had regained consciousness before Constable Forbes had reached the Royal Melbourne Hospital. He'd been confused and his vision had been blurred, and he was only partly aware of the activity going on around him. He was in the back of a car, then he was on a stretcher and then a trolley, and finally, somehow, he was in a bed, and his outer clothes had been removed. People had shone torches into his eyes, asked him questions, felt about his head, and checked his heartbeat. Slowly, everything came into focus. There'd been no pain initially, but as the morphine had worn off, a headache of monumental proportions began to assert itself.

Helen Lord sat in a chair beside the bed, and Inspector Lambert stood at its foot. They'd arrived within minutes of each other. Helen had come into the ward first. She tried, and failed, not to cry.

'I've brought you some pyjamas,' she said, and managed to get her voice under control. Joe was puzzled by her tears. He assumed she must have heard bad news about Guy.

'It's Guy, isn't it?'

'No, you stupid man. It's you. Seeing you in a hospital bed again is upsetting. You could have been killed. You would have been killed.'

She began to cry again, and Joe was so embarrassed by her tears that he said nothing for a full minute. As her sobs subsided, Joe thanked her for the pyjamas.

'I thought I'd have to be here in my underwear until they discharged me.'

'Shall I call a nurse to help you change into them?'

'No, no. I'll do it later.'

These banalities helped restore calm between them, and when Titus arrived he noted Helen's red eyes, and was glad to see Joe sitting up and coherent.

'You're a magnet for people who want to injure you, Joe Sable.'

'I need to thank you and that young constable. And you don't look so good yourself.'

The blow to Titus's nose hadn't broken it, but it had caused two black eyes to bloom.

'The person who saved your life was the young woman who calls herself Justice. If she hadn't helped us, we'd never have found you.'

'What happened to me?'

'Joe, we can talk about that later. We have Prescott and the young man in custody, and the two women are cooperating. Abraham is still at large, but we'll find him.'

Joe was about to speak, but Titus interrupted him.

'Joe, please. All the other stuff can wait. I'm afraid I have bad news about your friend Guy Kirkham.'

Helen whispered, 'Oh,' and reached out and clasped Joe's hand. His fingers closed around hers.

'I sent men in to search the area where Abraham had dropped you. I thought he must have chosen the place for a reason. High up the slope, in a depression you can't see from the road, we found Guy's body. I'm so sorry.'

Joe stared at Titus.

'No,' he said quietly. 'No, that can't be true.'

'I'm sorry.'

'How? How did he die?'

Titus had been told the vicious nature of Guy's death, but he wasn't willing to burden Joe with this yet.

'Like you, he'd been hit from behind. The autopsy will reveal the actual cause of death.'

Helen understood that Titus had deliberately left out some vital details, but Joe felt himself caving in under the weight of what he'd been told, and he failed to notice the omission. He lay back and stared at the ceiling.

'Joe?' Helen asked, and squeezed his hand. Joe turned to her.

'It can't be true, Helen. It can't be true, can it?'

She nodded gently, and her lips quivered. Joe began to weep soundlessly. Helen wanted to climb onto the bed, lie beside him, and hold him. She didn't do this. She leaned in and kissed his bandaged forehead.

'We'll find him, Joe. We'll find the man who did this.'

'It can't be true,' Joe said again. 'Guy will come home. He will, won't he?'

WINSLOW FAZACKERLY DIDN'T know the streets of St Kilda well. The suburb's proximity to Port Phillip Bay meant that its briny air reminded him of South Melbourne. Here, though, there was also the faint whiff of rotting vegetation. Here, in Dalgety Street, several gardens had been let run riot, and the effect was oddly tropical and lush.

The address Winslow had been given was a flat below street level, which must have been the servants' quarters of the large house above it. It would have been converted some time in the 1930s into a boarding house. There were lights on in some of the windows, including the window of the flat to which he'd been directed.

Coming here was foolish. He knew it was foolish. He walked the length of Dalgety Street twice before stopping outside number 64A. Who was behind this door? Whoever was here, Winslow couldn't imagine how he or she could have information about his wife. There was one possible channel that he'd thought of. Japanese prisoners were held at Cowra in New South Wales. Winslow couldn't see, though, how a captured soldier or naval officer could have specific information about Etsuko, let alone know to whom this information might be of interest.

As far as Winslow knew, all civilian Japanese men had been interned, so was this contact in St Kilda someone's wife? Conscious that this was potentially the worst decision he'd ever made, he knocked on the door. It was opened by a man whose bulk was shocking to Winslow. Absurdly, his immediate thought was how this man maintained his obesity in the face of wartime austerity. It wasn't as if there were no overweight people around, but this was something else. The voice that came out of this flesh mountain ought to have been deep. It wasn't. It was high, and propelled by a wheeze. It was also brusque.

'What do you want?'

'That depends on who you are.'

In another person, the small snigger might have been just that — small. In this man, the heave required to produce it shook his whole body.

'Oh, I know who you are. I've been expecting you. You'd better come in.' The man was observant: he had detected a tentativeness in his visitor. 'I'm the only one here. Do come in.'

His voice was educated. Guy recognised that his vowels had been rounded by training. An actor perhaps? The man repeated his invitation in Japanese. It was heavily accented, but it was spoken with the confidence of someone familiar with the language.

The flat was untidy. Tidiness required an effort. It was a kind of exercise, and this man didn't look like exercise was part of his daily routine.

'Clive Kent is the name.'

He didn't extend his hand, but instead lumbered to a sideboard, where he opened a bottle of red wine. Without asking if Winslow wanted a glass he poured him one, and handed the smeared vessel to him. Winslow liked red wine, but he hadn't had many good glasses of it recently. He expected this to be undrinkable. It was excellent.

'Know a chap,' Kent said. 'Good, eh? I can tell you're surprised. Have a seat, my friend.'

Winslow sat in an armchair that needed to be resprung. Clive sat across the room from him.

'Here's to you,' Kent said, and then in Japanese added, 'and to the heavenly sovereign Emperor Hirohito.'

Winslow's heart sank, but he raised his glass. Clive sipped and smiled.

'There are only a handful of us, Mr Fazackerly, but how comforting it is to know that we are not alone.'

'We?'

'Yes. Those of us who know that there is nothing to fear from the empire of Japan.'

'There are many, many thousands of people who know that that isn't true, Mr Kent.'

Clive Kent waved the comment away.

'Propaganda, Mr Fazackerly. You lived in Japan. No one knows better than you how civilised, how civilising the Japanese are.'

Winslow had heard that there were some Westerners who were hopeful of a Japanese victory. He'd never met one, and he didn't understand how they could be so wilfully blind to the brutality meted out by the Japanese military to conquered peoples. Did they think they'd be embraced by the victors? Surely, this late in the war, they'd read enough to lose any sentimental or romantic notions about the chrysanthemum throne.

'Have you ever been to Japan, Mr Kent?'

'I didn't learn to speak Japanese in this godforsaken country, Mr Fazackerly. I lived for many years in Kyushu. Satsuma pottery, that was my trade. It's all dried up now, of course. I know people who've taken a hammer to such beautiful pieces it would break your heart. Do you like Satsuma ware?'

All Winslow wanted was information about his wife. He didn't want to make small talk with someone whose loyalties, were they known, would attract the attention of Military Intelligence. He regretted his decision to come to this flat, and wanted to end the conversation.

'I have no particular interest in Japanese pottery, Mr Kent. I believe you have information about my wife's health. That's all I'm interested in.'

Kent's jovial demeanour evaporated.

'All right, Mr Fazackerly, we'll dispense with the pleasantries. I do have information about Etsuko, but I'm afraid this is going to have to be a *quid pro quo* situation.'

'Before we go any further, how could you possibly know anything about a particular woman in Hiroshima?'

'Ah, that is one of those strange coincidences that war sometimes throws up.'

'I don't believe in coincidence, at least not in this case.'

Clive Kent wheezed out a small laugh.

'Well, coincidence isn't the right word. Luck might be closer, and in some ways, Mr Fazackerly, to be perfectly frank, it's a piece of luck that is now more than six months old, so I can't tell you anything about your wife's health as it is now. I can only tell you how it stood six months ago.'

This was reassuring to Winslow, not because it eased his fears about Etsuko, but because it made Kent's story more plausible. Being in Kent's presence began to feel less like a trap. He relaxed a little. Kent noticed that Winslow unclenched his fingers and leaned back in his chair.

'Go on,' Winslow said.

'It really isn't as extraordinary as it sounds. Your wife was ill and needed medication that is impossible to get in Japan.'

'What do you mean by ill?'

'Oh, some female thing. Something uterine.'

His face suggested that he found this distasteful.

'She was experiencing a lot of pain, apparently. I don't know. Women's bits are a mystery to me.'

'That's very vague.'

'Yes, I'm sorry. Let me continue. There was a young man who lived near your wife's family. He's a naval officer. Now this is where it gets a bit odd. Your wife wrote you a letter in Japanese, telling you what was wrong and asking you for help. It's not just about her health. There's other personal stuff in it. I'm sorry to say it's a sort of farewell letter. She gave this letter to the naval officer, obviously never expecting that you'd receive it. I imagine she did it in the spirit that you'd put a letter in a bottle and throw it overboard. She knew that this man was about to do duty in the Pacific, and just the thought that the letter would leave Japan must have given her some comfort. There would have been no expectation that it would ever reach you. Why would it? For a start, there was no guarantee that this man wouldn't just screw it up and put it in the bin. However, he didn't. He put it in the pocket of his uniform, and maybe he forgot about it. He was captured by the Americans, and he was interrogated by them. He was cooperative. Japanese prisoners are surprisingly cooperative. You'd understand their character. To be captured is to be humiliated and to lose all connection with Japan. Surrendering means surrendering all your rights, not that Japanese prisoners know much about the Geneva Convention. The Americans had the letter translated, but didn't think it was of any real importance. They actually returned it to the man before sending him on to Cowra. And from there it made its way to Loveday, and here we are.'

'How? How did it get from Cowra to Loveday?'

'That I don't know. I do know it wasn't officially sanctioned. The fact is, Mr Fazackerly, I have the letter. What I don't have is any means to get a reply to your wife. I'm afraid I'm not that well connected.'

He reached into the voluminous jacket he was wearing and withdrew a piece of paper.

'I'm not going to lie to you and pretend I haven't read Etsuko's letter. I have. Reading Japanese isn't one of my strong points, but I got the gist. It's a lovely letter. Very touching.'

The thought that this man had run his eyes over his wife's words was as disgusting to Winslow as if he'd run his hands over her body.

'Show me Etsuko's letter.'

'I want you to do me a very, very small favour in return.'

'Go on.'

'I want this war to be over as much as the next man, Mr Fazackerly, and I think we can agree that Japan is rather on the back foot. I have tremendous sympathy for those men in Cowra.

They must feel so isolated, so cut off, perhaps permanently cut off, from everything that matters to them as men, as people. I believe I can get a letter into Cowra. Nothing seditious, you understand. I have no wish to foment any kind of dissent. I'm talking about sentiment, not politics.'

'Since when has blackmail been sentimental?'

Clive Kent smiled.

'It is true. I am blackmailing you, and to use a letter from your wife is despicable. I am not a despicable man, Mr Fazackerly, but the simple truth is my Japanese isn't sophisticated enough to draft the letter I want to write, and so I must, as it were, stoop to conquer.'

Winslow wanted to leave, but he also wanted to hold in his hands something that Etsuko had held in hers.

'What is it you want me to write for you?'

Kent, with some effort, rose from the chair and handed Winslow a piece of paper. On it was written a short passage: *Soldiers of Japan, we want you to know that there are in this country people who honour and respect you, people who would welcome you into our cities, our homes, our hearts. You are not the enemy we despise or fear.*

'You see, Mr Fazackerly, these are just a few words that will fit on a scrap of paper. They are not a manifesto or a call to arms. My only hope is that they might help one young man find solace in his capture, especially as he would know that his country has abandoned him and won't welcome him home after the war. He should have killed himself, not accepted the humiliation of capture. You see what I mean about sentiment.'

Winslow read the words again. He thought they were indeed sentimental and foolish.

'Who shall I say this note is from?'

'A friend.'

Kent gave Winslow a cigarette paper, a book to rest it on, and a sharpened pencil.

194

'Can you make it fit on this?'

'I think so.'

When he'd finished, the cigarette paper was crowded with characters, and he gave it to Kent, who read it, and took tobacco from a pouch and rolled a cigarette with it. He held it up to the light to examine it.

'The prisoners in Cowra are treated well. They are allowed cigarettes.'

'I would like my wife's letter, please.'

He stood up. Kent crossed to the front door and opened it.

'The letter will be delivered to your house. I couldn't risk having it here, in case you turned out to be a violent man who would simply take it from me. I assure you it will be there. I wouldn't lie to you. You know where I live. I will make a phone call, and it will be waiting for you when you get home.'

Winslow was torn between wanting to hurry home and wanting to find the cigarette, which Kent had put in his pocket, and crush it. *At least*, he thought, *I won't have to read Etsuko's words in this man's presence*. Suddenly he couldn't bear the sound of Kent's wheezing, and he left the flat. The air outside felt pure and healthy, and he set out for his house in South Melbourne. When he reached it, half an hour later, he noticed that the front gate had been left open. He walked to the front door and looked down. In the darkness, the corner of a white piece of paper stood out from where it had been pushed under the door. Had Kent actually been telling the truth? Had he kept his word after all? Winslow opened the door and picked up the folded paper. He went into the living room and switched on the light. Tom Chafer was sitting there, his legs crossed, in an armchair. Chafer said nothing. Winslow unfolded the piece of paper. It was blank.

'Did you really believe that a letter from your wife would get from Japan to you? Are you really that stupid, Fazackerly?'

As he said this, two men appeared in the doorway behind Winslow. Before he knew what was happening, his hands had been secured behind his back with handcuffs.

'You're a traitor, Fazackerly. I don't expect they'll hang you, but they'll certainly put you in prison, where you belong.'

Tom Mackenzie had read the material he'd been given on Loveday internment camp, but he hadn't been prepared for the camp's size. Given that there were more than 5,000 men interned there, he supposed he ought to have been. The amount of land under cultivation around and within the camp was impressive. It didn't look at all grim, although being separated from their wives and families must have been terrible for the Germans, Italians, and Japanese held here.

The running of Loveday was a source of pride for its administrators. Perhaps it was partly propaganda, although the information provided to Tom had come from internal documents and briefings. The camp was run according to the dictates of the Geneva Convention, and inmates were encouraged to work and were paid a small wage for their labour. There were surly and unco-operative internees, some of whom adhered unapologetically to their fascist or National Socialist beliefs. The majority, however, found that work helped create an illusion of normality — and the work was plentiful. Loveday produced large quantities of raw opium from its poppy crop. The morphine that quelled the cries of a wounded soldier in New Guinea, or somewhere in the Pacific, had probably begun as a poppy head picked by an interned man at Loveday. There was the daisy crop to harvest for its pyrethrum, guayule for latex, and every kind of vegetable, some for food and some for seeds. There was a piggery and a large chook run. Loveday was a business, and Loveday turned a profit. It was, in effect, a small town, policed by 1,500 army personnel. It had sportsfields and a golf course, neither of which extinguished the misery of internment, misery that crept up on men with the awful persistence of the sand drifts that threatened to smother Loveday's crops.

Yokito Torajiro spoke excellent, if accented, English. Tom Mackenzie walked with him around the perimeter of a grassless square in Camp 14. Japanese internees played baseball here. No game was in progress. Mr Torajiro was polite, and acknowledged without demur that he'd known Winslow Fazackerly for many years, and that he knew him because of his marriage to Etsuko.

'Did you like Mr Fazackerly?'

'He was a good man, I think, but ...'

'But?'

'But you can't become Japanese by marrying a Japanese person.'

Winslow had been honest in his acknowledgement that there would always be distance between him and the Japanese people he occasionally met. There was something, however, in Mr Torajiro's tone that made Tom think his disapproval of Winslow ran deep, much deeper than perhaps Winslow knew. Tom wasn't sure what questions to ask Mr Torajiro, because as he walked with him he realised he wasn't entirely sure why he was there. He'd been well briefed on Loveday, but had been given no guidance about how to proceed with the two men whose names he'd been given — Yokito Torajiro and Toshiro Akiyama, who was Katherine Hart's husband. Was Tom Chafer setting him up to fail? He wouldn't put it past him.

'What's life like here, Mr Torajiro?'

'Survivable.'

Yokito Torajiro stopped and ran his hand over his mottled bald head.

'Life is short,' he said. 'It should be better than this. It should be more than survivable, don't you think?'

'Are you treated well?'

'This is not my home. I was taken from my home. I am fed. I work. I can move around, but I am not permitted to leave. This is a prison, but I committed no crime.'

Tom became impatient.

'Would you rather this camp was run the way the Japanese run their camps?'

'Are you asking me to be grateful simply because my jailers aren't as brutal as some of my countrymen? Should I say thank you to the soldier more than half my age who watches me and tells me what I can and cannot do?'

'Surely you must know how Japanese soldiers treat the citizens of the places they occupy.'

'Of course I do.' Mr Torajiro's voice was sharp with anger. 'I haven't lived in Japan for more than 50 years. It is not my home. My home is in Melbourne. I haven't invaded anyone. I haven't treated anyone cruelly. I am guilty only of being Japanese. My face, my body, my ancestors — these are my crimes.'

Tom felt disinclined to continue this line of conversation.

'You wrote to Mr Fazackerly, is that right?'

'I have no loyalty to Winslow Fazackerly. I wrote what I was told to write.'

'What do you mean?'

Mr Torajiro laughed.

'Why did they send someone so naive all this way?'

This was beginning to make hideous sense to Tom.

'Someone told you what to write? Who?'

'Oh, it was very formal. I was called into an office in the administration building. There was a military man there, a colonel, I think, and a civilian was with him — a very, very fat man who spoke terrible Japanese. They handed me a note and told me to translate it into Japanese. I didn't really have a choice if I wanted my life here to remain tolerable. I was told, too, that Toshiro Akiyama's wife, who is an Australian, would suddenly find her life turned upside down if I didn't cooperate. As I said, I have no loyalty to Winslow Fazackerly, so I did as I was told.'

'And what did you write?'

'It was a note telling Winslow that his wife was very ill, and that was all. Just a few words. I was told to give the note to Toshiro, who would give it to his wife when she visited.'

Tom was anxious to end the conversation. He thanked Mr Torajiro, and decided that talking to Mr Akiyama would be pointless. The person he really wanted to speak to was Tom fucking Chafer.

Chafer wasn't at his desk when Tom's call was put through, so Tom waited half an hour before trying again. During this time he was obliged to listen to a lengthy encomium about Loveday's contribution to the war effort by a major who rattled off crop tonnages as if he were personally responsible for planting and harvesting every item.

Chafer picked up the telephone when Tom called again. The conversation was brief. Fazackerly had been arrested. Chafer had been right about him. He'd been prepared to betray his country at the first opportunity.

'Why did you insist that I come all the way to Loveday?'

'You needed to see how real intelligence works.'

'Winslow Fazackerly is no traitor. You set out to trap him.'

'I set out to test him.'

'You're a fucking prick.'

'I'm good at my job.'

Chafer hung up.

ON HER WAY home after nightshift, Clara called in to Helen's office and sat with her. It was clear that Helen had barely slept.

'Inspector Lambert told me what happened to Guy, Clar. Am I responsible for this? Am I?'

'If you keep asking yourself that, you'll start to believe it, and it's absurd. You might as well ask if you're responsible for the whole fucking war.'

'But I let Guy go out there. I employed him to go out there.'

'And he accepted the job. He knew what he was doing.'

'Did he, though? And Joe? Joe could have died, Clar. And his best friend is dead. Why did I think I could do this? I can't do this. I'm closing the business.'

'No, you're not. It's your investigation that's uncovered all the Church of the First Born bullshit.'

'Not in time to save Zachary Wilson, or Guy.'

'But maybe in time to save God knows how many other people.'

Helen looked blankly ahead of her.

'Helen, listen to me. If you give up now, Guy's death really will have been in vain. You can't do that to him. You have to be brave enough to accept the risk. You have to be as brave as Guy was.'

'Those are just words, Clar.'

'So turn them into something more, Helen. Turn them into actions.'

Helen stood up and walked the few steps to where Clara was sitting. Clara rose, and Helen embraced her. This sudden intimacy surprised Clara. In all their years of friendship, Helen had rarely made physical contact with her. They were close. They knew each other's secrets and private thoughts — although not all of them — but Helen had never been comfortable with touching others.

'Where do I go from here, Clar?'

'I don't know. You're the fucking detective.'

Joe was released from hospital at lunchtime, and was given strict instructions to go home. He was to take things slowly and to be mindful of any change in his vision or in the intensity of his headaches. He ignored the advice, and walked from the hospital to the office. He wondered why people were staring at him, and realised it was the bandage around his head.

Helen knew that he wouldn't go from the hospital to Kew, and she didn't admonish him when he came into the office. She wanted to tell him that he looked terrible, unwell, and that he shouldn't be here. She recognised, though, that Joe wouldn't appreciate being given advice. If he was here, it was because he wanted to be here, needed to be here.

'I can't tell you how sorry I am about Guy,' she said.

'His parents have been told. Inspector Lambert telephoned them. I don't know how they reacted.'

'They must have been devastated.'

'Oh no, I doubt that very much. They'd go through the motions, but Guy wasn't what they wanted in a son. They'll give him a decent funeral, the full requiem mass — there are people in the district to impress, after all — and then they'll tidy away their emotions and mention Guy less and less until they stop mentioning him at all.'

'My God, Joe, that's a bleak assessment. Will you go up for the funeral?'

'No. They don't like Jews, and I couldn't bear to sit through all that ritual that Guy despised. He was a good man, Helen.'

'I know he was.'

'But I hadn't seen him for a couple of years, and when he turned up a few months ago he wasn't entirely himself. Something was missing. Something was broken, and I feel guilty saying it, but I thought he'd take his own life, and in a way I think that's what happened. There was enough of the Catholic left in him to stop him from actually committing suicide, but putting himself at risk was the next best thing.'

Helen was surprised by Joe's calm rationalisation of Guy's death. She was relieved, but also disturbed. Perhaps it was a way for Joe to find consolation, but there was something chilly and intellectual about it. His emotions had been raw just 24 hours ago. Now they were disciplined. If she'd been more practised in expressing her own emotions, she might have challenged him. As it was, despite the traumatic events, they settled quickly back into a conversation that functioned to displace the personal in favour of the practical. Helen was suddenly loath to mention her decision to close the business. Indeed, when Joe walked into the office, she'd changed her mind. Helen Lord and Associates had to continue. The idea of dragging Joe down into her own sense of failure was appalling to her. Despite the romanticism of Clara's words, she'd been right. Guy Kirkham needed justice, and she and Joe would see that he got it.

13

When Clara Dawson tried the door of the house in Powlett Street, she was relieved that it was locked. Pat was finally getting the message. Clara had waited at some distance from the house, scanning the street for Kenneth Bussell. When she was satisfied that he wasn't about, she went inside. She checked each room and the backyard before going into her room. She read until lunchtime and then, unusually for her, she fell deeply asleep. The discordant jangle of the telephone woke her. It took a moment to disentangle the sound from a dream. She barked her shin on the way to answering it, so when she said, 'Hello,' into the mouthpiece it wasn't entirely cheery.

There was silence.

'Hello? Are you there?'

Silence.

'I know you're there. I can hear you breathing.'

This was true. Clara could hear breaths being taken and released.

'I can hear you, Mr Bussell. How did you get this number?'

As soon as she uttered his name, she heard the click of disconnection. She found that she was shaking. It was as if he'd been in the room with her. Her first instinct was to check yet again that the front door was locked. It was just before 5.00 pm. Should she telephone Inspector Lambert? Was she being hysterical? Maybe it hadn't been Bussell after all, but a wrong number, or a child playing a random prank. It hadn't felt like that, though. Why had the phone gone dead at the mention of Bussell's name? She telephoned Russell Street, and was told that Inspector Lambert was unavailable. She left her name and the simple message that Kenneth Bussell had contacted her. She decided not to ring Helen. She had enough to worry about without adding news of an anonymous call to her list.

ANTHONY PRESCOTT HAD requested that his solicitor be present for his formal interview. He'd been detained in custody for the past 24 hours. He'd been offered a change of clothes, but he'd insisted on wearing the tunic he'd been wearing when he'd been brought in. He was unshaven, and was beginning to look slightly dishevelled. He'd declined to shave, and had said that the remand cell was his wilderness and that he would shave again only when he'd come out of the wilderness. Apart from this, he'd made no complaints about the accommodation. He'd borne it with equanimity.

The young man named Nepheg, whose real name turned out to be John Ogilvy, had been released on bail into the care of his family. This arrangement had been accepted with reluctance on both sides.

Constable Forbes had brought Prescott across Russell Street from the watch house cells to the interview room on the third floor of police headquarters. Prescott's solicitor, a thin man in his fifties with horn-rimmed spectacles and oily hair, hadn't admitted to being a member of Prescott's church, but the subtle deference he paid Prescott suggested to Alexander that he was an acolyte. Neither he nor Prescott was aggressive or uncooperative. The sight of a man in a tunic, bare-legged, in an interview room was peculiar, but Prescott was utterly unselfconscious.

With the preliminaries dispensed with, Inspector Lambert began his questioning.

'Are you a murderer, Mr Prescott, or the accessory to the murder?'

'I am neither of those things, Inspector.'

'And yet Guy Kirkham is dead, and Joe Sable would have been killed if the man named Abraham hadn't been discovered and interrupted. I'd like to deal with the assault on Joe Sable first. Where were you when this happened?'

'I was in the kitchen.'

'So you didn't witness it?'

'No, of course not. Joe Sable had come to see his friend, Mr Kirkham, who as far as I knew had left us the previous evening. We had a conversation in the chapel, and at some point I offered a cup of tea, which Mr Sable accepted. I left to make it, and when I returned there was no one there. I heard the truck start, and came outside to find that Abraham had driven away in it. I wasn't sure what had happened, and then your car appeared, which confounded me even more.'

'Are you asking me to believe, Mr Prescott, that this man, Abraham, struck Joe Sable on the head, carried his unconscious body out of the house, loaded it, single-handed, into a truck, and that you heard and saw nothing?'

'I am asking you to believe that, because that is what happened.'

'Joe Sable says that the last thing he remembers is talking to you. You were in the room when he was assaulted.'

'He suffered, I believe, a severe blow to the head. His memory, I'm afraid, is faulty.'

'The woman named Justice — is her memory faulty, too? She saw you helping Abraham with Joe Sable's body.'

'She's mistaken. I think you'll find that the death of her sister has addled her brain somewhat.'

'Who is Abraham?'

To Titus's astonishment, Prescott didn't repeat the Church of the First Born guff he'd indulged in previously.

'He came to us out of a bad marriage and a failed business venture. It wasn't my place to inquire about either deeply. The Church of the First Born offers sanctuary, not interrogation.'

'And his name? His real name?'

'Walter Pinshott.'

Alexander Forbes left the room briefly. Titus held off asking further questions until he returned.

'You understand that Walter Pinshott murdered Guy Kirkham?'

'I find that shocking.'

'Do you doubt it?'

Prescott looked at his solicitor.

'No,' he said. 'No, I don't doubt it. I'm shocked by it, but I don't doubt it. He must have believed that he was doing the righteous thing. I wish he'd come to me. I would have counselled him.'

'Why do you think he killed Guy Kirkham?'

'How did Mr Kirkham die?'

Prescott's calm irked Titus. The ease with which he lied, and his measured, mellifluous tone lent him a disturbing credibility.

'Mr Kirkham didn't die quickly. He was tied to a tree, and three six-inch nails were hammered into his heart.'

Prescott didn't appear to be surprised by this. He leaned back in his chair and crossed his left leg over his right.

'Ah, I see.'

'You see what?'

'Abraham named Mr Kirkham when he came to us. He called him Absalom, and at the time I thought this was premature, but Abraham was adamant — adamant that this young man wasn't what he said he was. He said that he'd betray me, betray us.'

'So the name was significant?'

'Absalom was one of David's sons. He betrayed David, and died when three darts were fired into his heart. I think Abraham might be guilty of being rather literal.'

'He's guilty of murder!'

Inspector Lambert's fierce exclamation stunned Alexander, and caused Prescott to blanch. It only took a moment, though, for him to recover.

'I apologise if that seemed like a trivial thing to say, Inspector. I, like you, am trying to understand Abraham's actions.'

'Let's agree to call this murderous man by his real name, Walter Pinshott.'

Titus's voice was now quiet.

'Yes,' Prescott said. 'The Church of the First Born does not give sanctuary to murderers. As soon as I return, we will conduct the necessary ceremony and declare Walter Pinshott anathema.'

Alexander began to wonder how much of this was performance and how much insanity. Prescott must know, surely, he *must* know that the evidence for his involvement in these crimes was strong: two witnesses, and possibly three if the young man spoke against him, had declared that he'd been present when Joe Sable had been assaulted.

'Where would Pinshott go?'

'What do you mean?'

'Where will he hide?'

'Once he's been declared anathema he'll have nowhere to hide. It's forbidden to give shelter to someone who has been declared anathema.'

'Where will he go *now*?'

Alexander worried that Inspector Lambert might lose his patience.

'I suppose he might go to someone in our congregation.'

'Do you have a list of the people who form your congregation?'

'Oh no, nothing like that.'

'How large is your congregation?'

'It's growing, but at the moment I think there might be about 100 people who have been saved.'

'But you don't know who they are or where they live.'

'Not all of them, no.'

'I want the names and addresses of everyone you *can* remember.'

Prescott slipped his hand under his tunic and scratched his thigh.

'No, Inspector, I'm afraid not. There is no reason to harry my followers.'

Alexander knew, and he was certain Inspector Lambert knew, too, that there was a list of worshippers. The Church of the First Born raised funds for itself efficiently, and that required knowing who'd paid and who hadn't.

'I'd like to take a short break,' Titus said. In the corridor outside the interview room, he asked Alexander if John Ogilvy, who called himself Nepheg, had been fetched for questioning.

'He should be here now, sir. A car was sent to pick him up.'

'Good. I don't want Prescott to know that he's here. Set him up in another room. I'll tell Prescott that I'm suspending the interview for half an hour. And we need to go back out to Nunawading and turn that place inside out. There's a list of names — nothing is more certain than that.'

JOHN OGILVY WAS wearing clothes that weren't his own. They didn't fit him. The trousers were too large and were tied around the waist with a piece of rope. Unlike Prescott, he was freshly shaved, although the small nick on his chin suggested he'd shaved hastily. His solicitor gave every appearance of being annoyed at having to be here, a situation that didn't bode well for Ogilvy.

Perhaps, Alexander thought, *he's doing a favour for someone in Ogilvy's family. An angry lawyer is not the ideal advocate.* Ogilvy seemed dazed, as if he wasn't entirely sure where he was, let alone why he was there. After some preliminary questions about Ogilvy's decision to join the Church of the First Born, Inspector Lambert asked him what he knew about Walter Pinshott.

'I don't know who that is.'

'Abraham.'

'Oh, is that his godless name?'

'Tell me about him.'

'He wasn't kind, but the Master favoured him, and so I suppose he was a better man than I thought he was. When am I going back to Nunawading?'

'That depends on what you tell us and whether or not we believe you. Guy Kirkham was murdered by Walter Pinshott, and there are four other victims, some or all of whom may have been murdered by him as well.'

'No. The Master wouldn't allow it,' he said quietly.

The solicitor looked at his client, but said nothing. Titus allowed the silence to build.

'But there was a young man who came to our sanctuary. I don't know his name. I didn't meet him. I left to do work soon after he arrived. I was in the orchard and I stopped work to ... to relieve myself, and I saw this young man come out of the women's hut. I knew Justice was in there for her body to be cleansed of its foul bleeding. I was shocked, and as he walked away — and I think he was crying — as he walked away Abraham fell upon him. I couldn't see exactly what happened, but the young man's body went limp, and Abraham picked him up as if he was a broken puppet. He put him in the front of his truck and drove away.'

'Emilio Barbero.'

'I don't know that name.'

'That's the name of the young man who you saw Pinshott kill.'

'Who says he killed him?'

'He was strung up like a carcass on Peter Fisher's veranda. He was 17 years old.'

'And Absalom?'

'You know what happened to Absalom. You were there.'

'He left.'

'No, he didn't leave.'

Ogilvy shook his head and whispered, 'Though I should receive a thousand shekels of silver in mine hand, yet would I not put forth mine hand against the king's son.'

He looked at Inspector Lambert, and his eyes filled with tears.

'But he did, didn't he?' Ogilvy said.

Titus took a piece of paper from his pocket and read from it: '*And he took three darts in his hand, and thrust them through the heart of Absalom, while he was yet alive in the midst of the oak.*'

Ogilvy slumped in his chair, and Constable Forbes believed that whatever else this young man might be guilty of, being an accessory to murder wasn't among his crimes. Perhaps his only crime was credulousness. Ogilvy rallied briefly and said, 'The Master will be filled with grief for Absalom when he hears about this.'

'Mr Prescott is in custody. We have no doubt whatever that he knew precisely what had happened to Guy Kirkham.'

'No. That can't be right. That won't be right.'

'I assure you, Mr Ogilvy, that it is right.'

'No,' Ogilvy said simply.

Inspector Lambert had organised the return of Peter Lillee's car from Prescott's property. By midafternoon of the day of his release from hospital, Joe had convinced Helen that they had to drive out to the orchard. Helen had been reluctant and had argued that the police mightn't approve of them poking about what was now a crime scene. Joe pointed out that Helen Lord and Associates was a licensed inquiry agency, and that, as a victim of a crime carried out there, he had something of a personal interest.

There was no police presence when they arrived at Prescott's orchard. They were invited into the house by Prudence, who had watched their approach from the veranda. She offered her condolences to Joe for the death of his friend, and expressed her regret over his head injury. Prudence was not in the least obfuscatory. Helen introduced herself as a private inquiry agent, and Prudence offered to answer any questions that she might have. It was in everyone's interest, she agreed, that Abraham should be found and taken into custody.

'He is no longer a member of our community, so he is now just plain Walter Pinshott,' she said. 'He has forfeited the right to sanctuary here. I have already spoken at great length to detectives, and they have invaded the privacy of this place and taken away material which I hope they'll treat with respect and return. This includes your friend's clothes, Mr Sable. His loss must be terrible for you, and I will honour your grief by giving you as much information as I can.'

In the course of a long conversation, Prudence told them all that she knew of Peter Fisher, his apostasy, and the fact that Sean Fisher was Anthony Prescott's son — although she called Prescott David. She acknowledged that Emilio Barbero had come to see Justice and had broken the taboo of entering the women's hut. She couldn't explain the circumstances of his death. She acknowledged, too, that Guy had broken this taboo.

'And what,' Joe asked, 'is the penalty for breaking this taboo?'

'There is always room for absolution through penance in the Church of the First Born.'

'So not death then?'

'No, Mr Sable, not death. This is 1944, not 944.'

'And yet Guy is dead.'

As these words were spoken, Justice entered the room carrying a tray with a teapot, cups, a milk jug, and a bowl of fruit on it. Until this appearance she hadn't made her presence known. Having placed the tray on the table, she crossed to Joe, leaned down, and kissed the bandage that was wrapped around his head. This was done so swiftly that it was accomplished before Joe had time to pull away.

'Please stay,' Prudence said to her.

As Joe watched Prudence pour the tea, he realised that every movement, and that every word, was a deliberate and self-conscious act of metamorphosis. Prudence was changing before their eyes from Prescott's handmaid into … into what? Prudence smiled benignly and emanated calm. Joe believed that Prudence had been watching, studying Anthony Prescott for a very long time. She was trying Prescott's mantle on for size. In an attempt to goad her out of her studied tranquillity, he asked, 'What is your relationship to Anthony Prescott?'

Without demur, she said, 'He is my husband.'

'According to whom?'

Prudence stood and opened the drawer of a small side table. She retrieved a document and passed it to Joe.

'According to the state of Victoria, and more importantly, much more importantly, according to the congregation of the Church of the First Born.'

Joe looked at the marriage certificate, which revealed that on the 2nd of May 1940, Anthony Prescott had married Bethany Hudson. Joe passed the certificate to Helen.

'And you're Bethany Hudson?'

'I was that person.'

Helen decided that indirection was pointless.

'Your husband slept with your sister. How did you feel about that?'

Prudence, not yet pitch perfect in her poise, displayed a slight affront in the narrowing of her eyes.

'I was unable to give my husband children. David lay with Truth with my blessing, and we rejoiced when she fell pregnant.'

'How could you be certain that it was his baby and not Peter Fisher's?'

'Because my husband withered Fisher's testicles with the power of his mind.'

Prudence declared this with some force, as if daring Joe and Helen to doubt it.

'That's absurd,' Helen said. 'It's so absurd it's laughable, and I don't believe that you believe it. If he could make a man sterile, why couldn't he make you fertile?'

With *sang froid* worthy of Prescott, Prudence said, 'My faith isn't touched by your ridicule.'

'If he can dry up a man's testicles, getting himself out of prison should be a cakewalk,' Joe said.

Prudence turned her gaze towards Joe. There was heat in it, but no warmth. That was something she needed to work on, Joe thought. At the moment, her gaze was bland and empty.

'I don't expect my husband will get out of jail for some time. He came to me last night in a dream. He called me the mother of our church, and said that I must look after our congregation. He passed his wisdom into me. I'm in charge here now.'

Prudence was no fool, Helen thought, although she wasn't convinced that Prudence had the charisma to dupe people into believing that she'd been anointed as the mother of the church.

'Are you saying that Mr Prescott will plead guilty to being an accessory?' Joe said.

'No. But I'm a realist, Mr Sable. Anthony was in the room when Pinshott attacked you, and Justice saw him help carry your unconscious body to the truck. I also was a witness to that and, when called, we will testify to that effect. Anthony helped Pinshott remove Mr Sable's body, and I have no doubt now that he did the same with your friend.'

The use of 'Anthony' didn't go unnoticed by either Helen or Joe.

'You'll testify against him, even though you're his wife?' Helen said.

'Yes, I will.'

'As will I,' Justice said.

Helen was aware that she and Joe had just been privy to a sort of coup d'état. Perhaps these women believed the nonsense they spouted, but Helen was convinced that however strong their faith, their business sense was stronger.

When Prudence rose to see Helen and Joe out, she made an attempt at majesty. Maybe with practice it would appear less ridiculous. She went for noble graciousness, but landed on clumsy haughtiness. This would change. She would hone her skills — Helen had no doubt about it.

WALTER PINSHOTT WOULDN'T have harmed either of the Master's wives. Nevertheless, he was glad to find the house empty when he entered it. He hadn't missed them by much. A police car had collected them — Inspector Lambert was to interview them at Russell Street — just half an hour before he arrived. There was no sign of Nepheg either. This suited Pinshott too. He could go about his business undisturbed. He needed food, fuel, and clothing. He shaved his beard and cut his hair so that he looked less like a cut-rate prophet and more like a not particularly successful accountant. He couldn't stay at the Master's house, but he knew a man, another of the Master's followers, who would take him in. He disturbed nothing in the house. He took only what he needed, and before he left he went into the chapel, prostrated himself, and prayed to the Master, who was, after all, God incarnate.

TOM CHAFER PUSHED the letter that Winslow Fazackerly had written, along with its translation, across the desk to Tom Mackenzie.

'Traitorous correspondence with the enemy in a time of war is tantamount to treason. Fazackerly will be court-martialled. Unfortunately, the death penalty will probably not be invoked. He can, however, expect to spend time in prison and then be dishonourably discharged without benefits.'

Tom Mackenzie picked up the cigarette paper.

'Be careful with it,' Chafer said.

Tom turned the paper over in his fingers.

'You might care to read this as well.'

'This' was a document comprising two typed pages detailing the meeting that had taken place between Winslow and Clive Kent. Underlined, doubtless for Tom's benefit, was the claim that Winslow had raised a glass in a toast to 'the heavenly sovereign, Emperor Hirohito'. The report stressed that Winslow had made the rendezvous without any pressure being applied to him, and that in the course of the conversation he had freely offered support and sympathy for both the people of Japan and for their military representatives. The language was carefully unemotive. Tom Mackenzie had no way of knowing that it didn't, in fact, represent the truth of the meeting and that it contained damaging statements that Winslow had not uttered. He was confused. Nothing in the report correlated to the man he thought he knew.

Did he know him, though? How could he really? He'd worked with him for a brief period, and socialised with him once or twice. He'd seemed so decent and honest about his love for Japan, but he'd also made his loathing for its militarism clear. Maude had liked him, and Tom trusted his sister's judgement about people. He pushed the material back across the desk to Chafer. 'I don't believe any of this. Can I talk to Winslow?'

'Of course not. He's being detained pending a court martial. And let me give you some advice, Mackenzie. I wouldn't go about defending Fazackerly if I were you. You might get a reputation that won't do you any favours.'

'Are you threatening me, Chafer?'

'I'm giving you a friendly warning. I'd heed it. Don't imagine for a minute that you're above suspicion.'

'You're a real little Napoleon, aren't you? One day you might need friends. Do you have any?'

Chafer's lips moved in the approximation of a smile.

'I have enemies,' he said. 'You know where you are with them.'

'You're a sad little person.'

Tom stood up and left Chafer's office. When he returned to his own office, he telephoned Maude Lambert. He needed to talk to her.

Inspector Lambert had taken statements from the two sisters, who gave their real names but insisted on being called Prudence and Justice. Their frankness had been unexpected. He'd assumed that they would try to secure Prescott's release by covering for him. Instead they each gave evidence that allowed him to formally charge Prescott with being an accessory to murder. Prudence revealed that Emilio Barbero had been at Prescott's orchard just a day before he was found hanging on Fisher's veranda. She said that she'd only realised that Pinshott might have killed him after Guy Kirkham's body had been found. Emilio and Guy had one thing in common, she said: they'd each entered the forbidden space of the women's retreat. Pinshott did nothing without Prescott's direction, so if he murdered Emilio, it was because Prescott had ordered him to, and the same went for Guy. And Nepheg? Oh, poor, silly Nepheg. No, he wasn't implicated in any of this. He was a bit dull-witted and easily led, but not bright enough to be trusted with anything demanding or important.

Titus interviewed each of the women separately, and released them, letting them know, however, that he would need to speak to them again. With Prescott charged, Titus allowed himself to feel some satisfaction, but nothing could assuage his sense of having failed Zachary Wilson. He telephoned Maude after Prescott, whose equanimity had been unruffled by the charge, had been taken back to his cell in the watch house. It was Maude who suggested that he bring Constable Forbes home for dinner.

'Tom rang me,' she said. 'He's coming, too. He's had a bad day, although he wouldn't say why over the telephone.'

'He mightn't appreciate a stranger being there if he wants to talk.'

'He might appreciate some decent conversation. I'll ring him back, though, and let him know there's going to be another person here. He can make up his own mind.'

Titus was relieved that Maude seemed to have moved on from being overprotective of her brother. It meant that she felt secure in his recovery from the ghastly injuries he'd suffered the previous year.

'I'll try to be home by 6.30. I'll bring Constable Forbes with me.'

14

WHEN CLARA DAWSON arrived at the Royal Melbourne Hospital to begin her shift, she found a message from Adelaide Matthews, asking her to telephone at her earliest convenience. She did so at 9.30 pm. It was clear from the slight slurring of her words that Adelaide had been drinking. She wondered if Clara might like to come to the house the following afternoon. She'd make afternoon tea. Nothing fancy, and Clara could meet the children. Clara declined the offer, saying that after a week of night shifts her plans for the weekend involved nothing more demanding than sleep.

'I see,' Adelaide said, snippily. 'Perhaps another time. I didn't realise afternoon tea was considered demanding.' She hung up.

Clara had no time to analyse the oddness of this response, as she was immediately called to an emergency. Later, when she was able to think about the telephone call, she wondered if that one meeting with Adelaide had created an erroneous impression that some sort of friendship had been forged between them. She felt vaguely guilty, as if she might be failing to support Adelaide in her grief. But she barely knew her. The only connection between them was the death of her husband, and that wasn't a pleasant connection. Both Titus and Helen had warned her about creating any sort of relationship with Adelaide Matthews. Perhaps they'd been right after all.

✳

Tom Mackenzie had half an hour alone with Maude Lambert before Titus arrived home with Alexander Forbes. It was enough time to tell her all he knew about Winslow Fazackerly's situation. He'd remembered the note, word for word, and Maude agreed that if it was authentic it was an extraordinarily clumsy and risky expression of disloyalty.

'My problem with it,' she said, 'is that it simply doesn't *sound* like Winslow. There's nothing of his voice in it.'

Tom pointed out that Chafer had said that it was a translation from the Japanese that Winslow had written, and that would account for the strangeness of the tone.

'There's also the witness,' Tom said. 'There's no question in my mind that it was entrapment. It was a set-up. The bloke who laid the bait is an Intelligence agent, but Winslow took the bait, and walked into the trap.'

'The bait was his wife, if the people you spoke to at Loveday were telling the truth. Do you know this Intelligence person?'

'No. I haven't come across him, but if he's in cahoots with Chafer, I wouldn't trust him as far as I can throw him.'

'Why was Chafer so suspicious of Winslow? Are we missing something, Tom? Did he fool us? Was his charm and openness an effective disguise?'

'Chafer tried to recruit him, and he wasn't interested. As far as Chafer was concerned, Winslow was guilty of treason at that point.'

'I honestly don't know what to think.'

'You know what I hate, Maudey? I hate feeling like I've been played.'

'By Chafer or Winslow?'

'Possibly by both of them. Definitely by Chafer. I wish I could talk to Winslow, but that's not going to happen.'

'He must be feeling dreadfully alone.'

The conversation about Winslow Fazackerly came to an end when Maude told Tom that Guy Kirkham had been murdered and that Joe Sable had come close to losing his life.

'Why wasn't I told about this?'

'I telephoned your house. There was no answer, and the only information I could get out of Victoria Barracks was that you were interstate. They wouldn't tell me where or for how long.'

Maude gave Tom as much information as she had, and as she spoke his feelings about Chafer turned blacker than ever. It had been Chafer's fault that Tom had been in South Australia when these dreadful things had happened. He'd been sent on a wild-goose chase. No, it hadn't even been that — it had simply been a way of getting him out from underfoot when the trap that caught Winslow was sprung. Had he been here in Melbourne, he might have been able to do something for Joe. He had no idea what, but *something*. He would certainly have been able to give Helen Lord some sort of support. What must she think of him? His preoccupation with Winslow had pushed thoughts of Helen to the back of his mind. Now they tumbled forward, and he recognised again that there was something about Helen Lord that interested him. It was suddenly important that she understand why he hadn't been in contact. A telephone call didn't seem sufficient. He'd ask to borrow Titus's car and drive out to Kew after dinner.

Alexander Forbes looked out of place over dinner. This was simply the result of his being in uniform. Undoing the top buttons of his jacket helped a little. His presence constrained Tom from talking about Winslow Fazackerly, but it didn't constrain Titus from revealing details of that day's interviews. The fact that Titus had invited him for dinner — an indifferent meal, given Maude's limited culinary skills — and that he permitted

Alexander to see how unguarded he was in conversation with Maude about his work was evidence enough of Titus's level of trust in the young man.

'Do you prefer Alexander, Alex, Alec?' she asked.

'Family and friends call me Alexander. I rarely get called Alex, and whenever I do it takes a moment to realise it's me.'

Alexander didn't find Maude's questions intrusive, although he was aware that she was inserting them into the conversation at discreet intervals to avoid any feeling that this was an interrogation. He knew the bare bones of Tom Mackenzie's history with Joe Sable — Titus had sketched this in. Without this, he would have wondered at Tom's intense interest in the case.

'So you met this Pinshott character?' Tom asked.

'Briefly. Inspector Lambert and I spoke with him and Anthony Prescott.'

'Did he seem crazy?'

Alexander thought for a moment.

'No. He was dressed like a cut-rate prophet and he was protective of Prescott, but he seemed like a businessman to me. I think he saw Prescott at least partly as a financial asset. That might be because I can't bring myself to believe that anyone with a modicum of intelligence would accept Anthony Prescott as the incarnation of the Messiah.'

'History is littered with people who do believe such things,' Maude said.

'They're always damaged in some profound way, I think. The exploiter and the exploited, although I suppose it might not always be that straightforward.'

'For Pinshott to murder Guy with such ritualistic care and relish has more than a whiff of religious fanaticism about it.'

'That's true,' Alexander said. 'I have a tendency to over-simplify.'

Maude could see that Titus was exhausted, so the evening wound up at nine o'clock. Titus was happy to lend Tom his car. There was half a tank of fuel in it, which would be plenty to get Tom to Kew and back, as well as to drop Alexander off in Fitzroy on the way. Maude and Titus left the dishes, and were in bed by 9.30.

'Alexander seems like a very sharp man,' Maude said.

'I won't have him for long. I wouldn't have him at all if we weren't undermanned. He's ambitious. As soon as the war is over, he'll go to detective school. I wouldn't be surprised if he ended up being commissioner.'

'He'll be wasted. He'd make a brilliant detective, and we need brilliant detectives. We need people who can protect us from the Prescotts and the Pinshotts of this world.'

'Those people are rare. How do we protect wives from their husbands? I've said it before, and every day confirms it, we are a truly ghastly species.'

'Don't despair, Titus. Please, please don't despair.'

At 11.00 pm, Clara was called down to the ground floor desk at the Royal Melbourne Hospital. The duty nurse told her that a man had left her a package. He hadn't stayed. He'd said it was a gift and that he didn't want to trouble Dr Dawson while she was on duty.

'Are you sure he's gone?' Clara said.

'Oh yes, doctor. He left as soon as he handed me the package.'

'Did he leave a name?'

'No. I got the impression he thought you'd know who it was from.'

'Thank you, sister. I'll be right down.'

Clara put down the telephone. She hadn't liked the slightly

lubricious tone of the duty nurse's final remark, as if she'd discovered that Clara had an admirer.

When Clara came downstairs, Sister Kelly handed her the small package. Clara didn't much care for Sister Kelly. She was an untidy woman, slovenly, and she was among those nurses who disapproved of women doctors. Clara didn't know it, but Sister Kelly, on more than one occasion, had speculated during her tea break that Dr Dawson might be a lesbian. The idea had shocked and titillated her listeners. Now she had a morsel of proper gossip to impart.

'The man who left this, what did he look like?'

'Well, quite presentable, although he needed a shave, and he had a bruise on his face. Dark hair. Nice eyes. He seemed quite nervous, like a suitor.'

'Like a what?' Clara snapped.

Sister Kelly blushed.

'I didn't mean anything by that, doctor. I just meant I got the impression that the parcel was a gift, a personal gift.'

Sister Kelly was hoping that Dr Dawson would unwrap the parcel in front of her. It was obviously a book, wrapped in brown paper and tied with string. It hadn't been carefully wrapped, but men were hopeless at that sort of thing, Sister Kelly thought. Still, it was romantic, wasn't it, to give someone a book? It might be a book of poems. That would be doubly romantic. If it was poems, she'd know for sure that the man with the bruise was in love with Dr Dawson.

Clara took the parcel and returned upstairs. In her small office, she placed it on the table and looked at it. She was called away before she could open it, and didn't have a spare moment for another three hours. It was well after midnight when she picked it up and weighed its heft in her hand. She turned it over. There was no writing on the brown paper. She handled it as if it were a bomb, feeling along its edges, reluctant to discover its identity. Finally, she cut the string and tore away the paper. It was a volume of Shakespeare's sonnets. It had every appearance of being second-hand. There was no dust jacket, and the cover was battered. On the flyleaf was the name 'Kenneth Bussell' and an address in Rockhampton, in Queensland. There was a handwritten note poking out from among the pages. Clara pulled it out, and then worried that she ought to have been more careful about preserving fingerprints. The note was short, and written in a well-formed hand:

My dear Dr Dawson,
This isn't much, but I don't have much. I move around and can't afford the burden of things. I always carry this with me. I consider it my most precious possession, and so I wanted you to have it. It's just to say thank you for your kindness at the hospital and for your graciousness in dealing with that awful other doctor. He was a terrible man. I've met many like him. I despise them.

You were gentle. I was boorish; more boorish than normal. I can't help thinking, for example, that you've seen my private parts, which makes the intimacy between us unequal — a situation I'd like to correct. Please read sonnet 29. It tells you all you need to know about me. I'll be in touch, Kenneth Bussell.

Clara re-read the note, disturbed by its disorienting mix of careful phrasing and casual obscenity. It was a confession of sorts, too. The reference to Dr Matthews was unambiguous in its hatred of him. That final 'I'll be in touch' was terrifying. What was in sonnet 29? Clara found it. It was one she remembered from school:

When, in disgrace with fortune and men's eyes,
I all alone beweep my outcast state,
And trouble deaf heaven with my bootless cries,
And look upon myself and curse my fate ...

She hurried through to the final two lines:

For thy sweet love remembered such wealth brings
That then I scorn to change my state with kings.

She'd never thought of this sonnet as sinister, but its association with Kenneth Bussell made it so. It was a declaration of love, and that opening verse was as good as a confession to murder. How else could you interpret 'disgrace'?

HOSPITALS AT NIGHT, even with wards filled with snoring patients, are unsettling places. There are dark corners and empty corridors, and they produce sounds whose echoes come from unexpected places. Kenneth Bussell's love token — for that was clearly what it was — created an air of disgust that played on Clara's nerves. She kept expecting him to emerge from a shadow, or touch her shoulder, or breathe down her neck. She ought to have felt safe inside the hospital. She didn't, and so she spent the rest of her shift moving to wherever she could see a nurse or orderly. The privacy of her office, even though she shared it with two other doctors, and which she valued as a place she could retreat to, now made her feel isolated and vulnerable. Should she ring D24? No. This was hardly an emergency.

An unexpected consequence of Bussell's gift was that Clara felt guilty about declining Adelaide Matthews' invitation to afternoon tea. Perhaps the intensity of her feelings made her sympathetic to the intensity of Matthews' feelings. It was just afternoon tea, after all, and having it with the one other person with a connection to Kenneth Bussell (a grim one) felt like it might be reassuring somehow. She'd telephone Adelaide as soon as she got home. She wasn't looking forward to the walk home. Maybe she should telephone Helen before she left the hospital and ask her to drive in and take her home. Yes, she decided, yes. Helen wouldn't mind.

Tom Mackenzie dropped Alexander Forbes in Fitzroy, and drove on to Helen's house in Kew. He'd only been there on a couple of occasions, and its size and extravagance still amazed him. It was 9.30 pm when he knocked on the door. He was expected. Ros Lord opened the door and welcomed him, unexpectedly, with a kiss on the cheek.

'I kiss people now,' she said. 'Life is too short not to kiss people I like.'

That simple kiss shrank the grand dimensions of the entrance vestibule to comfortable domesticity. When Ros took Tom into the library, the first thing he saw was the back of Joe's bandaged head.

'The bandage has become an item of clothing for you, hasn't it?'

'You can talk,' Joe said, getting up from his chair.

Helen stood and greeted Tom, and said that she'd go upstairs to bed and leave them to it. Tom said, 'No, no. please stay. I'd like to talk to you as well as Joe.'

Ros Lord reappeared, carrying three brandy balloons on a tray.

'I'm trying to teach my palate to like brandy,' Helen said. 'So far, I'm not succeeding.'

'I, on the other hand, have met with considerable success,' Joe said.

Ros declined the offer to join them, claiming a prior engagement with a radio serial on 3UZ. Throughout the conversation, Tom watched Helen surreptitiously. He liked her face. Expressions moved across it easily. Was she pretty? Most people would say no, but it was a face that was better than merely pretty. It was a face animated by intelligence and curiosity, and the more he looked at it, the stronger his attraction grew. As he watched her, he began to realise that her eyes were focused on Joe. Perhaps it was a sympathetic response to his injury. Or was there something else in her gaze? Tom pressed this thought down. Joe and Helen spoke about the Church of the First Born and about the strange characters who peopled it.

'Are they all capable of murder,' Tom asked, 'even the women?'

'Well,' said Joe, 'remember Voltaire's observation. Those who can make you believe absurdities can make you commit atrocities.'

'That's the history of religion in a single sentence,' Helen said. 'We watched Prudence turning herself into a version of Prescott. I found it disconcerting. There'll be people lining up to be duped by her. She calls herself the Mother. It sounds benign, doesn't it?'

'It's a long, long way from the benign,' Joe said.

'Alexander Forbes said he got the impression that the Church of the First Born is essentially a business.'

'That's what we thought,' Joe said, 'and that was an underestimation that cost Guy his life. It's a business, of course it is, but a man like Walter Pinshott believes — genuinely, insanely believes — that Prescott is the chosen one. He's invested his whole intelligence, his whole sense of self in the bullshit that Prescott peddles.'

'No one knows better than you two where fanaticism leads,' Helen said.

'The Jews in Europe are finding out all about where fanatical belief leads,' Joe said.

Tom was tempted to tell them about Winslow Fazackerly. It wasn't the restrictions imposed by the *Crimes Act* that stopped him doing so. It was the sense that there was no room at this moment for a story that competed with the awful gravity of Guy Kirkham's death.

'How are you going to find Pinshott?' Tom asked.

'Someone is sheltering him,' Helen said, 'and that someone is likely to be a member of the Church, and somewhere there is a ledger with all their names and addresses. It's a small congregation, so Prescott would want to keep track of the ... what's the word?'

'Tithes,' said Joe.

'The police would have done a full search, but they might have missed it. It might be a single piece of paper or a thin notebook, tucked away somewhere.'

'I'd like to see inside the women's hut,' Joe said.

'You're not going near that place again, Joe, at least not on your own.'

'What about me?' Tom said. 'No one knows who I am out there. I could ...'

'No!' Helen said with a fierceness that was sudden and that neither Tom nor Joe was expecting. 'No one is going out there alone, or under cover. We don't know how dangerous these women are, and we know nothing about that young man.'

'He hasn't been arrested,' Tom said. 'Titus doesn't think he was involved in any of the violence.'

Helen took a sip of her brandy and made a face.

'It's cough medicine.'

Tom left the Lord house at midnight. He was glad he'd come. He felt reconnected with Joe, and he was now certain that his feelings for Helen were real. This didn't feel like a schoolboy crush. Her focused attention on Joe was a concern, although he was convinced it wasn't reciprocated. Joe seemed unaware of it.

He thought all this over on the drive back to the Lamberts' house, where he was to spend the night. Suddenly, it occurred to him that there might be something he could do to help find Walter Pinshott. He understood Helen's admonition that no one should go out to Prescott's orchard, but it sprang from her fear for Joe's safety and probably some guilt about Guy Kirkham's death. Such feelings of guilt would be misplaced, but Helen was the type of person who would shoulder the blame, not shift it onto someone else. He, Tom, wasn't an employee of Helen Lord and Associates, so he was under no obligation to follow her directions. The thought of actually doing something energised him. He was feeling miserable about the whole Winslow Fazackerly affair. He hated his job, and he loathed Tom Chafer. The possibility of finding that list of names offered a sense of redemption. In a way, he convinced himself, this wasn't just to impress Helen Lord; it was also an opportunity to prove something to himself.

As DAYLIGHT BEGAN to drive out the shadows in the hospital corridors and corners, Clara felt less trepidation about walking home. She'd intended to telephone Helen, but decided it wouldn't be necessary to bother her. She checked the street before she set off. There was no sign of Bussell. She walked quickly to Russell Street Police Headquarters, and left the copy of Shakespeare's sonnets at the desk, with a note for Inspector Lambert. It was just after 7.00 am, and although he was expected, he hadn't yet arrived. *Does he ever take a day off?* Clara wondered. When she left the police building, she again checked the street for Bussell. There were a handful of people on the pavements, each walking purposefully. As Clara began to walk towards East Melbourne, a car slowed down as it passed her, which made her heart race. It stopped just ahead of her. She, too, stopped. The passenger door opened and a woman got out, waved goodbye to the driver, and closed the door. The relief made Clara smile at her jumpiness.

When she reached home, she was glad to discover that the front door was locked, even though it was Saturday morning. Pat, God bless her, had got the message about keeping it locked. When she entered the house, the smell of bacon frying calmed her nerves. She dropped her bag in her room and went into the kitchen. Susan was there. Pat, apparently, was still asleep. This was the normal, comforting routine. On the weekend, Susan never slept in, and Pat almost always did. There was, however, something rather tense in Susan's face.

'There's a letter for you,' she said. 'It was pushed under the front door. There was no name on the envelope, so I'm sorry, but I read it.'

'That's all right. I would have done the same. It's from him, isn't it?'

Susan nodded.

'We're not leaving here, Clara; just so you know. We're not going to let this man scare us out of our house.'

'Thanks, Susan. I do feel as though I've brought this bastard into all our lives.'

Clara picked the envelope up from where Susan had placed it on the table. Inside it was a folded piece of paper. It was good-quality paper, as if it had been taken from an expensive stationery box. Printed in purple ink were the words, 'Ungrateful bitches are as useless as arrogant bastards.' Clara's first thought was that Bussell must have expected her to go looking for him outside the hospital as soon as she received the book. This ugly little note was how he dealt with that disappointment. The volatility of his emotions was frightening.

'I feel like I'm under siege. Why is the world so full of arseholes?'

'Because half the world is made up of men,' Susan said.

Clara managed to laugh, and it felt so good she hugged Susan in appreciation.

'I'm going up to Carlton in a few hours. I'll drop this in to the police on the way. I'm going to try to get a couple of hours' sleep. Are you and Pat going to be around?'

'I don't know about Pat, but I'll be here, and I'll keep an eye out for any men loitering out the front.'

Clara telephoned Adelaide Matthews. She sounded groggy, as if the call had woken her; given how early it was, Clara supposed that this was the case. It took a moment for Adelaide to understand that it was Clara Dawson whom she was speaking to. When Clara said she could come for afternoon tea after all, the tone of Adelaide's simple 'Oh' was indicative of having been taken aback.

'I'm sorry, have you made other plans?'

'No. It's just …'

'Well, another time perhaps.'

'No, no. This afternoon would be lovely. I'm half-asleep.' She laughed. 'You must think I'm a slug-abed.'

'Not at all, Adelaide. Saturday mornings should be for sleeping in. Only barbarians and shift workers should be awake at this hour.'

It was a mollifying thing to say, considering that it wasn't really very early at all. They agreed that Clara would arrive at 2.30 and that there was no need for her to bring anything.

The presence of Susan and Pat in the house meant that Clara felt sufficiently secure to lie on her bed, close her eyes, and attempt to relax.

When, in disgrace with fortune and men's eyes,
I all alone beweep my outcast state …

These verses insinuated themselves into her dozing brain, and she couldn't shake them.

Tom Mackenzie didn't own a car. His brother-in-law had been generous enough to lend him his car to drive from Brunswick to Kew and back. Even this distance made a significant dent in the amount of fuel in the tank, and Tom knew that Titus wouldn't be keen on his petrol ration being exhausted by a further drive out to distant Nunawading. In any case, Titus wouldn't sanction Tom's idea of snooping around Prescott's property in search of a registry of members of the Church of the First Born.

Having stayed the night in Brunswick, Tom shared breakfast and the newspapers with Titus and Maude. Amongst the news of an Allied victory at Cassino was the more mundane excitement that the first consignment of new season's navel oranges had arrived in Melbourne. Tom mentioned this as he turned the pages. Maude was interested.

'The thing I like about oranges,' she said, 'is that you don't have to cook them.'

Tom's eye fell on an advertisement on page four:

Hire cars are obtainable, for business purposes only. 'Drive Yourself' cars from Latrobe Motors Pty. Ltd. 182 Exhibition Street.

There was no telephone number, but the exchange would find that for him. This would be expensive, and he'd have to manufacture some sort of ersatz business, but money would encourage the proprietors to suspend due diligence. Maude asked him if Winslow Fazackerly's imprisonment was preying on his mind as actively as it was on hers.

'It bothers me, but it's not preying on my mind.'

'I've been thinking about it all night. I know I only met him once, but I loved the way he spoke about his wife, and the clear-

232

headed way he talked about Japan. Whatever he did was driven by his love for his wife, not hatred for his country. He's not a traitor, Tom. Please don't abandon him. This is a terrible injustice.'

'Is it? I was just getting used to the idea that I'd been taken in. I prefer that to worrying about an innocent man. I have no way of finding out anything. I can't even find out where he's being held.'

'Can't you break into Chafer's office and rifle through his drawers?'

'Not unless I want to share a cell with Winslow. There are a couple of decent blokes in Intelligence, though. Maybe I can make discreet inquiries.'

On the tram down Sydney Road, Tom thought about approaching either Benjamin Newman or Vincent Deighton. They'd been polite to him and they shared his opinion of Tom Chafer. But he had no real relationship with either man, and what would be in it for them to risk censure by giving him information? He wished Maude hadn't been so adamant about Winslow's innocence. He trusted her judgement, so now he couldn't comfortably consign Winslow to the pariah status of traitor.

When he reached home, he telephoned and was put through to Latrobe Motors. They'd be open until 5.00 pm, and Tom would need to bring proof of his legitimate business. He needed a car, he said, to run out to see a client in the eastern suburbs, and his own car was off the road.

'I had two blowouts,' he said, 'and I just can't get replacement tyres.'

The man on the other end of the line assured Tom that their cars were reliable, although they weren't new cars, and the tyres were reconditioned. Fuel would have to come out of Tom's allocation, which was fine as he hadn't had reason to use it, and he was able to purchase fuel to cover at least 80 miles. There were two small hitches. The first was that he wasn't in any sort of business; the second was that he didn't know where Prescott's orchard was. Money would overcome the first, and he hoped that his friendship with Joe Sable would solve the second.

The proprietor of Latrobe Motors was a man in his late sixties. He was smartly dressed, and his small selection of cars were polished and looked to be in good order. He'd been in the business before the war, and, with the recent relaxation of regulations around the use and availability of commercial vehicles, he thought he'd reopen the enterprise. Uptake had been slow, he admitted. As they weren't permitted to hire out cars for recreational purposes, they depended on businesses whose own vehicles had become unroadworthy or undrivable. He made a feint at checking Tom's credentials, but allowed him to fumble in his wallet and declare he'd forgotten to bring his paperwork without pushing him too hard. He accepted Tom's verbal assurance and the £10.00 above the hiring fee that Tom included.

Tom had chosen to visit Latrobe Motors close to 5.00 pm. He thought this might encourage the owner to squeeze in a sale before closing. He decided not to give Joe advance warning of his intentions, and drove out towards Kew without telephoning first.

15

CLARA WAS HALF-EXPECTING Adelaide Matthews to answer the door with a drink in her hand. As it happened, when she opened the door she wasn't drunk, but she was definitely angry. In fact, she was so angry she didn't speak. She simply retreated into the house with the expectation that Clara would follow. In the front room, Adelaide stood with her hands clenched at her sides, and composed herself.

'I'm sorry, Clara, what must you think of me? You caught us at a bad time.'

'Us?'

'I'm afraid my children have been misbehaving, my son especially. He's been impossible. I've sent them upstairs.'

She didn't elaborate, and Clara didn't press her to. Other people's children were of little interest to her.

'Thank you for coming,' Adelaide said. Despite her best efforts, a small quiver of hot rage remained in her voice. 'I'll get the tea things.'

When she returned and began pouring the tea, she said, 'The funeral was ghastly, really ghastly.'

'I'm sorry. I didn't know the funeral had happened.'

'It was yesterday. There was hardly anybody there, which isn't surprising. Gerald didn't have many friends, and I don't think his colleagues liked him much. It was all rather grim. But at least it's over and done with.'

'It must have been difficult.'

'To be perfectly honest, Clara, I was more embarrassed by the small turnout than upset.'

The brutal honesty of this remark embarrassed Clara. It was the kind of thing you might say to an intimate friend who would know you well enough to interpret it sympathetically.

'How did your children manage?'

'Well, they hardly knew their father, so I think they found it all rather boring. I didn't bring them to the cemetery. What would have been the point of that?'

Clara had no answer. She saw that no pictures had been put up to replace the Norman Lindsays that had been taken down.

'You haven't chosen your pictures yet.'

Adelaide looked around the room.

'No. I rather like the blank walls, actually. Gerald would have hated the way this room now looks.'

'You must miss him.'

Adelaide laughed.

'Oh, Clara. I don't miss him at all. He's dead and buried, and suddenly I like living in this house. I feel like I can breathe. I know I told you that he loved me and that he loved the children, but as soon as he was safely in the ground, I realised that he didn't really.'

'Surely he loved the children?'

Adelaide suddenly seemed slightly drunk, although Clara hadn't seen her drink any alcohol.

'He was pleased when Cornel was born. A boy, you see. He made no effort to hide his disappointment when Violet was born. He was so disdainful of females that he couldn't see the point of them. Here was Violet, this beautiful child, and all Gerald could do was moan about the pointless expense of educating her. As Cornel began to grow up, Gerald dismissed him from his affections too. He got it into his head that Cornel was queer.'

'How old is Cornel?'

'He's just turned ten. Gerald began to insist that he was homosexual when the poor child was only six. It was the way he held his cutlery, and then it was the way he walked, and how timid he was.'

Clara began to feel out of her depth as this confessional rush poured out of Adelaide. Surely this wasn't the sort of thing you shared with someone on just a second meeting. It was so awful, and so private.

'Adelaide, are you sure you want to tell me these things?'

The question startled Adelaide.

'Why, of course. You're the only person who really knows what sort of man my husband was. I know I can trust you, and if I don't talk to someone I think I might burst into flames. You do see that, don't you?'

Clara didn't see that at all, and at this moment what she wanted most in the world was to be anywhere but here.

'I didn't really know Gerald,' she said.

'You know he hated you. So that's something about Gerald we have in common. He hated me, too.'

'His opinion of me honestly didn't bother me.'

'It bothered *me*.'

Adelaide seemed on the edge of hysteria. 'He went on endlessly about you. Every night. You were like the third person in our marriage.'

'I'm sorry.'

'Oh please, don't be sorry. The more he railed against you, the closer I felt to you, and I'd never even met you. It's odd, isn't it? I should keep my voice down. Cornel and Violet shouldn't hear their mother talking about their father like this. They're hanging onto the childish belief that Gerald loved them. I'm afraid I tried to disabuse them of this just before you arrived. Cornel said some awful things to me. I hate to say it, Clara, but I could hear Gerald in his voice, and I lost my temper.'

'Are they all right?'

'Oh yes. I'll fix it all up after you leave.'

Clara began to feel slightly dizzy, and decided she couldn't bear to be in the room with Adelaide Matthews a moment longer. She stood up, and said simply that she needed to get home in order to sleep. Adelaide stood, too, and made no attempt to detain her. She walked her to the door.

'I'm afraid this hasn't been very enjoyable,' Adelaide said, 'but I'm so grateful to you for listening. You will come around again, won't you? We'll only talk about amusing things, I promise.'

Clara said nothing, and offered only a weak smile. Adelaide kissed her on the cheek.

'You will come again, won't you?'

'Yes, of course.'

Clara took the gamble that Helen might be in her office despite it being Saturday. As she made her way there, she cursed herself for having said, 'Yes, of course,' in answer to Adelaide Matthews' question, instead of, 'You have to be fucking kidding me.'

CLARA TOLD HELEN that if she drank any more tea her kidneys would collapse.

Helen made herself a cup while Clara told her about Bussell's gift and his subsequent brutish note. Helen insisted, yet again, that Clara move into the Kew house until Bussell had been found, and Clara, yet again, refused.

'He's not going to drive me out of my home, Helen. Besides, he hasn't actually threatened me, has he? He's allegedly in love with me.'

'It's a dangerous kind of love, though, isn't it?'

'Speaking of dangerous kinds of love, how's Joe?'

Helen let that pass, and said that she'd insisted he stay home. He'd said at breakfast that he had a slight headache, and, as he never complained of pain, Helen took this to mean that the headache was severe. Clara said that she was worried by this and that she'd like to check on him. They decided that she should sleep in the office for a few hours, and go home with Helen for dinner.

Clara tried to make her summary of afternoon tea with Adelaide Matthews amusing, but the unsettling nature of it resisted humour. Adelaide was as frightening in her way as Bussell.

'I don't know if her husband's death has unhinged her, or if she was hingeless before he died. I'm pretty sure she's an alcoholic. Her children are probably safer in their boarding school than they are at home.'

'You think they're in danger?'

Clara thought about this for a moment.

'Not physical danger, no, but psychological danger, definitely. Those poor bloody kids. They really lost the lottery when it came to parents.'

'You should have no further contact with her, Clar.'

'Should I warn her about Kenneth Bussell?'

'No, absolutely not. Why would you even think about doing that?'

'I don't know. In case he shifts his attention from me to her.'

'He probably doesn't even know she exists. Bussell killed Dr Matthews because of the way he treated you. He made that perfectly clear when he left that little trophy outside your door, and that book of sonnets just adds to the creepiness.'

'I'm not having much luck with men, am I? You know I had dinner with Guy.'

'I did not know that.'

'I liked him. I would have gone out with him again, I think.'

Helen found this news rather astonishing.

'Why didn't you say something?'

'Well, you know, it was all very tentative and uncertain, and then he died.'

They sat in silence for a moment.

'He was a bit of a mess,' Clara said. 'Narcolepsy is a strange condition.'

'He had the most terrible nightmares. I never said anything, but you could hear him crying out, all through the house.'

'Does Joe have nightmares?'

'I don't know, Clar. I've never spent the night with him. If he does, they're not loud enough to hear.'

'Tell me, Helen, what do you see in Joe Sable?'

Only Clara could have asked that question and not been rebuffed.

'I see a decent man, and I've seen him hold on to his decency in awful circumstances. He's brave.'

'Bravery matters to you, doesn't it?'

'Not if it means taking foolish risks. It's old-fashioned, but one of the things I most admired about my father was his steadfastness.'

'Now there's a word you don't hear very often.'

'And before you jump to any amateur psychological conclusions, I don't like Joe because he reminds me of my father. He doesn't. He looks nothing like him, for a start.'

'Is he good looking, do you think?'

Helen laughed.

'Your tone suggests you don't think he is.'

'Guy was better looking, you have to admit.'

'Well, Dr Dawson, your essential shallowness is finally out in the open.'

Clara shrugged.

'I'm easily seduced by shiny things, Helen.'

'And Joe isn't sufficiently shiny for you?'

'Well, he has no idea how to talk to women, and that takes the shine off.'

'What do you mean? He's never rude.'

'That's not what I meant. He's awkward, like a schoolboy. I know he's well educated and knows a lot about art and books, but honestly, have you ever had a proper, decent conversation with him?'

'Of course I have.'

'I don't mean about work. I mean about, I don't know, life.'

Helen's silence made Clara think she'd gone too far. She wasn't sure why she'd begun asking these questions.

'I'm sorry. It's really none of my business.'

'You're right, though, Clar. We only ever talk about work, but that's not just Joe's fault. It's mine, too. I find it difficult not to correct other people's opinions.'

Although this was said with seriousness, it provoked a burst of delighted laughter from Clara, and Helen joined her.

'Oh, Helen, that is so fucking funny.'

'I don't think Joe finds it funny.'

'If you wait for him to make a move, you'll wait till hell freezes over. If you want anything to happen between you and Joe, you're going to have to be grown-up about it and take charge.'

'Oh, God, Clar, what if he's appalled?'

'Then you'll know he's a moron, and you can stop mooning over him.'

'You're a wise woman, Clara Dawson.'

As Tom Mackenzie walked up the path towards the Lord house, Joe called his name and emerged from behind a tree, a set of hedge-clippers in his hands.

'Ah, the nobility of physical labour,' Tom said. It was just before 5.00 pm, and the air was cool. It was getting darker earlier with each passing day, and a thick cloud-cover added to the gloom.

'How can you see what you're doing?'

'I was just finishing up. What are you doing here? It's good to see you. Come inside. I'll clean myself up and we'll have a drink. In fact, stay for dinner. Ros won't mind, and Helen should be home any minute.'

Once inside, Joe went upstairs to wash and change his clothes. Ros Lord sat with Tom, and asked polite questions about his life and how it was all going. He decided to relieve her of the need to be discreet.

'I'm almost fully recovered, Mrs Lord, apart from this.' He held up the strapped fingers of his left hand. 'This is annoyingly slow to heal.'

'You look very well.'

'Underneath this shirt is the unsightly legacy of a scald. It's not painful anymore, except to look at.'

'My husband had a dreadful burn scar across one shoulder. He was caught in a house fire when he was about 12 years old. I always thought it was a part of the biography of his body. He hated it. I couldn't have imagined him without it.'

'It's hard to accept your own ruined flesh.'

'I suppose that's true. I'm very sorry about your friend, Guy Kirkham.'

'He was Joe's friend, really. I only met him a handful of times.'

Somehow this seemed mean-spirited, so he added, 'I'm sure we would have become good friends, although he might have found my lack of culture irritating.'

'I liked having him here in this house. It's far too big for just Helen and me. Thank goodness Joe is here, but he'll get his own place eventually. My brother, Peter, lived here on his own for years. I think he was very glad to take me and Helen in, though. He liked his own company, but he liked mine, too. We would talk and talk.'

'You must miss him.'

'Terribly. Every day. I know Joe misses Guy. He doesn't talk about it, but you know, don't you, when there's sadness behind a person's eyes? He's angry, too, and anger sometimes makes people do reckless things.' She lowered her voice. 'Will you watch out for him, Tom?'

Tom marvelled at Ros Lord's intuition. Somehow she knew that this wasn't just a social visit. No wonder Helen's intelligence was so sharp, given that she'd grown up in this woman's orbit.

'I'll do my best, Mrs Lord.'

'Promise me.'

'I promise.'

Ros smiled and patted Tom's knee. 'Thank you. I'll get some sherry.' As she walked away, she turned and said, 'Don't be too hard on yourself when you break that promise, Tom. I'll put the sherry in the library.'

When Joe came into the library he was wearing clothes that were both casual and expensive.

'I thought you lost all your coupons when your flat burned down.'

'Peter Lillee doesn't own any cheap clothes. I've just assumed complete control of his wardrobe now. As Helen said, trousers and suits don't look good on her.'

Ros Lord returned with the sherry, and then discreetly left the two men alone.

'I'd never drunk sherry in my life,' Tom said, 'until I visited this house.'

'Neither had I. It's amazing how quickly it seems essential to daily life. How are you, Tom?'

'It's you with the bandage around your head. How are *you*?'

'I'm fine, I think. I woke up with a pounding headache, but it's pretty much gone now.'

They talked about Guy, with Joe acknowledging that Guy's mental state had been fragile.

'He was almost the same Guy Kirkham who I knew at university, but he wasn't quite.'

'There was that incident in New Guinea, wasn't there? An accident.'

'Yes, but there'd been something before that, something he never told me about. It gave him night terrors, and it may have precipitated his narcolepsy. He was drinking quite heavily, but he was getting back to something like his old self, I thought.'

'I would have liked to get to know him better.'

'I want to catch the man who killed him, Tom. I mean, I don't just want him caught, *I* want to catch him.'

Tom leaned forward in his chair and told Joe why he'd come. Joe's face showed his excitement.

'Helen won't lend us the car unless we can convince her to come with us, and I'm not sure she'll agree. She's very down on herself about Guy's death, and I feel like she's wrapping me in cottonwool.'

'I have a car. I hired one, would you believe?'

In order to avoid Helen's opposition to a visit to Prescott's orchard, they decided to leave for Nunawading then and there. Joe let Ros know that they wouldn't be in for dinner after all. She didn't ask why. The manner in which Tom avoided catching her eye told her they were doing more than just 'going for a spin in a hire car'.

'Don't worry about dinner,' she said. 'It was just mince on toast, and I may have been too generous with the curry powder.'

Ros Lord had indeed been too heavy-handed with the curry powder — a culinary error that bothered neither Helen nor Clara, particularly as both were distracted by the news that Joe and Tom had gone for a 'spin' in a hire car. All three women knew that they were headed for Prescott's orchard in Nunawading. Helen was quietly furious.

'I told Joe to stay away from that place.'

'You sound like a prefect, darling,' Ros said. 'Joe is a grown man, not some girl in the lower fifth.'

Helen felt the reprimand.

'He's also an employee.'

As soon as she'd said this, she realised how pompous it sounded.

'I'm just worried about him, Mum. I know he's desperate to find the man who killed Guy and who nearly killed him, but he has a head injury. It must have been his idea.'

'No. I think it was Tom's, but I'm sure Joe didn't need persuading.'

'Why on earth would Tom Mackenzie want to get involved in this?'

'The motivations of men are usually depressingly simple,' Clara said. 'Instead of speculating, why don't we ask them?'

It took Helen a moment to understand. She smiled.

'What a brilliant idea, Clara. Let's drive out to Nunawading.'

'I don't think women's motivations are any more complicated than men's,' Ros said, looking directly at her daughter.

It was a long drive to Nunawading, and Joe talked easily about Guy and his difficult relationship with his parents.

'His mother is a real piece of work. All Catholic rectitude and no Christian compassion. His friendship with me was incomprehensible to her.'

'Why?'

'I'm Jewish. I killed Jesus. They thought they'd raised a nice, obedient Catholic boy. Guy turned out to be something of a disappointment to them. If they knew half of what he got up to, they'd spontaneously combust. He wasn't interested in farming, which was unmanly of him. I think his father was one of those awful proponents of muscular faith. *Mens Catholica in corpore Catholico.*'

'Is that an expression?'

'I just made it up.'

'I like it. Do we have a plan?'

'It will be well and truly dark by the time we get there. Do we announce ourselves, or do we commit trespass and look inside the women's hut before anything else?'

Working on the assumption that only Prudence and Justice would be on the property, and that the hut would be unlikely to be in use, they decided that an examination of its contents might be quite straightforward.

'Prudence didn't strike me as having surrendered herself to Prescott. I think they were a team, and if there are any documents that might be sensitive, the best place to hide them would be in a place with highly restricted access. No such documents might exist, of course. Still, this feels like I'm doing something.'

Tom parked the car where Joe knew it couldn't be seen, and they walked up the driveway towards the house. There weren't any lights visible, but perhaps they still put up blackouts, or perhaps the women were in the back of the house and saving on electricity by illuminating only the rooms they were in. There was no moon, and the darkness was deep. Joe turned on his torch, but covered much of the light with his hand. They needed its feeble glow to find their way. They crept slowly and carefully to the back of the house, and kept going till they reached the taboo building that was the women's hut. There was no light on in the hut. The blind in the single window was up. It wasn't late, so if either Prudence or Justice was inside, surely she wouldn't be sitting in the dark? They listened for any sound. Nothing. After a minute or so, Joe took the risk of trying the handle. He turned it, half-expecting an exclamation from within. There was silence. There was a bolt, above the door knob, but it was pulled back. The door opened soundlessly, and Joe and Tom slipped inside. They closed the door and stood for a moment in the silence.

'That wasn't too difficult,' Tom whispered.

'Let's do this as fast as we can,' Joe said. They each had a torch. Joe pulled the blind down, and they turned their torches on. As Guy had discovered before them, the room had very little furniture in it. There was a bed, the prie-dieu, and a small table. There was a single drawer in the table, but it contained a Bible and nothing else. Tom flicked through it, but no loose pages fell out. Joe lifted the mattress and felt it all over. Nothing. He examined the prie-dieu, looking for a cavity or secret drawer. It was solid.

'If you wanted to hide something in here, where would you put it?' Joe asked.

'Under the floor, in the ceiling, or behind the walls.'

The hut was a simple construction. The walls were lathe and plaster, the floor timber, and the roof space open to the rafters. It must have been stinking hot in here in summer with nothing under the corrugated-iron roof to provide insulation. Joe swept his torch over the room. A dado ran the length of one wall.

'Is that just for decoration, do you think?'

Tom looked at it closely.

'It's not actually flush with the wall. It's built out slightly.'

They tested each of the wood panels, and each was secure until they moved the bed to get to the panels behind it. There were four panels, which gave a little when pressed, and it didn't take long to discover that if pushed up they came out easily from the skirting board beneath them. There wasn't much room behind them, but there was enough to hold a couple of folders and a bound notebook. Joe took them out and put them on the table. As he opened one of the folders, both he and Tom heard a sound outside. They snapped off their torches and listened intently. What they heard was the unmistakable sound of the outside bolt being pushed home. Two other bolts, which they hadn't noticed — one at the top and the other at the bottom of the door — were also slid into place. Then there was silence.

'Oh fuck,' said Tom. 'I bet that window doesn't open.'

'THIS IS SUCH a beautiful car,' Clara said.

'It's the car I learned to drive in, so I take it for granted, which I shouldn't do.'

Tom's hire car appeared in Helen's headlights as she rounded a corner on the unmade road to Prescott's orchard. She stopped the car and got out. She and Clara walked around it and shone torches into its interior. The doors were unlocked, and the hire papers in the glove box confirmed that this was definitely Tom Mackenzie's car. It was Clara who noticed that the air had been let out of all four tyres.

'That doesn't happen by accident,' Helen said.

'They've been deflated, not slashed. That suggests restraint, I hope.'

'We're going to drive up to the door. I'm certainly not leaving the car here.'

There was a light on in one of the front rooms, and as Helen parked the car a light came on the veranda. The front door opened, and Prudence came outside, followed by Justice. Helen noted that Prudence was wearing a pale-blue cummerbund that cinched her tunic at the waist. Justice's tunic was unadorned.

'You're welcome,' she said disarmingly, and invited Helen and Clara inside. This was disconcerting. One of these women had disabled Tom Mackenzie's car; unless, of course, there was someone else on the property. The room they entered was well lit and familiar to Helen from her earlier visit. There was no sense of threat. Helen introduced Clara, and an offer of a cup of tea was accepted. Clara decided that she'd only drink hers if all their tea was poured from the same pot, and if Prudence drank from her cup first. She'd seen enough movies where someone was slipped a Mickey Finn to be wary.

'You must be wondering why we're here,' Helen said.

'You did say you might return. I presume it's about Walter Pinshott. He isn't here, I can assure you of that. Only Justice and I are here at the moment. Are you also a private inquiry agent, Clara?'

'No. I'm a doctor.'

Prudence's eyebrows shot up.

'A doctor? A medical doctor? How marvellous, although I imagine you meet men every day who disapprove of you.'

The benign look she bestowed on Clara needed a little more rehearsal, Helen thought, but clearly Prudence had begun to inhabit the role she'd created for herself.

'It's not only men who disapprove,' Clara said.

Prudence nodded sympathetically.

'So many women have lost the knowledge that all power flows from the mother. She raises the men who usurp her power.'

This sounded like an inchoate manifesto for the new Church of the First Born, a church without a messiah, but with a divinely ordained mother at its head. To avoid any further sermonising, Helen said, 'We passed a car on the way up here, near your gate.'

Prudence didn't miss a beat.

'Yes. Two men entered our property, uninvited and unannounced. One of them is your employee, the man named Joe. The other I don't know. Justice let their tyres down because their trespass should inconvenience them more than it does us.'

'Where are they?' Clara asked.

'No one knows better than you, I imagine, how the first tendency of men is to underestimate women. Joe and his friend thought they were unobserved as they crept up the path. They compounded their trespass by entering the most private place here. That's where they are, locked and bolted inside the room we withdraw to when we bleed. They've shown no respect, and have been shown none in return.'

'You can't keep them locked in there,' Helen said. 'That's a crime.'

She realised how lame this sounded. Prudence smiled.

'Do you want us to rescue them?' she asked.

'How long have they been in there?'

'About an hour.'

'Let's leave them for another half an hour,' Clara said.

Justice entered the room with the tea things, and, forgetting her suspicion that the liquid might be drugged, Clara sipped it as soon as it was handed to her.

'I want to find Pinshott as much as you do,' Prudence said. 'But this is my home, and although I have nothing to hide, I don't like people, men, creeping around it, looking for stuff that isn't here.'

'So you know what they were looking for?' Clara said.

'I presume they're looking for a list of all the people who belong to our church. The inspector I spoke to didn't believe me when I said there was no list.'

'Prudence, Guy Kirkham was Joe's closest friend. He came here because …'

Prudence's face lost its studied calm.

'My sister and my nephew are also dead!'

She said this with some force, and Helen caught a glimpse of a formidable quality in Prudence, a quality she'd need if she wanted to lead and control others.

'Where do you think Walter Pinshott is now?' Helen asked.

'I have no idea. All I can tell you is that he isn't here.'

'Do you have a photograph of him?'

'No.'

Joe had described Pinshott to Helen, and she had a clear idea of what he looked like. 'A poor man's Old Testament prophet,' Joe had said. 'Thick white beard, long hair. The full cliché, only he doesn't look biblical. He looks like a tramp.'

Clara wanted to ask Prudence and Justice if they genuinely believed that Anthony Prescott was the Messiah. The idea was so ludicrous to her that it seemed inconceivable that these seemingly intelligent women could embrace it. She wasn't in a position, though, to ask such questions. She didn't want to compromise Helen's work.

'How are you managing the orchards with just the two of you here?' Helen asked.

'Nepheg will come back.' It was Justice who said this. These were the first words she'd spoken since Helen's and Clara's arrival.

'He telephoned. He doesn't like the people he's being forced to stay with, and they don't like him. He can't return until this is over, though.'

'Who actually owns the farm?' It suddenly occurred to Helen that she'd always assumed it was Prescott's property, but maybe it wasn't.

'I share ownership,' Prudence said.

'With your husband?'

'With my sisters, and since Truth's death, just with Justice.'

'It seems very prosperous.'

'Our congregation is generous, but what price can you put on salvation?'

'Your husband must be good with money.'

Prudence laughed, and so did Justice.

'Accounting wasn't one of Anthony's strong points. His mind was on higher things. I, on the other hand, am an excellent accountant.'

'So Anthony Prescott has no financial interest in this farm at all?'

'None, and when we married he made no claims to assume any. He is a spiritual man, chosen by God.'

Clara couldn't prevent a small snort of disbelief from escaping. Prudence turned her gaze upon her.

'They crucified Christ,' she said, and offered nothing more, as if this observation contained enough wisdom to make further discussion unnecessary.

THE BATTERY IN Tom Mackenzie's torch was failing, and his bladder was full. He tried the window again, just in case it gave way on this, the fifth attempt.

'I really need to piss, Joe. This never happens in the movies, does it? Humphrey Bogart never needs a piss.'

'All I can think of is how angry Helen is going to be. This is just going to confirm her poor opinion of my skills.'

'Seriously, Joe, I'm nearly at the point where I'm going to have to wee in the corner, or in the drawer of the desk. I can't do that, can I?'

'Why didn't you go before we left Kew?'

'I did. It's the adrenaline. Is there any sort of container in here? A bottle? Anything?'

'There's a jug and wash basin at the foot of the bed. No chamber pot. No need for one with the washhouse so close by.'

'Which would be the least disrespectful, the jug or the basin?'

Joe picked up the jug and turned it upside down. The light from his torch picked out two crossed swords on the base.

'It's Meissen,' he said. 'You're going to defile beautiful Meissen porcelain.'

'Given that these people may have murder on their minds, I don't think I care, actually.'

Joe returned to the disappointing documents he'd removed from the wall cavity. There was no list of church members. It was a collection of poems, adolescent diary entries, and sketches. They were precious, no doubt, to the person who'd written them — precious and private enough to justify hiding them — but of no real interest to anyone else. Perhaps buried amongst the welter of material were juvenile reflections on love and attraction, but reading the small scrawl by torchlight was difficult, and Joe's torch, too, began to fade. Both he and Tom switched the torches off and stood in the darkness. Joe pulled up the blind to allow whatever vestiges there were of cloud-obscured moonlight to seep in. They each became aware of the taint of urine in the air.

'Sorry about that,' Tom said.

'This is so humiliating. We can't just stand here. We have to smash the door open.'

'It's a pretty solid door, Joe.'

As he said this, they heard the sound of the centre bolt being drawn back, followed by the top bolt and then the bottom one. The door was pushed open, but no one appeared in the doorway and no one spoke. It was as if it had been opened magically. Tom thought he heard retreating footsteps. Was this another trap? If they stepped outside, would they be struck down? The hideous murders at Fisher's farm made the idea of an axe-wielding maniac less ludicrous than it might otherwise have been.

'What do we do?' Tom whispered.

'I'm going first. If there's anyone there, they'll be expecting us to be standing, so if they've got some sort of weapon, they'll swing it at head height.'

Joe crouched and scuttled through the door. No one attacked him, and he stood up.

'There's no one out here,' he called, and Tom joined him.

'What's going on, Joe?'

'I have no idea. Someone's playing a game.'

The back of the farmhouse could be seen from the women's hut, and in the surrounding darkness the rectangle of light from an open door was dramatically visible.

'We're supposed to go into the house, aren't we? We're supposed to be attracted to the light. They're treating us like moths,' Tom said.

'Based on our performance so far, they're right to think we've got the brains of moths.'

'We could leave.'

'Oh no. I'm not leaving here with my tail between my legs, and with no information.'

'Do moths have tails?'

'Let's at least go around the front of the house. That back door might be booby-trapped.'

Neither of them supposed that an approach from the front would take the occupants by surprise. Clearly, they were way ahead of Joe and Tom, and when they reached the front they found the door invitingly open. The biggest surprise was Peter Lillee's car.

'Oh, God,' Joe said, 'Helen's here. Why?'

There was no sound from inside the house, and the silence made Joe's heart pound. *Oh, Christ, not now*, he thought, *not now*. The familiar nausea didn't arrive.

'They've got Helen,' he said. 'We have to go inside.'

The thought that Helen Lord might be in danger galvanised Tom, and he broke away from Joe and headed for the veranda.

'Tom!' Joe hissed, but he was ignored, and Joe followed him, aware with every step that this was reckless and foolish. They had no idea what they were dealing with, although what they did know was that whoever was inside was ready for them. Tom had thrown caution to the wind, and Joe had no choice but to follow him into the house. They burst, one after the other, into the front room. The four women, all seated and holding teacups, looked up at them. None of their faces registered surprise. Justice stood and said, 'I'll make another pot of tea.'

16

CLARA WAS SURE that Tom Mackenzie's and Joe Sable's embarrassment and discomfort would be a source of anecdotal joy for years to come. When Tom confessed to defiling the Meissen water jug, Clara thought her own laughter was unseemly. His shame-faced offer to clean the jug was, she thought, priceless. She had to get to the hospital by 11.00 pm for her shift, so she and Helen left Prudence's orchard at 9.30. Tom and Joe had been told that their tyres had been let down, but that there was a pump on the property that they could use to reinflate them. The image of them sweating as they manually pumped air into the tyres entertained both her and Helen on the way to the hospital.

'Poor Joe,' Helen said. 'He looked so crestfallen.'

'He and Tom both looked like naughty little boys who'd been caught misbehaving.'

'And they thought they were being so brave. I *am* angry with them, Clar, especially Joe. This could have ended very, very badly.'

'In a way it did, for them.'

Helen drove Clara first to her flat in East Melbourne, where she changed her clothes, and then to the Royal Melbourne Hospital. She waited until Clara had crossed the road and entered the hospital. She sat for a couple of minutes longer, just in case

Kenneth Bussell turned up. There was no one on the street, and so she drove home to Kew.

SISTER KELLY WAS on the front desk, as she had been the previous night.

'No visitors tonight, Doctor.'

Was that a small smirk on her face as she said this? Clara was certain that it was. Perhaps she should tell Sister Kelly that her 'suitor' was a murderer. That would put the wind up her. No, she'd save that for another time.

Upstairs in her office she went over the notes left by the doctor she was relieving. There was nothing that threatened to turn into an emergency tonight. That was a relief — she felt like she'd had enough excitement for one night. She began her rounds, finding the wards mostly quiet, apart from the snoring of a couple of patients. She walked the length of the last ward, checking charts. In the last bed the patient was snoring excessively. For everybody's sake, she needed to get him to shift his position. She picked up the chart from the foot of the bed. It was blank. That was an oversight that would require a reprimand. She moved to the top of the bed and pulled down the blanket that was obscuring the patient's face. The snoring stopped, and Kenneth Bussell smiled up at her.

'Sorry about the noise. I had to get your attention.'

Clara was curiously calm.

'What are you doing here?'

'The sister at the front desk is £5 richer.'

He sat up, and Clara took a couple of steps back, as if he were an uncoiling snake.

'Did you get my book?'

'You know I did.'

Bussell swung his legs over the side of the bed and made to stand up. He stumbled, either accidentally or deliberately, and fell towards Clara, who instinctively opened her arms to prevent his fall. He quickly detached himself and apologised. Clara knew how volatile this man was, so she took the apology to be strategic, not genuine. She did notice that he smelled clean, which suggested that he wasn't living on the streets.

'I wanted to let you know in person what that book means to me. It's a part of me. Now it's a part of you.'

'Mr Bussell …'

'Ken, please. We've moved beyond formality, surely.'

Every word he uttered struck Clara with sinister force. She felt unsafe, despite being surrounded by patients, some of whom were well enough to come to her assistance or raise an alarm if Bussell attacked her. There was something in Bussell's casual assumption that lying in wait for her like this, under a hospital sheet in a vacant bed, was either amusing or, worse, romantic that made Clara's anger flare with sufficient heat to overwhelm her fear. She wanted this man out of her life, and preferably behind bars. She didn't want him hanging from the end of a rope. She was opposed to public executions, although anyone who murdered someone in Victoria ran the risk of suffering that fate. She had to find a way of incapacitating him long enough for the police to arrive to arrest him. Thinking quickly and not knowing if the strategy would work, she asked Bussell to sit on the edge of the bed.

'I'd like to take a look at your wound, if you don't mind. I'll draw the curtain around the bed for you. If you could take off your coat and shirt.'

Bussell smiled.

'Should I take off my pants as well?'

Clara smiled back at him, and hoped that her face didn't betray the rush of disgust she was feeling.

'That won't be necessary, Mr Bussell. I need to get some swabs. I'll be back in a moment.'

Bussell began taking off his coat. Clara hurried to her office, hoping and praying that no patients needed her urgently. She telephoned D24, but the operator told her that the lines were busy. Did she want to hold? Clara tried to calm herself and think clearly. The man who had murdered Gerald Matthews, the man who had brought her a bloodied trophy of the crime and who had demonstrated that he could shift from admiration to vituperation if crossed, this man was just a few feet from her. She couldn't let him leave the hospital.

'I'll call back in a minute or two,' she told the operator. With some trepidation, but with clarity of purpose, she decided to do something that would have been unthinkable in any other circumstance. She decided to incapacitate Bussell with an injection of morphine. She'd have to be careful with the dose, to avoid respiratory depression, but she wanted the dose to be large enough to work quickly. She didn't need Bussell to be unconscious, just disabled sufficiently to keep him in the bed until the police arrived.

She prepared a tray with swabs, disinfectant, and bandages, loaded a syringe with morphine — she carried a key to the drug cabinet when she was on duty — and hid it beneath the swabs and bandages. When she returned to Bussell, she found him lying on his back, bare-chested, with his hands behind his head. The bandage she'd applied to his knife wound was still in place. She was a little surprised by this. She'd have expected Bussell to have been more cavalier about his hygiene. She'd based this on his unwillingness to stay in hospital on the night he'd presented, and she realised, looking at him, that nothing about him made any sense. Why did she think he was some sort of drifter? Possibly because the police couldn't find him.

As she removed the bandage, she assessed him again. His clothes were of good quality, he was clean-shaven, with no nicks or razor burns, his hair was clean, and his body gave off no offensive odours.

The book of sonnets suggested that he was an educated man, and yet he was unable to suppress expressions of lewdness. It was as if he believed that Clara would find these expressions attractive.

The wound was uninfected.

'My trouser belt isn't in the way, is it?'

'Actually, yes.' She smiled as if to encourage him.

'Cheeky,' he said.

'Would you mind lowering your trousers?'

Clara kept her voice steady. Kenneth Bussell, smiling broadly, undid his belt, unbuttoned his flies, and asked Clara if she'd edge the trousers down, as he found it awkward while lying in this position. Clara pulled the trousers open, and discovered the cause of Bussell's grin: he wasn't wearing any underclothes. She went ahead and lowered his trousers to his knees.

'Well, it's not like you haven't seen it before, is it?'

'I'm a doctor, Mr Bussell. I've seen more penises than you've had hot dinners.'

'So how do I compare?'

Bussell's penis began to swell.

'You should take that as a compliment,' he said. In response to this, Clara took the syringe and plunged it into the muscle of Bussell's hirsute thigh.

'Fuck me!' he yelled. 'What are you doing?'

He threw his legs off the bed and tried to stand, but his trousers caught around his ankles and hampered him. He sat down and tried to pull them up. He managed to get them halfway when the morphine hit. It was a large injection, but even so it shouldn't have worked that quickly, and Clara, horrified, thought she'd miscalculated the dose. Bussell fell back, his eyes open, disoriented, immobilised. His shouted obscenity had woken two patients, one of whom, an elderly man, began calling out. The duty nurse, who ought anyway to have been on the ward, but who'd been in the lavatory, walked quickly towards the distressed man. Clara appeared from behind the screened-off bed and gave the nurse rushed instructions. She then telephoned D24 again, and this time the operator connected her. As calmly and as clearly as she could, she explained that a man named Kenneth Bussell, who'd murdered Dr Gerald Matthews, was temporarily incapacitated in the Royal Melbourne Hospital. The police needed to come and arrest him. The officer who took her call asked a couple of questions, and Clara could hear the scepticism in his voice.

'Should I telephone Inspector Lambert at home and tell him that his officers have allowed this suspect to get away?'

Her crisp impatience had an effect, and she was assured that officers would be dispatched immediately.

Clara felt ill as she walked back to where Bussell lay. Had she killed him? Was he allergic to morphine? The duty nurse stood by Bussell's bed, her face an animated mix of confusion and fear.

'Why are his pants around his knees?' she asked.

'Is he breathing?' As she said this, Clara moved to check for herself. Bussell's breathing was shallow. She checked his pulse. It was strong. His eyes remained open and unfocused.

'Let's make him decent before the police get here,' Clara said.

'The police?'

In order to galvanise the nurse into action, Clara said, 'This is the man who murdered Dr Matthews. I've given him a shot of morphine.'

The nurse drew back as if Bussell might suddenly lash out at her.

'Trousers!' Clara snapped, and the two of them managed to pull the trousers up and do up the flies. It was Clara who wrestled with the buttons, and she shuddered when her fingers brushed against Bussell's penis. As soon as she could, she'd wash that sensation away. They manoeuvred him into his shirt, but didn't attempt to dress him in his coat. The police could deal with that.

When the police arrived, Bussell was still semi-comatose. They couldn't arrest and take away an unconscious man, and Clara couldn't release him until she was sure that he was in no danger of dying. The situation was awkward, and the police were uncertain how to proceed. One of them made a telephone call. He was away for some time, and when he returned he said that Inspector Lambert had been rung and that he'd given clear instructions that Bussell was to be guarded, and had advised that he'd be at the hospital as quickly as he could manage it. The two constables, who'd been frankly annoyed, were now more impressed than they had been by Clara's claims. The fact that Inspector Lambert was prepared to get out of bed at this hour was compelling proof that this semiconscious man might indeed be a murderer.

Clara knew that she might face disciplinary action over her use of morphine to subdue Bussell, although, if she'd done no lasting damage, surely the medical board would applaud her quick thinking. She kept checking Bussell's vital signs every few minutes, knowing that the drug's effects wouldn't fully wear off for many hours. To her relief, Bussell began to come around, and by the time Inspector Lambert arrived, Bussell was groggy and incoherent, but clearly out of physical danger.

Titus sat with Clara in her office, leaving the two constables with Bussell. They were to call him as soon as Bussell showed any signs of alertness. Clara discussed the book of sonnets and the significance of the sonnet that Bussell had claimed as his favourite.

'It was the poisonous little note he left at my house that really frightened me, Titus.'

'Infatuations are disturbing enough at the best of times, but when the infatuated person is unstable you have every reason to be frightened. Bussell's obsession seems to have been getting more intense and out of hand.'

'I hate to sound Edwardian, but his indecency really bothered me. He seemed to think that, because I'm a doctor, anything goes. It very much doesn't. Does that sound prim?'

'Certainly not.'

'Will you arrest him?'

'I think we can. It's all a bit circumstantial, but there's a pattern of behaviour that is worrying. And we certainly need to speak to him as a person of interest.'

'It will be such a relief just to know that he's not out there.'

'I can't presume that he won't be bailed. If that happens, I'll let you know.'

Titus was called to Bussell's bedside, and Clara accompanied him. Bussell was coherent, but bewildered. He couldn't make sense of what had happened to him, and when Titus declared his intention to arrest him and read him his rights, he struggled into a sitting position and was immediately restrained. It was clear that he hadn't understood the reason for his arrest, and when Titus repeated that he was being arrested on suspicion of having murdered Dr Gerald Matthews, he began to laugh. He looked at Clara, and she recoiled automatically, but his gaze wasn't filled with hatred, only puzzlement.

'I couldn't help the erection,' he said.

As she watched Bussell being led down the ward, Clara thought that whatever disciplinary procedures were invoked against her, they would be worth it. Now that he was safely off the street, she realised how the threat of him had been hanging over her, detracting in some way from her enjoyment of every day.

JOE SAT OPPOSITE Helen at the breakfast table. Helen couldn't bring herself to berate him, what with his bandaged head and general air of the crestfallen. He looked so pathetic, her heart melted.

'How long did it take to reinflate the tyres?'

Her lips refused her internal instruction not to smile.

'Half an hour. It was exhausting.'

'I'm sorry I was out when you got back. I was driving Clara to work.'

'I was glad you were out. There's only so much humiliation a person can take in a single evening.'

'Oh, Joe, it wasn't that bad.'

'Wasn't it? I can honestly say, without a shadow of a doubt, that walking ...'

'Bursting.'

'Yes, all right, bursting. Bursting into that room is the low point of my life.'

Helen laughed.

'Now I know you're exaggerating, unless you're suggesting that facing four women drinking tea was more daunting than being tortured, and almost killed.'

Joe had to acknowledge that both those events in his life had put the previous night's fiasco into perspective.

'Nevertheless, I feel foolish, and that is an extremely unpleasant feeling.'

'Given what's happened recently, if all that's been hurt is your pride, I'm happy.'

She was teetering on the brink of saying more when the telephone rang. Ros stuck her head around the door.

'Clara,' she said.

'Oh, God, I hope everything's all right.'

Helen was on the phone for so long that Joe finished breakfast, washed his dishes, and went upstairs to change out of his pyjamas. When he came downstairs, Helen told him Clara's astonishing news: Kenneth Bussell had been arrested.

'It's one thing I can stop worrying about,' Helen said. 'Now, if she'd stop all contact with Adelaide Matthews, I'd feel even better.'

Helen gave Joe a précis of Clara's description of afternoon tea with Adelaide.

'She's clearly an emotional cot-case, and Clara shouldn't be ministering to that. It's too draining, and her job is already draining enough.'

'She's an amazing person.'

Helen was looking away when he said this, so she missed the slight blush that spread over Joe's face. He felt keenly that his chances of impressing Clara Dawson had diminished severely. He was trying not to blame Tom for this, but he did harbour some resentment that Tom had rushed unthinkingly into that house and had obliged Joe to follow. Blaming Tom was absurd, of course. However, that small, ugly feeling was definitely there.

'Clara's coming over here later this morning. I told her about your headache. She wants to check on you.'

'That really isn't necessary. I feel fine.'

Helen looked at him, his head bandaged, unshaven, dressed in her uncle's beautiful clothes, and her eyes welled with tears. It happened, just like that, and she didn't turn away. Joe watched her face, astonished.

'Are you all right?'

She nodded, stood up from where she was sitting at the table, and walked around to him. She leant down and kissed the top of his head. His hair smelt faintly of Hungary Water, Peter Lillee's favourite cologne, and now one that Joe used often. She said nothing, and left the room. The contact had been so small and fleeting that Joe didn't understand its significance. For Helen, the gesture represented a shift in her relationship with Joe. Surely now he'd have some notion of her feelings for him.

THE LAST PERSON in the world that Clara wanted to speak to was Adelaide Matthews. Unfortunately, she hadn't mentioned this to Susan, and Susan had said, 'Yes, she's here,' when Adelaide telephoned. With a feeling of dread, Clara took the receiver from Susan.

'Adelaide. Is everything all right?'

There was silence, and then a deep, racking sob.

'I can't believe he said those words to me,' she said, pulling herself together. 'I can't believe he called me those names.'

'Who? Who called you names?'

'Cornel.' Her voice lost all expression when she uttered her son's name. Clara closed her eyes and cursed her initial curiosity about Gerald Matthews' wife. Why, why had she made that first visit?

'Is there someone close to you whom you can talk to? Someone who can give you some advice?'

The ensuing silence had a stunned quality to it.

'Well, yes,' Adelaide said. 'There's you. You understand. You're the only person I know who truly understands.'

Clara had no idea what it was that she supposedly truly understood.

'He's run away, Clara. He ran out of the house, and he said he was never coming back.'

'Children say things like that. They don't mean them.'

'Cornel means it. Can you come over? I'm frantic here.'

'I don't think I can, Adelaide. I have to visit a friend in Kew this morning.'

All Clara could hear were sharp little intakes of breath on the other end of the line.

'I've tried, Clara,' Adelaide said, after the prolonged silence. 'I've tried, but I'm at the end of my tether.' She hung up.

'You look like you've had bad news,' Susan said.

'I'm sick to death of crazy people, Susan.'

'You're not usually a magnet for them. That's me. I sit on the tram, and the mad person heads straight for me.'

'Adelaide Matthews is a problem of my own making, but I can't take responsibility for the emotional mess she's in. I mean, I've met her, what, twice?'

Susan agreed that Clara had no obligations to Adelaide, however distressed she'd become since the death of her husband. Clara was glad of this reassurance, but the phone call nagged at her. She'd talk about it with Helen.

She set out for Kew with a determination to cease all contact with Adelaide. When she arrived there, she found Joe on his own. Helen and her mother had gone for a walk. This was something they'd taken to doing recently, Joe said.

'They walk and they talk.'

Joe didn't really understand that this intimacy between mother and daughter was new, and that for each of them these walks had become precious interludes.

'They've got a lot of catching up to do,' Clara said.

'Have they? They've always lived together.'

Clara wondered yet again what Helen saw in this man. Joe reluctantly submitted to Clara's shining a torch in his eyes and to her checking the wound on the back of his head. She changed the bandage and examined his face closely.

Despite feeling unnecessarily fussed over, Joe found himself aroused by the touch of Clara's fingers as they pressed gently around his scalp. The excitement was brief, and he was sure that Clara was unaware of the effect she was having on him. He was right in this. However strong his response was to Clara's touch, it failed to register with her. She sat near him when she'd finished her examination, and asked if Helen had told him that Bussell had been arrested.

'Yes, she did. You must feel very relieved.'

Clara laughed unexpectedly.

'I'm sorry, Joe. I know it's mean of me, but the look on your and Tom's faces last night was fucking priceless.'

Joe made a feint at rallying to his defence, but gave it up and simply laughed.

'You should have seen us pumping up the tyres. Oh, and God help us, Tom pissing into the Meissen jug.'

'Now *that* is funny.'

'You and Helen must think we're a couple of Keystone cops.'

'It is incredible that two grown men can be so ... what is the word?'

'Incompetent?'

'That's not the word I was looking for, but it'll do.'

Clara was pleasantly surprised by Joe's willingness to park his pride and not resent her obvious enjoyment of his discomfort.

'You know,' she said, 'Prudence saw you coming up the road to the house. The bandage on your head was like a searchlight.'

Joe put his head in his hands, and then looked across at Clara.

'It is funny,' he said.

Clara realised that this was the first proper conversation she'd had with Joe, and she found herself liking him. He was amusing, and there was something about him that was actually charming. She could see why Helen might be so attracted to him. For his part, Joe had never felt so at ease with Clara. Clara, who liked to test the mettle of men she conversed with, told Joe about Kenneth Bussell's erection.

'He said I should take it as a compliment. What do you think?'

'I think God created trousers to protect women from the awful spectacle of what goes on inside them.'

Clara was so delighted by this response that she thought a complete reassessment of Joe Sable might be necessary.

When Helen and Ros returned, they found Joe giving Clara a guided tour of the pictures on the library wall.

'The Goya is the standout,' Joe said, 'although there's a good Dobell sketch. Peter knew Dobell. There are a few of his sketches here in the house.'

The Goya etching, which Clara found ugly and disturbing, made her think about Adelaide Matthews. It wasn't the subject matter, but its capacity to alter her mood somehow. She needed to talk to Helen, and with an abruptness she hoped wouldn't offend Joe, she said, 'Helen, I need some proper advice, and I need you to give it to me. You don't mind if Helen and I talk in private, do you, Joe?'

'No, no, of course not. I do bang on about pictures.'

Clara touched his arm.

'That's not true, it's just that something a bit urgent has come up.'

Joe left the library, and didn't feel in the least deflated. Quite the contrary.

AFTER A LENGTHY conversation about Adelaide Matthews, including an admission that she should have taken Helen's advice in the first place and stayed well away from Adelaide, Clara said, 'In my defence, Helen, how could I possibly have known that she was disturbed to begin with? Clearly, she was mentally unstable before Dr Matthews died, but he was such an arsehole. I don't doubt that he was unpleasant to live with, and probably abusive, psychologically if not physically. I thought I was offering consolation, not stepping into a vast pile of emotional horseshit.'

'When you first met her, at Russell Street, didn't you notice anything odd about her, apart from the obvious oddness of asking you around for afternoon tea?'

Clara sighed.

'I don't have your powers of observation.'

'Your job is about observing people, Clar.'

'Being able to tell the difference between a bubo and a pimple doesn't require subtle observational skills.' She paused. 'I have a bad feeling about this. I didn't like the way she spoke about her son.'

'Well, let's go around there.'

Clara was startled.

'I thought you said I shouldn't have anything more to do with her.'

'I've got a bad feeling, too, and if her children are in some sort of danger, we can't sit by and do nothing. Tell me, honestly, is Adelaide Matthews capable of harming her children?'

Clara thought for a moment.

'I honestly don't know. It seems unlikely. I mean, it's such a neat, ordered household. It's hard to believe that anything savage could happen in it. Should I have told her that the man who murdered her husband had been arrested? Maybe that would have given her some sort of solace.'

'I doubt it. I'll drive you there, and wait in the car while you assess the situation inside the house. The children go to boarding school, don't they?'

Clara nodded.

'See if you can find out when they're due back there. I imagine it will be in a couple of days. Once that's happened, you can relax. This should be the last time you have to have anything to do with her. If the children are okay and they're going back to school, you can stop worrying. You have no obligations to this woman.'

In the car on the way to the Matthews' house in Carlton, Clara was so preoccupied that she didn't mention her change of opinion about Joe Sable.

17

INSPECTOR TITUS LAMBERT didn't often conduct interviews on a Sunday. This wasn't out of respect for a religious notion that it was a day of rest, dedicated to worship. It was because it was one of the precious days that he and Maude got to spend together. Today, he made an exception for Kenneth Bussell. Bussell had initially declined to have a solicitor present, but Titus had insisted, pointing out that the charge against him was so serious that to be unrepresented would be foolish.

The solicitor provided by the court was a man Titus respected. He was in his sixties, and close to retirement. He was a competent lawyer who provided even the most dismal clients with good counsel. With the preliminaries over, and with Alexander Forbes taking notes, Titus said, 'We've been looking everywhere for you, Mr Bussell. You've exercised an extraordinary amount of police time.'

Bussell wasn't belligerent. He was calm, which made Titus think that talking to police in an interview room wasn't a new experience for him.

'You understand why you're here, Mr Bussell?'

Bussell shook his head.

'No. No, I don't.'

'It has been explained to you.'

271

'That's not what I meant. You reckon I murdered a bloke I've never even heard of. That's what I don't understand.'

'My client is mentally competent, Inspector. He simply vigorously denies the charge.'

Titus acknowledged the solicitor's interruption with a nod.

'What happened on Thursday, the 11th of May?'

'I got stabbed, and the bloke who stabbed me wasn't this Gerald Matthews character. I suppose you think it was, and that I killed him in some sort of fight. Didn't happen.'

'What did happen?'

Bussell looked at his solicitor, who nodded.

'It's not my proudest moment. I hope you're not too prim and proper.' He looked across at Alexander Forbes. 'I'd hate to shock that young bloke. You're not going to hear my story in church.'

'I think we can hear what you have to say without falling into a swoon,' Titus said.

'Well, as you know, sometimes a man needs, you know, a release, and if a man doesn't have a wife, or his girl, if she's willing, he's going to have to pay for it. Now, I don't mind paying for it. A man's gotta do what a man's gotta do, and when he has an itch he's got to scratch it, and sometimes the hand just won't cut it. Am I right?'

Titus declined to answer.

'If you blokes think you're on top of prostitution in this town, you're kidding yourselves. The gardens opposite the circus? It's like Bourke Street in there. When there were more Yanks in town it must have been swarming. It was dark. I found a sheila, and we went off for a bit of a knee-trembler against a handy tree. She was bit stand-offish, I have to say. Not so much as a fumble before she got paid. That's reasonable, I suppose. What is she going to do if I fuck her and then refuse to pay? Maybe she's got a pimp nearby, maybe not. A lot of these women are working solo, just trying to pay the bills. I respect that, so I paid what she asked. She wasn't as forthcoming as I thought she should be, given that she had my money. I got a bit, you know, willing, and slipped my hand under her dress. She was a good-looking woman, from what I could see of her. Looked about thirty. Smelled nice. I got my hand inside her pants and felt about in her bush. I was raring to go. That's when she opened her thighs, which had been clamped together, and you know what's coming, don't you? Suddenly I've got a cock in my hand.'

Bussell looked at his solicitor again.

'Now, this could have gone a number of ways. If he'd had the courtesy to tell me that he was a bloke, I would have left him to it. If that's how he wants to earn a quid, it's none of my business, and I'm sure there are plenty of blokes who are looking for what he offers. Good luck to him. But he didn't, and I ended up touching another bloke's cock, which is not my idea of a good night out, so I wasn't happy, and I shouldn't have grabbed him by the throat, because the bastard had a knife and he used it. I wasn't sure what had happened, so he told me. "I've slit you," he said, or something like that, and this time the voice was a couple of octaves lower. I must have been in shock, I don't know, but then he did me over. I was beaten up by a bloke in a frock. I mean, Jesus. I'm not going to dine out on that story, am I? And I tell you what, he could throw a punch a hell of a lot harder than I can.'

'So he left you for dead.'

'Well, at this point I don't think he was too concerned about my welfare. He defongerated as soon as he was satisfied that I was in no condition to chase him.'

'And then what happened, Mr Bussell?'

'I got up off the ground, discovered that I wasn't too badly hurt, and took myself off to the hospital.'

'You walked all the way up to Lonsdale Street after being stabbed?'

'Well, there were no trams, and it isn't actually that far.'

Titus didn't want to hurry him.

'And then what happened?'

'I was admitted and seen to. I was cleaned up, stitched up, and I left.'

'Who stitched your wound?'

'A woman, believe it or not. Dr Clara Dawson.'

'Was there another doctor present?'

Bussell gave every indication of being genuinely puzzled by the question.

'There was a male doctor, now that you mention it. He was a bit of a prick, actually. He was rude to the lady doctor. It was obvious he didn't like her. She handled herself well.'

'You didn't like the way he spoke to her?'

'No, I didn't.'

'So you waited for his shift to end the next day, and you killed him.'

Bussell looked stunned.

'This is the bloke I'm supposed to have murdered? You have to be fucking kidding me.'

'Where did you go after you killed him?'

Bussell looked at his solicitor.

'Do I have to sit here and listen to this?'

'You can answer the charges by answering the questions, Mr Bussell,' the solicitor said. 'If I feel there's a question it's not in your interest to answer, I'll step in.'

'So where did you go after you'd killed Dr Gerald Matthews?' Titus repeated.

'I didn't fucking kill him. When I left the hospital that morning, I went straight to my digs, and I stayed there all day and all the next night, too.'

'And where is home?'

'Sixty-four Frederick Street, Yarraville. I'm not going to come all the way back into town to lure a bloke I met for two minutes into a park and kill him. I mean, come on.'

Titus decided to change tack.

'You've been bringing Dr Dawson unwelcome gifts.'

'Not gifts. Just one. I wanted to thank her for cleaning me up. I thought we had a bit of a connection.'

'Just the one gift?'

'Correct. I waited outside the hospital for her once, but I lost my nerve. I think she saw me.'

'And the phone calls?'

'Why would I telephone her? Where would I get her number?'

'What about the first gift? What about Dr Gerald Matthews' wallet left outside Dr Dawson's bedroom door? What about that little trophy?'

'How the fuck would I know where she lives? Jesus Christ. She thinks I murdered this bloke too, doesn't she?'

Titus asked a few more questions, establishing what Bussell did for a living (odd jobs, not a railway employee, which is what he'd told the hospital), and who he lived with (his younger brother), and then paused the interview.

Back in his office, he asked Alexander for his impressions.

'I wouldn't say that Mr Bussell is a diamond in the rough. I think he's a bit of a sleaze, but is he also a bloody good actor?'

'When people realise they could end up dangling from the end of a rope, it's amazing how often they discover hidden theatrical talents.'

After a break of 15 minutes, they returned to continue the interview with Bussell.

CLARA AND HELEN sat in the car outside Adelaide Matthews' house in Drummond Street. Clara wound down the window and listened, half-expecting to hear Adelaide raging within. The house was quiet.

'Do you want me to come in with you?'

Clara said that the sudden appearance of a stranger would be hard to explain.

'I'll go in and talk to her, find out what's going on, and with any luck it will all be fine. Cornel will have come back home, and everything will have settled. I'm glad you're here, though. Just in case.'

'You can't just confiscate her kids, Clar. You do know that?'

'Thank you. I do know that arcane little fact.'

Helen watched as Clara walked up to the front door. There was no twitching of the curtains in any of the windows. Clara knocked, and waited. She knocked again. She turned to Helen and shrugged quizzically. She knocked a third time, and then tried the door handle. The door opened. She looked back at Helen and raised her hands in a 'What do I do now?' gesture. Helen waved her inside.

As soon as she stepped over the threshold, she called out, 'Adelaide! It's me, Clara Dawson.' There was no response. The silence in the house was unsettling, and it took all of Clara's courage not to flee. Something was wrong here; she could feel it. She checked each of the rooms downstairs. Nothing. At the bottom of the stairs, she strained her ears. There was something — it might have been a whimper — but it was so small it might have been a timber settling. She climbed the stairs and heard another whimper, this one distinct. It was coming from a room to the left of the landing. Clara reached it and, absurdly, knocked.

'Adelaide? It's me, Clara.'

She turned the door knob and leaned against the wood. The door opened without a sound. Adelaide Matthews stood facing her two children, who were also standing. The little girl, Violet, was crying softly; the boy, Cornel wasn't crying. His cheek bore a red mark that could only have been raised by the flat of Adelaide's hand. Each of the children was tearing pieces of paper in half, and in half again.

'Oh, you decided to come,' Adelaide said. 'How very nice. We're having a lovely time, aren't we, children?'

Neither Violet nor Cornel responded.

'Aren't we, children?'

Each child looked at the floor. Adelaide's arm swung back, and she delivered a vicious slap to the side of Cornel's face. He dropped the paper he was holding, and cradled his cheek.

'Adelaide!' Clara was so shocked that she remained rooted to the spot. Adelaide immediately took Cornel in her arms and cooed how sorry she was. She kissed his cheek and stroked his face. He stood, rigid in her arms, and so she pushed him away.

Adelaide smiled at Clara.

'We're making confetti,' she said. 'I've taken every Norman Lindsay drawing out of its frame, and I've collected all Gerald's Lindsay prints, and we're tearing them up into confetti. We're having a lovely time.'

Those final words chilled Clara. Adelaide's eyes were dull, either because of alcohol or medication, or a mixture of both. Clara had treated patients who looked as Adelaide now looked, and they'd been beyond the reach of reason.

'Let's go downstairs and have a cup of tea,' Clara said. Adelaide laughed.

'But we haven't finished making confetti out of daddy's pornography, have we, children?'

This time, Violet managed a shake of her head.

'And I've been telling the children all about their daddy and what sort of a man he was. It's a sad story, but it has a happy ending, because now he's dead.'

Cornel began to cry.

'See, Clara, see. He doesn't believe me when I tell him his father hated him. Not as much as he hated Violet, of course. She's a girl. Half a brain. Just a womb on legs. Just an incubator for the next glorious man.'

These words appalled Clara. Perhaps the children didn't fully comprehend them.

'Adelaide, the police have arrested the man who murdered Gerald.'

This seemed to strike Adelaide with the force of a blow.

'What?'

'The man who killed your husband, the police have arrested him.'

Adelaide moved towards Clara, and ushered her out of the room and onto the landing.

'What do you mean?'

'They've caught him.'

'There is no *him*!' Adelaide seemed to be swelling into a rage.

'I don't understand, Adelaide.' In fact, she *was* beginning to understand.

'How could you believe that this man, whoever he is, killed Gerald?' Her anger was increasing. 'Are you stupid? Did I waste my time? I brought you Gerald's wallet. It was a gift, a token to let you know that you'd never have to suffer my vile husband ever again.'

'You?'

'You *must* have known. Why else would you begin a friendship with me?'

'You killed Gerald for me?' Clara couldn't manage more than a whisper. Adelaide put her hands on her hips.

'Don't be ridiculous, Clara. I hadn't met you. I killed that bastard for me and for my children. The fact that I'd never have to listen to another tirade about women doctors, specifically you, was a bonus. If he'd made your life as miserable as he'd made mine, I thought you'd like to know he was — how shall I put it? — permanently knobbled.'

'How did you know where I lived?'

'I found that out months ago. I just asked, and, because I was Gerald's wife, they told me. I thought I might visit you, warn you that Gerald was undermining you. I just never got around to it, until that night. It was rather thrilling, hiding in the shadows in your house, waiting for the other two women to go to their rooms.'

Clara was backing away, towards the stairs.

'How did you …?'

'Oh, Clara. My husband was a vain and selfish man, and so easy to fool. We used to walk in that park when we were courting, and sometimes, late at night, he'd force himself on me there. He found the risk of discovery exciting. I suggested we meet there that night, after his shift, and go for a romantic stroll.' Adelaide snorted. 'Gerald didn't really do romance, but he was excited by the prospect of sex by moonlight in a public place. That was his sad notion of something illicit. He was unbelievably easy to kill. Do you know what his last words to me were?'

Clara shook her head.

'He called me a name I can't bring myself to say, and then he died. I'd like to think that was his ticket to hell.'

'I'm going downstairs, Adelaide.'

'You're not going to call the police, Clara. No, no, no. This is just between you and me. They can hang the man they've arrested. I wanted you to know the truth. I wanted you to know that it was me who ended your misery and mine. No one else has to know. The children need their mother, after all.'

Adelaide seemed calm, but as Clara put her foot on the first tread of the stairs, Adelaide rushed at her. Her hands closed around Clara's throat, and her momentum threatened to topple Clara backwards. Somehow — afterwards she could never explain it, perhaps it was the fact that Adelaide was drunk or drugged — as their bodies twisted, it was Adelaide who lost her footing, and, propelled by the action of Clara grabbing her wrists and thrusting them away from her, fell heavily down the stairs. The dull thud as her body tumbled was a sound that Clara would never forget.

The house was perfectly still and quiet, apart from a strange panting sound, which Clara realised was her own breathing. Adelaide Matthews lay still at the bottom of the stairs, one shoulder dislocated into a sickening position.

The door to the room that the children were in opened, and Cornel stepped onto the landing.

'Go back inside,' Clara said, and to her surprise he did as he was told. She wasn't sure if he'd seen his mother. She descended the stairs and felt Adelaide's pulse, half-expecting that there wouldn't be one, but it was there, and it was strong. Adelaide was unconscious. Clara hurried into the street and called Helen into the house. Without asking what had happened, Helen went straight to the telephone and rang the police and an ambulance. As Clara continued to check Adelaide's vital signs, she told Helen everything.

'Good God, those poor children,' Helen said. 'Shouldn't we move her off the stairs, Clar?'

'No. She may have damaged her neck. We'll need to stabilise her first.'

'I'll check the children.'

'Helen, I almost killed Kenneth Bussell with an injection of morphine.'

'He's alive, Clar, and he's about to get good news.'

Clara closed her eyes and concentrated on the pulse in Adelaide Matthews' neck.

18
three weeks later

'THE FIRST THING I'm going to make when this war is over is a proper Irish stew.'

Both Maude and Titus assured Tom Mackenzie that the stew he'd served them was fine.

'Suddenly there are potatoes in the shop, but no onions, not a single bloody onion. Unbelievable,' he said.

The three of them were in Tom's house in South Melbourne. The newspapers that day had been full of the continuing inquiry into the identification of the Pyjama Girl. Although the mystery surrounding this murdered woman had gruesomely entertained Australia since the body's discovery way back in 1934, these proceedings had assumed an interminable quality. As always on this subject, Titus remained resolutely discreet. He shared his knowledge with Maude — Tom had no doubt about that — but it was off-limits as dinner-table conversation.

Titus had got over his annoyance with his brother-in-law's little adventure at Prescott's orchard, partly because it had yielded, through Helen Lord's intervention, the useful knowledge that Prescott did not in fact own the property. His marriage to

Prudence was legitimate, and whether or not Justice also shared his bed, there was no evidence that he'd entered into a bigamous marriage with her. A marriage sanctioned by the Church of the First Born was no marriage before the law, so that at least was one charge that hadn't been included in the list of charges laid against him. The most serious of these were attempted murder and being an accessory after the fact. If Walter Pinshott ever turned up, the charges, depending on Pinshott's evidence, might be upgraded. Pinshott, however, had avoided capture.

Prudence, in her new role as the Holy Mother, had been unexpectedly cooperative. She'd given the police the names and addresses of several members of the church, and these people had in turn provided further names and addresses. All in all, more than 100 people had accepted Anthony Prescott as the Messiah. None of them was harbouring Walter Pinshott, and several of them had expressed the view that they didn't like him. According to the report that Titus read, one woman said that when Pinshott looked at her, he did so with lewdness in his gaze. A male member of the congregation claimed that Prescott had the power to make this man's son sicken and die, and that £50 would prevent this from happening. He'd paid the £50, but regretted doing so. Nevertheless, he continued to attend services. Why, Titus had asked Maude, why were people so immoveably stupid? Maude's theory was that people, some people at least, preferred to let others do their thinking for them. They wanted a Master.

Tom had heard from Joe about Clara and about Adelaide Matthews, and Titus didn't think that it was breaching anyone's confidence to say that Clara had been badly shaken by her misjudgement of Kenneth Bussell.

'He's not going to press charges about the morphine injection, although it undoubtedly constitutes assault. He's a strange man.

A small part of him is charming. The larger part is unappealing.'

'And Adelaide Matthews is alive and well?'

'She's alive, Tom. She's far from well. I suspect her counsel will go for an insanity defence.'

'God knows what her husband subjected her to,' Maude said. 'You don't start a marriage hating your husband. You get there by degrees.'

Titus raised his eyebrows.

'That isn't a universal truth, darling,' she said. 'Just a depressingly common one.'

Tom cleared away the dishes, and, as she almost always did, Maude asked for the recipe. She had yet to actually make one of Tom's dishes in her own home. She followed Tom into the kitchen to help with the washing-up.

'It's been a few weeks since Winslow was arrested,' she said. 'Have you heard anything?'

'Not a thing. I've asked Chafer, and I've asked a couple of other people, but the answer is always the same. He's out of harm's way, the army will court-martial him when they see fit, and no one, other than official people, is allowed to visit him, or even know where he is.'

'That amounts to torture.'

'Chafer told me he was well watered and well fed.'

'That makes him sound like a farm animal.'

'Chafer wouldn't rate him so highly.'

'And what about you, Tom? How do you rate him?'

Tom stopped what he was doing and faced his sister.

'You know what, Maudey, and this will sound awful, but the initial shock of Winslow's arrest wore off pretty quickly. I liked him, but I didn't know him, except briefly and superficially, and the evidence that Chafer got on him was pretty damning. I say that without budging an inch from my position of loathing

Chafer. Given Winslow's situation, I can sort of understand that his loyalties might be divided, but maybe loyalty to a Japanese wife when we're at war with her country is a dangerous luxury. That's certainly Chafer's position.'

'E.M. Forster said that if he had to choose between betraying his friend and betraying his country, he hoped he'd have the guts to betray his country.'

Titus came into the kitchen with a plate that had been left on the table.

'Titus,' Tom said, 'answer this without thinking about it. If you had to choose between betraying Maude and betraying Australia, what would you do?'

'I'd betray Australia, and I'm pretty sure I wouldn't have a single pang of conscience.'

Tom looked at his brother-in-law, and wasn't immediately sure whether he was shocked or impressed by what he'd said.

CLARA SAT WITH Helen in Helen's office. She'd escaped disciplinary action for her use of morphine on Kenneth Bussell. The nurse who'd taken £5 from Bussell and allowed him into the hospital had not been so fortunate. She hadn't been dismissed, but she'd been suspended from duty, and the note on her record would ensure that she'd never make matron. Naturally, she blamed Clara for this, because taking responsibility for her own actions had never been in Sister Kelly's repertoire of virtues. Clara wasn't looking forward to Kelly's return to work — although, as she said to Helen, Sister Kelly had always been a bitch.

Helen and Clara agreed that it was amazing how quickly things had returned to what passed for normal, given the state of the world. There'd been no word from or about the Church of the First Born. Anthony Prescott was locked up, awaiting trial, as was Adelaide Matthews. Her children had been given over to the care of Adelaide's parents. Helen had driven out to visit Meredith Wilson, and had found her among her pear trees, grieving for her husband, certainly, but not blaming anyone for his suicide. Helen had a long conversation with her, and felt at the end of it that Meredith Wilson would be all right.

Joe wasn't in the office when Clara arrived. Helen Lord and Associates had begun to pick up paying work. A toolmaker had asked them to investigate the cumulative losses of small pieces of equipment. Someone on the floor was pocketing stuff — equipment that the thief obviously thought no one would notice, and which he could sell on the black market. The missing nuts, bolts, screws, and drill bits were costing a significant amount to replace.

There was also a restaurant owner who suspected his chef of diverting supplies from the kitchen into the black market.

'It's small beer,' Helen said, 'but it's proper, paying work.'

They spoke about Joe — they often spoke about Joe, especially since Clara had begun to warm to him. Helen hadn't made any declarations. She felt much more at ease around him, much less afraid that she might blurt out her feelings. They laughed together now, and she believed there was a developing intimacy that would make a declaration unnecessary.

'I feel like there's an inevitability about it now,' she said, 'and that I should just let it happen in its own time.'

Clara was sceptical, but after her disastrous misreadings of Kenneth Bussell and Adelaide Matthews, she felt disinclined to offer Helen advice.

'So long as you're happy, Helen.'

'I am, Clar. Truly, I am. I don't feel the need to hurry anything. With the business finding its feet, I'm glad not to complicate things.'

'Do you keep in touch with Inspector Lambert?'

'He's keeping me up to date as much as he can without breaking police rules. They're preparing the case against Anthony Prescott, and against Walter Pinshott, although he seems to have fallen off the face of the earth. Prudence has assured the police that Pinshott hasn't made any contact with her, and Titus believes her.'

'What about the young man who lived out there?'

'Oh yes. I asked about him. He hasn't gone back. They're keeping an eye on him, but he seems to have lost interest in the Church of the First Born. He volunteered for the army, but they knocked him back. He has a history of psychological problems. Manpower has placed him in some menial job. I don't know what. Titus didn't say. He did say that, as far as they know, Pinshott hasn't made any attempt to contact him. Prudence thinks he's gone north.'

'Are you and Joe still looking for him?'

'No. Joe was reluctant to let it go, but, realistically, we've done all we can. At least there's no mystery about who killed Guy. That would have been unbearable for Joe. Sometimes people who commit terrible crimes get away with it. Wouldn't it be nice if everything got tied up with a neat bow?'

'The world is full of knots. Bows are harder to come by.'

Helen laughed.

'Clara, you're a philospher. Come around tonight for dinner.'

Clara agreed, and as she walked back to her room in Powlett Street, she realised that for the first time in a very long time she felt happy. She smiled and almost hoped that Pat hadn't locked the front door. Somehow that would represent a return to normalcy.

TOM MACKENZIE'S POLICY was to avoid Tom Chafer if at all possible. With Winslow Fazackerly waiting to be court-martialled,

Tom's secondment to Intelligence had come to an end. His day-to-day duties were once again overseeing the management and distribution of essential materials for the armed forces. He wasn't alone in this, of course. The supplies that the army, navy, and airforce required demanded an enormous number of support personnel. Nevertheless, sitting alone in his office, trawling through requests, demands, and invoices, he often wondered if there was in fact anyone else doing similar work. Why did a request for 800 pairs of shoelaces come across his desk and not that of his counterpart in Sydney, which was where the shoelaces were needed? Fortunately, he knew where to source the laces, so this was an uncomplicated order. He'd just placed it when Tom Chafer walked into his office. He didn't knock. Any form of courtesy was seen by him as being somehow demeaning. Tom therefore felt no obligation to be polite.

'What do you want? I'm busy.'

Chafer was unaffected by Tom's dismissive tone.

'Your mate Fazackerly will spend the rest of the war in prison.'

'The court martial has happened?'

'Yes. What? Did you think you'd be kept personally informed of the procedures?'

'Well, you must be very happy, Chafer.'

'I'm happy to have been proved right. I'm not happy that they didn't hang the bastard. They went soft on him. Someone pulled some strings.'

'Maybe they thought one letter did not a traitor make.'

Chafer's face turned red, but his voice remained measured.

'When the war's over he'll be dishonourably discharged, and he won't be able to hare off to Japan, and his wife won't be able to come here. I don't know what sort of work he'll be able to do. Who'll hire a traitor?'

'His parents have money.'

Chafer's face assumed an ugly sneer.

'I detest people like Fazackerly.'

'I'm sure he's not having a very nice time in prison. Where is he, by the way?'

'That's classified. I can guarantee you, though, that he's not enjoying himself. He's not getting special treatment.' Chafer produced a harsh little laugh. 'Although in lots of ways he is getting special treatment, if you get my drift.'

Chafer left Tom's office, and Tom decided that he wouldn't include this final piece of information when he told Maude that Winslow had been tried and sentenced.

IT WAS AN unpleasantly cold day. The disadvantage of living in a house the size of the house in Kew was that its rooms were impossible to heat. All of the bedrooms had fireplaces, but the shortage and the expense of fuel led Ros and Helen to heat just one room — the library. It was the most used area, and in winter it doubled often as the dining room. Both Helen and Joe were due home at 6.00 pm, and she wasn't sure, but she thought that Tom Mackenzie might be coming for dinner. At any rate, Joe had said on his way out that morning that he might invite him. Ros always cooked for an extra person. She'd done this all her adult life. The meal was mainly leftovers from the previous night's meal, but she was quite happy with the resultant thick barley stew, loaded with turnips, potatoes, lamb broth, and a few scraps of lamb meat. It was hearty and filling.

When there was a knock on the door at 5.30, she supposed it was Tom. The thought of chatting to him as she set the table was delightful. She liked Tom Mackenzie, despite his having not been entirely honest with her on his previous visit. It was a shame that Clara wasn't coming tonight. Ros wasn't a natural matchmaker, and she'd never actively attempt it, but if Clara and Tom saw more of each other, well, who knew what might follow? They'd make an attractive couple, as the Hollywood magazines would say.

Ros wiped her hands on her apron, and turned on the outside light. She opened the door, and there was a man standing there, smiling. He had a satchel slung across one shoulder, and he removed his hat politely so that Ros could see his face plainly. He was clean-shaven, and his hair was cut very short. It was neatly done, probably by a good barber. He held his hat in one hand and a book in the other. Ros knew immediately that he was a Bible salesman. He smiled at her benignly and said, 'Good evening. I hope this isn't an inconvenient time to call.'

Ros had turned away Bible salesmen before. They hadn't all been as polite as this man. She had some sympathy for them. Jobs were hard to come by, and this man looked to be in his early sixties. For many of these men, the Bible was a product, no different from a cutlery set or a garden tool. It was something to sell.

'I'm sorry,' she said, 'but it is rather an inconvenient time. I'm just in the middle of getting dinner ready.'

The salesman didn't betray any annoyance.

'Perhaps I could make an appointment to come back at a more convenient time, or is there someone in the house I could talk to instead?'

He held the Bible out to Ros, and she took it automatically.

'It's very best quality,' the salesman said. 'Leather bound. Is there perhaps someone at home who might be interested?'

'No. I'm sorry. There's just me home at the moment. I'm expecting my daughter and her friend any minute, but I'm afraid we're not a religious household.'

'I understand perfectly.' Again he smiled, and Ros moved to give the Bible back to him. He reached to take it, but instead his hand shot out towards Ros's throat and closed around it. The Bible fell onto the step, and the weight of the man's body propelled Ros back into the house. She clawed at the fingers pressing into her throat, lost her balance, and dropped to her knees. He let go of her. Ros, gasping for air, tried to stand.

'I don't like hurting women, but if you don't do exactly as I say, I will hurt you very badly. Do you understand?'

Ros nodded, her pain and shock rendering her unable to make any sense of what was happening.

'I want you to get up, and I want you to take me into a comfortable room where we can wait.'

Ros tried to speak, but her throat produced little more than a gurgle. She stood up and took the intruder into the library, where a fire was burning and where the table was partly set for dinner. The man indicated that Ros should sit in one of the armchairs, and he withdrew into a darkened corner and simply stood there. Ros massaged her throat and in a whisper asked, 'Who are you and what do you want?'

'I want justice and I want retribution.'

'Why?'

The man walked across to Ros and crouched down in front of her. Light fell full on his face. It was, Ros thought, the face of a disciplined man. It wasn't an ugly face. It was lean, with no hint of jowls. The eyes didn't seem to her to be unkind. Was he a disgruntled husband, the victim of one of Helen's or Joe's investigations? No. Helen Lord and Associates didn't do divorce work.

'All flesh is grass, missus,' he said, 'and tonight Joe Sable will be gathered to the Lord. No one else needs to die. I am Abraham, and I've come to make this sacrifice. The Master is persecuted and imprisoned because of this man's actions. And he is a Jew.'

Ros was astonished that Abraham's face retained its air of calm as he said these words. It was as if he believed there was nothing unusual in what he was saying. At least she now knew who this man was.

'Are you a Christian, Abraham?'

'I am a chosen Christian.'

'Jesus was a Jew.'

'Jesus stopped being a Jew when he rose on the third day.'

'Why do you think that Joe lives here?'

'This address was in his wallet. I read it. I've been watching the house. I know he lives here.'

Ros's eyes left his face and looked to either side of him. He noticed.

'Are you looking for something to strike me with, missus?'

He reached into his satchel and pulled out a revolver.

'I use it to kill vermin on the farm. It will be just as effective killing vermin in Kew.'

Ros could smell the gun oil as Abraham moved it about in the air. She recognised it. Her husband had had the same gun. She hated it. It was American, a Colt .45 calibre pistol.

Abraham stood up and resumed his position in the deeply shadowed corner. He wasn't well hidden by any means, but if anyone walked into the library and wasn't expecting him to be there, that person might not immediately see him.

'Joe comes home at night with a woman. Who is she?'

'She's my daughter.'

'Is she his wife?'

'No. She's his employer.'

Abraham laughed.

'He takes instructions from a woman. Yes, of course he does.'

They both heard the car as it drove into the garage.

'When they come in here, say nothing.' He raised the Colt. 'If you make a single sound, I will shoot your daughter, and then I will shoot you. Understand?'

Ros nodded. She ought to have been terrified, but all she felt was a sort of numbness as if all this was an anaesthetic dream. This man standing opposite her, holding a gun, it couldn't possibly be real, could it? Nothing like this could happen in such a beautiful room. There was the sound at the rear of the house of Joe and Helen entering through the back door. The reassuring smells of cooking would be in their nostrils.

'We're home, Mum,' Helen called, and not waiting for a reply, both she and Joe went upstairs to change. Abraham and Ros stared at each other. The wait for them to come downstairs seemed interminable.

When they came into the library, Helen saw Ros in the chair and moved across to her, while Joe stood near the dining table. They were talking to each other, and didn't register Ros's silence. Helen leant down to kiss her on the cheek. She froze when she saw her mother's staring, unblinking eyes, and her heart seized as she thought that Ros might have had a stroke and died.

'Mum?'

Ros blinked, and Helen followed her gaze. Abraham stepped into the light. He didn't point the gun at Helen or Joe. He pointed it at Ros.

'Stand back over there, near Judas. I will shoot your mother if either you or he does anything foolish, and you know already that as an instrument of the Lord's vengeance I am not afraid to take a life and condemn its soul to eternal damnation.'

Helen heard this as a blather of words without meaning, but there was clarity in the steel of the gun. Joe wasn't able to identify the intruder until he spoke. He looked nothing like the man Joe had met at Prescott's orchard, but his voice was unmistakable.

'Walter Pinshott,' he said.

'My name is Abraham, and your name is Judas. Judas Iscariot, the traitor Jew.'

Joe took two steps forward.

'And who have I betrayed?'

'The Master.'

Joe's instinct was to keep Pinshott talking.

'Why doesn't the Master throw open his cell door and walk free?'

'Why didn't Christ climb down from the cross and turn the people who nailed him there to stone?'

'I don't know. Why didn't he?'

'Because it was his father's will that he should come through suffering before entering into his glory.'

Helen knew that if she spoke, it would be a mistake. A woman's voice was not what this deranged man wanted to hear. She stood perfectly still so that nothing would distract Pinshott from his focus on Joe.

'I sent your friend to his judgement. I stuck him with three darts, like his namesake. He suffered, oh, he suffered.'

Joe clenched his teeth, aware that Pinshott would shoot Ros Lord without batting an eyelid.

'Come closer to me,' Pinshott said. 'I like to see into a man's eyes before I kill him.'

'What did you see in Emilio Barbero's eyes?'

'I took him from behind and broke his filthy neck, but I saw the final fade to death, and then I strung him up like a side of pork, to warn the apostate Wilson that he'd be next.'

'And was he?'

'No, although perhaps the sight of Barbero hanging there drove him to commit his barbarous acts.'

Pinshott's eyes left Joe's face and moved to Helen's. They remained there only briefly. She was of no interest to him, but something occurred to him, and he asked, 'Do you have any rope?'

'Yes. In the garage, I think.'

'Judas hanged himself,' Pinshott said. 'It would be a sight, wouldn't it, if you hanged yourself, here in this room, in front of us? Would you do that to save the lives of these women?'

Helen's hand covered her mouth, and her eyes widened.

'Go and get the rope. I'll give you exactly one minute. If you're not back in one minute, when you do return, you'll find your mother dead.'

Keeping control of her voice, Helen said, 'It might take longer than that to find the rope.'

'Ninety seconds then. Go!'

Feeling sick, and bereft of options, Helen ran out of the room and down to the back door. Perhaps, she thought, she could find some kind of weapon to bring back with her. In the garage, she turned on the light, and immediately saw the rope. There was no time to hunt for anything else. She raced back into the house, so desperately afraid that the ninety seconds was ticking over that she didn't go into the kitchen to get a knife. Had she done so, she was certain she'd have heard the hideous explosion of the gun being fired.

When she returned to the library, Pinshott said, 'That was closer to two minutes. Fortunately, I'm a merciful man. Give Judas the rope.'

Helen, her hand trembling, gave Joe the coil of rope. He took it from her, and she saw that his face was composed.

'Make a noose. A loop will do.'

Pinshott looked around the room.

'There's nowhere to hang yourself in here. But there's a staircase. You can climb the stairs, tie the rope to the banister, jump over and dangle at the end of it.'

'Why are you doing this?' Ros whispered.

Pinshott was startled by her voice, but his gun never wavered.

'Me? My conscience is clear. Judas will take his own life. Put the loop around your neck.'

Helen began to shake. Why was Joe so calm and still? Did he have some sort of plan, or was he going to do this? Joe raised the rope and slipped the loop end over his head. He let the rest of the rope drop to the floor. He stared at Pinshott defiantly, and for a moment Pinshott wondered if he was about to rush at him. He placed the gun barrel against Ros's temple. She gasped.

'I think we're ready. You should ask forgiveness of God for what you are about to do.'

'There is no God, Pinshott. Your existence and God's existence are incompatible notions.'

Pinshott smiled grimly.

'Stand up, missus.'

Ros was halfway to her feet when the large window behind Helen and Joe shattered with astonishing violence. Had Pinshott fired the gun? The noise was shocking. It was Ros who moved first. Without knowing what exactly had happened, she snatched the gun from the distracted Pinshott's hand. She had it before he knew what she'd done, and she found its balance quickly and fired a bullet into Pinshott's knee. His scream was barely heard over the crash of the gunshot, and he fell to the ground. Ros stood away from him, calculating whether or not to fire a second bullet into him.

Helen's first action was to grab the rope from around Joe's neck and toss it from her as if it were a venomous snake. They all stood dazed and uncertain about had happened.

Tom Mackenzie's head appeared in the space where the window had been.

'That seems to have worked,' he said. 'Sorry about your window, Ros.'

They all turned to Ros and took in the sight of her, gun in hand, ready to fire again if Pinshott tried to stand. He didn't. His body was going into shock, and he lost consciousness.

'We need the police and an ambulance,' Ros said. Helen went to her mother, and held her tightly. Joe went across and gently took the gun out of her hand.'

IT WAS THE Bible on the doorstep,' Tom Mackenzie said. 'It was lying open and face down, which I thought was peculiar. Just weirdly out of place. I was about to knock when I thought I'd just do a quick reccy of the house. I felt a bit like a peeping Tom, looking in the windows, but when I got to the library and saw what was going on, I knew I had to do something desperate. I mean, what I was watching was so bizarre. I couldn't hear anything, but here was this man, holding a gun to Mrs Lord's head, and Joe was putting a noose around his own neck. Smashing the window seemed like the only way to cause a major distraction. It could have gone badly wrong.'

It was very late. Walter Pinshott had been taken under police guard to the Alfred Hospital; Ros and the others had been questioned separately, and statements had been made. Inspector Lambert had gone with Pinshott to the hospital. The hours that had passed since Pinshott's arrival and removal had, with the help of brandy, allowed each of them to sit and calmly discuss what had happened. Helen sat close to her mother, who was amazingly sanguine for a woman who'd just shattered a man's kneecap.

'Where did you learn how to shoot, Mum?'

'Oh, I recognised the gun. Your father had one in Broome. I hated the thing, but he taught me how to use it.'

'Are you sure you're all right, Mrs Lord?' Tom asked.

'I'm fine, Tom. Really I am. I might sit bolt upright at three this morning, but for the moment I'm fine. I'm more worried about poor Joe and what that man forced him to do.'

'I honestly don't remember the action of putting that rope around my neck, Ros. All I could see was that Pinshott was pointing a pistol at your temple.'

'You were so calm, Joe,' Helen said. She couldn't bear thinking about it.

'I was struggling to think of a way out for us all. All I could think was that if I went along with it, maybe somehow he'd take that gun away from Ros's head, and then I'd have a chance, or Helen would have a chance. And yet I was shocked to find I had a rope around my neck when it was all over.'

Helen leaned across and kissed her mother on the cheek.

'You deserve a medal, Mum. I don't know if I'd have had the guts to take that gun out of Pinshott's hands. If you hadn't, Joe might …' An image of Joe dropping over the balcony at the top of the stairs and snapping his neck at the end of that rope crashed into her mind, and she turned white.

'I'm sorry, I'm going to be sick.'

She rushed from the room, and Ros followed her to the bathroom. Tom closed the library door to muffle the sound of her violent retching. This was for her sake, not his.

'How bloody extraordinary all this is,' Tom said.

'I owe you my life, Tom,' Joe said.

'You owe Ros Lord your life.'

'Would I have just meekly gone up those stairs and hanged myself, do you think?'

'No, I don't. There would have been a moment, even just a split second, when Pinshott would have moved that gun. Helen would have been watching for that moment, too.'

'And Ros. Pinshott underestimated Ros.'

Ros put her head around the library door and said that she was taking Helen up to bed. The brandy, she said, had disagreed with her. Both Tom and Joe knew that Helen would hate feeling that being sick might be seen by them as being weak and female. To spare her this, Tom said that he was about to go home anyway, and Joe said that he was more than ready for bed.

No one slept well that night, and Joe barely slept at all. Over and over again, he put his hand up to his throat; each time he took it away, it was shaking.

THE FOLLOWING DAY, Helen wanted to stay home with Ros, but Ros insisted that she go to work.

'I'm fine, darling. Maybe if I'd killed that dreadful man I'd have lost more sleep. As it is, he might limp for the rest of his short life. They will hang him, won't they?'

'Probably. He might make an insanity defence, but I don't think that will wash. I just don't think you should be here on your own, Mum.'

'Don't be silly. I have a lot to do. I have to get the blood out of the rug, for a start.' She smiled. 'That's false bravado, but I would actually like to potter about here by myself. If I get lonely or jumpy, I'll pop next door. I'll do that anyway. Barbara must have heard the gunshot last night. The least I can do is liven up her day.'

Reluctantly, Helen agreed to treat the day like any other. Joe, too, insisted on going to work, and they drove into East Melbourne together. Before they got there, Helen pulled the car over. She turned to Joe, and her eyes filled with tears.

'I thought you were going to die last night, Joe. Every time I think of you, standing there, with that rope around your neck, I want to be sick.'

Joe reached across and put his hand on Helen's shoulder.

'I would never, *never* have walked up those stairs and just jumped over the edge. I wouldn't have let it happen; you wouldn't have let it happen, and Ros didn't let it happen. We were all buying time.'

'What if Tom hadn't smashed that window?'

'You know what I believe, Helen, what I truly believe? I believe you would have done something extraordinary.'

Helen felt her chest heave, and surrendered to a racking sob. With her eyes streaming and her nose running, she was unable to say a word. Joe, taken aback by the effect his words seemed to have had, and certain that Helen wouldn't appreciate him seeing her in such distress, offered to drive the rest of the way. He could watch the road while Helen composed herself. She agreed with a nod, and they changed places.

When they reached the office, Helen gave no indication that she was embarrassed by her tears. The telephone rang as soon as they were inside the door. Helen answered it, glad to delay an examination of Joe's words, but confident now that she might be able to express her feelings for him without suffering a humiliating rebuff.

It was Inspector Lambert. Walter Pinshott was expected to live, although his running and jumping days were over. He'd be interviewing him at his bedside later that morning. Anthony Prescott hadn't been informed of this new development, and neither had the press. On an impulse, Helen asked Titus if he and Maude would like to come around that night for dinner. He agreed. She then telephoned Clara and invited her, and asked Joe to telephone Tom and invite him. It suddenly felt important to Helen that all the people who'd come through this investigation should get together. She rang her mother with the news that she'd be cooking for seven instead of three, and asked if she could cope with this. Ros was unfazed. In fact, she was happy. She'd head out to the butcher's immediately. This would certainly take her mind off the horrors of the previous evening.

There was no time to talk to Joe. He had to leave to continue the surveillance he was doing. Helen's mood was buoyant, and Joe noticed this. On his way out, he poked his head around her office door and asked, 'You know Clara really well. If I asked her out to the pictures, do you think she'd say yes?'

Helen, who'd been smiling at him, kept the smile in place. She said nothing. She just shrugged. No words would come. Joe took the shrug to be a simple, 'I don't know,' and left.

Tom Mackenzie shaved for the second time that day, and ironed his shirt and a dark-blue linen jacket. He decided against wearing a tie. He wanted to look neat, tidy, and well put together. He was having dinner with Helen Lord, and with five other people, it was true, but he hoped that he might get an opportunity to speak with her alone.

Over dinner, Titus told them as much as he felt able to about the progress of the case. Now that it had moved beyond investigation into prosecution, he was constrained as to details, especially given that everyone at the table, apart from Maude, would be called on to give evidence. This constraint also applied to information about Adelaide Matthews. If she pleaded guilty, it would be a simple matter of sentencing. If she claimed she was of unsound mind, Clara would have to be called.

A toast was raised to Ros, who insisted that people should stop making a fuss. Throughout the meal, Helen looked at Joe from time to time and saw that his eyes were directed at Clara. She contrived to meet with Clara in the kitchen, on the pretext of clearing the table before dessert. She pressed her mother's shoulder — and Ros understood that she was to keep her seat — and denied Maude's offer of help.

'Joe is going to ask you out, Clar.'

'Oh, fuck. You're not serious.'

'He's hoping you'll say yes.'

'Honest to God, Helen, I was starting to like him, but that man is so fucking dumb.'

Helen had thought she might cry when talking to Clara. She didn't.

'And speaking of not paying attention, Helen, what are you going to do about Tom Mackenzie?'

'What do you mean?'

'He hasn't taken his eyes off you all evening. He's like a lovesick puppy.'

'Don't be ridiculous.'

'You and Joe have one big thing in common, and it's the thing that will probably bring you together. You're each as blind as the other. You're both stumbling around in the dark, or at any rate staring stupidly in different directions. Eventually, you're bound to bump into each other.'

She hugged Helen, and when they'd separated she said, 'I'm tempted to say yes to Joe just so I can set him straight.'

Helen looked appalled.

'Oh, don't worry. I won't do that. But Helen, when you've dashed poor Tom's hopes, don't give up on Joe.'

There was the sound of conversation and laughter from the dining room.

'If I've learned one thing out of all of this, Clar, it's that I'm much, much stronger than I thought I was, and much stronger than you think I am.'

'Oh no, Helen. I've never doubted your strength. Never.'

Acknowledgements

WHEN YOU WRITE a book there's no one looking over your shoulder. If there is, you need to reassess your situation, and maybe call the police. When the book has been written, however, writers need a Roman legion of people to get it between a beautifully designed cover. These are the people I need:

First and foremost, a great publisher. I have one in Scribe, and my gratitude is boundless, and includes Henry Rosenbloom, who edited this book and who has taken Scribe to remarkable heights.

I also need early readers who will tell the truth. Helen Murnane is first among these. I have relied on her judgement for many, many years. If she says take that bit out, out it goes. The friendship of other writers is precious, so thank you Jock Serong, Sulari Gentill, Emma Viskic, and Tony Thompson. Thank you Jo Canham, whose bookshop, Blarney Books and Art, has become one of Port Fairy's true treasures. Thank you Jon Gray for your gorgeous covers; it is a privilege to have your name on my book. Lastly, thank you to my parents, my mother, Maurene, and my late father, Kevin. Books mattered to them and my reading was never censored, despite a tendency towards the louche and tasteless as a teenager.